P9-CMT-161

By Tom Piccirilli

THE
LAST
KIND
WORDS

THE
LAST
KIND
WORDS

A NOVEL

Tom Piccirilli

BANTAM BOOKS

New York

Copyright © 2012 by Tom Piccirilli

Published in the United States by Bantam Books,
an imprint of The Random House Publishing Group,
a division of Random House, Inc., New York.

BANTAM BOOKS and the rooster colophon are
registered trademarks of Random House, Inc.

Library of Congress Cataloging-in-Publication Data

Piccirilli, Tom.
The last kind words: a novel / Tom Piccirilli.
p. cm.
ISBN 978-0-553-59248-1 (acid-free paper) —
ISBN 978-0-553-90635-6 (e-book)   1. Criminals—
Fiction.   2. Families—Fiction.   3. Long
Island (N.Y.)—Fiction.   I. Title.
PS3566.I266L37 2011
813'.54—dc23   2011029745

Printed in the United States of America on acid-free paper

www.bantamdell.com

2   4   6   8   9   7   5   3   1

First Edition

Book design by Donna Sinisgalli

For Michelle

&

Jim D'Angelo

&

Anna Weitzell

"Fear and hope are alike underneath."
—RICHARD FORD

"Can't do it, simply 'cause underneath 'em is too ugly."
—BILLY GIBBONS

Part I

MAKING GHOSTS

I'd come five years and two thousand miles to stand in the rain while they prepared my brother for his own murder.

He had less than two weeks to go before they strapped him down and injected poison into his heart. I knew Collie would be divided about it, the way he was divided about everything. A part of him would look forward to stepping off the big ledge. He'd been looking over it his whole life in one way or another.

A different part of him would be full of rage and self-pity and fear. I had no doubt that when the time came he'd be a passive prisoner right up to the moment they tried to buckle him down. Then he'd explode into violence. He was going to hurt whoever was near him, whether it was a priest or the warden or a guard. They'd have to club him down while he laughed. The priest, if he was still capable, would have to raise his voice in prayer to cover my brother's curses.

I was twenty minutes late for my appointment at the prison. The screw at the gate didn't want to let me in because he'd already marked me as a no-show. I didn't argue. I didn't want to be there. He saw that I wanted to split and it was enough to compel him to let me stay.

At the prison door, another screw gave me the disgusted once-over. I told him my name, but the sound of it didn't feel right anymore.

"Terry Rand."

The fake ID I'd been living under the past half decade had become a safe harbor, a slim chance to better myself even though I hadn't done much yet. I resented being forced to return to the person I'd once been.

The screw made me repeat my name. I did. It was like ice on my tongue. Then he made me repeat it again. I caught on.

"Terrier Rand."

Expressionless, he led me off to a small side room where I was frisked and politely asked if I would voluntarily succumb to a strip search. I asked what would happen if I said no. He said I wouldn't be allowed to proceed. It was a good enough reason to turn around. I owed my brother nothing. I could return out west and get back to a life I was still trying to believe in and make real.

Even as I decided to leave I was shrugging out of my jacket and kicking off my shoes. I got naked and held my arms up while the screw ran his hands through my hair and checked between my ass cheeks and under my scrotum.

He stared at the dog tattoo that took up the left side of my chest, covering three bad scars. One was from when Collie had stabbed me with the bayonet of a tin Revolutionary War toy soldier when I was seven. I got a deep muscle infection that the doctor had to go digging after, leaving the area a rutted, puckered purple.

Another was from when I was twelve and my father sent me up the drainpipe to a house that was supposedly empty. A seventy-five-year-old lady picked up a Tiffany-style lamp and swatted me three stories down into a hibiscus tree. A rib snapped and pierced the flesh. My old man got me into the car and pulled the bone shard through by hand as the sirens closed in and he drove up on sidewalks to escape. The scar was mottled red and thick as a finger.

The last one I didn't think about. I had made an art of not thinking about it.

The screw took pride in his professional indifference, courteous yet dismissive. But the tattoo caught his attention.

"Your family, you're some serious dog lovers, eh?"

I didn't answer. One last time he checked through my clothes for any contraband. He tossed them back to me and I got dressed.

I was taken to an empty visiting room. I sat in a chair and waited for them to bring Collie in. It didn't matter that there was a wall of reinforced glass between us. I wasn't going to pass him a shiv and we weren't going to shake hands or hug out twenty years of tension. The only time we'd ever touched was when we were trying to beat the hell out of each other. I'd been thinking hard about the reasons for that on the ride back east. How could it be that I had such resentment and animosity for him, and he for me, and yet when he called I came running?

They led him in, draped in chains. He could shuffle along only a few inches at a time, his hands cuffed to a thick leather belt at his waist, his feet separated by a narrow chain, bracelets snapped to his ankles. It took ten minutes to unlock him. The screws retreated and Collie twirled his chair around and sat backward, like always.

Like most mad-dog convicts, prison agreed with him. He was a lot more fit than he'd ever been on the outside. The huge beer belly had been trimmed back to practically nothing, his arms thick and muscular and covered in twisted black veins. There was a new gleam in his eye that I couldn't evaluate.

He had old scars from drunken brawls and new ones from the joint that gave him a sense of character he'd never exhibited before. Like me, he'd gone gray prematurely. He had a short but well-coiffed mane of silver with a few threads of black running through it. I noticed he'd also had a manicure and a facial. He glowed a healthy pink. He'd been moisturized and exfoliated and closely shaved. The nancies on C-Block could open up a salon in East Hampton and make a mint off Long Island's wealthy blue-haired biddies.

I expected that with his execution only two weeks off, and with five years gone and all the uneasy blood still between us, we would need to pause and gather our thoughts before we spoke. I imagined we would stare at each other, making our usual judgments and taking each other's measure. We'd then bypass trivial concerns to speak of extreme matters, whatever they might be. With a strange reservation, a kind of childlike hesitation, I lifted the phone and cleared my throat.

Collie moved with the restrained energy of a predator, slid forward in his seat, did a little rap-a-tap on the glass. He grasped the phone and first thing let loose with a snorted, easy laugh. He looked all around until he finally settled on my eyes.

He usually spoke with a quick, jazzy bop tempo, sometimes muttering out of the corner of his mouth or under his breath as if to an audience situated around him. This time he was focused. He nodded once, more to himself than me, and said, "Listen, Ma hates me, and that's all right, but you, you're the one who broke her heart. You—"

I hung up the phone, stood, and walked away.

I was nearly to the door when Collie's pounding on the glass made me stop. It got the screws looking in on us. I kept my back to my brother. My scalp crawled and I was covered in sweat. I wondered if what he'd said was true. It was the best trick he had, getting me to constantly question myself. Even when I knew he was setting me up I couldn't keep from falling into the trap. I wondered if my mother's heart really had broken when I'd left. I thought of my younger sister, Dale, still waiting for me to read her romantic vampire fantasy novels. My father on the porch with no one to sit with. My gramp losing his memories, fighting to retain them, now that there was nobody to stroll around the lake with and discuss the best way to trick out burglar alarms.

Collie kept on shouting and banging. I took another step. I reached for the handle. Maybe if I'd made my fortune out west I would have found it easier to leave him there yelling. Maybe if I'd gotten married. Maybe if I'd raised a child.

But none of that had happened. I took a breath, turned, and sat again. I lifted the phone.

"Jesus, you're still sensitive," he said. "I only meant that you need to stop thinking about yourself and go see the family—"

"I'm not going to see the family. Why did you call me here, Collie?"

He let out a quiet laugh. He pointed through the huge glass window off to the side of us, which opened on an area full of long tables. His gaze was almost wistful. "You know, we were supposed to be able to talk over there. In that room, face-to-face. On this phone, talking to you like this, it's not the way I wanted it to be."

"How did you want it to be?"

He grinned and shrugged, and the thousand questions that had once burned inside me reignited. I knew he wouldn't answer them. My brother clung to his secrets, great and small. He'd been interviewed dozens of times for newspaper articles and magazines and books, and while he gave intimate, awful details, he never explained himself. It drove the courts, the media, and the public crazy even now.

And me too. Words bobbed in my throat but never made it out. The timeworn campaigns and disputes between us had finally receded. I no longer cared about the insults, the torn pages, the girls he stole from me, or the way he'd run off on short cons gone bad, leaving me to take beatings from the marks. It had taken a lot of spilled blood to make me forgive him, if in fact I had. If not, it would only matter another few days.

On the long night of his rampage, my brother went so far down into the underneath that he didn't come back up until after he'd murdered eight people. A vacationing family of five shot to death in a mobile home, a gas-station attendant knifed in a men's room, an old lady beaten to death outside a convenience store, a young woman strangled in a park.

None of them had been robbed. He hadn't taken anything, hadn't even cleaned out the register at the gas station.

It wasn't our way. It had never been our way. I thought of my grandfather Shepherd again. One of my earliest memories was of him telling us all around a Thanksgiving dinner, *You're born thieves, it's your nature, handed down to me, handed down from me. This is our way.* He'd been getting ready to cut into a turkey Collie had boosted from the King Kullen.

Collie turned on the charm, showed me his perfect teeth, and said, "Been a long time, Terry. You look good. Trim, built up. You're as dark as if you'd been dipped in a vat of maple syrup."

"I work on a ranch."

"Yeah? What, busting broncos? Roping cattle? Like that?"

"Like that."

"Where? Colorado? Montana?"

That question made me frown. I'd been eager to know how he'd managed to track me down. I'd been off the grift for years, living under an assumed name, doing an honest job. I thought I'd covered my tracks well, but four days ago, after coming in from digging fence posts, I'd received a phone call from a woman whose voice I didn't recognize. She'd told me Collie wanted to see me before he died.

"You already know. How'd you find me?"

"I put in a call."

"To who?"

"Who do you think?"

He meant our family, who had connections all over the circuit. I'd half-expected that they'd somehow kept tabs on me. They must've gotten in touch with the people I'd bought my fake ID from and shadowed me through the years. I should have realized my father wouldn't let me go so easily.

But that voice on the phone didn't belong to anyone I knew. I wondered if my other identity had been completely blown and I'd have to start over again, rebuild another new life. How many more did I have left in me?

"It's been good seeing you, Terry. I'm glad you came. We both need a little more time."

I'd barely slept over the last four days, and all the miles gunning across the country suddenly caught up with me. I felt tired as hell. "What are you talking about, Collie?"

"Come back tomorrow or the day after. They gave you shit at the door, I can tell. Rousted you, strip-searched you? If they try that again, tell them to fuck themselves." He raised his voice again and shouted at the screws. "Dead man walking has at least a couple of extra privileges!"

"Listen, I'm not—"

"Take some time to settle yourself."

"I don't want to settle myself. I'm not coming back tomorrow, Collie."

"Go home. Visit the family. I'll tell you what I need when I see you again."

I started breathing through my teeth. "What you need. I'm not running drugs for you. I'm not icing anybody on the outside for you. I'm not sending around a petition to the governor. I'm not coming back."

It got him laughing again. "You're home. You're going to see the family because you've missed them. You've been gone a long time and proven whatever point you had to make, Terry. You can stick it out on your own. You're your own man. You're not Dad. You're not me." He cupped the phone even more tightly to his mouth. "Besides, you love them and they love you. It's time to say hello again."

Life lessons from death row. Christ. I felt nauseous.

I stared hard into my brother's eyes, trying to read a face I'd always been able to read before. I saw in it just how plagued he was by his own culpability. He was shallow and vindictive, but he rarely lied. He didn't often deny responsibility and he never cared about consequences. There was absolutely nothing I could do for him.

"I'm not coming back," I told him.

"I think I need you to save someone's life," he said.

"What?"

"Tomorrow afternoon. Or the day after, if you want. And don't be late this time."

I hung up on his smile and let out a hiss that steamed the glass.

Already he'd bent me out of shape. It had taken no more than fifteen minutes. We hadn't said shit to each other. Maybe it was his fault, maybe it was mine. I could feel the old singular pain rising once more.

I shoved my chair back, took a few steps, and stopped. I thought, If I can get out now, without asking the question, I might be able to free myself. I have the chance. It's there. The door is three feet away. I can do this. I can do this.

It was a stupid mantra. I'd already missed my chance. I'd turned back once already, and I was about to do the same thing again. I knew Collie would still be seated, watching me, waiting. I turned back, grabbed the phone up, stood facing the glass, and said, "The girl in the mobile home."

He almost looked ashamed for an instant. He shut his eyes and swung his chin back and forth like he was trying to jar one memory loose and replace it with another. He pursed his lips and muttered something to his invisible audience that I wasn't meant to hear. Then he grinned, his hard and cool back in place. "Okay."

"So tell me," I said.

"What do you want to hear?"

"You already know. Just say it."

"You want to hear that I did it? Okay, I aced her."

"She was nine."

"Yeah."

"Tell me why."

"Would you feel better if she was nineteen? Or twenty-nine? You feel better about the old lady? She was seventy-one. I killed her with my fists. Or—"

"I want to know why, Collie."

"You're asking the wrong questions."

"Tell me or you'll never see me again."

His icy eyes softened. Not out of shame but out of fear that I would leave him forever. He licked his lips, and his brow tightened in concentration as he searched for a genuine response.

"I was making ghosts," he said.

"What the hell does that mean?"

"I appreciate you showing up. Really. Come back tomorrow, Terry. Okay? Or the day after. Please."

I thought of a nine-year-old girl standing in the face of my enraged brother. I knew what it was like to be caught in that storm. I imagined his laughter, the way his eyes whirled in their sockets as he made her lie down on the floor beside her parents and brothers, pointed a .38 at the back of her head as she twisted her face away in terror, and squeezed the trigger.

I made it to my car and threw up twice in the parking lot. I drove through the prison gates and waited on the street until I spotted the guard who'd made me repeat my name three times.

He eased by in a flashy sports car so well waxed that the rain slewed off and barely touched it. For a half hour I followed him from a quarter mile back, until he turned in to a new neighborhood development maybe ten minutes from the shore.

The rain had shifted to a light drizzle. I watched him pull in by a yellow two-story house with a new clapboard roof and a well-mown yard. There was an SUV in the driveway and the garage door was open. Two six- or seven-year-old boys rolled up and down the wet sidewalk wearing sneakers with little wheels built into them.

I drove to the beach and sat staring at the waves until it was dark. I'd been surrounded by mountains and desert for so long that I'd forgotten how lulling the ocean can be, alive and comforting, aware of your weaknesses and sometimes merciful.

Five minutes off the parkway I found a restaurant and ate an overpriced but succulent seafood dinner. I'd been living on steak and Tex-Mex spices for so long that it was like an exotic meal from some foreign and romantic land. The lobster and crab legs quieted my stomach and loosened the knot there. I listened in to the families around me, the children laughing and whining, the parents humorous and warm and short-tempered.

The wind picked up and it started to rain harder again. Streams of saturated moonlight did wild endless shimmies against the glass. I drank a cup of coffee every twenty minutes until the place closed, then I sat out at the beach again until the bluster passed.

It took me three minutes to get into the screw's house. I stood in the master bedroom and watched as he and his wife spooned in their sleep. She was lovely, with a tousled mound of hair that glowed a burnished copper in the dark. One lace strap of her lingerie had slipped off her shoulder, and the swell of her breast arched toward me.

I found his trousers and snatched his wallet. He had a lot of photos of his children. I left the house, drove to the water, and threw his wallet into the whitecaps. I didn't want his money. I didn't want to know his name. I didn't even especially want to hurt him. I was testing myself and finding that I'd both passed and failed.

I was still a good creeper. The skills remained. My heart rate never sped. I didn't make a sound.

I hadn't broken the law in five years, not so much as running a yellow light. My chest itched. My scars burned. The one where Collie had stabbed me. The one from my broken rib. And the largest one, made up of Kimmy's teeth marks from the last time we'd made love. She bit in so deep under my heart that she'd scraped bone.

I drove home through the storm, thinking of the ghosts I had made.

My old man was waiting for me on the front porch. The rest of the house was dark, and the wet silver lashed the yard with dripping, burning shadows. Gutters pinged and warped wood groaned like angry lovers.

He had a twelve-pack on ice and had already killed off eight bottles. He wasn't drunk. He never lost control, not even when he was tugging bone slivers out of his own kid.

John F. Kennedy sauntered out from his usual position at my father's feet. JFK was an American Staffordshire terrier, a second cousin to the pit bull. He was nine now and I could see the gray of his muzzle lit up in the moonlight. He recognized me immediately and met me on the top stair, got up on his hind legs, and greeted me with savage kisses. He remained muscular and his breath was just as bad as I remembered. I hugged and patted him until he eased away, returned to his spot, circled and dropped. Besides Collie, JFK was the only member of the family to ever kill a man.

My father proffered me a bottle. Our hands touched briefly but it was enough. I could still feel the power within him. He barely came up to my chin, but he was wiry and solid. By the yellow porch light I could see that he still had all his hair and it was still mostly black. I had more gray in mine. I had more gray than even the dog.

I sat beside my father and took my first drink in five years.

I knew he wouldn't ask about Collie. We hadn't discussed the murders when my brother was brought down and we wouldn't talk about them now. The urge would be there but my old man would keep it in check, the way he kept everything in check.

He wouldn't ask me about my life away from home unless I brought it up. I might be married. He might have grandchildren. I could be on the run from the law in twelve states, but he'd never broach the topic. We were a family of thieves who knew one another very well and respected one another's secrets. It was dysfunction at its worst.

Still, I knew what would be bothering him more than anything else. The same thing that filled me with a burden of remorse that wasn't mine to carry. It would eat at him the way it ate at me. We'd flash on the little girl a couple of times a day, no matter what we were doing. Step through a doorway and see her on the floor of the mobile home, intuit her terror. We would suffer the guilt that Collie either didn't feel or couldn't express.

My father had never been comfortable as a thief. He was a good cat burglar but wasn't capable of pulling a polished grift. He couldn't steal from someone while looking him in the eye. He disliked working with the fences and the syndicates that the Rand family had always worked with. He stole only to bring home cash to the family, and so far as I knew he hardly ever spent a dime on himself. He didn't live large, had no flash, preferred to be the humble and quiet man that he was by nature.

After I took my thirty-foot fall, my father slowly withdrew himself from the bent life. He pulled fewer and fewer scores until he was no longer a criminal. I knew it was my fault, as much as having a busted rib pulled through your flesh can be your own fault. But having my blood on his hands eventually forced him out of the game. He played the stock market frugally, took three or four trips down to Atlantic City a year and sometimes hit big. He wrote his travel expenses off on his tax forms. So far as the IRS was concerned, my father and uncles were professional gamblers, and they each paid out a fair hunk of cash to Uncle Sam every year to keep the feds off their backs.

I finished the beer and he handed me another. We could go on like this for hours. The silence was never awkward between us. I sipped and listened to JFK sputter and snore.

My father said, "I wish he hadn't put out the call to you."

"You didn't have to pass it on, Dad."

"Yes, I did. He's my son. You didn't have to answer."

"Yes, I did. He's my brother."

"I thought you hated him."

"I do hate him."

That actually got my old man chuckling. I knew why. He was thinking about how he'd lived in the same house his entire life alongside his father and two older brothers, Mal and Grey. The four of them under the same roof for more than a half century and a sour word had never passed between them. They were partners, trained to function as a gang on the grift. My father had once taken a bullet meant for my uncle Mal. It had done little more than clip the top quarter inch off his left pinky. The wound had been sutured closed with three stitches. He'd lost maybe a squirt of blood. But none of that altered the fact that Mal owed his life to my dad. He recognized the truth of it every day since the incident had occurred more than twenty years ago.

And here I'd despised my brother since I was old enough to walk and get knocked down by him. And here we'd never had a kind word for each other. And here we'd slugged it out and crashed through the porch railing together. And here I was home again, answering the whistle.

The rain overloaded the gutters and poured over the edge of the roof in vast sheets. It never rained like this out west. I'd forgotten how much I missed it. The chill spray felt good against my face.

My father said, "You doing okay?"

"Yeah."

"You look healthy. Fit. Your hair's a little longer. Suits you. Hard to tell out here but you seem tan."

"I work on a ranch."

"When you were a kid you always said you were going to own one someday."

"I don't own it, but I help run it."

He nodded. "Herding sheep? Breaking broncs? Moving cattle through rivers, like that?"

I held back a sigh. When I first got out west I thought I'd be busting broncos too. Sitting around campfires eating beans. Being a hero of the rodeo. What the fuck did I know. I'd ridden one bronc and he threw me off in half a second and gave me a concussion.

And yet I somehow pined for my own ignorance. "Like that."

He continued drinking and the grin never left his face, but I could feel his brisk inspection of me even though he didn't turn his head. This was as playful as he was likely to get. We danced around any important topics. Stepped to them, rejected them. The silence was full of our unvoiced conversations.

He understood that I'd never gotten over Kimmy and never would. He consoled me without a word. In the darkness I could hear his fierce heart stamping in his chest.

"Reporters hassling you much?" I asked.

"A little, with Collie's, with his"—he couldn't say *execution*—"with all the hustle and activity surrounding him again. They come in groups. Channel 3, Channel 7, Channel 21, all these vans pulling up out front. And then they stand around whiling the time away, eating bagels, drinking coffee. They put the prettiest girl with the microphone out in front, let her lead the charge. And she stands at the door and says, 'How does it make you feel?' She asks it like it's a real question, with her eyes full of false sympathy. Licks her lips like she's waiting for an answer."

"They bother Ma?"

"No, I don't let it get that far. The lawyers say I shouldn't slam the door in their faces, but if I try to respond I sound like an idiot. Mal and Grey handle it better, so they field for us."

"Cops?"

"Same as usual, no more or less. You remember Gilmore?"

I remembered Gilmore.

"He still comes sniffing around. Sits in and plays cards, has a beer or two."

"How much do you let him win?"

"We rob him blind. He doesn't much care, figures he's learning something trying to spot the four-card lift, the third-card bottom deal. He hardly even questions us about stolen goods anymore."

"He thinks he's rattling you just by showing up, reminding you that someone's always watching."

"That's something I'll never forget."

"He's making sure."

"We all have to spend our time somehow. He's a detective now."

I nodded. Gilmore had always wanted the gold shield. It made sense that he'd still come prowling around even now. If Collie could cross the line then so could I. It must keep him up, wondering if I was out there, going shitstorm crazy.

"How much pressure does he put on you to tell him where I am?"

"A little in the beginning, right after you left. Not so much anymore. He asks in passing, tries to get someone to confess something out of turn. 'So, how's Terrier holding up? You get a Christmas card from him this year?' It doesn't amount to anything. I think he's genuinely curious. He always liked you. He's different now. Has no real edge to him anymore. His wife left him and took the kids. He's got too much time on his hands. I don't know what he does with it all."

"How's everybody else?" I asked.

"Old Shepherd is worse." My father's grief was under control but it still hung heavily in his voice. "Most days he can't recognize anyone. He doesn't really talk anymore. He watches a lot of TV. It's what fills his days now. He likes cartoons. If you get the chance, I hope you'll sit with him. He might rouse a bit."

I knew my dad's subtle nuances. He had more to say, but he was superstitious. He didn't want his words to give life and form to whatever he was holding back. I waited. It took him a few more minutes. JFK whined in his sleep. The rain started and stopped again. "I think your uncles have a touch of Alzheimer's too. I've found them out in the yard in the middle of the night a couple of times, looking dazed, like sleep-walking."

I had to move. I got up and put my hands on the rebuilt rail and hung my head over enough so that the rain fell against the back of my neck. I couldn't imagine Mal and Grey watching cartoons, drooling, unable to crack wise or shuffle and cut a deck eighteen times in ten seconds and still pull four aces from the bottom. Or would those skills last long after they couldn't form a cohesive sentence anymore?

As much as I loved my grandfather and uncles, my reaction was as selfish and full of fear as it was anything else. I didn't want to think that in my DNA I had a predisposition to losing my mind. I didn't want to believe I might one day end up like Gramp, just as I didn't want to believe that I might one day end up like my brother.

I turned and my father said, "Dale is doing good in school, spends a lot of time performing in plays. She's always practicing around the house, puts on a southern belle accent and acts out *Cat on a Hot Tin Roof* or *Streetcar.* Your uncles help. Mal does Newman, Grey does Brando. They walk around asking for lemonade and patting their foreheads, talking about how sultry the steamy south is. She's a natural. She's always taking the train into the city to see something on or off Broadway. Has a fondness for Albee and Ibsen. Williams. Surprising for her age, I'd say."

Ibsen and Albee and Williams. Jesus, it had been a long time since I'd read her little vampire fairy tales to her.

"You must be tired. Your room's the same as you left it."

I hadn't expected anything else. "I'll see you in the morning, Dad."

"Good night, Terry."

I started inside but turned before the screen door closed behind me. "Have you ever gone to see him?" I asked.

"No. None of us." I could hear the steel in his voice. "I wouldn't allow it. You understand that, don't you?"

I understood my own reasons but I wasn't sure his or anyone else's were the same. But I said, "Of course."

I stepped in and moved through the darkness of my own home the way I'd crept the prison guard's. With the same strange sense of quelled excitement and personal dominion. I slipped up the stairs into my bedroom.

My old man hadn't been kidding. My room was the same, untouched except for maybe the monthly sweep of a feather duster. I checked some of my stash spots and found my old burglary tools and a couple wedges of cash that totaled three grand. I counted the bills. Most were fresh, printed within the last year or two. Somebody had discovered my money, taken it as needed, and then later replaced it. For all I knew, every one of them had riffled through it.

It was good to know that a few rules still hadn't been broken. Chief among them was that we didn't steal from one another.

I laid back on the bed and listened to the rain and tried to empty my thoughts, but there wasn't a chance. I turned over and opened the nightstand drawer. It was too common a place for anyone to look for anything of value.

I took out the last photo of Kimmy and me together. We're at Jones Beach. I'm grinning because I'm with her. I'm grinning because the latest set of burglary charges against me have been dropped due to insufficient evidence. I'm grinning because the night before I scored over a grand from Gilmore's house while his wife and kids were out at the movies. He thought he was slick, keeping a chunk of skimmed cash at the bottom of an old cereal box. Always check the dates.

In the photo we're happy. We'd been talking about getting married. Most of the hardness was out of Kimmy's eyes by then. It would be another couple of weeks before she miscarried and the grief brought it back and shoved us apart. Another month before Collie would be found drinking beer at a corner dive called the Elbow Room, a trail of fire and blood behind him.

I woke to see my mother on the edge of the bed, staring at me with her hand pressed to my heart. She had a bad habit of doing that kind of thing.

Dawn sliced through the blinds. I blinked twice into the glare and she was there with the barest lilt to the edges of her mouth, hazel eyes intense and a little solemn. When I was a kid this had felt comforting. When I got older it started to spook me a bit. Right now it felt somewhere in between.

The pulse in her wrist beat back against the snap of my heart. The wash and pound of our blood made for a strange internal music. She shifted and with two fingers plied my gray patch.

"You get that from my side of the family," she said. She shook out her auburn hair. She was using some kind of dye that brought out the red highlights.

I'd never met anyone from her side of the family. Apparently, after she and my father started becoming serious, her parents asked what kind of a boy he was. She told the truth. They ordered her to stop seeing him immediately. She showed up one last time to pack her belongings and found the pictures of her turned to the wall. She never went home again.

Except for that one story, she never spoke of them.

I realized with some surprise that I didn't even know her maiden name. I always wondered why she hadn't just covered and lied about my father's occupation. Was it because she knew that the truth would eventually come out anyway? Because she had imagined Thanksgiving dinner at her parents' house, everybody sitting down to the turkey and, just as the mashed potatoes were being passed around, the cops raiding the house? Her parents with their mouths half full of corn and yams being shoved up against the wall, frisked, billy-clubbed in the kidneys, cuffed, *Freeze, dirtbag.*

My mother remained a beautiful woman even at an age when such women were often called handsome. Her lips and chin had softened a bit more but she was still lovely, with a natural smile that always made you feel better.

"I started finding gray strands when I was in junior high. I went wild plucking them. My mother would find them all about the house and say, 'Ellie, being bald is worse than having your face framed by silver.' " She curled more of my hair around her fingers. "Looks good on you, Terry, gives you character. If you're hungry I'll make you something."

I was, but I shook my head. Sleep hadn't done anything to wear away the tension in me. I wanted to burn it off a little. "It's early."

We spoke in whispers.

"I just wanted to look in on you."

"You should go back to sleep."

"So should you."

"I'm used to getting up at dawn."

"So am I. I have to check on Gramp. He sometimes wakes up early and doesn't do anything but sit and stare until someone at least turns the television on for him. Kids' shows, if you can believe it. He gets upset with anything else, but you put on cartoons and he settles."

"Christ, he's really that bad?"

"The doctors can't do much. He's too far gone with Alzheimer's." She shrugged, a lissome and graceful movement. "That and being shot in the head."

"Well, yeah."

My grandfather had been shot in the back of the head when he was sixteen, and the bullet had never been removed. You could feel the entrance wound, which had never fully scarred over. He'd made everybody do it at least once. When I brought Kimmy home for the first time, she'd grinned, pressed her purple-painted fingernail to his gunshot hole, and said, "If you think nasty thoughts about me now, Old Shep, I'll know it. *I'll feel them.*"

He claimed it never bothered him until he was in his sixties and the headaches started. They grew worse the older he got until they began to fade along with his mind. He'd been getting a touch forgetful and had just started walking in his sleep when I left.

I swung my legs out of bed.

"I'm glad you came back," my mother said. "I've missed you. But I'm sorry it had to be like this." She shut her eyes and worked her mouth silently for a moment before her voice caught traction. "I'm sorry it was for *him*."

"It's all right."

"It's not all right. He shouldn't have . . . they . . . he . . ." She caught her breath and a sheen of tears brought out the flecks of gold in her eyes. "Sometimes I hate him like a poison. I think about what he's done, what happened, and I wish . . . I wish they'd hurry up with it. And then I feel guilty for thinking it, and I remember who he is, that he's my son, and that I love him, and I want him out of there, I want him home again, I want you all home again, and I think, I think . . ." Her face firmed. "It can never happen, and I'm glad for that. I'm glad we don't talk about it, even though we'd all be better off if we would. Especially your father. Did he ask you anything?"

"No," I said.

"Then I won't either."

"You can."

"No, I won't make you discuss it. You're like all the Rands, you can't talk about it. Sometimes I'd give my right tit for one of you to get in a gabby mood, be garrulous just for ten minutes."

"Ma, listen to me." I made myself form the words. "Collie, he wanted—"

"Shhh . . . it's okay. Now that you're done with him, you can—"

"I'm not done. He wants to see me again."

"For what reason?"

"He's got more to tell me."

"Don't listen."

"I have to."

"You don't, and you shouldn't."

"I do, I have to."

"Why?"

There was no way to start talking about it and then stop. You couldn't just explain a piece of it, unwind one thread from the knot. The little girl, the strangled teen, the nights awake, the miles that lay behind.

My mother loved me enough not to expect an answer. She said, "I understand."

"It wasn't just Collie. It was time I came back anyway."

"For Kimmy."

"I don't know."

"Of course you do."

Maybe I did. I wanted to ask her if she'd seen Kimmy, heard anything about her or her family. What she was doing, if she was married, if she was still in New York. My chest grew heavy with the number of questions I had, all the unfinished business.

But my mother was right. I had gray in my hair from her side of the family, and from my father's side I learned to keep stony and mute about anything of real importance. It's how I'd lost Kimmy in the first place.

While I tried to somehow slip around my own silence my mother kissed my forehead and left the room.

I was used to hard work and exercise now. I felt wired and antsy and decided to take a run. There were some old sweats and sneakers in my closet. I put them on. Everything was tight on my larger frame but manageable.

I walked downstairs and felt some of the old familiarity start to ease back into me. I knew that in ten minutes it would be like I'd never left at all.

The house had been in our family for four generations. Construction had been started by my great-grandfather and his brothers, who'd been adept architects and carpenters but piss-poor thieves who were always breezing in and out of the joint. Because they were often caught and incarcerated together, it took forever to raise the roof beams. The place had been completed a decade or so later with the help of my grandfather and his brother, who were starting to learn what to do in order to stay out of the can.

They'd purchased three lots' worth of land so that our nearest neighbor was a quarter mile up the road. Only a comparatively small section of the yard had ever been cleared. The rest remained wild and overgrown with trees and brush. As little kids, my best friend, Chub Wright, and I would camp back there and talk about car chases in action movies, listening to my uncles come and go through the house, unloading goods after midnight.

Unless you were an ace heister who pulled in multi-million-dollar scores, owning a house was almost unheard of on the circuit. Thieves by their nature and calling were usually on the move. They had warrants out on them in one state so they ran to another. The heat came down so they moved to cooler climes. They never stayed put. Except that we did. It made things a little hinky. All the cops knew us. All the undercover journalists would show up at our door trying to sell us soap or vacuum cleaners, carrying cases with hidden cameras and digital feeds inside. We could spot them from fifty feet away.

That was another reason why it took so long for the place to be built. The house was a well-crafted magic trick. Unless you were intimately familiar with its interior, you'd never guess just how many crawl spaces, hidden rooms, extended root cellars, and attic areas the place actually had. Whole sections of floorboards could be peeled back, but you had to know where the locking mechanisms were. Walls slid aside. Built-in staircases unfolded and let you climb eight or twelve feet up into recessed chambers. You couldn't use a hammer to find a hollow spot, because damn near every inch of the extra space was filled with loot. Some of it went back fifty years. My grandfather and his brothers had boosted a lot of shit back in the fifties that they weren't able to fence. But you never dumped hot property. You sold it or planted it or kept it. When your whole family was made up of grifters and gaffers and second-story men, that meant a ton of excess haul: old machinery, bicycle parts, busted record players, eight-track tape decks, old TVs with missing vacuum tubes, furniture, worthless silverware, and literally tons of other crap I'd never even seen.

Under the living room where my grandfather sat in his chair, with the quiet strains of cartoon characters taking frying pans to their heads, was a cache of unfenced curio bric-a-brac going back decades. My father had never been able to resist small trinkets and novelty gadgets that he felt might have an interesting history. In the middle of a job he'd pocket broken shillelaghs, nutcrackers with busted hinges, dinged Zippo lighters, music boxes with cracked dancers, chipped Dresden dolls, and old tools whose purpose eluded him. He had a healthy respect for hands and couldn't resist anything that looked like it had been caressed and fondled or well applied.

The irony of a useless man in a room stationed over useless hidden things wasn't lost on me. I figured if my grandfather grew lucid at all anymore, it wouldn't be lost on him either. Gramp's hands twitched and trembled. His eyes never left the television screen.

My mother came in holding a bowl of oatmeal and said, "Do you want to feed him?"

"No."

So she sat on the loveseat and fed him instead. I stood close to his shoulder and watched. She kept up a running monologue of childish banter, and Gramp never reacted in any way. During commercials his chin would droop and his gaze would lower, his whole body slumping forward. When the cartoons came back on he'd sit a little straighter. He'd make noises that might have been laughter.

I took it for as long as I could and then I started out of the room. I made it two steps and knew something had happened but I wasn't sure what. I turned and Old Shep looked exactly the same, still making his sounds but a little louder now. I looked at the floor. I scanned the room. Then I checked my pocket. My wallet was missing.

Even with the Parkinson's and the Alzheimer's he was an ace pickpocket. It took me a minute to find my wallet deep in the folds of his robe. He was still in there somewhere.

I said, "Sweet action, Gramp," but a commercial was on and he was slumped in his seat with his strings cut.

As I trotted down the drive into the road, JFK came lumbering after me. I ran back inside and got his leash. I didn't know if his knees would hold up, but I didn't plan to do more than a few miles. I wasn't even going to pretend to be heading anywhere except Kimmy's place.

The area had changed some. A few more housing tracts had gone up, a couple of new strip malls. We clung to Old Autauk Highway, which broke through a few small neighborhoods down by the bay, then circled Autauk Park and my old high school. We cut north and covered a couple of miles of the back trails that still surrounded Shalebrook College. I saw there was a new building on campus, looked like a science hall. They'd completed the bridge expansion that connected the dorms to the library with a glass atrium that arched over the parkway.

We reached Shalebrook Lake and JFK took a long drink and then hunkered down in the shallows, the small waves stirred by the wind breaking over his ridged back. He turned his face to me with a regal expression, all of his usual attitude back in place. I'd worried about him, but he was handling the run fine and actually looked healthier for it.

I sat on a nearby bench and almost unconsciously started counting the number of houses that I'd robbed. I only realized what I was doing when I hit twenty. Most of the burglaries had been for pocket change. Even the crappiest joe job would've paid better and without the hazard of going away for a three-year jolt.

"You going to be like them?" Kimmy had asked me after meeting the family, while she shook out about half a pound of hot pepper onto a slice of pizza. "For the rest of your days?"

"I'm a thief. Thieves steal."

"You're a cat burglar."

"That just means I steal shit while people are home sleeping."

"Someone's going to shoot you in the head too."

"Then you'll be able to feel my naughty thoughts."

She took a bite and her face flushed. "Those I'm already well aware of."

"Some of them."

We were nineteen. The world was a contradiction. It seemed both wide open to possibility and set in tracks we'd never be able to alter.

Of course Kimmy knew all about the notorious Rand clan. Everyone in the area did. Sometimes it helped Collie and me in our romantic lives. A lot of girls liked the bad boys, and they'd expect us to take them on scores with us, let them get a feel for what the bent life was all about. Two girls I dated practically begged me to rob their parents' houses. They knew where the stashes were, codes to the alarms, combinations on the safes. I'd say, "Where's the fun in any of that?"

If they pushed too hard I tossed their phone numbers. I never knew when one of them might sneak off with her mother's jewelry and try to blame me for it.

I wasn't the only criminal around, so I lost some cachet. There were meth cookers on their way up and a few syndicate princes and princesses from the last couple of mob families in the area. Chub was already a first-rate crew mechanic. By the time he was nineteen he owned his own garage and was known for souping up stolen cars for strings putting together bank heists. He'd fine-tune engines until they sang and help the drivers plot out their getaways.

I'd been arrested twice by the time I was seventeen but I was never held for more than a couple of hours. In some eyes, that meant I was just a wannabe outlaw. That was how I liked it. Being someone on the outside but no one really knowing if I deserved the rep I'd been saddled with. It was one way to keep off the radar.

Kimmy was an outsider too, someone who hung around the lake at night with the other kids but was never quite part of their pack. Living at home, taking classes at the college, she was smarter and more sensitive than the rest of them. I could see it in the way she held herself, a hint of lower-middle-class sorrow and hushed desperation in her eyes but hanging on to the chance for something else. She was beautiful but didn't want to be. She dressed down. She tied her brown hair back, hid it beneath hats and scarves. Others felt the crush of mediocrity and resigned themselves to it with booze or crystal, floating around the fields until it was time to show at their minimum-wage labors the next day. Kimmy bucked the trend, studied harder, glared at you harder, talked harder.

Sitting on the hood of a '66 Mustang, holding in a lungful of Acapulco Gold, Chub wheezed out, "That one, she'll send you up or set you straight."

"Might be worth the risk."

"Don't you believe it."

Like most teens who shared an attraction, Kimmy and I danced around each other for weeks before moving in tight enough that we had to say hello.

First thing she ever said to me was, "My aunt, she manages an organic-health-food-and-vitamins store. Six months ago somebody held her up and cleaned out the register. Was it you?"

"No. I don't do armed robbery."

"They didn't get much cash but they made her give up her jewelry. Everything was junk except for a gold pendant given to her by my grandmother. Inside were two tiny photos of my great-grandparents, taken in Hungary back in the thirties. It's the only thing left of them. It wasn't just sentimental, you know? It's more meaningful than that."

She wasn't talking about a pendant but a locket. I nodded. "I think I understand."

"Any chance you can help me get it back?"

A stickup already six months old. Unless the piece was exceptional and really stood out, there wasn't going to be much of a shot. But I knew all the fences and could probably get a line on the punk snatcher. I looked into Kimmy's eyes and liked what I saw there. They were almost mean but I could see a little softness tucked deep inside. I wondered what had happened to her to give her such a hard shell so early on and decided I wanted to hang around long enough to find out.

"If your aunt's got a photo of herself wearing the locket, give it to me. If not, have her describe it in detail. Any extra information can only help."

Kimmy was a step ahead. She handed me a photo. There was a stickum note on the back with all the relevant info, including the name and address of the shop and the date and time of the robbery. "This is it."

"Give me four days. If I can't get a line on it by then there isn't anything that can be done."

She said, "Thank you," without an ounce of real gratitude. "So . . . Friday night then?"

"I'll pick you up."

She frowned, came this close to hitting me with a sneer. "You don't know where I live."

"Sure I do."

When she climbed into my car four days later the locket was waiting for her on the dashboard. She checked the tiny photos inside, then stuck it in her pocket.

"What did it cost you to get it back?"

"Nothing, the fence owed me one."

"Did you talk to the guy who stole it?"

"No."

I couldn't read the expression on her face in the shadowed interior of the car. I turned up the dash lights.

"I thought maybe you'd have to fight him for it," she said.

"You wanted me to fight him for it, that right?"

I watched as her lips parted into a grin and then a smile. She kissed the side of my face. It was nothing more than a peck but it started to do its thing.

I said, "Take off the scarf."

"Why?"

"I want to see your hair."

"Why?"

"Take off the fucking scarf, right?"

She pulled it down until it was around her neck, then shook out her hair. It was shorter than I'd thought, but the way it framed her face added to everything else I liked about her. My breathing began to grow rough. So did hers. I leaned in and she backed away until the side of her head pressed against the passenger window. I got my hand looped through the scarf and used it to draw her to me. I drove to the dead end at the bottom of the block and then we kissed and she giggled against my chest, and when she bit my neck I growled and we fell into the backseat, tearing each other's clothes off.

Twenty minutes later I lit us both cigarettes and asked, "You're beautiful but you don't like it—why?"

"I do. I just never felt that way before."

"Before what?"

"Before you, asshole."

Crawling out of the shallows JFK growled while his fur dripped mud and water. I spotted a black Mercedes filled with dark suits and rigid faces at the curb. It was starting already.

Wes Zek got out from behind the wheel. That showed me right there that the Thompson crew were still second-raters. Your driver is never the muscle. Your driver never gets out of the car. Wes had taken the keys out of habit and held them in his left hand. Now if anything happened to him, the others were stranded at the curb.

He looked like he'd been promoted from crew to captain and wasn't pleased with it. A hundred-and-fifty-dollar haircut, wraparound shades, and a fancy black sports jacket to hide his piece. Couldn't have been anything larger than a .32 considering how small the bulge was under his arm. Despite the kick up in what he earned, he looked stressed, harried. He'd lost weight but it didn't look good on him.

I said, "Hello, Wes. A little early in the day for you all to be doing business, isn't it?"

"We're still up from last night. Terry, you got a few minutes?"

"Not right now."

"Eager to get back to your run?"

"I'm going to see someone."

He shrugged. "She doesn't live there anymore. She took up with Chub. They got a kid now and live over—"

Before I realized it, I was off the bench and way up close to Wes. I saw my teeth in his sunglasses.

"Heya," I said, "how about if you stay out of my business and I'll keep out of yours, right?"

He looked a little embarrassed. "Sure, Terry, sure. Mr. Thompson would like to speak with you."

"Junior or Senior?"

"Senior had a coronary three, four years ago and retired to Arizona. The big one hit him in Phoenix, on a golf course. We don't call Junior Junior anymore, though. He likes Daniel or Mr. Thompson."

My family had been doing business with the Thompsons since before Danny's grandfather had Americanized the name from Tompansano. Danny and I were the same age and had run around together for a while in our teens.

"Fine," I said. "My dog sits in back with your muscle. Don't give me any shit about him muddying up your Mercedes."

"This the beast that snuffed Bernie Wagner?"

"Yeah."

JFK lolled his tongue and let out a belch that smelled like lake silt. I opened the back door and he hopped in and climbed over the thugs as they bitched and cursed, their suits already flecked with wet fur. Wes climbed behind the wheel and said, "Christ."

We drove over to the Fifth Amendment, Big Dan Thompson's bar that fronted all the real action. The name of the place was Big Dan's way of giving the finger to the feds, who'd been trying to build a RICO case around him for years, and doing it the way he had done almost everything, with a cocky defiance.

"Leave the dog outside, all right, Terry?" Wes asked.

"He comes with me," I said.

Wes groaned but let it slide. "Well, wait here for a minute, okay? Will you at least do that?"

"Sure."

It gave me time to take in the rhythm of the old place again.

I glanced at the photos on the walls. Big Dan with various celebrities, politicians, sports heroes. Some of the pictures of the old crews had been changed out, probably because so many wiseguys had flipped over the years. Big Dan once told me he'd never pulled the trigger himself unless he was shooting a rat. He said it the way my mother had said she hated Collie like poison. A thing to be mentioned, understood, held on to, then put away.

I'd had my first drink of hard liquor, seen my first thousand-dollar bill, and had my first woman here at the Amendment, all on the same day. In the back room they held private card games, where some of the waitresses earned extra cash by taking the major hitters to the private lounge. When I turned fourteen, Big Dan had invited me in and shown me the delights of that back room, all on his ticket, the same way he'd shown Danny a few weeks earlier on his birthday.

I couldn't help grinning thinking about it again.

Now Danny Thompson sat at his father's station, holding court at the corner table where all the real business got done. He was surrounded by a crew of five. I didn't recognize any of them. All the old-timers had either kicked off, been sent to the bin, or retired when Danny rose up to take over. I wondered what that said about the way Danny handled the operation now.

He was giving hell to one of his captains. I picked up a few words here and there. It sounded drug-related. Danny talked loud, much too loud for discussing business. His father had never raised his voice, not even when he was furious.

Danny hadn't aged well the last five years. He'd put on thirty pounds and looked uncomfortable as he shifted in his seat, packed into a suit a couple sizes too small for him. I could see the sweat gleaming on his face. His silky blond hair had started to recede and he had a nervous habit of brushing the back of his thumb across his prominent widow's peak. I could imagine what it must be like for him, sitting in that chair and seeing his father everywhere he looked. He should've sold the place and set up shop somewhere else.

The meeting broke up and a couple of Danny's boys walked past. The one who'd been under the gun was flushed from the berating he'd received. He had no idea who I was but he couldn't meet my eyes. He rattled way too easy. If he was in charge of the drug trade, I could see why there were problems.

Danny looked up from the table and waved me over with two fingers, the way Big Dan used to allow passage to his corner. His son couldn't even make that his own. I wanted to tell him, *Wave someone over with one finger, with three, use your chin, your left hand, anything except the same thing your dad did.*

JFK heeled at my left leg as we crossed the bar. I got to the table, put out my hand, and said, "Hello, Danny."

He tightened up. First words out of my mouth and I'd already made a mistake with him. I wondered what it would cost. His eyes clouded and then immediately cleared, and he let his lips hitch into a thin smile.

He shook my hand. "Terry. You look tan. Sit down."

Again with the fucking tan. Like Long Island didn't have two hundred miles of shoreline beaches.

I slid into the chair across from him. JFK dropped at my feet. Wes stood nearby, ready to take orders. The rest of Danny's men headed to the back room. The door was open and I could see the remnants of a big game, a lot of beer bottles, and a woman sleeping on one of the sofas.

"Sorry to hear about your father."

"Thanks for saying so, even if you don't mean it."

Except that I did mean it, and it surprised me that Danny would think I didn't. I'd always liked Big Dan, even if I didn't agree with some of his practices. He scooped up a lot of my family's goods and cut a few side deals along the way, sending me after certain specific items he wanted from rivals and occasionally even associates. He knew I could keep my mouth shut.

In all the time I knew him, I'd gone up against him only once. Chub had tuned the getaway car for a crew that had taken down a massage parlor that Big Dan fronted. The heisters blew town with fifty large, and Big Dan thought Chub ought to pay back with cash, his garage, or his legs. I asked Dan to let it slide, explaining that Chub had known nothing about the heist beforehand, even though I was certain he had. Big Dan didn't like my asking and gave me a chance to change my mind. I didn't. I put my hand on his wrist and asked him to let it go.

He ordered four of his men to kick the shit out of me in the parking lot. He added that if I fought back, they should break my arms.

I didn't fight back.

But Big Dan had let Chub slide anyway, as a favor to me. It was two weeks before I stopped pissing blood, but I didn't take any of it personally. He had to save face and had to make sure that back talk didn't become an everyday occurrence. He knew I was a pro and that I'd understand, and afterward we continued our amiable relationship right up until I left.

But somehow Danny didn't realize it. He thought I harbored resentment against his old man. That showed me he was still a piker even though he ran the show now.

"We've got a lot to talk about," he said.

"Do we?"

"Sure, old friends. We've got some years to cover."

He looked at JFK and beckoned the dog by patting his gut. JFK stood and planted his big head on Danny's thigh. Danny made good-doggie noises, scratching JFK's ears and jowls. He kissed the dog and the dog licked him back.

"Jesus, I think I can still smell Bernie's cologne on his breath."

The death of Bernie Wagner was an open secret, one I didn't like being reminded of. Bernie had been a two-bit hood turned meth-mouth tweaker who thought it would be a good idea to score a house full of thieves one night. Everyone was asleep except for me and my father. We were out in the garage, putting a new starter in his car. Oddly enough, everything from the car to the parts to the tools had been bought and paid for.

JFK had never so much as growled at anyone. He didn't even growl when Bernie sneaked around the side of the house and put a .22 to the back of my father's head. "Your stash, I want all of—"

In an instant, JFK lunged and champed his fangs in Bernie's throat and with a small wag of his head tore out Bernie's windpipe. My old man made the effort of trying to wrap the spurting wound with his own shirt and he even performed mouth-to-mouth as Bernie's life ran down his chest. There was nothing that could be done. It was already over. JFK sat there whining, his muzzle soaked with bloody foam.

My uncles packed Bernie up and drove him to the emergency room and dropped his corpse off at the curb. It was cold but there wasn't much else that could be done, and no matter how you looked at it Bernie Wagner had called the play.

Turned out Bernie had told a lot of people that he was going to try to boost the Rand house. Even though Gilmore and a few other cops had come around, no one could make anything stick.

Danny said, "Wes, go in back and get the prince of Camelot here a couple of burgers."

Wes did as he was told but I could see where some of his stress was coming from. He'd been promoted but was still stuck flipping hamburgers. And for a dog.

"So, Terry," Danny said, trying to look hurt. "You never said goodbye to me."

"I never said goodbye to anyone, Danny."

"You needed out that bad?"

"Yeah."

"I suppose I can understand that. After what happened with Kimmy. And Collie. Talk about a one-two punch. Still, I wish you'd stuck around. I could've used a good man like you."

"I never would've fit in as a member of a crew."

"What member? You could've been my lieutenant."

It was empty talk, but I smiled graciously. "Still not my thing. You know that."

"I suppose I do. But anyway that's in the past. Something else isn't. Listen, Terry, we have a problem."

It didn't surprise me. It was only blind luck that I'd gotten up for an early run. Wes must've been on the street in front of our house this morning and shadowed me to the lake. I was angry with myself that I hadn't spotted the Mercedes behind me. I had too much on my mind.

Danny tried to nail me down with a glare that was equal parts indignation and disappointment. It was another trick he'd stolen from his father.

I was committed to playing dumb. "How's that even possible? I've been home one day and you've already got a problem with me?"

"Not with you. Your uncle. He owes me money."

"Which one?"

"Malamute."

"You mean he beat the bank at one of your private big-gun card games."

"Yeah."

"And you let him play for what reason?"

"Someone thought it would be accommodating to extend a professional courtesy."

"Who would that someone be?"

He pulled his chin in. "Me. So you see the problem."

"Not yet. Was he dealing?"

"What difference does that make?"

"Was he?"

"Of course not."

"Then he wasn't cheating."

I was talking out my ass. There were a hundred ways to cheat at cards without ever laying a hand on the deck. Mal could have loaded his jacket, palmed high cards out of dead hands and hidden them until they were needed. He could have marked the deck with his thumbnail in ways nobody else ever would have spotted.

"He doesn't cheat if he's not dealing?"

"Not if he's alone," I said.

"Explain that."

"He and my uncle Grey can pull all kinds of grift if they're partnered. Their cross chatter alone can keep the marks distracted enough that they can slip a full house in. But they need each other. Either one of them alone, without the deck in his hands, isn't cheating."

"I'm out almost forty g's."

"That's why they call it gambling, Danny."

He studied me and I made sure he saw exactly what I wanted him to see. A liar who could lie and never be found out but who, *in this particular case,* right now, was telling the truth. I was a master of self-composition. No one could read my face, except, of course, my family. And Kimmy.

"I'm not sure if I believe you."

"I really don't give a shit."

"Don't talk to me that way, Terry."

You had to play Danny Thompson with a soft touch but not too soft. I could sense his insecurities still running wild inside him. He owned the shop and had men who would cave if he so much as cast an irate glance in their direction. But for all the old-friend bullshit he'd been tossing around I knew he also had to hate me, at least a little. I remembered when his father used to slap the hell out of him with his ham-hock hands. Senior had worn a diamond pinky ring that would sometimes catch Danny across the cheek and open him up like a razor slash. If I didn't go hard, Danny would run me to ground.

"I might have to come by and talk to Mal," he said.

"Is that how you run the show now, Danny? You invite old men to play in the game, then you muscle them if they beat you?"

"If they're cheating."

"You'd better be sure if you come after my family."

"If I was sure, we wouldn't be having this discussion. You'd be at the cemetery saying your goodbyes to Mal."

Big Dan never would've made such a threat. He might've popped somebody in the back but he never showed his hand.

Danny at least had the good sense to appear sorry for his strong-arm tactics. "Times are tougher than when my old man was chief of this crew."

"I doubt that, but you play the game however you like. I'm out."

"You're not out. You'll never be out. You Rands stick together, don't you?"

"Not always."

"Seems like it. You even went to visit your brother."

News traveled fast on the circuit. I figured JFK's reputation hadn't been the only thing holding his men back from bracing Mal this morning. Danny wanted to get a look at me too, see if I might roll over or become a problem.

"He asked me to visit," I said.

"Why do you care what a child-killing prick asks you to do?"

"Because he's my brother."

"Is that supposed to be an answer?"

"As much of one as you're going to get out of me."

I stood. From the lounge, Danny's men kept their attention focused on me until JFK lumbered to his feet. Then they watched the dog. They tried not to appear worried.

Wes stepped out of the kitchen carrying a plate with six or seven cooked burgers on it. I said, "Come on, Wes. We're leaving now."

With that thin smile still hanging in place, Danny Thompson openly appraised me. He thumbed his widow's peak. His eyes were hard but bright, his skin ashen as he sweated out last night's liquor. If nothing else I wanted him to know that I really was sad that Big Dan was gone, but I didn't know how to make him believe it. A part of me felt sorry for him. I could imagine how shaken I was going to be the day my father died and what kind of lasting effect it would have on me.

But all I said was, "Don't hang around at my curb anymore, Danny. You might get picked up for loitering."

"See you soon, Terry."

"Sure."

I turned my back on him. Wes had fed the burgers to JFK and JFK's nub of a tail was twitching, his muzzle pink from the juice. It was a good enough image to leave behind. I marched out with the dog heeling and Wes trailing behind us, his hands covered in grease.

I opened the back door of the Mercedes and JFK hopped in. His knees were still holding up but he looked run-down and overfed. He circled once and with a contented snort fit his chin between his paws and fell asleep.

Wes put on his wraparound shades, got behind the wheel, and asked, "You want me to take you back to the lake?"

"No."

"You want to go to Kimmy's place?"

"Just take me home, all right?"

"Okay, Terry."

We said nothing the rest of the ride. When we pulled up in front of the house, I asked, "Chub still got a garage?"

"Yeah. A different one from before. This one's bigger and on the other side of town."

"He still helping out heisters?"

"I don't think so," Wes said, shrugging. "But I don't really know."

Chub had won Kimmy's heart. He had stuck by her. He had fathered a child. He'd stood firm where I'd failed.

But if he was still plotting getaways he'd eventually be taken down. I pictured Chub on the six o'clock news, dead or in chains, Kimmy alone again, a kid in her arms waiting for a daddy who might never come home. The guy had to have gone straight, I thought, he wouldn't risk Kimmy and a baby for anything. But I wanted to be certain.

I stood on the front porch and listened to my family talking over breakfast. They were in a good mood. My father said something that had the quality of an anecdote and the others yapped comebacks. My mother allowed herself a strained but genuine kind of singsong laughter.

I needed a hot shower and a little more time to brace myself. I slipped off the porch and around the side of the house and in through the back door. I took the stairs three at a time, grabbed some fresh clothes, and hit the upstairs bathroom.

My head was louder than the steaming water blasting down. I shut my eyes as the past broke against me—snippets of old conversations, whispers in the dark. Flashes of Kimmy's face seen as dawn muscled through the curtains, sunlight catching the stray downy hair beneath her ear. I thought of Chub on top of her. Imagined her screaming in labor with Chub crouched next to the doctor, waiting for his baby to crown. Collie's victims turned their eyes on me. I scrubbed until my stomach burned from tasting too much soap and my skin felt raw. I tried to remember anything about life on the ranch and came up empty.

I got dressed and realized I didn't want to see anyone except Collie. He'd known his story would get under my skin, that I wouldn't be able to hide from it.

I think I need you to save someone's life.

I stared in the mirror and wondered who the hell he might be talking about. My eyes were shot with red and I checked the cabinet for drops. There weren't any.

I stood at the top of the stairs and listened to my family talk. I wanted to run again but I didn't know where. I sat on the top step and looked down through the railings, which gave me a view of the living room and the kitchen.

My father was leaning against the screen-door jamb, having a smoke. He stood silhouetted in the sun, as dark and powerful as he had been last night in the rain.

Mal and Grey were at the table, practicing their card grifts and cross chatter. I knew what to look for and I could still barely see when they pulled five-card lifts and bottom- or third-card deals. They'd played half a million hands of poker but never tired of the game.

Grey still had his ladies'-man looks. He projected a boyish charm, smiling with fifty thousand dollars' worth of first-rate dentistry, his head cocked and his perfectly combed silver hair falling just right. He always put on a show even when no one was watching. He'd had hundreds of women, owned them, cared for them even, but the one he truly loved had left him at the altar when he was seventeen and he'd never gotten over it. There was the faintest glint of regret in his eyes, which made him even more attractive to women who liked that sad puppy-dog look.

Mal had the hard appearance of a stone killer. There was no softness in his face at all. It looked like it had been sandblasted out of rock and then pounded at by storms for centuries—craggy, coarse, and crudely fashioned. He had a generous laugh and a warm, beaming expression, but his teeth were yellowed by years of smoking Churchill stogies. It hadn't only been JFK that made Wes and his boys too afraid to bust in and take him on. Mal looked vicious enough to ice a pregnant schoolteacher.

But so far as I knew, he'd never even thrown a punch. When I was a kid he used to take me to the park and we'd feed the ducks in the lake. On the occasional weekend he'd lead me around town until we found some children's party somewhere and crashed it. We'd load up on cake and ice cream and watch clowns, magicians, and puppet shows. He'd sometimes even work the grill and barbecue for the kids and their parents. No one ever dared ask him who he was or what he was doing there. They either knew he was a Rand or they took one look at his face and decided to shut the hell up and stick to the other side of the yard and hide behind the toolshed.

Grey took little notice of me until I hit twelve or so. Then he was the one who showed me the correct way to shave, how to dress, how to tie a tie. I'd already been given the birds-and-the-bees speech by my father a few years earlier. It had mostly scared the hell out of me. Grey reinterpreted the information for me and made me realize it sounded sort of fun. He told me, "The next couple of years you're really going to learn what it means to sting and burn, kid. I envy you getting to go through it for the first time, but I wouldn't trade places with you for anything."

Mal and Grey's banter at the kitchen table was quick and fun but with a slight angry undertone, the way the best long green chatter is played out. No one suspects that two people who sound as if they don't like each other might be working together. It was already getting on my nerves. I wondered how my parents could live with that noise day in and out. I wondered how I'd lived with it for so long.

My father turned from the front door and called to Grey, "Your girlfriend's back."

"Taking a beautiful woman out for a night of dancing doesn't make her my girlfriend," Grey said.

"Maybe not," my father admitted. He drew deeply on his cigarette and exhaled smoke as he spoke. "But what about the three, four weeks of courtship that have followed?"

"That's not courtship, Pinscher, it's infiltrating the enemy."

"That what they calling it nowadays?" Mal put in. "Infiltration? You write that on the notes you leave on her pillow? 'Before you, my life was an unfinished poem. You complete me. I shall always remember our wondrous night of love and song, what with all that infiltration of your sexy bits.' Now it makes sense why she keeps coming around. She can't live without the romance." Mal grinned. If anything, it made his features seem even more brutal.

"And what did all your spy work lead to?" my father asked.

"Exclusive rights to my life story," Grey said.

"So she wants her money's worth."

"Or her money back," Mal said.

I realized they were talking about the pretty reporter my father had mentioned, the one who stuck a microphone in his face and asked him how he felt now that his son was about to be executed. He stood at the door watching her now, defending the house. Grey sat thinking of his time in bed with her even while he dipped into the cards and tried to give himself a straight flush. Mal slipped aces out of the deck and I thought behind his open expression he must still be jealous of his brother, staring into that handsome face every day knowing he had the power in his fists to crush all the beauty from it.

A young woman I didn't know was washing dishes with my mother. She moved with a kind of gentle swaying, as if dancing to music only she could hear. I tilted my head to get a better look.

She said, "I can go give a statement. They'll take a few photos and screw up my comments but at least it'll move them along for a little while." Her voice stopped me. She was the woman who had phoned me at the ranch and told me that Collie wanted me to visit him. I looked harder and saw it was my younger sister, Dale, who'd been only ten when I left. I had spoken to her and hadn't even known it.

"No, I don't want you talking to them," my mother said.

"I don't mind."

"I know you don't, but I don't like the way they *descend*."

"It's their job."

"That's not their job. This deathwatch isn't their job."

"That's where you're wrong, Ma. It is."

"It shouldn't be."

Dale shrugged.

"Grey, can you get your girlfriend out of here?"

Grey did a five-card lift and shuffle and dealt Mal two deuces and himself two aces. "Ellie, Vicky and I have spent many pleasant evenings in each other's company over the past month or so, but she's still a journalist and—"

"That one is not a journalist."

"—and she mostly hangs around me hoping to get a story anyway."

"That one hangs around for more than that."

"I said 'mostly.'"

"The rest is about the roses, the chocolates, and the infiltration," Mal said.

"And you, Pinscher," my mother said, directing her attention to my old man, "do you always have to stand in the door like that, watching them? It makes you look guilty."

"I *am* guilty," he said.

"I know you are, but they don't need to know it."

"They already know it."

"They don't have to know it so much."

"So for the last five years I should've smoked in the house?"

"You should have given up cigarettes when you had your infarction."

"That was heartburn."

"Come inside, Dad," Dale said. "She's in a mood."

My sister had blossomed into a beautiful young woman. She held herself with an air of maturity and refinement. Her soft features were highlighted with a touch of makeup. She'd gotten her height from my mother and stood an inch or two over my father, which made her almost as tall as me. She had a casual grace, though, and seemed to prance around the room.

I slipped out the back door and walked around the side of the house, feeling more like a thief in my own home than I had while robbing others.

Two news vans were parked out front. My father was right. They liked to eat their donuts and have coffee before they hassled the family. There was no way I could get to my car without dealing with them. I thought of cutting through the woods and realized how stupid that was and how rattled I'd become. I was running from the warmth of my family so I could visit prison and listen to my brother talk of mad-dog murder.

The pretty blond newscaster with startlingly bright azure eyes came rushing up at me, followed by her film crew. The soft scent of citrus wafted along with her. I pictured her dating Grey, saw him taking her out to the best places on the island as she prodded him for information and he prodded her for pleasure.

She stuck the microphone in my face and licked her lips, her gaze full of false sympathy, exactly as my father had said. There was a lot I wanted to tell her. I had a few questions of my own that I felt like asking. I thought about this deathwatch, as my mother called it, and wondered if anyone really cared at all about the victims. When Collie got the needle there would be hundreds of folks out in front of the prison who would cheer. Maybe they had the right. Maybe I would be one of them. The idea of it made my guts twitch.

"You there, hello!" she shouted, somehow still smiling. "Who are you?"

It was a righteous question. I held my chin up. I stammered out the other name I'd been living under the last five years. It didn't come easily to me. I think I might've botched it. I could barely hear my own voice. There was too much running wild inside me. If I started talking I might not ever stop.

"I'm from Freddy's Fix-It," I said. "This house here, their hot-water tank burst, flooded the basement. A real mess."

"But you don't have a truck."

"Emergency call, came here straight from home. Heading back to the shop now. I'll be back in a little while with parts."

"It's the other one," the cameraman said. "The younger son. Terry. Terrier Rand. He looks just like his brother."

"Is it?" she asked. "Are you?"

"Freddy's Fix-It, lady."

The other news crew caught wise and started shouldering me. Their newscaster wasn't nearly as pretty but she had a real gleam in her eye. She wanted to spike me to the ground, pin me there, and force me to fess up.

I yanked open my car door and ducked behind the wheel, but they didn't let up. The camera guy leaned over the front hood and pressed the lens into my windshield. Azure eyes tried to make some kind of contact with me. I knew she didn't give a shit about the news. She had the expectant expression of all of Grey's former lovers. I could practically hear her thoughts. Has he talked about me? Will he see me again?

"Your brother is scheduled for execution in eleven days. What do you think about that? Do you have a message for the families of his victims?"

"How about if you back the fuck off me?"

That was going to look great on the six o'clock news, edited down to me saying "fuck off" to the victims' grief-stricken families.

The sharper reporter and her cameraman had already turned back to their van. Channel 14. They were going to pursue me. I shook my head in disbelief and cursed Collie under my breath. I'd sworn that I wouldn't visit my brother again, but I had to find out what the hell he needed from me. I wanted to see Kimmy. I wanted to see her child. I wanted to protect her from men like Collie and men like me. But I'd lost my chance. I'd abandoned my girl. I'd failed her and myself. I'd sacrificed my own happiness to the underneath. I wasn't ready to be a part of my own family yet. I knew the truth of it, I really had broken their hearts. I glanced at the front door and saw my sister standing there, watching me run away from home again.

Kimmy had finally decided to embrace her beauty. She'd grown her hair long and allowed it to lap over her shoulders and drift in the breeze. It whirled to a rhythm I could hum along with. She was dressed comfortably but fashionably in summer clothing that accentuated her contours. I wasn't close enough to look into her eyes, but I could tell from the way she moved, more carefree than I'd ever seen her move before, that the hard shell had been peeled away.

I should've been happy for her but I was a miserable selfish prick. My fingers trembled against the steering wheel.

She and Chub lived in a new development. Once this area had all been pumpkin fields. Kimmy and I had taken a hayride through the thick trails one Halloween while an old farmer told ghost stories that smacked of truth. He was so intently fixed on his own tale that his dentures worked themselves free every so often and he had to press them back in with his fingers. It gave us the giggles. Afterward he let us off to pick as many pumpkins as we wanted for free. We were late to the patch and the choosings were slim, but we found a few fairly sizable pumpkins that we brought home to her family and carved on her kitchen table. We tried to retell the ghost stories but we couldn't finish without laughing. One jack-o'-lantern sat in the front window, while the others perched out on her front stoop. She kept them lit through most of November, even after the first snow fell and they began to rot and sink in on themselves.

I shut my eyes and tried to place where the house stood in relation to that hayride. I thought I had the spot down and remembered the two of us snuggling beneath a blanket, my hand on her warm belly.

She'd picked up a knack for gardening. Most of the morning she spent trimming azalea bushes and clipping roses while the baby staggered around the lawn, playing with various objects, none of which appeared to be a real toy. She pawed a plastic bowl, a flyswatter, and a chain of pink barrettes clipped together.

I listened to Kimmy talking to the baby. Every time her daughter toddled away too far Kimmy would chase after her and say, "Here now, Scooter, don't you motor off." The sound of her voice made my chest hitch. She dug deep in rich soil, planting new roses, and I thought of all the desert dust I'd breathed in over the past five years. I'd been a coward. I deserved to be alone. The fact of it made me squirm behind the steering wheel.

I could picture the inside of their home. I could feel myself moving through it the way any good thief could. I took one look at the place and immediately started plotting, deciding which tools I might need, what time I would go in. I'd enter through the quaint French doors that opened up to the patio deck, where Chub had actually staked tiki lamps ringing the yard. The outer edges of the doors didn't match the house paint, meaning they'd been installed after Kimmy and Chub had moved in. Any alarm system probably wouldn't be attached.

I'd slip into the dining room where a large breakfront would have Kimmy's mom's china on display. It was the kind of thing her mother would do, handing the good stuff down. Family history had always meant something to Kimmy. We'd met because of it.

No chimney, so no fireplace. So no mantel. But there'd be shelves for the photos. A huge wedding portrait hanging on the far wall. They would've been married out at Shalebrook Lake. A smallish gathering of only close friends and Kimmy's family. Chub had been on his own since he was sixteen. I had no idea who his best man might've been. Kimmy's father? That sounded right. Chub in a white-jacketed tux, Kimmy in a subdued but still breathtaking dress. The photographer telling them to gaze into each other's eyes, hold up the champagne glasses as if in a toast, stand at the rim of the water. They would've had to be careful because of the duck shit.

The opposite wall would be devoted to Scooter. A few large and fancy baby pictures. At least a couple of those family portraits with the child looking one way and Chub and Kimmy with faraway expressions and faintly perplexed smiles. One or two of the hanging frames would be slightly askew. I'd straighten them as I passed by.

The living room would have formal but comfortable furniture, the kind that had no real personality but that you could lie on without fear of wrecking it. Scooter's toys would be piled in their own corner. Dolls and stuffed animals and pull-string gadgets that would teach her a cow said moo, a cat went meow. All of them neatly stacked. Chub was a neat freak in his own way, carefully organized and meticulous. It's what made him such a good mechanic and getaway planner. The carpeting would be gray, something to hide dirt. There would be doormats to wipe your feet on and a small tiled foyer where you were expected to leave your shoes.

The banister leading upstairs would be polished and glossy, the corners of the stairs well vacuumed. Their bedroom would have a little more character, at least a couple of pieces of antique furniture. The headboard from some nineteenth-century captain's home on the North Fork, with a carving of a three-mast square-rigged blowing-mainsail whaling ship dead center. When they made love, they'd have to prop the pillows just so, to keep from getting welts.

At around three in the afternoon Chub pulled into the driveway. I slid farther down in my seat even though he didn't glance in any direction except Kimmy's as he crossed the lawn. She brushed her hair back with the side of her glove and left a dirt smear across her forehead. For some reason it made me groan.

Chub had lost a little weight and grown a Vandyke that he kept well trimmed. It suited his face. He'd started losing his hair as a teenager and now kept his head shaved. He walked with a light step. He practically skipped after Scooter, who squealed with laughter and tried to run away. He scooped her up, set her on his shoulder, and spun around while she held her arms high, fingertips brushing blossoming buds on the ends of tree branches. She slid down into his arms, where he held her tightly against his chest and marched over to Kimmy. They kissed and then he pressed his forehead to hers for a moment.

Nothing they did was out of the ordinary, but it seemed exceptional to me. I saw the life I wanted, or the life I thought I wanted. The only part that was ugly was the creeper parked on the other side of the street, staring at them.

Chub had put in only a half day. His clothes looked too clean and fresh for a grease monkey. Maybe he'd gone legit and let other mechanics work under the hoods and transoms at his garage, but I couldn't see him stepping out of the game completely. He certainly hadn't crawled under any soccer mom's SUV today. So what else was he doing with his time? Paperwork? He'd still be known on the circuit. Crews and strings would still be coming to him for engine work and plotting getaway routes. Was he turning them away? Or did he just pick and choose more carefully now?

I grabbed the door handle like I might climb out. And do what?

I could step up their brick path and watch as Chub turned and saw me, hit his usual pose of cool, sort of locking his legs and leaning back. He'd invite me in and it would be awkward at first, Kimmy unsure of what to say or how to act, ill at ease that I was there at all because I'd be staring at her. I wouldn't be able to stop myself. But soon things would loosen up. We'd act a little stupid, joke around, and share old stories. Nothing serious would be broached until later, after the beer bottles started to pile up. Chub would be thankful I'd deserted Kimmy. It had allowed him to step in. But he'd still resent me and consider my leaving a betrayal of our friendship if nothing else. His face would fall and that wounded expression would cross it inch by inch, starting with the frown lines in his forehead and down to his lower lip, which he'd be chewing on. Eventually he'd taste blood and stare at me for a lengthy time, steeling himself to either grab one of the bottle necks and crack me across the temple or let most of his anger slide and give me a hug.

Kimmy wouldn't have any of it. She would still hate me. She would always hate me. I didn't blame her. I hated me too.

Even as she said, *It's good to see you. How've you been?* I'd know what was really moving through her heart. The real questions she wanted to ask, the honest indictments she would make. I'd left her alone to wallow through the misery of the miscarriage and our broken engagement. I'd left her to endure the onslaught of questions and insinuations by her family and friends as they snapped open the headlines and came at her, saying, *This mass murderer, this sicko. He's your boyfriend's brother, isn't he?*

All those bodies left behind in Collie's wake, but the only one that meant anything to her would be ours, the one that hadn't come to full term, which she'd lost without anyone knowing, without anyone to console her. Not even me.

With a sharp tug I angled the rearview mirror so I could see them in it. See myself with them. I ran different scenarios. I saw other ways to impress myself upon the world. I could ease out of the car, move across the lawn as if it had been me who spent a thousand hours pushing the mower back and forth, using the edger to trim the borders, the way my father did, the way Chub did. Drop him with a shot to the kidneys. Kneel before the baby and hand her a teddy bear, get her to giggle, draw her into my arms. Lift her up and move to Kimmy, then press my forehead to hers, smell the loam, taste her life. Turn my back to Chub coughing in the grass and dream him gone. It's what we all did when we wanted something badly enough. Let the irrational thoughts slip through, the idea that by sheer force of belief we could make things change, adjust, divert, back up. It's what a thief does in the shadows, willing himself to vanish.

Step inside with my family and put the baby in her crib and take Kimmy by the hand to the bedroom and love her the way I would've if I hadn't run away in my weakness and fear. I clutched the door handle until my fingers were white and cramped. I forced myself to let go. I cocked the rearview mirror back to where it belonged. When I looked over again, the front lawn was empty except for one pink barrette and the plastic bowl, tilted on its side.

The screw whose house I'd crept made me go through the same regimen as the day before. I spoke my true name. He led me to the small side room where I was frisked. He was a little rougher this time and clenched my nuts hard enough to make me grunt. Again I was politely asked if I would voluntarily succumb to a strip search.

I thought, I know what your wife's lingerie looks like. You drove to work today without a license, without any credit cards in case of an emergency.

He repeated the question.

I told him to fuck himself.

Instead of telling me to leave, the screw moved me along.

I was led to the visiting room full of long tables that Collie had pointed out to me yesterday, where we could talk face-to-face. It was rough enough talking to my brother on a phone with reinforced glass between us. I wasn't sure I wanted to get so close to him.

The screw held me in place with his palm against my chest. I could see Collie seated across from a woman who was talking animatedly. Pages of open books and legal pads in front of her flipped to and fro. She tapped them angrily. When she tossed her head a lash of glossy black hair whipped through the air. She wore a dark business suit with killer heels and glasses with thin black frames that accentuated the sharp Asian angles of her face. No matter how she turned I couldn't see her eyes, only the glowing reflection of the ceiling lights in her lenses. Collie looked cowed, his chin down like he was a berated child. I thought, What in the fuck. I'd never seen my brother shrink like that before. It simultaneously elated and unnerved me.

"Don't shake his hand," the screw told me. "Don't pass him anything or take anything offered."

"Right."

Three minutes later the woman gathered up her belongings and packed them into a briefcase. She leaned in to say goodbye to him and their lips met briefly. She pushed her seat back and moved to the door. It opened and she walked past me. She stepped like a thief, her footsteps silent.

I was ushered in. Collie stood and sort of jumped forward just to spook the screw. It worked. The tension thickened. Then Collie let loose with a laugh. The sound of the door slamming and the lock turning bothered me worse than it had yesterday.

Collie gripped me in a bear hug.

"We're not supposed to touch," I said.

"I'm going to die in less than two weeks. If I want to hug my own brother I goddamn will." He pushed me off, took me by the shoulders. "Thanks for coming back. I knew you would."

"Yeah, how?"

"Because you're a good man."

I didn't know what the hell to say to that. He gestured to the visitor's chair like we were about to have a beer and watch a ball game together.

"Who was that woman?" I asked. "Your lawyer?"

"That's Lin. My wife." He tried to grin but all it did was bring out the deep furrows in his face. "I got married a year ago. I didn't tell the family about it, figured they wouldn't want to know. In the beginning I just thought she was another one of these jailbird pen pals. I get boxes of mail a week. Everybody on death row does. It's a weird cultural phenomenon, the way some women get turned on by—" He knew enough not to go on. "Well, anyway. But something in Lin's letters reached me. She started visiting and one thing led to another."

I tried to process everything he'd just said. "One thing led to another?"

"Yeah."

A demented lonely hearts reads about a mass murderer and decides this is her psycho soul mate, this is the man she's been waiting for all her life? A guy who butchers children?

I thought, Jesus Christ. What if he goes out with a bang and gets her pregnant? I could see the woman showing up on my parents' porch, holding a half-Asian baby, going, *Say hello to little Li, your grandson.*

My father wouldn't even sigh. My mother would turn away, grit her teeth, steel herself, then smile and feed and welcome them. Later, perhaps years later, she would lock herself in the bathroom and fold herself up in the corner and cry silently until someone needed something from her.

Collie let out a chuckle. "Well, say something."

My tongue felt covered in moss. I fought not to glare. I pushed off my disgust. "Congratulations."

"Thanks."

"What was she so angry about?"

"We'll get to that."

"All right."

He showed those teeth and I loathed his smile. It said that he had me in his hand, that he could make me come to him whenever he called. I'd thrown a hundred fists into that smile and I'd never hit it even once. Collie was faster than me, stronger than me. I could feel the superiority in him bleeding through even under these circumstances. I listed the things he might say that would force me to leave.

If he mentions Kimmy, if he asks me to help pay for a new attorney, if he talks about my fucking tan again. I thought, The minute he opens his mouth I'm out of here. It took me another moment to realize that I didn't have to be here. That I wanted to be here. That I needed to be here for some reason I didn't understand but my brother did. Maybe I hated him. Maybe I wanted to see him die. Maybe I wanted to pull the switch.

"You saw the family," he said.

"Yeah."

"How's it been?"

"Fine. It's been good."

"Everybody okay?"

"They're fine. They're good."

"You're lying."

"I'm not lying."

"You're lying, Terry."

"So fucking what?"

"Don't break Ma's heart again."

"I don't take advice from dead men walking."

He was making me question myself again. I wondered how he managed to swing it so easily.

His smile dropped and he ran a hand through his gray hair and a lot of my rage receded. He looked like an elderly man to me now. His manicure had dimmed, his nails had dirt under them. Then I realized they were paint chips. In the long night he probably scratched at the walls or the bars. What else was there for him to do? His freshest scars shone pink in the light. I wondered if he'd fought with other cons or the guards or both. For an instant it seemed to matter. I wanted to ask him who his enemies were. If the victims' families ever tried to see him, if he ever spoke with them. If the rest of his mail was from people wishing him slow agony or a quick pop of city-grid voltage. I wanted to ask him about his nightmares. I knew he had them. I wondered if they were worse than mine.

"Collie, you said you wanted me to save someone."

"Yeah."

"Who?"

"I don't know." He muttered under his breath, like he was speaking to someone else in the room. "The next one."

"The next one?" I said. "The next one what?"

"The next girl."

"What are we talking about?"

"Rebecca Clarke."

The girl he'd strangled in Autauk Park a mile from the Elbow Room, where he'd been drinking, a couple miles from the trailer park where the mobile home had been parked. "I don't understand. She's already dead."

"Listen to me, Terry, this is important. I need you to do something for me—"

"I need something from you first, Collie. I want you to tell me about that night."

The temperature in the room felt like it dipped twenty degrees. My flesh started to crawl. Our gazes caught and held. I had once loved him more than anyone else in the world. I had once feared him more than anyone else as well. Maybe I still did. We were too much alike. There are sibling rivalries that dissipate and others that become wars of wills and knives. I remembered all the faces of all the girls he'd stolen from me. I recalled their names, the taste of their lips, the feel of their bodies in my arms. I knew my brother wouldn't recollect any of them. The nerves in my fingertips tingled. My tongue was too large for my mouth. My teeth were too sharp. I needed to know the answer.

"You've already read about it," he said. "You already know most of it."

"I want to hear about it from you."

"What's that going to give you except nightmares? You remember how you used to wake up screaming as a kid?"

I leaned forward. I thought, We could do it. We could cut loose and kill each other in less than a minute. The guards wouldn't be able to get in here fast enough.

"How about if the child-killer doesn't fucking analyze me, huh?"

"Hate me if you want but—"

"What, you think I need your permission to hate you? You think this is something new?"

"No."

A vacationing family of five shot to death in a mobile home, a gas-station attendant knifed in a men's room, an old lady beat to death outside a convenience store, a young woman strangled in a park.

"The little girl. Say her name, damn you."

"Susan Coleman."

"Suzy."

"Suzy Coleman."

"Say the rest."

"There's no point to this, Terry."

"Say them or I'm out of here forever."

He spoke without expression. The words dropped from him like he was reading a baseball lineup. "Paul Coleman. Sarah Coleman. Tom Coleman. Neal Coleman. Suzy Coleman."

"The rest."

"Doug Schuller was the guy I knifed in the gas station. Mrs. Howard I pummeled with my fists. I hit her four, maybe five times."

No remorse. No scourging of conscience. It wasn't hidden in the folds of his face, it wasn't hovering beneath the surface of his calm. His eyes were the eyes of my brother, no different than they'd ever been.

"None of them was robbed, Collie. You didn't even take anything from the register at the gas station."

"No."

"Then why?"

"There is no answer. I just did it."

"That doesn't make any sense."

"I didn't say it did."

Gramp Shepherd had called it going down into the underneath. That moment when desperation, rage, or momentary madness drove you out of your head and forced you to do something stupid and terrible. He'd always warned us. He told us to be aware of it, to watch for it, to know that when that trapped feeling hit, you couldn't let it make you lose control.

"What made it happen? What provoked you?"

"There was no provocation, it just happened."

"You went mad dog for nothing?"

"It just happened."

"Suzy Coleman. The girl in the mobile home—"

"Why are you hung up on the girl? Not the old lady? Nobody else? Only the girl, huh?"

Saying it like I should be ashamed.

"You told me you were making ghosts. What's that mean?"

"Don't talk about them. Don't think about them. That's not what you're here for."

"Don't think about them?"

"No. It'll just be distracting for you. There's only one person you need to wonder about, that you need to ask about. Rebecca Clarke."

"Why only her?"

"Because I didn't kill her."

I rubbed my eyes. I made a scoffing sound.

"So why didn't you say anything about it before now?" I asked.

Collie looked at me with a mischievous expression, almost wearing a sad grin. He said nothing.

"What? You thought maybe you didn't remember strangling a teenager?"

He said, "I wasn't sure."

"Then how can you be sure now?"

"There have been more."

"More?"

"More young women who look an awful lot like Rebecca Clarke have been killed."

I couldn't look at him anymore. I stared over his shoulder at the wearisome white stone walls and tried to make sense of what he was saying. "How do you know that?"

"Lin's been doing research. There have been other women murdered in similar ways since I've been in here. And at least one that happened about six months before I—"

"Tell the cops."

"They don't believe me."

"I don't either."

He paused and the pause lengthened into a heavy silence, and finally he snapped his fingers to get my attention again. "I want you to look into it."

"Look into what?"

"Becky's murder. And the others."

"*Becky?*"

He pursed his lips and turned away to say something to his audience. His stony eyes focused on me again. His tongue prodded the inside of his cheek. He cleared his throat.

"Talk to Lin, she has notes for you. She's been investigating."

"Oh, Christ, Collie."

He started getting excited. The jazzy bop rhythm worked back into his voice. "Young women strangled around the island. Some even near the park, like Becky was."

"Stop calling her Becky as if you were friends."

"There's been at least three more since I've been in here."

"Collie, what the hell are you saying?"

"Someone else murdered Rebecca Clarke. And it looks like he's been snuffing others. As many as five in the last six or seven years, maybe more, I don't know. But the others, they all looked like her. Brunettes, pretty."

I couldn't hold back a bark of laughter. "That's the description? Pretty brunettes? Someone's killing pretty brunette teenagers?"

"They weren't all teenagers. But they all looked similar, from what they tell me."

"From what who tells you?"

"Lin."

The new wife. The new psycho wife. If it was true and other women were being murdered, I figured that maybe she would be doing it. Trying to put the whole case in doubt. Strangling young girls because she'd always been turned on by the thought of murder. It was why she married a murderer. And now she had the perfect reason. She was killing for love.

"Fuck this," I said.

"Listen to me, Terry. You've got to listen." He pawed at his face but he wasn't sweating. I was. "Someone's out there snuffing women."

"What do the cops say about all this?"

"They still think I did her."

"So do I."

"Check with Lin."

"Check with Lin?"

"Stop repeating everything I say, Terry. Just do it."

"Why? Why should I?"

"Because I'm asking you to."

I slumped back. "You haven't actually asked me anything, Collie. And that's how I know you're bullshitting. You're giving orders, you're pushing me around the way you always do. Fuck this nonsense."

"Please, Terry. Please. I'm begging you."

"You're not begging me. You're simply saying that you're begging me. But why? Why do you care so much?"

Collie leaped up in frustration and I slipped out of the chair, put some space between us, got my fists up. My brother could be a fearsome sight, the way he moved like a caged beast waiting for the proper moment to strike. His eyes settled on me and he frowned, like I was an idiot to be afraid of him. He was detached from the horror of his own crimes. He had no idea how intimidating it might be for me to sit across from him, from those hands. They were powerful and menacing. They could strangle a young woman easily. They could do the same thing to me.

"Why wouldn't I care?" he asked.

"Why didn't you say anything about this before?"

"I did. But no one believed me. Look, you've got to trust me on this."

"Wait a second," I said. "Wait. Wait." I mouthed the word again but nothing came out. Then there was a trickle of sound that turned into a chuckle thick with revulsion. "I have to trust you? And what the hell am I supposed to do?"

"Ask questions."

"Ask questions? That's what you're telling me to do? What does that even mean?"

"Find out who did it. Stop them."

"Why do you care? What difference does it make now? Five years later?"

"I've been thinking about it a long time."

"But it doesn't make any sense. You iced one young girl but you want to see justice for another you claim you didn't kill?"

"It's not a claim, Terry. I didn't kill her. I man up for my own crimes."

"You're not even sure!"

"I am sure now. Find Gilmore. You remember Gilmore?"

"Jesus fucking Christ, I remember Gilmore."

"He still hangs around the house. He can probably put you in touch with the dicks who handled my case and the cases involving the other girls."

"Why the hell would I want to surround myself with cops?"

"Because they think I'm lying."

"I think you're lying too."

"No, you don't. You think I was wrecked out of my mind and can't remember, but you don't think I'm lying."

I didn't like being corrected. "Actually, Collie, I do think you're lying and I think you're setting me up to take some kind of fall here. I don't think you want to go out of the game alone."

My brother didn't have the capacity to look hurt. It wasn't in his nature. I wasn't sure if it was in his nature to even *be hurt*. But the look that crossed his eyes came as close as I'd ever seen.

I knew every muscle and vein and scar in my brother's face. I'd seen him with a 106-degree fever and his eyes rolling back and showing only white from the agony of sepsis. I'd walked in on him more than once while he was *in flagrante delicto,* usually with one of my girls. I knew every twitch and tell he had.

I got in close. "Say it again."

"I didn't kill her."

Maybe it was the truth. I just didn't understand why he was bothering to tell it now. It earned him nothing. He couldn't buy his freedom or his life for it. And a mass murderer couldn't possibly care about justice for a victim that wasn't even his own.

The exhaustion and miles and edginess caught up to me in that moment. I slumped into the seat and dropped my chin to my chest, and before I knew it I felt tears on my face.

"Are you crying?" he asked.

"No."

"You are. For me?"

"Fuck no. I want to know what set you off."

"Nothing."

He'd spent the evening drinking at the Elbow Room. He'd gone on his spree and then returned to the bar, ordered a beer, and casually informed the bartender and patrons that he'd just murdered several people. He'd cracked open the .38 and unloaded the weapon. His knuckles were bruised but not bloodied or torn. It didn't take much to beat an old woman to death. He waited without incident for the cops to show up. He confessed on the spot to what he had done.

I lifted my shirt and wiped my face. I breathed deep. I tried to calm myself. I could be cool and steady burgling the house of a cop while he slept six feet away from me. But my own brother made me a heaving mess.

"Something had to," I insisted.

"No."

"You had no drugs in your system. You'd only had a few beers."

"Yeah."

"So you were sitting in the Elbow Room, minding your own business, having a pilsner by yourself—"

"A Corona."

"—having a Corona by yourself, and you decided, *Hey, I need to go out and kill a bunch of people.*"

"It wasn't a decision," he said. "It just . . . happened. I'm not lying. I haven't lied to you yet, Terry."

"You told me you were making ghosts. Why did you do it?"

"Stop asking."

"Was it because of a woman?" I asked.

"What woman?"

"How the fuck do I know what woman? Any woman."

"Why would a woman make me—"

"How the fuck do I know why? For any reason."

"No, it wasn't a woman, Terry. Listen to me."

"Listen to you!" I jumped out of the chair. His voice, or my own, was too loud inside my head, and I couldn't hear myself anymore. "You listen to me!" I shouted. "Are you . . . ?" The words caught in my throat. I tried to cough them free. I couldn't catch any air. I tried again, my voice sounding nothing like me, sounding, in fact, more like him. He stood and reached for me. I backed away. "I mean, I know you're crazy, you had to be, you have to be . . . but man, Jesus, Collie, really, just . . . just . . . *are you fucking insane?*"

"No."

I stumbled toward the door while he continued to plead with me. He said her name again. Becky Clarke. It's all he cared about. Not the other kills on his conscience, not what he was doing to our family. I hammered at the door like a terrified child. It brought the screws running. I was so pale that they checked me for shiv wounds.

My Christ, I thought, I have the same blood running through my veins.

You walk into a department store and there are security cameras and undercover employees everywhere. You try to creep an apartment building and you have to get past a front door, a security door with an automatic lock, closed-circuit television, and a doorman who gets paid by the pound. You want to score a warehouse and you've got a couple of twenty-year-old fuckup minimum-wage rent-a-cops patrolling the grounds just waiting to pull their revolvers, dive and roll, snap off six wild shots, and blow somebody's face away.

But if you want to slip in somewhere that's full of people, action, money, drugs, weapons, where no one even looks at you much less questions you, then try a police station about six P.M., dinnertime.

Cops are hungry and tired and wanting to get home. They're sloppy and sign out early. The ones left around figure that if you're in the squad room you must have a good reason. You're a victim, you're waiting to make a complaint, look at mug shots, sign a statement. If they don't recognize you and you're not part of their caseloads then they don't want anything to do with you. They're already burdened with unsolved crimes and vics and pains in the ass of every stripe. They pretend to be busy and refuse to meet your eye. They don't check up on you. They hope the next cop down the line will take care of you instead.

First thing I did when I walked into the squad room was scan the on-call board. Gilmore had the late shift and wouldn't be on until midnight. I went looking for his desk.

I recognized the framed photo of his two daughters, Maggie and Melanie. It was an old picture. No snapshots of his wife. A happily married man always puts a photo of his wife on his desk. He changes the pictures of his kids and keeps them up-to-date, unless they no longer live at home with him. Like my father had said, Phyllis had finally walked out and taken their daughters with her.

I sat in his chair and went through his desk hoping I might find Collie's jacket or files on the case. It was a long shot and I came up empty. I did find an old rent receipt that gave me Gilmore's new address. I knew the apartment house. The neighborhood was good, but he wasn't paying much. Police discount.

Cops walked past me by the boatload. They dragged in suspects who whined and complained and tried to look menacing. They threatened to sue, wanted their lawyers, proclaimed their innocence. The cops ignored them. So did I.

Under Gilmore's phone was a directory sheet of extension numbers. I called the archives room and asked them to bring up Collie Rand's file. Some old-timer gave me static about proper channels.

I kept my voice quiet but filled with a self-righteous sharpness. "Move your wrinkled ass, pops. Protocol takes time and we don't have any to waste."

The geezer sputtered. I told him to leave the file on my desk in the next ten minutes, even if I wasn't there. That brought another round of protests. I cut him off. "If you don't get moving now you'll work the last of your thirty on the bay this winter. It'll be the boat for you. You got insulated drawers, old-timer? You ever seen hypothermia of the ball sac? You want to go out of the game with your ex-wives knowing you've lost your package?"

I hung up.

The desk next to Gilmore's was also unoccupied. I went and sat over there and watched the squad room fill and empty. I went to the little kitchenette area and got myself a cup of coffee and a stale bagel. It wasn't until I took the first bite that I realized I hadn't eaten anything all day and I was starving.

Gilmore was one of those cops who had more in common with the criminals he was trying to put away than with the rest of the joe-citizen world. He'd been in trouble himself as a teenager, orphaned early and kicked around the foster-family system, spent some time in the juvie reformatory and then county lockup later on. He'd steal a car, go joyriding, get laid in the backseat, then return it a couple of days later.

He had his big turnaround when he tried to outrun a statie with his girlfriend riding shotgun and got into a minor crackup on the LIE that cost her the full use of her right arm. He did a nine-month jolt, came out, and started going to a community college. Must've stood on tippy-toes to get him over the police height requirement and graduated middle of the pack at the academy. For years he kept changing divisions— bunko, vice, narco—but they all brought him around to Big Dan Thompson.

Big Dan had a way of working his magic on a cop like Gilmore. Gilmore wasn't dirty but he was just bent enough to help Big Dan out on occasion. So if Dan knew a little about one of the rival syndicates— the Chinese, the Colombians, the Russians—maybe what time a shipment was coming in or who pulled the trigger on some witness for the D.A., he'd turn Gilmore on to it for some kind of trade. Nothing that couldn't be considered a legal gray area. Maybe Gilmore would let one of Big Dan's boys off on a leg-breaking rap or he wouldn't get around to popping one of the big games even when he knew about it. I never found out if Big Dan gave Gilmore a monthly envelope, but it wouldn't surprise me if Gilmore had a wedge of Dan's cash hidden in a lockbox buried in his yard someplace.

Gilmore hooked on to me when I was sixteen because he suspected I was the one pulling burglaries in Dix Hills, a ritzy neighborhood where some of the residents had clout with the town council. He was right, I was. He followed me for days, trying to catch me climbing into someone's window. He dragged in known fences and tried to get them to roll on me.

He braced me hard the first time—cuffs, twelve hours in the holding tank without a phone call, no food or toilet break, threats against the family—and then later he tried playing soft, telling me about his own run-in with the law, giving me his whole life story. I thought he was lying but later on found out it was all true.

While he chased after me, I watched him. He was a little bulldog who seemed to be running from himself. It was written in his face. He eventually caught on that the Rands were satellite members of the Thompson crew and started coming around the house. At first he just rousted my father and uncles and Collie, trying to pick up information in exchange for favors. Except the Rands didn't play that kind of game.

For some reason, he seemed to like the family. He couldn't hide his interest in us. I knew it was because he'd never had a family of his own, no father to talk to about guys like Big Dan. He rousted us less and less and started hanging around. Eventually he began sitting out on the porch, having beers with my father. My mother knew the birthdays of his kids and would send cards.

One time Gilmore found me reading to Dale and said, "That's not how you do it. You have to work the voices, put on a show. When the vampires bite, you have to pull back your lips, show teeth." He told me how he read children's books to his two daughters, the way he'd get into character, the different voices he'd use. At the time his daughters were three and four, and Dale was ten. He didn't think it mattered.

When Collie dove into the underneath Gilmore actually came around and tried to console my parents. He hugged my mother and patted my father's arm. He brought flowers like he was attending a funeral. He didn't cry with them but I could see that he was trying to. I thought, even then, Gilmore, he's going to be the one in the end who gets close enough to stick in the knife.

I finished my bagel and scarfed down two more. When I returned to Gilmore's desk Collie's file was there. Five files, actually, stuck inside a huge accordion folder. I photocopied everything. I had a stack of about a hundred pages. I found a couple of thick rubber bands in Gilmore's junk drawer and snapped them around the bundle. I called the geezer back and told him to come pick up the file. He started yelling and I said, "You did good, pops, you may have just saved a life," and walked out.

JFK met me at the bottom of the driveway. He looked regal and aware, his eyes lit by the setting sun. I got the sense that he knew there was potential trouble coming down from different quarters and he planned on being ready for it.

I left the thick sheaf of paperwork under the passenger seat and slid out of the car. As I moved up the walk I called JFK to me, but he remained staunchly on guard, continuing his watch.

I passed the trash can and thought of chucking all the pages in and forgetting my brother had said anything at all. I thought I could very easily live in denial back at the ranch or at another one like it. I had already done it for five years. I could do it for another fifty. If anyone asked if I had a brother I could say no or say yeah, he lives back east, or say he was dead without explaining anything more. I could sleep well without any remorse for never following up.

My old man was inside with my mother, watching television with Gramp. My uncles and sister were nowhere in sight. I could hear my dad talking to his father as if he might get coherent responses. My mother did the same thing. They were having a lively conversation that would sound buoyant to anyone else but sounded strained to me.

They weren't doing it just for Gramp's benefit, hoping to keep what little personality he had left alive for as long as they could. They were doing it for themselves because it was the only way they could possibly accept the burden of caring for him. Pretending that it mattered. I imagined that when my father spoke to Old Shep he heard the man's deep voice talking back to him. His thunderous laughter so forceful that you had to lean away from it.

I tried to figure out how much I should tell them. Would it make them feel any better that Collie now admitted to killing only seven people instead of eight? Hell, I decided to say nothing. It wasn't much of a decision. It was the path of least resistance. When you heard someone at the door, you dove out the window. Avoid confrontation, hide or run away. I'd been doing it my whole life.

I walked in and my parents immediately quit their little performance. I vibed that there was a darker subtext to their benign chatter. I wondered if the news crews had been more aggressive after I left, banging on the door, asking my mother where I'd been these last few years, why I was back, if I'd been in prison too. If I had blood on my hands too.

My father asked me, "Hungry? Got some leftovers. Steak and mashed potatoes, yams, corn on the cob. Your favorite."

It was my favorite. It was also Collie's favorite. I had no doubt he'd ask for it for his last meal. All I'd eaten today were the rubbery stale bagels. My guts were knotted and I had cramps. My stomach made a weird sound and I said, "Maybe later."

"You know where the fridge is."

My mother was watching me intently. I could tell that she knew I'd visited the prison again despite her warning not to go. Her eyes flashed and I could feel her reading exactly where I'd been each minute of the day. The meeting with Danny, the stalking of Kimmy, the face-to-face with Collie. I wondered if I should tell her that Collie had gotten married behind bars like all the rest of those death-row douche bags.

She tucked a few coarse strands of Gramp's hair back behind his ear, then did the same with her own soft auburn curls. She was gathering herself.

"What's the matter?" I asked.

"Nothing."

"Jesus Christ, considering you've lived with second-story men all your life, you're a really awful liar. What is it, Ma?"

"You should rest, Terry, you look tired."

"I should rest? What is it? Dale?"

She glanced at my father.

So there it was. "Okay, it's Dale. What about her?"

My mother pulled a face. I looked at my father as he sipped his beer. He grinned at me in that way that said, *Your ma, you know how she is.*

My father took the lead. "Your mother found a pack of condoms in Dale's jeans in the wash."

"Okay. That just proves she's being careful."

Ma shook her head. "It's not that she's having sex . . . well, all right, I'm having some issues with that, but it's natural and we've had our woman-to-woman talk already. But—" She drew air through her teeth.

My father and I waited. We kept waiting. I cracked before he did. "But what?"

"We don't like the boy very much."

I looked at my dad. He shrugged.

"The Rands are now judging character?" I asked.

"No, I'm not saying that, not at all. Not really. But there's something about him, Terry. I don't trust him. I don't like him. He's older. Technically it's statutory rape."

"We calling the cops?"

She wasn't being overprotective and wasn't really worried about Dale because she'd found a pack of condoms. I could see that in the way my mother was forcing the issue. This was something else. She turned, and her gold-flecked gaze not only pinned me to the wall but frisked me as well.

"Go talk to her," she said.

I let out a small nervous laugh. I didn't know my teenage sister. I couldn't imagine talking to her about her boyfriend. "Ma—"

My father drained the rest of his beer. "It might not be such a bad idea."

"No," I said. "It's a very bad idea."

"You're her brother. The only one she has left. She wanted to have breakfast with you. She saw you book out."

He stopped short. I knew what was supposed to come next, those things my father would never say. *We all wanted to have breakfast with you. We waited. We were in good spirits. But you ran off. What does Collie want with you? Why did you choose him over us?*

"Where is she?" I asked.

"Where else?" my mother said. "The lake. It's still the place where all the kids go. That boy, he'll be there. See what you think of him. Whether I'm just being overly concerned." She hit me with a hard gaze. "Or whether he's trouble. Real trouble."

I nodded. I trusted her. It wasn't about the condoms. It wasn't her being clingy. She knew he was bad news and wanted me to check it out.

Dad got up, went to the fridge, and made me a steak sandwich. "Here, eat this. Those ranch hands might not mind listening to a man's guts growling, but you don't want to embarrass your sister in front of her friends."

But that's exactly what I was going to do. You don't just show up to check out your little sister's boyfriend and wind up on her good side.

My dad sat again and my parents started talking to Gramp as if the hollow conversation had never stopped.

I thought, We as a family, we Rands, we have some significant issues.

I ate my sandwich in five bites and then raided the fridge for whatever else I could find. I made two more sandwiches, finished up some potato salad, two slices of apple pie, and a half gallon of milk.

I needed to regroup. It had been a long and emotional day already and my head was still ringing like a call to vespers. I sat on the porch digesting and looked out over the yard thick with shadows. There were a lot of places I wouldn't let my mind go. Too many bear traps that made any kind of reflection difficult to maneuver. I couldn't think of Kimmy and Scooter any more tonight, couldn't imagine Collie's victims for another minute. I didn't want to think that Chub might still be working with strings pulling scores, that he was going to go down hard one day and leave his family all alone. I didn't want to be faced with the realization that I almost hoped it would happen soon, that I'd have my chance with her again once he was tucked away for twelve to fifteen.

I got in the car and forced my attention away from my brother's files stuffed under the seat. I called JFK to see if he wanted to come along to the lake. He took a step forward like he might clamber in, shook his head as if he'd thought better of it, then marched up the porch steps.

It wasn't until I was on the road that I realized I didn't know what kind of car the boyfriend drove, or if he drove at all. I didn't know what he looked like. I didn't even know his name. Worse than all that, I feared I might not recognize my own sister.

The kids had taken over the parking area of Shalebrook Lake and spread out with their cars, pickups, and Jeeps across the back fields. They'd set up mini tailgate parties the way we used to do it, truck radios on, milling around coolers packed with beer. The park lamps did a fair job of illuminating the paths and picnic grounds.

I started searching among the groups for Dale. I had no idea where to look. There had to be two hundred kids drifting about. I wandered among them. I was young but not quite young enough, and the gray patch made me stand out. I caught some glowers and scowls. I looked just like what I was: an edgy older brother.

Heavy bass tracks and guttural lyrics moaned from car to car. They kept their radios low so there wasn't a war of music, just a low humming and groaning punctuated by an occasional caterwaul or whine.

So long as no one started a bonfire and everybody threw their beer bottles in the trash cans or took them back home again, the cops wouldn't come down too hard. Cruisers usually stopped in a few times a night on the weekends just to make their presence known and keep the peace.

Chub and I used to get badgered by the cops a little more frequently than everyone else. It didn't matter. It helped to build the legend, something that seemed important when I was seventeen. I had some small claim to fame and hung my hat on it. I wondered if Dale did the same thing.

I'd glimpsed her for only a minute this morning, and I knew how different a girl could look hanging out with the crowd at night than she did at home in the daylight. I imagined walking up to a teenager and discussing condoms, only to get hauled off by the cops for talking to the wrong girl.

Those teen-vampire romance novels she adored so much had left their mark on her generation. Most of the girls were dressed in black and red, tight low-slung jeans, lace and velvet blouses, long leather coats. A lot of makeup attentively applied to accent lips and eyes.

I made two complete circuits of the area before I finally homed in on her.

Dale seemed to be in her element among the crowd, weaving between tribes, drifting. I took up a perch beside a tree, lit a cigarette, and watched. She was the popular chick, everyone focusing on her, circling her, asking her opinion. She held a bottle of beer but sipped from it rarely. She was offered a joint and a cigarette and passed them both by. She laughed quaintly, almost shyly, but with a gorgeous smile and her neck tilted back. Her lips were strikingly red, cheekbones heavy with purple makeup that almost looked like bruises. Boys put their arms around her but only briefly. She kept on the move. I couldn't tell which might be the boyfriend, if any of them.

Beneath a tight, short leather jacket she wore a skimpy black T-shirt that left her midriff exposed. She had a lot of shake when she walked. I saw that she'd gotten a small tattoo near her navel. At this distance I couldn't make the tat out. You couldn't get a tattoo if you were under eighteen, not even if a parent said it was okay, and my mother never would have. That meant she had a fake ID. That sort of shocked me and it shouldn't have. Damn near everyone had fake identification. Fifteen seemed so much younger to me now than it once had.

I kept trying to see my little sister within the young woman before me. I'd missed out on some of the most important years of her life. I wondered how well she remembered me. I thought she must hate me. Not only had one of her brothers totally fucked himself and the family over and then vanished from her life, but almost immediately afterward so had the other. I wondered how I could have done it to her. I wondered how I could have done it to any of them.

A thousand fatuous questions wafted through my head. I tossed the butt and lit another cigarette. A hard breeze made the branches flap and residual rainwater shook across the field. Kids laughed. A bottle broke and hysteria-laced giggles erupted. Car engines rumbled. A drunk kid took a header and almost fell into the lake.

Dale was breaking from one group and heading toward another. I made my way toward her on an intercept course. She sensed me before I'd taken five steps and turned. She made a beeline for me. I saw that her tattoo was of her namesake, an Airedale. She had a ring through her navel, and the dog was posed as if leaping through it. I thought that was kind of cute. She wore no expression but her eyes blazed.

"What are you doing here, Terry?" she asked.

"You called me, remember?"

"Not here in New York. I mean what are you doing here right now. At the lake."

"I just—"

"Mom sent you."

I'd be stupid to deny it. After all this time the first words out of my mouth shouldn't be lies. "Yeah."

She sneered. The flickering golden light threw pools of shadow across her face. "Did you really come two thousand miles just to check on me?"

"No," I said.

"But you're going to do it anyway."

"I thought we could talk a little."

Her lips flattened. They were as red as if she'd just chewed through her wrist. "Now you want to talk?"

"I do, Dale."

"About what?"

She was like the rest of the Rands. Her anger and hurt had been locked so far down inside that when they sluggishly awoke and crawled out they became a monstrous and frightful thing. I saw them emerging. I turned my face aside.

It was my own fault. I shouldn't have cut out and run this morning. And I definitely shouldn't have let her catch me doing it.

"I'm not sure," I said. "Anything."

"Anything." The word hung there. "I don't know that I like you following me. You've been watching me, haven't you? You've been here for a while watching me. What gives you the right? You haven't even said hello. You haven't even asked me how I am, how I'm doing. You never called, Terry. Not even on my birthday. Never. You could've called." Her voice was a low growl. "Even if you didn't want to see any of us, you could've picked up the phone. You could've written. You could've let me know you were alive. You could've shown some concern, for even one minute. You could've done any of a thousand things, Terry, and you didn't. Now you want to talk?"

I reached out and drew her into an embrace. My timing was off, as usual. I should've let her vent longer, but I thought that once she got started it might never stop. I was still avoiding responsibility.

She didn't resist. She didn't hug me back either. It was like holding on to a mannequin dressed like a young woman who sort of looked like my little sister. I kept at it, but there was no point. I let her go.

She said, "Is this where I'm supposed to forgive you?"

"No," I said. "It's just that I wanted to hug you, all right?"

"You going to give me a lecture?"

"About what?"

"I don't know."

"I don't know either."

"About whatever you think I need lecturing on, Terry. That's really why you're here."

"You're confusing me, Dale."

I wanted to ask her what she felt about Collie. I wanted to know how his reputation had affected her in school and elsewhere. If instead of being known as a child of the nefarious Rand clan of thieves she was now marked as the sister of a thrill killer. I stared at that smear of blood-colored wax over her lips. I was as bad as the rest of my family. I didn't want to ask anything of real consequence for fear of being asked something meaningful in return.

"What did Mom and Dad say?"

"They found condoms in the laundry and they don't like your boyfriend."

"Ah, shit. So that's where that pack went."

"Always double-check your pockets, Dale. Always."

"So now you're reporting back to them."

"I'm here because I wanted to see you and say I was sorry for running out this morning."

We locked eyes. I tried to let her read me. I didn't know what it would mean or how it would go down, but I made the effort. She seemed about as satisfied as she could be under the circumstances, and her lips eased into a small, soft smile. She turned aside for a moment, and when she turned back the smile was gone.

"You really came back for Kimmy, didn't you? Not us. Not Collie."

"I don't know why I'm here, Dale."

"At least you're telling the truth now. That's something. Did you see her yet?"

"I saw her. I didn't talk to her."

"Why didn't you say anything?"

I shrugged. It was my father's gesture. It was meant to deflect honesty, intimacy, and insight. I couldn't make it a habit. "She's married to Chub now. They have a kid. It's not my place."

"But you watched her."

"Yes," I admitted.

"So what was the point of that?"

"Good question," I said.

"Five years out there on a ranch beneath the big blue sky, lots of time to clear your head, and you come home with a brain as full of snakes as when you left."

I lifted my chin and studied her face. "Fifteen and you know everything there is to know, eh?"

"Not quite."

"Right."

"Okay, so she found condoms. What parent is going to like the guy who's having sex with their little girl?"

"That's a mature way to look at it, Dale."

"I do my best."

"I'm glad. So how about if you introduce me to the guy and we leave it at that?"

"And if I don't?"

"Then you don't."

The wind grew stronger. I could smell more rain in the air, another storm rolling in. Dale's hair flapped in the breeze and for a second I saw the little girl I remembered, slipping off to sleep with her head on a Princess Lilliput pillowcase while I read about hepcat James Dean–looking blood drinkers who romanced the ladies across deep black fields beneath a hunter's moon. A twinge of regret banked through me.

"Okay," she said. "Let's go meet the beau."

"Jesus Christ," I said, "seriously, that's what you call him? The beau?"

"I do."

She locked arms with me and drew me along as we threaded through the parked cars and the kids talking and getting wasted. She took me to a '69 Chevy that looked like a 396—a speed demon, a racer with wide tires to hug the curves. Only the parking lights were on, glowing bright yellow as we approached. The radio groaned with a heavy bass.

The beau was propped up on the hood, laid out across his windshield, holding a beer and taking in the starshine. He was much older than I'd expected, maybe twenty or twenty-one. He shouldn't have been dating a fifteen-year-old girl. My shoulders hitched.

He had darting eyes, and his nose had been broken at least once and badly set. It lent him a touch of character he hadn't earned. He went shirt-less and wore four black leather wristbands on his right forearm. Jeans cinched his waist, the seams straining as he slid off the hood. He was so skinny he looked half starved. He smelled of oil, acne ointment, and second-rate pot. A tattoo of foreign words was scrawled in black script along his left shoulder. His nose and bottom lip were pierced. He had a pencil beard that rode around the very edge of his jaw, no mustache.

"Butch, this is my brother Terry." She gripped him around the waist so tightly he let out a little gasp. She glanced back at me. "Terry, meet Butch."

We shook hands.

His voice had a focused edge to it, strong and clear, which I wasn't expecting. "You're the one who's been out west," he said.

"That's right."

"What's that like?"

I had a hard time remembering. I strained to come up with an an-ecdote, a yarn, some kind of an accounting that would be good enough to tell to anyone who asked. But the harder I tried to recall the last half decade the less substantial it seemed. Fences, a lot of fencing, always in need of repair.

Luckily Butch didn't really give a shit. He hadn't waited for a re-sponse. "I think about heading out that way. You know, just getting on the road. Hitting three or four states in a couple days. Prairies. Farms. All those highways, all those exits. That's got to be the life, right?"

I said, "Sure."

I knew one thing. Dale and Butch might've hung around the lake most nights but they did a lot of cruising too. Nobody kept a machine like that and didn't let out the clutch and tear up the streets. I could see them burning down Sunrise Highway, out past the barrens, flipping off the Hamptons and heading down to the beaches.

He was territorial the way most young men were, and he put on the same show. He kept a hand around her waist, rubbing his knuckles against her bare midriff, telling all the other punks around that she was his and his alone. I'd done it myself. I couldn't hold it against him, except I did. A part of me wanted to kick his teeth out, but I supposed that was about par. It was his way of proving he had a bloom on her that her own flesh and blood never would.

He asked, "Hey, babe, can you get me another beer?"

"Of course. You want one, Terry?"

"No thanks," I said.

She climbed into the backseat and I could hear her rattling a cooler. "We're out. You want a Mike's Hard Lemonade instead?"

Butch said, "What do you think?"

"I'll be back in a minute."

"That's my girl."

Dale slipped off, walking briskly but with a sexy sashay. As she moved across the area I could see her silhouette appearing every so often in the blaze of headlights.

A fine drizzle started. I liked the feel of it. Trees bucked and branches swept to and fro, the lake showing small whitecaps.

"I might have a job for you," Butch said.

"A job?"

"Yeah. I can't say too much about it now, not until I get all the details. It's not a bank or anything. A jewelry store. Family-owned. We take it a week from Tuesday."

Now I understood what he meant about hitting three or four states in a couple of days. All the highways and exits. He was fantasizing about a crime spree, taking down scores across America, being a real outlaw. Like you didn't have to plan as much. Like it was easier to escape the cops on the I-25 in the middle of Wyoming, twenty miles to the nearest exit, than it was dodging the staties on the Wantagh Parkway. I realized why he smelled like oil. It was gun oil.

My mother had good instincts. She knew a criminal when she saw one. This kid stank of trouble. I should've been sharper.

"I've got three men already," Butch went on. "We need another for crowd control. It's a small shop, but they've got a lot of employees. Like I said, family-owned, so they've got Mom and Dad in back, a couple of uncles doing inventory, sisters and cousins up front working the counters. The hardware will be clean, untraceable. Unless you've got your own piece you'd rather use. In and out in under four minutes."

"I don't do that," I said.

He frowned. "You don't do what?"

"That."

"Hit jewelry stores?"

"I don't carry a gun."

He smiled like I'd just told a joke that hadn't quite come off. "Since when?"

"Since always."

"But you're a Rand."

"And we don't do that," I said.

"Are you kidding me?"

"I'm not."

For some reason I was suddenly offended by the fact that he was standing here without a shirt. That scrawny chest on exhibit. His naked nipples steered toward me.

He bounced like he was being tickled and let out a small burp of a giggle. "You're old-school thieves. You're famous. Everybody knows what you're all about."

"No armed robbery."

He cocked his head. "No exceptions, huh?"

"None."

"Not even for a big enough payday? Let's say, six figures?"

The kid was a fucking idiot. Jewelry was always the hardest thing to unload on a fence. Some pieces could be identified as readily as fingerprints. It had to pass through a lot of hands before anyone could turn it into cash. You saw maybe a dime off every dollar. For a five-man crew to see a hundred grand each you had to pull down a five-mil score. This mook would never be involved with that kind of a major haul.

In this town he wouldn't even think about it unless he was in the good graces of the Thompson syndicate.

I asked the obvious question. "You do any work for Danny Thompson?"

"A little of this and that," Butch said.

"What kind of this and that?"

"You know—things. Stuff."

I watched Dale across the way, returning with a couple of beers. She could make it only a few steps before someone stopped her, chatted her up, got her laughing. She was pretty and popular and shouldn't be hooked up with a twenty-year-old hood talking armed robbery. The rest of them looked like punks and assholes but at least they weren't getting ready to take a five-to-seven rap.

I wondered if she was drawn to Butch because he was a thief like her brothers and father. If she felt more comfortable with him than some straight-A joe working at the Walmart and putting himself through night school. If she liked the smell of gun oil on him. I thought of this mutt on top of my sister. My fists tightened and my knuckles cracked. The pounding bass from his radio beat into my feet and moved up my legs, into my chest, and up through my brain.

I got in close, went nose-to-nose with Butch as he backed up and became trapped against the Chevy's grille. He turned his hip to me as if to climb away.

He frowned and said, "Hey, man, hey—"

A little of this and that. Butch was one of the hangers-on. Back in Big Dan's day I watched them come and go, guys trying to mob up who Dan would take advantage of for as long as he could. Get them to do some extra dirty work, the stuff he didn't want to lay out on his own crew. But he'd always pay them something for the risk and trouble, even if they didn't get any of the respect they were hoping for. Danny, though, I could see him running guys like Butch out to do everything from shining shoes to cleaning his rain gutters to pulling heists, just so he could skim off the top, paying them nothing and letting them drop wherever they fell.

"Stay away from him."

"Why?"

"Because he uses guys like you."

"You shouldn't talk about Mr. Thompson that way, it's not healthy. He's got a lot of ears, even out here, you know what I'm saying?"

"I know what you're saying."

He hissed a laugh. He thought he was on the inside track, hip to the action, impervious to injury. I considered proving him wrong, chopping him in the throat or shattering that already ugly nose, but it would hurt Dale, and I couldn't make my sister suffer any more than I already had.

It took him a few more seconds to realize how badly he'd fucked up. He'd presumed too much, spilled too much. His smarmy expression froze.

"Hey, man, hey. It's cool, right? We're cool?"

"Sure."

"You're a Rand. It's not like you're going to cause any trouble, am I right? Tell me if I'm wrong."

I was a Rand. "Old school, Butch. I don't blow anyone else's scores."

"Righteous."

I backed away from his car, let the throbbing hum ease out of me, taking some of the agitation with it.

Dale returned and handed me a beer even though I hadn't asked for one. What the hell. I drank quickly while Dale discussed how she and Butch met. It was my story. It was the same story as most of the kids here and the ones from my day and before, going back to my old man and my uncles and maybe to the Indians who'd originally owned the land. You hung around and eyed one another until someone eyed you back and then you decided if it was worth your time to launch ahead.

She hugged him. She mothered him. She cared about him. When the drizzle grew a bit harder, she got in the backseat and pulled out a shirt for him. He put it on reluctantly. She fixed the collar for him. I wasn't going to be able to talk dirt with her.

"I've got to run," I said.

Butch and I shook again. I looked at him like he was already in the can, his head shaved, tattooed with swastikas, on his knees for the Aryans.

"Good meeting you," he said.

"You too."

Dale took my hand and walked me back to my car. I found myself almost unconsciously studying the texture of her palms and the pads of her fingers. Had Dad sent her scurrying up drainpipes too? Could she pull a five-card lift?

She gave me a hug. "I'm glad you came out here to see me."

"I am too."

"What are you going to tell Ma?"

"That of all the things there are for her to worry about, you're not one of them."

"That's sweet, but do you believe it?"

"I believe you're smart and sharp. It won't help, though. You know she'll keep on her course."

"I don't expect anything different from her. That's what we all do. Stay our course."

I wanted to ask, *And you? How are you handling everything?*

"Love you," she said, and spun away.

I got in behind the wheel and snapped the dome light on. I opened Butch's wallet. I'd picked his pocket when he'd turned his hip to me. I hadn't even intended to. It was as if he'd offered me the chance and my body had reacted.

I found out that his real name was Joe Cassidy. Now I knew where the Butch came from and probably where the crime-spree fantasies had originated too. He had six dollars in singles. A suspended driver's license with a Freehold address. No condoms. That's why Dale made sure she always kept a pack on her, because our good friend Butch here just didn't give a shit about protection.

He also had no credit cards. That meant either Dale was fronting him pocket change for beer and gas and the like or he had a problem. Gambling or drugs or something else. I wondered if she had a part-time job or if she was nimble-fingered and following in the rest of the family's footsteps.

The question became: Did Dale know what Butch was up to? Or, worse, was she in on the score with him? The idea of it made the back of my skull ache. But she was fifteen. At fifteen, the rest of us Rands had been creeping around second-story bedrooms and stealing silverware and jugging tiny safes.

I pocketed his six bucks and tossed the rest out the window as soon as I hit the highway. Butch Cassidy. Motherfucker. I gunned it down the road, thinking, When Butch went down, would he take Dale with him? What was I going to have to do to protect her? How far was I willing to go? And how many of these kinds of questions had filled my brother's head before he got caught in the underneath and never came up again?

My head was full of the dead. I sat at the bar in the Elbow Room with the photocopied files and ordered a Jack and Coke.

The place was a dive. It had gotten worse since the last time I'd had a drink here. The men looked the same except maybe a bit more desperate. The drinks were watered down, the felt on the pool tables that much more worn. The mirror behind the bar had a thick film of grime on it so you could barely see your own face. Maybe it was a blessing.

The whores worked the losers a little more brazenly. They didn't bother with subtlety. They didn't play the buy-me-a-drink-and-maybe-I'll-go-home-with-you-and-oh-by-the-way-I-cost-a-C-note-sorry-I-didn't-mention-that-sooner game. It was all out front. I wasn't sure if I liked it better or not. At least you didn't waste time or get your heart chipped away when you realized the girl with the cool blue eyes and the slow smile wasn't really turning it on because you might be Mr. Right. You knew at the start you were wrong, and so was she.

The cops had interviewed the owner and two bartenders who had been working the night Collie went on his spree. All three swore he hadn't been drunk. That he hadn't started any kind of a ruckus or been involved in any sort of disturbance. That he hadn't been pestering anybody. There had been no fights. He hadn't pawed any of the girls. He hadn't tried to rob the place. No one reported having their pockets picked.

The juke purred a trio of female voices, low and tempting. The speakers beat at my back. I chowed on cocktail peanuts and sucked beer. My concentration skittered around the room, picking up pieces of conversations and lonely muttering. Men were talking standard shit. Who'd been ripped off by the boss, the government, the wife. Men with preteen sons talked proud. Men with older sons talked about intense disappointment. It was times like these that I was glad my family was full of men who kept quiet.

Someone bumped my shoulder and I spilled a quarter glass down my shirt. He didn't say excuse me. I turned and glowered. I wondered if this could start a chain reaction that would land me on death row.

I glanced at the register. I could have it cleaned out in under ten seconds. I could wait for the bartender to go get another case of beer from the storeroom. Or I could sucker-punch him and nab the cash. No one would try to stop me. That kind of draw was always there for me. Knowing I could reach out and grab what I wanted at any time. Of course it was. I was a thief. The devil had to be in Collie's ear all the time as well.

I wondered what set of circumstances would have to come together to send me on a spree where I would kill old women and nine-year-old girls. I knew my rage could send me into barroom brawls. But Suzy Coleman. I just couldn't imagine anything pushing me to murder a little girl.

I stood and moved toward a table in back. As I passed the end of the bar, a middle-aged pro with greasy eyes put her arm out and grabbed my wrist. She smelled of Four Roses and stale hamburger. I thought if she was making a play for me this was the wrong way to go about it. She held on tightly without so much as lifting her gaze or saying a word. She was sitting with a john who either hadn't been buying her whiskey fast enough or was taking too long cracking open his wallet and paying for her services. Now I saw she was using me to make him jump. He glanced up as if I was disturbing him and gave me the death glare.

I thought about Collie. I was going to be thinking about Collie for a long time to come, but especially in this place. Every scent, motion, action made me wonder. Was this what did it? Could this do it to me?

She opened her mouth to say something, then changed her mind when she looked into my eyes.

I walked on, snapping her grip.

I got a table and eased into the bench seat and thought about my brother doing the same thing. It would've been a tight fit for him five years ago. He'd had a substantial gut. He would've had to suck it in. The table edge would be cutting into him. He'd try to ignore it, throw back another Corona.

I didn't want my brother in my head, so why was I so desperately trying to get into his? It was a setup. I knew it. I could feel it. He was positioning me in some kind of a play in a game that wasn't even mine.

I started to slide out of the booth just as the waitress came around. She was thin-lipped, frizzy-headed, bony-shouldered, and small-breasted, yet somehow exuded sensuality.

"Get you?" she asked.

"Nothing."

"Nothing?"

Was there any possibility Collie was telling the truth? He seemed to believe it, but what kind of proof was that? He was at least as nuts as everyone else on death row, and that was a heap of crazy.

I slid back into the booth and knew I had to make a decision. Read the files or burn them. Stay or book. Give in or get the hell out. I'd gone this far for reasons I didn't understand. Maybe I should head back out west. Maybe I should pull the job with Butch. Maybe I could show up at Kimmy and Chub's front door and invite myself in. Had I come home to flame out like my brother?

"Fuck," I said.

"What's that?"

The waitress was watching me. She didn't seem bored waiting. A hint of talcum powder trailed across her cleavage. She probed a bad back tooth with her tongue and winced but didn't stop.

"Sorry. Give me a Dewar's and Coke. A lot of ice."

"You okay, man?"

"Sure."

She tilted her head back toward the bar. "Flo over there wants you to buy her a dirty martini."

I could guess who Flo was. "And why would she expect me to do that?"

The waitress shrugged. "It'll make her more friendly to you, you know?"

"I've got all the friends I can handle."

"The guys like her. Some of them anyway."

"Not tonight."

"Okay, man."

I spent the next forty-five minutes reading and slowly getting drunk. My stomach was empty by now, and the liquor hit me harder than it should have. It didn't slow me down. I kept knocking them back, hoping to disconnect. The pages flashed before me. Facts, dates, blood-spatter patterns, interviews. I knew the picture but details kept adding color and texture. More than I wanted to know.

The reports were about as cool and dry as they came. There wasn't a hint of emotion anywhere, not even in my brother's confession. He'd told the cops the same thing that he'd told me. There was no reason. He explained what he'd done that night step by step. How he'd moved from one victim to the next. He named the seven. He didn't name Rebecca Clarke. She'd been completely left out. No one seemed to care.

The victims soon emptied of whatever personality I'd instilled them with. Paul Coleman. Sarah Coleman. Tom Coleman. Neal Coleman. Suzy Coleman. Doug Schuller. Mrs. Howard.

He said he hadn't known any of them prior to that night. He'd had no grudges with any of them. He didn't even know their names. He'd never seen them before. He'd chosen his victims completely at random. He'd driven around town until he felt the urge to kill and then he'd climbed out of his car and headed off on foot. When he was finished with one he'd proceeded to the next. He hadn't done a thing to hide his crimes. He hadn't muffled the gunshots. The noise awoke other vacationers in the trailer park, who'd called the police. Collie had been long gone by the time they arrived.

Why go on a spree and end it of your own accord? Why not go out in a blaze? Had his rage really been vented? Had he been angry at all? The papers described him as coldhearted, methodical, meticulous.

Collie hadn't taken the stand. He'd never attempted to explain himself in court. His attorneys hadn't bothered to dispute the Becky Clarke snuff. They figured he was already up for seven charges of murder so an eighth didn't matter. They were adamant on a plea of insanity. It was a bold and stupid play, but they were strapped—Collie refused to recant his confession. Still, they should have homed in on that dispute and made it the central theme of their case. If they could cast doubt on that one killing, then they might shake the D.A.'s case a little. Becky Clarke had been strangled with a sash of some kind. They hadn't pulled any fibers. Collie had used a blade and a gun and his fists to commit his other murders. When the cops arrested him they found the gun unloaded on the bar where he'd put it.

So where were the knife and the sash? Why would he toss those and not the pistol?

The whole fucking thing was ridiculous.

I went through the paperwork again. I had the feeling I'd missed something. I dug around and came up with one of the forensics sheets. I scanned it, and most of the terminology didn't mean anything to me.

And then there it was. No one had made a big deal out of it.

"Jesus," I whispered.

Saliva. They'd found dried saliva on each victim's forehead. No one suggested what it might mean. They only dealt in facts.

But I knew. Collie had kissed each of them on the forehead before, or after, he'd murdered them.

Every one of them except Rebecca Clarke. There'd been no saliva found on her.

I shut the folders and shoved them away from me. I sat back and listened to the juke crooning and droning. I kept seeing Scooter bolting across Kimmy's front lawn. I thought about Chub playing it on the straight and narrow, running a completely legit garage. I saw my brother press his lips to the old woman's brow an instant before he beat her to death.

No matter how I tried, that night didn't piece together right. Where had Collie gotten the S&W .38 and the knife? He was a Rand. Rands didn't use guns. It had been a clean drop. No serial numbers. Had he already been armed in the Elbow Room? I tried to picture it. If he'd been on the verge of going mad dog, why not start here, in this kind of crowd? Why drive around first? It seemed to me that he would've been cooling off then. Or had he run into one of his cronies and purchased the weapons then? There didn't seem to be enough time. Collie had left the Elbow Room at eleven P.M., and the murders began about twenty minutes later. He returned before closing at two A.M. and announced he was a murderer and someone should call the cops.

I didn't see him rushing around looking to buy a piece. It wasn't his way. But neither was knifing an old woman. Not until that night.

Where and when had he picked up the weapons? If it had been days or weeks before, then how could anyone consider his rampage a spur-of-the-moment occurrence? There were at least a couple of names I was familiar with who might have sold Collie an untraceable piece. I decided I'd pay them a visit.

A shadow crossed my table. I looked up and Flo was standing there, watching me.

The whiskey-and-hamburger smell had given way to tequila and bland salsa. Her lips appeared to be even more unnatural as she hit a pose beneath the weak barroom lighting. She had on a pair of diamond stud earrings that looked like the real thing.

"I know who you are," she said.

"Yeah?"

She nodded. "You look just like your brother. With that same white streak in your hair."

That got my attention. I drew the files back toward me in a display of something like protection. Then I took a final pull of my drink. When I finished I wiped my mouth with the back of my hand and stared at her. "What do you know about my brother?"

"It's a compliment. He's a nice-looking man. Looks like your uncle. That Grey. He still comes in here sometimes. Handsome. A touch of class. He knows how to treat a woman." Without any invitation she slid into the other side of the booth. "Are you sure you wouldn't like a little company? I can see that you're lonely. A young man like you, hurting so bad."

"I don't know where you're getting that, lady." I held the file close, like it contained a catalog of all my own sins. "I'm merry. I'm full of mirth."

"You're melancholy and you're pining for an old girlfriend, right? The one that got away. The one that you'd give anything to be with."

"That's not a bold guess, Flo. Everybody in here is pining for the losses of his youth. Including you."

"Not me, hon. I've got no sentiment left in me."

"You were going to talk about my brother," I said.

"Was I?"

"Yes. Did you know him? Collie Rand?"

"Everyone knew Collie."

I sat up straighter. "Were you here that night?"

"Which night?"

"The night he was arrested."

"Why don't you buy me a dirty martini?"

"Why don't you answer my question first, Flo?" I grinned at her. I hoped it looked like a john's drunken smile. The pulse in my throat began to burn. I leaned toward her as if she was beginning to arouse me.

"I can make you forget, you know," she said.

"Let's stay on topic, Flo. Collie, my brother. The night he was arrested."

"You won't even remember her name after me."

She reached for my wrist and held on. I didn't want to be touched. I wondered about these people who thought they had some kind of a right to put their hands on you, to pull and pluck at you. I felt a surge of anger. "How about if you quit working me like I'm a lonely-hearts drunk with a wife who won't suck my pud and answer my fucking question, right?"

She pulled her hand back. "You're an abrasive son of a bitch, you know that?"

"Yeah, I know that."

I pulled a twenty out and slapped it down in front of her. She snatched it away and tucked it into her bra.

"You got a bad temper," she said. "Just like the other one. We can't even sit here and have a friendly talk?"

It was a cheap shot but it hit home. I tried to let the tension out of me but it was a losing game. The waitress appeared and I downshifted to beer. Flo watched me expectantly. Jesus Christ, the corners you could get backed into.

I said, "Fine. And you can have a dirty martini."

The waitress nodded and went to get our drinks.

"Look, about my brother—"

"I was here," she said.

"Tell me what happened."

"He was around, then he left, then he came back and he said for somebody to call the police. The cops came and they busted him. Didn't even have to wrestle him, he just laid flat on his face on the floor."

"Think you can go into deeper detail than that?"

I'd shown too much interest. She thought if I started getting the answers I needed then she could hold out on the rest of the facts and reel in more cash. Her greasy eyes were full of hunger. She repeated the story and tried to flesh out the scene with minor specifics, but she couldn't remember much. I got the feeling she had been bored. Collie hadn't done much that was noteworthy. He put the gun on the bar, drank his Corona, and laid down. It was barely a ripple in her night.

She finally realized I wasn't going to turn over any serious cash, and she slipped back to the bar and found herself a new guy to hang on to.

I was too swilled to be disappointed that I hadn't gotten more out of her. I opened the file again, then closed it, then opened it. I hissed, shut it, and got to my feet. My stomach twisted with the alcohol. I headed for the door. I wanted to go home to my bed.

Why did it matter to Collie now five years too late, and why the hell should it matter to me?

Maybe it was in the blood, this thing that made us so bent, so wrong. The veins in my wrist ticked away, black and twisted.

I knew I'd have to talk to Gilmore eventually. I didn't expect him to come around the back of my car in the Elbow Room parking lot and give me a left hook to the kidneys.

The pain forced me to my knees. I puked up the liquor and nearly went over but managed to keep my face out of the asphalt. I made a noise that sounded like an animal about to start gnawing its leg out of a trap, then I vomited again. I'd tossed my cookies more in the last two days than in the twenty years prior.

Gagging, trying to catch a sip of air, I looked up and saw Gilmore standing over me. He wore a sorrowful grin even while he sucked on a cigarette. His eyes were dancing pinpoints of dejection. His hair was short and chopped across the front, messy but still fashionable. His face had some alcoholic bloat to it.

Maybe he'd been following me and had seen me duck into the Elbow Room. Maybe he watched as I turned pages, and he recognized the photocopied files. Or maybe the old man from the archives had left a message on Gilmore's voice mail and given him shit for circumventing protocol. Gimore would question the guy and eventually put it together. Who else would grab Collie's jacket except me?

My father had said that Gilmore had no edge to him now that he'd lost his wife. I couldn't quite agree with that.

I crawled forward a bit and tried to stand. Gilmore gave me another shot in the same place. He grunted a little like it caused him pain. It hurt me ten times worse than the first punch and I went down flat on my face.

He lit another cigarette and leaned back against the trunk of my car. He stared off in the distance like he couldn't bear to look at me.

"Terrier. Didn't think you'd ever come back. Been keeping your snout clean out there wherever it is you've settled?"

Cars drove by. The front door of the Elbow Room opened and closed. I heard hushed voices punctuated by mean girlish laughter. Gilmore took me by the arm and got me to my knees.

A few of the other patrons walked by on their way to their cars. Gilmore acknowledged them and said, "Evening."

I deserved what I'd gotten. I accepted it the way I'd accepted the beating from Big Dan's boys. I took my chances with my eyes open.

Still, I thought Gilmore was overreacting a bit. It was a petty move. He knew I'd never punch a cop, not even in self-defense.

He tried to help me to my feet, but I was still too wobbly. He left me kneeling on asphalt and patted my back tenderly.

"You know, Terrier, you broke your mother's heart."

Jesus Christ, I thought, here it comes.

He toed the paperwork scattered across the ground. He said nothing about it.

"I always liked you. You and your whole family. From the start, or nearly so, we understood each other. There are lines you cross and those you don't. Your grandfather knew that, your uncles, your father. But it got crossed up when it came to you and your brother."

I wanted to tell him I was nothing like Collie, but I still couldn't speak. The pain was lessening. I breathed deep. As I listened to him talking quietly behind me, I couldn't stop picturing him pulling his piece and popping me in the back of my head, execution style.

"I wish you would've called me. I wish you would have asked. I deserve that much respect, no matter what you think of me or cops in general." He rubbed my back again, took a deep drag on his cigarette, and let the smoke out over my shoulder. "I thought you were the bright one. I thought you might be going somewhere. I had hopes, Terry, I really did. I figured you and Kimmy would get out of that house and go your own way. You'd leave the life behind and raise a family. It would've been a good thing. I knew you had it in you." He sighed. "But then you ran out on everyone. You showed a real lack of character there, you know?"

I knew.

"You got a wife wherever you been living? Kids?"

I coughed and shook my head.

"That's too bad." He flicked his cigarette butt away, lit another. "Did you really come back just to stir up trouble?"

"No," I groaned.

"Well, that's good to hear. I'm happy to hear that. You still on the grift wherever it is you've gotten to?"

"No."

"Good, that's good to know. But there's something about home that brings it out in you again, huh?"

I thought it might be time to try standing. He slung one of my arms over his shoulder and helped me up. When I was on my feet again, I propped myself against the back bumper of my car. I slumped there for a couple of minutes, watching him smoke.

When I was able to, I bent and retrieved the copied files, opened the car door, and stuffed them back under the passenger seat.

"I bet you could use a beer right about now," Gilmore said.

My voice sounded exactly like I felt—sick, weak, trembling. "I think I'm done for the night."

"Then you can buy me one. Come on, Terry."

He turned away from me and headed into the Elbow Room. I followed him, limping along. I smelled like asphalt and vomit. I thought I might get sick again the second I stepped back into the bar. Gilmore breezed over to the table I'd been at and took the opposite bench. I sat exactly where I'd been sitting all night.

The waitress came by and Gilmore ordered us two beers. She returned with them and he paid her and said thank you. I grabbed the wet bar towel from her tray and wiped my face with it.

Gilmore sipped his beer and stared at me like I was a long-lost friend he'd been searching for and had finally found. "You look well," he said.

"I've been better."

"You deserved worse from me, but we'll let that slide for now."

His eyes were dark and lonely. His kids were gone. He probably saw them only on alternating weekends, if that. When he was forced to drop them off at their mother's again, the grief would try to drown him from the inside.

"You didn't hang around for your brother's trial," he continued. "You never got to see the evidence against him. Hear the witnesses. Listen to the testimony. Take the stand in his defense. Your mother did, you know. She wept the whole time but she tried to put in a righteous word. You could've said something too, if you'd cared."

"What would the point have been? He admitted his guilt."

"That's right, he did."

I started to feel better. Suddenly I wanted the beer that was in front of me. I took a swig. Gilmore finished his and ordered another round. He paid again. Our eyes met.

"You know what he says now?" I asked.

"That he didn't smoke the teenage girl. Rebecca Clarke."

"That's right. Is there any chance it's the truth?"

"None," Gilmore said. "He did them all."

"He never confessed to killing her."

"He didn't have to. Maybe he just forgot. Isn't that what he said? That he wasn't sure at the time? A night like that, a crazy murder spree. Who wouldn't want to forget?"

I nodded and sipped. "What about the kiss?"

He pulled that tight and wistful grin again. He couldn't help himself, his face fell into it so naturally now. It showed me how forlorn he'd become. He let out a false chuckle that told me even more about how his life had smashed up since I'd last seen him. "You spotted that, huh? Sharp eyes."

"Yes. He apparently kissed them all on the forehead. But not Rebecca Clarke."

"So he was too excited. So he was too juiced up on rage or adrenaline to perform that specific sick ritual that one particular time. He still choked her to death."

"Maybe not. What about the sash or cord? What about the knife? They were never found."

"So he ditched them. He admitted to knifing the gas-station attendant, Douglas Schuller."

"Right, he admitted it to me again the other day. But he said he didn't snuff Becky Clarke."

"Did his wife put you up to this?" Gilmore asked.

I drew my chin back. "You know about her?"

"Yeah, she haunts me on a weekly basis."

"But you never mentioned her to my mother or father?"

"They've cut themselves off from your brother. It wasn't my place to lay something like that in their laps. Have you told them?"

"No," I said. "You've met Lin?"

"She's made it her life's mission to cause me heartburn. She camps out in my office, brings me information. What she calls evidence. Jailhouse lawyers are bad enough, but jailhouse wife attorney-wannabes are much worse. You know who falls in love with death-row inmates?"

"Mentally unstable individuals."

"That's right. Imagine what Christmas dinner is going to be like if she ever shows up on your doorstep."

I took a pull of beer and propped myself up lengthwise in the booth. I swallowed a grunt of pain. I watched Gilmore. There was a certain air to him that it took me a moment to place. He was doing his best to assure and console me.

"He told me there'd been others," I said.

Gilmore angled himself closer. "What others?"

"Not others he'd iced. Other girls who fit Rebecca Clarke's profile, murdered in similar ways. Some while he was in prison."

"Three or four."

"Doesn't that make it suspicious?"

Gilmore held back a mocking laugh, the strength of it causing his body to shake. "You know how many unsteady drunken bastards kill their wives or girlfriends every year? You know how many do it by choking them to death? How many of those women are young, cute, and brunette?"

"You're saying they were all snuffed by their boyfriends?"

"No, I'm not saying that, Terrier."

"Then what?"

He threw back his beer and looked for the waitress. I wondered if he was going to step up to double shots of scotch. I wondered how much booze he had to kill every night to help him get to sleep. I was curious as to how often he was allowed to see his kids and if he could still come up with those unique and colorful voices to entertain them. I imagined Phyllis with a new boyfriend, trying to get on with her life, and Gilmore holding on to the past like so many of us did. I could picture him in the darkness, reaching out to clench a woman who was no longer there.

He caught the waitress's eye and she came by with another round. He pushed one to me and I pushed it back to him.

Gilmore's lips jacked up as if someone had jammed their thumbs into the corners of his mouth and pushed. "Listen to me," he said. He tapped a fingernail on the tabletop. It clicked as loudly as if he'd pulled the trigger on an empty gun. "One of those women was found behind a motel in Riverhead, garroted with her own bra. It looks like a rape job gone bad." He tapped his finger again. "One had her hyoid bone broken, which probably happened in an accidental fall. She was drunk at the time. She was nineteen and out of work. She'd spent an hour that night arguing with her father on the phone because he wouldn't send her enough money to pay her rent. Neighbors heard her stumbling around. When they found her she was lying on a futon, her throat crushed against the wooden arm." Again that click, like we were playing Russian roulette. "Someone used a belt on the last girl. She was a distributor for a low-level meth dealer. She was hooked on her own product and un-doubtedly shorted her supplier. That's why she bought it."

"Did you personally investigate those cases?"

"No, they weren't mine. But I looked into them when Lin brought me her concerns. I do my job. There's nothing there."

"Give me those files too. Give me names."

"No."

"Why not?"

His eyes went hard as shale. "You're a burglar, Terrier, like the rest of your family. You don't get to see police files. Let me amend that. Let's make that, you don't get to see any *more* files. I don't need you running around out there stirring up strife, putting your nose in business that doesn't concern you. You want to talk about Collie or discuss his case, I'm here to help. He's going to be gone in a week and a half. You need someone to give you an ear, I'll do that. But you have to keep away from the rest of it."

"The kiss," I said.

"I hate to tell you this, Terrier, but just in case you haven't realized it yet, your brother is out of his goddamn mind. Anytime you get too curious about what was going on in his head, remember where that kind of thinking leads. You really want to start down that road?"

Gilmore stood. I could tell he wanted to shake my hand or give me a hug. His eyes were full of regret and remorse and a hope toward friendship. He walked away and took his fucked little grin with him out the door.

Like the last lone soldier defending a fort, my father stood guard on our house. He leaned against the veranda railing. Backlit by the porch light, he was lent a kind of mythic presence. He had the grave bearing of someone thinking hard on a particular subject. He showed no sign of restlessness at all, but I knew it was there. Maybe his tension was merely calling to my own.

Pinscher Rand had become a criminal for the same reason that I had. Because he'd been born to it. I wondered if he ever pulled a cheap score nowadays just to keep the old skills sharpened and to remember how exciting and awful it had once been. I imagined him picking a wallet and not pulling the money, just poking around the contents, looking at the driver's license photo, the credit cards, the carefully folded sheets of paper that rarely made any sense. A note from an ex-girlfriend that the mark valued, a frayed motto or private joke that had gone through the wash a couple of times. He'd pass by a mailbox and dump the wallet in. He'd feel some strange sense of accomplishment, knowing his fingers were still supple enough to get the job done.

He should've been a carpenter. It was the only other skill that was in the Rand blood. Maybe I should have been too. I imagined us razing the house and building another one, a smaller one, without the hidden caches, maybe with a nursery.

I wondered what he did with himself now that he'd quit creeping houses. What shit he wasted his time on. He and my mother should be out enjoying themselves, making the most of life. Except that I knew the burden of the murders tore him up with guilt in a way that none of his own crimes ever had. My father hid himself away out of shame.

JFK lay across the top stair and I had to jump over him. My side hurt so badly that I almost flubbed it. He gave me a resolute eye roll and coughed out a small belly bark.

I lit a cigarette and sat in a chair, trying to hide my discomfort. It was too late. My old man had already noticed.

"Someone worked you over," he said.

"I'm okay."

"Not Dale's boyfriend?"

I frowned. "Hell, no."

"Didn't think that one would get over on you."

"Not likely."

He nodded, took a step toward me, and looked me deep in the face like he was checking for bruises. "That's not what's on your mind, though."

"No, Dad, it's not."

My father sat, opened his cooler, and handed me a beer. I shook my head. He dug around in the ice chest until he came up with a small carton of orange juice. I drank and felt a little better.

We relaxed and watched the road and the black brush beyond it. JFK had picked up on my mood. He came over, circled and pawed and collapsed. His ears kept snapping up and he let loose with a deep-throated whine. I wanted to do the same.

We nodded. We sipped. We smoked. We took turns patting the great beast at our feet who'd once been young and fierce and was now only well muscled, noble, and old. The immense topic of our lives loomed between us.

We've failed. We've failed to hold our family together. We've failed to protect one another.

My old man started to clear his throat like he wanted to say something but couldn't find the proper words. I turned and watched him until our eyes met.

He said, "You want to talk about it, Terry?"

I sat up like someone had just lobbed a grenade. It was a question that my father never asked. I thought, Christ, I must look *really* bad.

Or maybe it was just his way of getting me to start a conversation that he himself needed to have.

I listened to my mother inside murmuring to Gramp, the way new parents talk to infants. She sounded elated. I waited for her to say, "Look at these chubby cheeks. Who's got such chubby cheeks? So big!" I thought about the toll it must be taking on her. If ten years ago Gramp had been able to see himself in this state, he would've put one in his head. Another one, that is.

Clouds swarmed the moon. JFK got up and wandered down to the lawn, parading back and forth like a fitful ghost.

I said, "Collie says he didn't strangle the girl. He says someone else did it and that they've racked up at least four or five other murders before and after he was arrested. He says the killer is targeting young women of the same description. He wants me to look into it with his wife."

My father waited. The information sank in. "His wife?"

"He got married in prison."

"To a guy?"

It almost made me smile. "No, to a pen pal."

"One of those," my father said with a disgusted nuance. "Celebrity stalkers, but they only like the mass murderers. They're just as psychotic."

"He says she's been trying to help him. Gathering evidence, I suppose."

He waited. "If it was anybody else I'd say it was a ploy to get a stay of execution, an appeal, or a new trial."

I shook my head. "He doesn't want any of that, he says. He just wants me to find out who's killing these women. He doesn't even want his own name cleared of that one killing."

"So why's he care? Why now?"

"He says it's because he wasn't certain if he'd killed the girl or not, but now his wife's been bringing him information and he knows for sure there's someone else out there."

"He's manipulating you."

"I get that feeling too, but I can't see any reason for it."

"Your brother doesn't need a reason to do things anymore. Maybe he never did."

"Does Fingers Brown still sell clean pieces?" I asked.

"Haven't heard much about him in a while. But I can't picture him retiring and doing a lot of fishing."

"Still got the bowling alley?"

"As far as I know. You're going to pay him a visit?"

"I want to ask him a few questions."

My old man finished his beer and took another, held the bottle to his chest. "You've decided to help Collie?"

"It's for me. I want to figure out as much as I can about what happened."

He went to the porch railing, stood against it, and looked at the moon. "Can you let it go?"

"No."

He was a sensitive and astute man, but I was still surprised that he was able to slice to the heart of the matter.

"You're not him, Terry."

I got up and took my place beside him. We watched JFK sniffing around the yard, lumbering across the grass, chasing moths. I said nothing because I had nothing to say.

"I'm sorry I put the call through, son."

"You were only doing what you had to do."

"I should've let you stay out west on your ranch."

"It wasn't my ranch. And it's all right. I never should've left. The last five years were a waste, Dad. I'm sorry I went. I'm sorry I left the family. I never should have gone. It was a mistake to run."

"Because of Kimmy."

"Because of everyone."

He put an arm around me and ruffled my white patch. It was a caricature of what your average American father might do to his son, but I appreciated the effort he was making. I only wished I could make more of one myself.

He whistled and opened the screen door. JFK galloped out of the brush and up the porch stairs, made sure he licked at my hand as he passed, and then rushed into the house.

I said, "Good night, Dad."

"Good night, Terry." My old man followed the dog inside. But my father, who wasn't a talkative man, who had lost one son forever and another for five years, who was worried about his teenage daughter, who had a phantom of a father waiting for him hunched in the corner as a constant reminder of what the future might make of him, still wasn't done speaking his mind. He hovered in the shadowed entranceway and turned back to me. I couldn't see his eyes. Silhouetted like that, silent as stone, he seemed more myth than man.

"Finish whatever it is you have to do," he said. His voice was hard, stoic, and indignant. "And let him go forever. Don't allow your brother to take you with him."

Then I was alone in the night.

Part II

BEAST
ON THE
LOOSE

Out of sheer exhaustion I was able to catch a couple hours of sleep, but the pain in my kidneys woke me in the deep darkness. I was slathered in sweat and spurred on to the bathroom. I gritted my teeth, pissed blood, and popped five aspirin.

I took a shower and let the cold water wash over me.

I'd dreamed of Kimmy. I was surprised and bothered by the clarity of the memory. We were in the Commack Motor Inn, one of several pay-by-the-hour motels we used to duck into so we could be together. Intimacy and privacy weren't among the benefits of living in a large house with an extended family. The backseat of a car got old quick. We were catching our breaths, lying back in each other's arms. Her hair was wet and scoured my cheek. She pressed her lips to my ear.

"Terry, I'm pregnant."

It was dark. I couldn't make out her face. Her voice was steady and I couldn't tell if she was glad or terrified or excited or indifferent. I knew that was why she'd chosen this precise moment to tell me. She wanted my own honest reaction not influenced by her own.

I said, "We're not naming her after a fucking dog."

It made her giggle, a sound that transformed me and lightened me and always seemed to make me float to somewhere safe. "Her? You want a girl?"

"I suppose I do."

"Why?"

"I like the idea of saying, 'I'm going home to my girls.'"

She let go with a relieved quiet laughter that soon turned into tears as we muttered our sweet somethings and made love again. I thought of the child growing inside her, and we were gentler and somehow more generous than we had been in a while. Afterward I looped my arms around her and kissed her belly. Our breathing was in sync, which meant our breathing was in sync with the baby's. I'd never felt quite so significant or so vulnerable.

"We'll get married tomorrow."

"No," Kimmy said. "I don't want to rush it. We can take our time."

"This summer? On the beach? We can rent the Montauk Lighthouse, have the ceremony at the top."

"You've been thinking about this?" she asked.

"Yeah."

"Since when?"

"Since I met you," I said. It was the truth. "We can buy a house out east. Something nice and affordable, but private, maybe near the Hamptons."

"You don't have that kind of money."

"Not *too* near. But, you know, *nearby*."

"Don't I get any say in the matter?" she asked.

"No. I'm going to take care of my girls. You just sit back and let me run the show and love you both. This summer, at the top of the lighthouse. I'll carry you up the steps."

"There's got to be two hundred of them, Terry. I'll be fat by then. You'll get herniated."

"I'll carry you very slowly," I whispered. "My girls."

I climbed out of the shower and held a towel to my face and stifled a moan, a groan, I don't know what, but it wanted out, and I wouldn't let it. After a minute the force of it began to lessen and finally subsided. I got dressed.

The sun wouldn't be up for another two hours. I got in the car, drove over to Chub's garage, and crept the place.

It had the innocuous name of Wright's Automotive Repair, with a logo that was a touch overdesigned. He'd apparently established a nice, legal business. Three rebuilt classic muscle cars were parked out front with FOR SALE signs in the windows. Four bays in the garage, two of them filled with soccer mom mini-SUVs, another with a Honda Accord in need of a new transmission. The last bay had a complete smashup laid out in it. I could barely make it out as a Dodge. It must've been towed there by some insurance company. That meant Chub didn't mind cops and insurance investigators sniffing around. Another sign that he'd gone completely straight.

I checked through his office cabinets and desk drawers and came up empty. Nothing that proved he was still souping cars for heisters and helping to plan their getaway routes.

I booted up his computer. It wasn't password-protected. The wallpaper was a photo of Chub, Kimmy, and Scooter all wearing Santa hats and smiling in front of a Christmas tree. Chub was on the verge of cracking up, his head tilted back, face slightly out of focus because he was already beginning to quiver. Kimmy stood there beaming, eyes crimped into an elated squint. Scooter had her mouth wide open in a guffaw, two tiny teeth poking up from her bottom gums. I could almost hear her wild baby giggling.

I was a head case. Jealousy ripped through me. That angry child's cry of I want, I want. Mine. Mine. Mine. Thieves were a covetous lot by definition, but I wondered if anyone in my family had ever been as green-eyed and greedy as I was now.

Did I want Chub on the narrow or was I hoping to find he was still in the bent life? Either way, what did it really mean to me?

I clicked through a few files. Spreadsheets of accounts and orders and inventories. If there was anything sneaky, I couldn't see it.

I searched for a safe. It took me two minutes to find it in the corner, tucked away under a set of shelves partially obscured by racks of motor oil and transmission fluid. It was a small, old, simple model that I probably could've cracked in a half hour. But I didn't even have to bother. Chub was a bit sloppy. He'd left the dial just a couple of numbers off, and the tumblers fell immediately into place.

There was nothing much inside. A few pink slips to junkers out back, some sales receipts, invoices, other old paperwork from before he'd bought the place. Copies of tax returns.

No, I thought, he wasn't sloppy. This was meant to be found by the cops or by thieves.

Chub had overplayed his hand. I knew now that there was another safe hidden somewhere on the premises. A sigh escaped me, maybe consolation or perhaps discouragement.

I walked the bays. There were a million nooks and crannies. The workbenches were covered with tools. In my own house there were hidden stairwells, crawl spaces, drop shafts. I knew I could hunt for his hiding spot all night long and never trip over it.

My thoughts cleared.

He wouldn't keep his real cache in the bays. He had legit employees working for him. He'd need a place all his own.

That meant the office. I scanned the area. Checked the ceiling, the vents, the air-conditioning ducts.

That wasn't how Chub would do it.

I bent to the safe again. It was heavy but shifted relatively easily. I shoved it aside and touched the boards of the floor. It took only a few seconds for me to figure out the proper way to lift them. When I did, they came loose without any effort.

The second safe was a lot newer and more compact. I could probably jug it with the right tools, but there was no need. This time Chub really had gotten sloppy. He'd played the same game as with the decoy safe. He'd left the combination only a couple numbers off.

I yanked the handle and the door popped open. Inside were maps of towns all over the island. Port Jefferson, Bayport, Bay Shore, Bridgehampton, St. James, Glen Cove, Bethpage. Different sets of charts and diagrams covered Brooklyn and Queens. There were notes about roadwork, detours, traffic buildup, and rush-hour congestion, likely spots where state troopers might be hiding on the parkways. Chub was expanding his operation, at least so far as the planning went.

There was ninety grand in thick slabs of cash. I knew this would be only one of his caches, escape-route money in case he ever needed to make a run for it.

"Goddamn it, Chub."

My voice was loud in the empty room.

I wondered if Kimmy would stand beside him the day he got pinched. Take the baby with her to visit him in Sing Sing, the little girl putting her hand up to the glass partition, Chub holding his up on the other side.

His girls.

I had made another ghost. I thought I might be one myself, revisiting a life that no longer wanted me.

I drove home, went to my room, and listened to JFK's powerful rhythmic breathing as he slept at the foot of my bed. I managed to shove him aside enough to crawl in under the blankets, and when I finally fell asleep I dreamed of Rebecca Clarke. When I awoke, my hands flashed out like I was trying to keep from falling. It spooked JFK and he barked once in my face.

I sat up and ran my hands through my hair. I needed to start taking sleeping pills, something that would put me out so I could wake up refreshed. Becky seemed so prevalent in my mind that I thought I should visit her, talk to her. Collie had been right. I'd always had extremely vivid dreams. I wondered if I'd sleep better or worse after my brother was dead.

The sun warmed my face. It was a little after dawn. I expected my mother to be up but she wasn't. I slipped through the house, going room to room and checking on everyone. I stood before the bed of my parents and watched them sprawled but still hugging each other. Mal was out. I hoped he wasn't scoring them at the Fifth Amendment. Grey slept like he always did, curled up in apparent great comfort as if he were spending the night at the Waldorf. His handsome face took on an even greater beauty in sleep—slack and innocent and genuine. Dale's teen anger and exasperation were gone from her face, and there was almost a small smile on her lips.

I stopped in Gramp's room and found him snoozing. It was a relief to see him that way. He looked like he'd just lain down after pulling a particularly exhausting grift. I had the intense urge to wake him up and talk with him. I had the irrational feeling that if I caught him at the right moment I might be able to sneak past his disease. Distract, divert, and

charm it. He'd yawn and look at me the way he used to and say, *Terry,*
we've got a good day ahead of us. A damn good day. Tight cooze and big
coin. He'd chuck me under the chin and give a wink. His hair would be
mussed from a night of tossing and the hole in his skull would be on
display, black and beckoning. *You with me?*

I stepped into Collie's room. It hadn't been changed either. I wondered how difficult it was for my mother to come in here and dust and
revisit his belongings. I looked around and tried to spot any sign of
madness. I slid a finger across the spines of the books on his shelves. At
least half of them were mine. I could almost feel Becky Clarke's breath
on my neck. I checked his caches. They were all empty.

I drove over to the address listed on the police report as the Clarke
house. It had rained during the night and a mist rose off the streets in
the growing morning heat. The family hadn't moved from Brightwaters
village. That surprised me. After a tragedy like the one they'd suffered
through, I'd assumed they would have wanted to get as far off Long Island as possible. But they'd stuck it out. I wondered if they'd left Rebecca's bedroom untouched the way I'd heard some families did when
they lost their children too soon. The way my own parents hadn't
changed a thing in my room.

I parked up the road and watched the house. It was two-storied and
gabled, painted a charming yellow.

The dream had begun to wear away. It felt distant and unknowable.
I didn't know why I was here. I was trying to reconnect to something I
didn't want to be connected to in the first place. But the only way to
learn what might have been going through Collie's mind, if he had
smoked Becky, was to start with her. I wanted to look at home photos. I
wanted to get a sense of her. I didn't know what I wanted to do.

"Jesus, what the fuck?"

I started my car. I felt like an idiot. I was about to pull away, when
the mother came out of the house, followed by the father. Their names
were in the file but I didn't feel the need to check. They were both pro-
fessionals, dressed in proper business suits, holding briefcases. He had
on a power tie and she wore a skirt that emphasized her lovely legs. He

was eating a cruller and trying not to get any sugar on his lapel. She sipped coffee. He finished in three bites and popped the code into the garage keypad. The door slid up. Inside was a two-year-old Lexus. The Clarkes said a few words to each other and climbed into the car together. She was behind the wheel. The train station was ten minutes away. They probably both worked on Wall Street within a block of each other. They'd take the LIRR into the city and sit side by side doing the *Times* crossword puzzle or double-checking yesterday's stock figures.

The front door slammed again. A nine- or ten-year-old girl carrying a backpack hopped off the tile stoop, followed by her teenage sister. Sixteen or seventeen and tall, nearly six foot. They walked over to the car and spoke to their parents but didn't get in. Mom and Dad waved and pulled out. The garage door closed. The sisters started walking together toward the corner bus stop. The teenager had no book bag, which made me wonder if she was a troublemaker at school, sitting in the last row, popping gum and sneering. Her little sister ran ahead, and she put an extra step in her stride. They both had black hair, shoulder length when it wasn't splayed and hooked by the breeze.

The Clarkes had a first-rate security system. I had the right tools for the job but it would take me a while to trip the system. It looked like I wouldn't need them. The back door was ajar.

Even after losing one daughter, they left the door open. She might've been killed in a park but they should've learned something about safety precautions. I shook my head.

I moved fast through the house. For the first time in my life I felt like an intruder. Scoring a place was one thing, but nosing around, being a snoop, hunting through the belongings of the dead, it somehow felt more corrupt.

I hit the master bedroom. Clarke had a .45 in his nightstand drawer. It was loaded. I thought that was a good thing. He might not have time to unlock the piece from a safety box and snap in the clip if someone tried to take his other daughters from him. My respect for Mr. Clarke went up a hair, even if he was a stupid bastard for leaving the door open.

There were three other bedrooms in the home. One was clearly the little girl's. It looked like a holdover nursery. There were block letters around the mirror, spelling out SHARON. Pink walls and white bookcases full of dolls. But she was getting old enough to assert herself. There were posters of the latest movie stars and a couple of boy bands. Beside her bed was a shelf full of paperbacks. She liked those 'tween vampire romances that I used to read to Dale. I recognized several of the titles.

Branching off from the end of the hall were the other two bedrooms. They were damn near identical. I couldn't tell which was Rebecca's and which was the other sister's. The parents not only kept Becky's room the same, they still dusted and sprayed air freshener.

Lots of prints of famous artwork on the walls. Looked like one or both of the sisters were interested in the likes of Manet, Jackson Pollock, Dali. I could check the dressers and become a fucking panty sniffer, see which one's underwear smelled fresher, but I already felt too ashamed. When even a thief feels embarrassed, you know something is way out of line.

I started with the room on the left. There were no photos. I didn't know what else I was looking for. Some connection between Rebecca and Collie? Between her and some boyfriend? Gilmore figured it was always the boyfriend.

The cops would've been through the place five years ago. They would've searched the drawers and found a diary or anything else that might've given them a lead. I stuck to the most likely places for a hidden cache. Most teens had one. A secret stash of cigarettes, joints, porn, boosted cash, self-taken nudie shots, or anything else they wanted to hide from their parents.

I checked the floor and ceiling of the closet. The air vent. The molding in the corners of the room. I pulled out drawers in case any of them had false bottoms or had been shortened to leave room behind them. I scored when I spotted a loose faceplate on one of the wall sockets.

The wiring had been disconnected. There was a cubbyhole about five inches deep. Inside was a dime bag of marijuana, half a bottle of what looked like Oxycontin, and several other bottles of Valium, Xanax, and Zoloft. The shit was serious. There were also stolen sheets of empty scrips. I pocketed a couple of them. You never knew.

The pot was skunkweed but it was fresh. This was the seventeen-year-old's room. She liked to mellow out and did what she had to do to follow her buzz and blunt her anxieties. After what she'd been through, I didn't blame her. But she was overdoing the self-medication. Too many antidepressants could have opposite the intended effect.

I crossed the hall to Becky's room, hating myself. I felt like a total fraud. Collie's name was stuck in my teeth. I'd been in the house almost ten minutes. That was a lot of time to be inside. I scouted the likely hot spots, tried the outlets first just to see if the seventeen-year-old had picked up the trick from Becky. There was nothing anywhere.

"Who the fuck are you?"

I spun and the teenage girl was there in the doorway.

If someone comes in the door, you dive out the window. That was one of the basic tenets of being a thief.

Except that she had her father's .45 trained on me.

They hadn't been as careless as I'd thought. She was just walking her sister to the corner stop, waiting with her until the bus arrived. That's why the door had been left open.

"Oh, hey there," I said, propping a high-wattage smile in place. "I rang the bell. And knocked, but no one answered. The door was open. I'm Freddy of Freddy's Fix-It. Seems like you've got some faulty wiring that your father wants me to check out."

"The front door was locked. The back door was open."

"Right," I said. "See, I was calling out and I decided to come around the side of the house over there and—"

"Where's your toolbox?"

"Oh, that's in the truck."

"So where's your truck?"

"We didn't have a flangella voltometer with us. Very important during electrical work, otherwise you can fry the frammistat. My partner left to go get—"

"Shove it. Who are you?"

"Everybody knows Freddy."

She was pretty, or had been once. Now her face was thin and drawn, with dark steaming eyes and heavy frown lines across her brow and around her mouth. In ten or twenty years they'd be deep as knife tracks. At the top of her arm, the hint of a tattoo edged out from beneath her black T-shirt. She was underage too. I wondered who this prick was that kept inking all these little girls.

She reminded me more than a little of Dale. The gun never wavered. It was a heavy piece of hardware. She held it with a two-handed grip, and the muscles in her forearms were tense and sharply defined.

I winced and waited for the screaming. I thought, Now Gilmore is really going to tune up my ass in a holding cell.

"I know you," she said.

"Everyone knows Freddy of Freddy's Fix—"

"No, I *know* you, fucker!"

I didn't like the way she said it. There was rage there as well as anguish and an undercurrent of vengeance. I never wanted to be around someone who sounded like that, much less someone pointing a large-caliber weapon at my heart. My back began to crawl with cold sweat. My breathing hitched.

"You're one of them," she continued. "One of those people. That family. Named after dogs."

Christ. I wasn't going to be able to cover the ground between us before she pulled the trigger. The window was closed and locked and there was a screen. I wasn't going to be able to duck through it and run away. I could only hold my ground and pray I didn't piss myself. I hoped she called the cops instead of taking her hate out on the wrong Rand.

"Which one are you?" she asked. "Tell me."

"Terrier," I admitted.

"You look like your brother."

"Right, but I'm not him."

"But you're in my house."

She had me there. "I found the piece in your father's nightstand drawer. I removed the clip."

"No, you didn't. I checked. I always check. My dad's taught me all about guns since I was twelve. I'm a good shot. Not that I'd have to be at this range."

"Shit. Look, I don't want to hurt you. I don't want to hurt anyone."

"You're not going to get the chance."

"Just let me explain."

"You people are thieves and liars and murderers. What makes you think I'm going to listen to you even one more second?"

It was a good question. If I came home and found the brother of the man who'd murdered my sister standing in the middle of her bedroom, I would've made my play by now, whatever it was.

But along with the low-slung burning fury and the distress and the dull edginess that comes when someone hooked on pills needs to pop another one, she was intrigued and wanted to know what the hell I was doing here.

I had to engage her. I said, "Your rooms are the same. Yours and Becky's. Why?"

"So you've already been in mine."

"Yes."

"Did you steal anything?"

"No."

"Not enough time?"

"There was plenty of time. But I'm not a thief anymore."

"Now you just break in to houses but don't take anything."

"Technically I didn't break in. I just—"

"Shut up!"

"Your rooms are the same, except you've got a hiding place for your goodies. You're hooked on antianxiety meds."

Her eyes widened and her mouth opened as if I'd just slapped her. It was an ugly expression on a cute face. Then she grinned without humor. That was worse. She studied me and was offended by what she saw. "Care to guess why, you prick?"

I nodded. "I already know why. You should just call the cops. Ask for Detective Gilmore. Don't worry, he'll definitely give me a good beating. He already has this week. He'll probably let you watch. Or help."

She was still calm, assured, centered, but the hate inside her was looking to get out, and it flickered in her eyes. They were at least a little crazy. I'd done that to her. My family had done that to her.

"Last chance to tell me why you're here. After this, I think I'm going to shoot you. I'm not sure where. Maybe in the knee. Maybe the balls. Maybe the head. I haven't decided. Did you think about dying when you were going through our things?"

"No."

"You should've. You must know something about last chances. Your brother's used all of his up."

I kept hoping she'd step farther into the room, or that her arms would tire, or that she'd drop her gaze and give me half a second to make some kind of a break. But it wasn't going to happen. I could usually make a lie sound like the truth, but I was floundering with her. I felt sheepish just being here. I wondered if I could make the truth sound like the truth.

I said, "I'm in your house because I was hoping your parents hadn't changed Rebecca's room."

"Why would you care about that?"

"I wanted to look at photos. I wanted to know a little more about her. My brother says he didn't kill her. He admits he murdered the other seven people but says he didn't touch her. He begged me to look into it."

She started to laugh very quietly. It was grotesque. I'd made a similar noise when I'd run from my brother, pale and shaking. Her pupils were very large.

The girl said, "First you called her Becky, then Rebecca."

I'd noted that too. "It was wrong of me to act so familiar."

"Your game doesn't even have any rules, does it?" she said. "You think it's wrong to call her Becky but you don't mind going through the drawers of a home you've invaded? Standing in a room of a girl murdered by your brother?"

"Actually, I do mind. I'm pretty ashamed. Listen, why don't you call the cops?"

"What makes you think I won't shoot you?"

"I was raised as a burglar. My whole life I've done nothing but take stupid chances. This is just one more."

She lowered the gun a fraction, then raised it again. I was hoping if she pulled the trigger she would only shoot me in the leg. I very carefully reached for my pack of cigarettes and shook one out.

She said, "There's no smoking in the house."

I put the butt back in the pack. "Where do you smoke your pot?"

"In the yard, when no one else is home."

"Fire your dealer. It's cheap weed."

"Your brother," she said. The word itself seemed to dry her mouth. She licked her lips and swallowed. "Do you believe him?"

"No," I told her. "Maybe. I don't know."

"Then why come around?"

"He's my brother. I've hated him most of my life. But he's my brother."

"Why do you hate him so much?"

The question flustered me. I wasn't sure that I'd ever thought about it before. I struggled for an answer. Long before the competition over women, even before the bad blood over incidents I remembered clearly—the times he ran out on me during a job, the taunts, the drunken posturing, the fights he started with fences that came back to cause me troubles—I had loved him. We had been friends. He'd protected me. I could remember riding on the handlebars of his bicycle while he kept one arm around my waist to keep me from falling. I thought he would never hurt me. But it had shifted somewhere, in a way I still didn't understand. He grew angry with me, seemed to always be on the attack. I thought of him stabbing me with the Revolutionary War figure that led to the awful scarring on my chest.

But I supposed that he had his reasons too, if someone had bothered to ask him. Maybe he was only reacting to something I put out into the world. He probably thought that I was distant, cold, a tightass. Maybe I didn't watch his back enough. Maybe he expected me to love him more, or better. Perhaps the truth was no deeper than the fact that Collie and I were simply wired to be enemies.

She squinted at me as if my hesitation was enough of a response. "You said a detective beat you up. That the truth?"

"Last night."

"I don't see any marks."

I lifted my shirt. The bruises on my kidneys were a mottled blue and yellow. She appeared to be impressed with either my asskicking or my dog tat. She seemed to come to a decision. She lowered the gun. I had no doubt that if I moved toward her or tried to run or said anything out of line she'd shoot me out of my shoes. I stood still in the center of the room.

"Why did he hit you?" she asked.

"Because I stole some files from him. I wanted to read the original reports."

"I thought you weren't a thief anymore."

"I've backslid a little," I admitted.

"And?"

"And Collie confessed to all the other murders but not your sister's."

"I know that. Of course I know that. That's why you're here?"

"Yes."

"So why didn't you look into this five years ago?"

"He only just asked me."

"Why?"

"I don't know."

She kept the .45 low against the side of her leg, the way the pros did when they walked into a place to knock it over. "He's crazy."

"Yeah, I think so."

"And you're crazy for helping him."

"Probably," I said. "Tell me about Rebecca."

"Tell you what? I don't know what to say."

"She was seventeen."

"That's right."

"The report I read said she was being tutored in an advanced physics class that evening. That she and several other students were at a teacher's home. Mrs. Dan—" I couldn't remember the name. It was Greek.

"Mrs. Denopolis."

"Who lived near Autauk Park. Your sister didn't drive?"

"She jogged. She was on the school track team. She ran everywhere."

"You must live at least eight or nine miles from the park."

"For Becky that was nothing. She was a long-distance runner. She'd run down Old Autauk Highway."

I thought I had a good poker face in place but she must've read something in my expression.

"What is it?" she asked.

"I just jogged that way yesterday morning."

"A lot of people do."

"Right. Did she ever mention Collie? That she knew him? That he was bothering her? Anything like that?"

"No."

"Did she mention having any trouble with anyone? An ex-boyfriend?"

"No. I was only twelve but we talked a lot and shared secrets. The same way Sharon and I do now."

It reminded me that I didn't know her name. I asked and she said, "Cara."

"Why aren't you at school?"

It made her scoff. "What are you, a parole officer? I quit and got my GED. I work part-time at Kohl's. I'm taking night classes at Suffolk Community."

"Cara, would it be all right if I called you in case I have any other questions about your sister?"

"I've told you everything I can. But if you want to come back you can talk to my parents. I think they might listen. But I'm not sure they could help at all."

"I doubt anyone can. I'm just spinning my wheels."

"So am I. That's how it feels. Like I'm wasting time. That's why I—"
She didn't have to finish. I knew she meant the pills. She was beginning
to tap the gun against the side of her leg. Her agitation was growing
worse. I could see the fear in her eyes. It had nothing to do with me.
The meds were wearing off. She had to be popping ten or twelve a day.
The charge of her emotions was overcoming her, and she needed to
deaden it.

"Where'd you get the scrips?"

"Like that's your business? I stole them from my mother's ob-gyn."

"You've been on the meds for too long. You're taking too many."

"I need them."

"But they're making you sicker now. You know it's the truth. You're
taking more and more pills and they're not working as well."

"Who are you to say that? You don't know me."

"I know when someone is an addict. You need to ease off. Slowly."

"Maybe I will."

"You can't do it on your own. Talk to someone."

"I think I might. Soon. One of these days."

"Listen, Cara, one final thing. Even if you're out of the house for a
few minutes, even if you're only walking to the corner. Lock your door."

She hadn't softened while we'd talked. A ribbon of hair had fallen
across her face and she brushed it away and it fell back again. She raised
the gun. I took a step back and a mean titter spilled from her mouth.
"You think I was kidding about using this thing? I hope someone does
try something. I hope you come back and try something. Next time I
won't chat. And I was lying about shooting you in the leg or the nuts. If
I ever pull the trigger, it'll be a head shot."

Jack "Fingers" Brown worked out of a bowling alley in Huntington Station. He held court on the last lane and never kept any hardware on the premises. If you wanted a clean, untraceable piece, you came to Fingers. Sometimes the serial numbers were filed off and sometimes they weren't. It didn't matter. They either were ripped off from a gun shop, had fallen off an army truck, or were police-academy-cadet fresh.

Collie had used a clean S&W .38 on his mad-dog outing. There were a couple of other guys on the island who might've been able to supply a piece like that, but I figured Collie would've gone to Fingers first. I wanted to know when Collie had decided to pick up a pistol. Had it been right after he'd left the Elbow Room or right before? Or had he nabbed it weeks in advance, preparing for his decline into the underneath?

Fingers was about fifty, with a smarmy leer, a snow tire around his middle, and a mountain of oiled hair that he kept swept to one side so it looked like he might topple over at any second. He'd been a gunrunner for twenty years or more and got picked up at least once a month by the cops, but they could never hold him for more than a day. He was smart and well connected, and word was he'd ace anyone who even looked like they might rat on him. His public persona of a bowling geek wasn't a persona. Fingers really did spend several hours a day knocking pins down. I looked around at the signs on the front door as I walked in. They'd been there forever. Senior citizens bowled free on Tuesday nights. Fridays the high school kids got in for half price. Special prices for parties of more than twenty. Ask about discounts.

My family had bowled here when I was a kid. Grey was a natural who regularly broke 250. My mother was damn good too. She had a deceptively soft way of throwing the ball. It would drop from her hand

and seem to barely have enough power to make it all the way down the lane, but once it got to the pins they practically exploded. Mal couldn't break 100 to save his life, and I wasn't much better. Collie had always been competitive but never with himself. Only with me. So long as he beat me by even a pin, he was happy. My old man would just sit and watch the rest of us and laugh while Gramp hung around in the bar and snatched enough pocket change to pay for his beer.

It was twelve-thirty. Fingers never came in before noon. He was working a four–six split in the fifth frame when I stepped up and sat behind his entourage. His right-hand man was an ex-con leg breaker named Higgins who stood six-three, weighed 230 of mostly muscle, and wore sunglasses day and night so you could never tell when he had a bead on you. It wasn't a bad guess to figure he was always watching. Word was he used a beaver-tail sap. I kept my hands on my knees.

Two young women were chattering, clapping, and urging Fingers on. They might have been twins or were just affecting the look. Short blond hair feathered across their eyes, lots of neck jewelry, both in muted summer dresses. The bowling shoes actually looked good on them. They each turned and gave me a beaming smile. I grinned back. Higgins kept his body angled toward me. If I made a fast move he'd find the sweet spot of my skull with that blackjack in no time flat.

Fingers had good form, a nice extension as he threw the ball, a solid curve that hooked the edge of the gutter and held on, breaking only at the last moment. He picked up the spare handily and the women clapped and woo-hooed.

He noticed me immediately but chose to ignore me until he and his lady friends had finished their game. Afterward, he gave each of them a juicy kiss that made me think this crew was a little kinkier than at first appeared to be the case. Maybe the bowling shoes should have been a giveaway. The women retired to the bar. Higgins kept focused on me the entire time.

Fingers finally turned his chin and waved me over. I got up and so did Higgins, who shadowed my every move. I stood before Fingers while he cleaned his ball with an oil-stained chamois rag.

"I know you?" he asked.

"We've never met," I said. "My name's Terry Rand."

He nodded. "Family's got a good rep, except for that one black mark on it."

"Right. That's what I wanted to talk to you about."

"I'm entertaining some friends right now."

"This will only take a minute."

"Not here." He stuck his ball in a bag. Higgins kept eyeing me. Whatever intimidation the sunglasses got him would eventually cost him. He'd be rough to take under these bright lights, but in a parking lot at night he'd go pretty easy. "Make an appointment with my partner here. Maybe we can set something up in a few days. Maybe next week."

"It can't wait."

"I told you. I don't do business here."

"From what I hear, Fingers, this is the only place you do business. No chance of the feds bugging you with all these pins flying."

"Like I said, I'm entertaining some close friends right now—"

"Yeah, I saw. They really twins or do they just like to play dress-up and pretend?"

It made him reassess me. He held his bowling bag on his lap and wet his lips.

"What do you need?"

"I don't need anything. I want to ask you a few questions."

"I don't answer questions."

"How do you get through life without answering questions?"

"I just do."

I put a little ice in my voice. "See that, Fingers. You just fucking answered one."

He checked over his shoulder at Higgins, to make sure he was still close by. "You don't want to be troublesome now, kid."

"You're right, I don't. But like I said, this can't wait. I think you know why."

"We're through here," Fingers said.

Higgins drifted nearer and began to brace me. He stuck his chest in my face and backed me up a step. Like most big bruisers, he underestimated anyone who wasn't as tall and thick as himself. He got in closer and angled a hip at me so he could yank his sap quickly. His right hand dipped into his pocket. He said nothing. What little of his face I could see held no expression. He started to draw the beaver-tail blackjack.

I grabbed the bowling bag out of Fingers's lap and hurled it down as hard as I could on Higgins's left foot. There was a crunch like a box of matchsticks snapping. He let out the first note of a yowl and bent over to grab at his mashed toes. I snapped a knee up into his chin. I couldn't see his eyes but they had to be rolling. He took one step backward and fought for balance. I knocked his other leg out from under him and he fell flat on his back.

While he was down, I kicked him twice in the face. His glasses cracked and sailed off.

The bowlers in the other lanes kept right on playing. I had to hand it to these folks. They certainly had dedication and passion. Jesus, were they focused.

Fingers didn't even try to take a swing at me. He just sat with a resigned air, sucking his teeth and shaking his head, probably already plotting how he'd snuff me.

"Did you sell a piece to my brother?" I asked.

"You're finished, you know. I can't let this go. Even if I wanted to, I can't."

"We'll cover that later. But for right now, focus. Tell me about my brother."

"I don't talk about my customers."

"Then you're admitting he was a customer. I'm not the cops, Fingers. It's not like I'm holding you responsible. But I need to know where he got his pistol."

He shrugged, his bony shoulders nearly spiking through his bowling shirt. "Why do you care?"

"How about if we don't chase each other around the track all night long? Did you sell him a clean piece?"

"Yes, I did."

"How about a knife?"

"That too."

My heart pounded and I crossed my arms over my chest as if to hold it in. "Right. When?"

"You want the date?"

"I do."

"How am I supposed to remember that?"

"You remember selling it. I bet you never forget a customer, a price, a date, or a caliber, especially if it's used in a spree like the one he went on. So tell me. When?"

Higgins let out a moan and started coughing blood. He blinked and tried turning over. I put a foot on his chest and said, "Shh."

Fingers kept wagging his head. It made that mound of hair waver and flap.

"Even if I wanted to let this go, you think he's going to?"

"What'd I say? Stay focused, right? Tell me when my brother came to you."

Fingers told me. It turned out to be the day before Collie went on his rampage. He said, "You're dead, you know."

"Bring along someone better than this goon."

"I will. See you soon."

I hit the door with my heart tripping. Collie hadn't gone off on a mad tear. It hadn't been anything that had happened at the Elbow Room to push him over the edge. He'd either been planning to drop into the underneath or he'd picked up gun fever once he'd held the piece in his hands. A fever that had risen by degrees through the night. My brother, a living storm of urgency and indulgence, sweeping across town.

I wondered if I'd been home, would he have saved the last shot for me?

I drew back my arm and tossed the stick. JFK brought it back and I tossed it onto the lawn again. He hung his head, looked at me like I was an asshole, and laid down at my feet.

I wanted to see Kimmy. I wanted to do more than that. I longed to fold up in her arms and beg forgiveness, but only if she would give it to me. I knew she wouldn't. I would stand there exposed and empty and begging and she would stare at me with no idea of what to say or do. Her eyes would be steamed with years of tamped-down puzzlement and hate. Scooter would jet around and I would want to call her my girl.

I had apologized to my old man for leaving, and now the urge to run was starting to overwhelm me again. In thirty or forty years my brain would turn to tapioca and I'd die in front of a television, watching cartoons and muttering about a dream I'd once had of carrying a woman to the top of the lighthouse.

I sniffed and smelled Mal behind me, standing in the screen door. I hadn't thought anyone was home. He was a damn good creeper even though his talents lay on the grift. If he quit the stogies, he could still be a solid second-story man.

I turned and said, "Heya, what's this?"

He pushed through and came out onto the porch. He had an unlit cigar butt tucked into the corner of his mouth. He pulled it free, peered at it for a moment, then replaced it. "I thought we should talk. You've been home for days and haven't even said hello to me yet."

His coarse, crude face was split by a smile. It looked like a deep fracture working through the side of a cliff. We hugged.

I said, "Nothing personal."

"I realize that. It wasn't an easy call for you to respond to. You've got a lot on your shoulders now that you didn't ask for. But it's still damn good to see you." He led me over to one of the thin trails cutting through the brush around our property. "Let's walk."

"Like when we used to feed the ducks at the lake."

"And bum-rush the neighborhood kids' birthday parties. Every one of those little fuckers used to have a clown or a magician, some asshole choking the shit out of long balloons and turning them into animals. And petting zoos. Monkeys and llamas and baby brown bears. Every other kid with some poor monkey in a cage staring through the bars, the kid trying to feed him ice cream and pizza. Talk about a crime."

JFK followed along as we moved through the woods. Mal picked up a stick and tossed it. JFK flicked his tail once but didn't move for it. I scratched at his ear. He let out a long, contented sigh.

Mal looked a little chagrined, which was hard to do considering the cruelty in his features. My shoulders tensed. So did his.

"When you cut and run you leave unfinished business. Don't think we all can't see it in you."

"I thought I looked trim and fit and tan."

"You do. You also look like twenty pounds of hammered shit."

I couldn't help grinning. "Look who the hell's talking."

Mal pulled the stogie butt from the corner of his mouth and let out a booming laugh that echoed through the undergrowth. "My beauty is for more refined tastes, that's all."

"Uh-huh."

"'..'re still a pretty emotional lot, you know," he said. "The Rands. All of us. I know this thing is bending you all out of shape. Visiting Collie. Listening to whatever crap he's pouring in your ear." He stuck the stogie back in. "You ever need any help, Terrier, I hope you know you can always ask me."

"Sure."

"You say that like you don't believe it."

"I believe it."

"Let's sit."

We sat on the trunk of a maple tree that had toppled over but wasn't quite dead. The leaves fluttered when we climbed on it. Squirrels clambered in and out of a knothole, and JFK dropped his chin and watched excitedly, then bolted after them. He could still really truck when he wanted to. He vanished into the brush.

Mal got up the nerve to ask me what Collie had wanted. I turned my chin to look at him and he was staring at the black soil under his feet. Maybe he wanted to know and maybe he didn't. I didn't bother to burden him with it.

I wanted to ask why he never married. It wasn't because he was so ugly. There had been women he'd cared about in his life, women who'd loved him. A couple that I remembered from the time I was very young. Their names and faces remained clear to me. At Christmas dinner twenty or so years ago I remembered calling one of them "Aunt Sally." She'd put down her silverware and laughed quietly and given Mal a sweet and open look of affection. Everyone else had chuckled pleasantly, but I could tell I'd done something wrong. I'd cried myself to sleep, thinking Mal would hate me forever. In the morning Grey had said, "Some of us aren't meant for wives and kids, Terrier. The only women we love are the black queens in a marked deck."

I tried to picture my life if Collie and I had been friends the way my father and uncles were. I saw Collie with a wife and three kids in that house and wondered if I would be able to live the way my uncles did. If a black queen would be enough for me.

I asked, "Did you juke Danny Thompson forty large?"

Mal shrugged his massive shoulders. "More like thirty-seven."

"Did you know that he's had men on the street—our street, out in front of the house—waiting for you?"

He pulled a lighter out of his pocket and lit the butt of his cigar. He blew smoke away from me. "Yeah, I spotted them."

"He's not Big Dan. He's insecure and edgy and fairly stupid."

"I know. He always was, even as a kid. I was surprised you took a shine to him when you were little."

"The kids of criminals tend to stick to their own kind."

"He liked to poke the monkeys with a yardstick, remember?"

I was getting annoyed. I got to my feet and turned to him. "Forget about the monkeys. Listen, do I really need to tell you this? You boost from the fish and from the pros, not from the twitchy fuckers."

"He made it too easy, I couldn't resist."

"You should have tried harder. He knows you worked him."

"He suspects. He doesn't know."

"A suspicion is all Danny needs," I said. "He's still trying to prove himself to his father's old associates. Taking you out would give him a little of the juice he wants."

Mal's jagged features flattened a little and re-formed into a grin. "He doesn't have the heart to move against us."

"He doesn't need heart. He just needs to put one of his hitters on it."

"None of them are pros either. Most of Big Dan's guys retired. Besides, we've got news vans covering the house all day long. You think they're going to want that kind of coverage? In a few days Danny will forget about it."

"Don't sell him too short."

Mal chuckled. Puffs of smoke drifted from his mouth. "Just short enough? His dealer had a three-card bottom drag and he kept folding the aces back into the deck to feed to himself. Big Dan was a psycho, but at least he always ran an honest game and I played him fair. His son's a mook who's already gaining a bad rep. Watch. Some of the other syndicates will come in and pull the Thompson crew apart piece by piece and Danny will wind up getting a cushy captain job in one of the other outfits. Either that or someone will plant one in his ear. He'll wind up in Shalebrook Lake, floating with the ducks."

He was probably right but I didn't like how easily he brushed the potential trouble aside. He was usually more practical than that, more cagey. He seemed to only be half paying attention, and I wondered if my father was right and early Alzheimer's was already beginning to grind away at Mal's memories. Being aware that you were losing your past, your own mind, must be the worst thing in the world.

JFK broke through the weeds and stood in front of us, panting. I massaged his jowls.

"You ever see Dale's boyfriend over at the Fifth?" I asked.

"That punk? What's he call himself? Butch Cassidy? Like he never saw the movie? He's got no idea what happened to Butch and the Kid in Paraguay?"

"Bolivia."

"Yeah, whatever the fuck. He comes and goes, runs errands for the guys. Picking up dry cleaning. Running people in and out to the airport. Nothing major. He doesn't have the heart for it."

"I think he might be stepping up."

Mal frowned, tugged his cigar loose. There wasn't much left of it. I thought I might finally see him light a fresh stogie. "To what?"

"I'm not sure yet. I met him last night. He offered me a job."

"What, a bank? He couldn't even open a checking account, that one, much less take down a bank."

"A jewelry store," I said.

"He was just talking out his ass, trying to show off to you."

"Maybe. Tell me about Dale."

"What kind of question is that?" He stood and the entire log shook. "What do you want to know?"

"Is she a thief?"

He held his hands up before him like I'd just pressed a .32 into his ribs. "Hey, hey, come on now, right?"

"Come on what? Is it a stupid question because I should know the answer is yes or because it's no?"

"You know your sister's not a thief!"

"How the hell do I know that?"

"Because your father would never let her go down that road."

Clouds began to cover the sun. The wind continued to rise. It whistled through the trees so loudly that JFK perked up and looked to see if someone was calling him. "How about if you save that kind of talk for John Citizen, Mal? What else would she know? What else has she been taught?"

"She's a smart girl," Mal said. "Straight A's. She's going to go to college."

"How smart? Smart enough to keep out of a big score or smart and capable enough to want in?"

"Jesus Christ, she's fifteen!"

"I know that," I said. "I want to make sure she's nowhere near the punk when he goes down."

He put a hand on my shoulder and squeezed it as a sign of reassurance, but it just hurt like hell. "I think you and her need to have a real conversation," he said. "As soon as possible. Today. But don't brace her."

"I won't."

Mal nodded but his mouth tightened. We were uncomfortably close to talking about things that the Rands did not talk about. It was almost enough for me to ask him what he was doing, what his own plans were. Did he ever intend on retiring from the bent life, getting off the grift, or were we all doomed to play the game until we wound up on death row or sitting around watching TV with holes in our heads? Did my father find a way out or was he just dying a different slow death, sitting on the porch drinking his beer, taking care of his family, and bored out of his fucking mind?

An almost undetectable expression of worry crossed Mal's craggy face.

"Have you seen Grey yet?" he asked.

"No." I waited, but that seemed to be the end of it. Another storm was building. Living in the desert, I'd forgotten what it had been like to get rained on all the time. JFK crawled under the downed tree limb and poked his nose out from beneath Mal's ankles and stared at me.

"Something the matter?" I asked.

Mal looked foggy, reached into his shirt pocket, and retrieved another stogie butt. He lit it, tucked it into the same corner of his mouth. "I don't know."

A vein on his forehead began to thicken and throb.

"What is it, Mal?"

My father had said he'd found his brothers on the back lawn, looking a little lost, almost like they were sleepwalking. Was this the beginning of an episode?

"Mal?"

I stepped to him and gripped his elbow, and he snapped away with a tiny fraction of the force he was capable of but I was still pushed aside. He shifted the stogie to the other side of his mouth. "Don't grab me."

"I'm sorry. You just looked a little out of it."

"I'm worried."

"About what?"

"I'm getting forgetful. I sleep like shit. I wake up with the sweats and I go sit outside and then I'm suddenly freezing. I lose my way around town. Places I've been to ten thousand times and now I'm getting lost. I read road signs out loud to help me remember. I think I might really be losing it like Old Shep."

"Mal, people who are going nuts don't think they're going nuts."

"That's what they say, but who knows if it's true?"

Good point, actually.

"It's hard to explain the way I feel sometimes."

"Try."

He held his enormous hands out before him and plied the air, trying to grab hold of something that had no form. He tried again, clutching at nothing, knuckles cracking. He let out a laugh that made my heart sink, fearing for my own future.

"Intense dreams. Nightmares."

A fierce shiver ran through me. Christ, don't tell me I was already showing signs of premature senility. Is that what had happened to Collie? Did he feel himself going crazy and just decided to go with it?

"I'm still sharp with the cards," Mal said, drawing a deck from his pocket. He did a one-handed quadruple cut and then walked the queen of spades across his knuckles. "I carry a deck with me just so I can see them, shuffle through them, and know that I've still got a four-card draw. That I'm still good at something."

"You been to the doctor?" I asked.

The cards disappeared. "Yeah."

"What's he say?"

"He's got me on medication and a whole health program. Valerian and kava. I drink chamomile tea and have a lot of herbal shit to take. Ginkgo biloba and fish oil. I'm supposed to eat a lot of green leafy vegetables. Me, your father, Grey. All of us. A fucking ton of salad. And your poor mother is always coming up with different healthy dressings for us. Cooking boiled cabbage. Stinks up the whole house. But we eat it. Watching Old Shep, it's a constant reminder, what we might be like one day."

He was telling the truth but not all of it. I could sense his desperation. It was way back there in the hard timbre of his voice and in the way he held his shoulders. The rain came down and we let it fall on us as we stood face-to-face. My white streak of hair hung in my eyes so that I didn't have to show him my own dread. JFK picked up on my mood and whined. He started back up the trail and we followed along almost reluctantly.

Now I understood what was really pulling Mal apart. Not simply the fear of what might be happening to him, but the idea that it might soon be time to take measures into his own hands. That's what he'd been groping for. He was struggling against the consuming terror that if he didn't time it just right he might actually become too senile to remember to do the job when the time came. We'd never let ourselves turn into Gramp. We'd fight rats for poisoned bait before we let that happen. I knew I would.

JFK hung his head out the passenger window and barked into the rain as I drove over to the high school. Mal was right—it was time Dale and I had a real conversation.

There was much more security now than when I'd attended class here. They'd gated the area up and there was a little booth with a semaphore arm blocking the road. I had to give my name and show ID and tell my reason for being there. I said my sister was feeling ill and I was picking her up to take her to the doctor. The security guard didn't give a shit so long as he got to mark it all down on his clipboard.

I drove through and parked outside the main set of doors. I didn't think I'd see Butch's Chevy around. I hadn't expected to. He was twenty-one and wouldn't want to get nabbed on school property with a fifteen-year-old. I was still surprised he'd been introduced to my parents. It seemed like the kind of relationship Dale would want to keep on the sly, but I suspected that Butch had pushed the matter, wanting to show off to my father, the infamous Pinsch Rand.

Within a few minutes the storm ended and the sun broke through again. A caravan of buses pulled up to the curb in front of the school. They blocked my line of sight. JFK was curled up and napping. I got out of the car, lit a cigarette, and took up position near the flagpole. Taped to it was a flyer stating that following the last period, open auditions were being held for *A Streetcar Named Desire*. It was a good guess that Dale would be there, so I steeled myself and decided to check out the auditorium.

The bell went off and the corridors crowded with students and teachers. A din of chatter, lockers banging shut, and running feet filled the place. I was heading upstream and kept getting pressed back by the current, but eventually I got to the auditorium.

There was a bigger turnout than I'd expected. A lot of jocks milled about in torn T-shirts, trying to ramp themselves up into Stanley-screaming-"Stella" mode. Several girls going out for the Blanche DuBois role had overdone their makeup and set their hair in wild curls. You couldn't get away from the movie.

I saw Dale off stage right, practicing lines with some other girl. I couldn't tell if she was doing Stella or Blanche. A flood of warm pride filled my chest. She looked lovely, assertive, and in command.

I went to take a seat and noticed someone in back waving at me. I squinted and saw it was my mother.

"Ma?"

"Terrier, come sit."

"What are you doing here?"

"What do you think? I'm waiting to watch my baby perform on-stage."

I sat beside her. "It's an audition."

"That's still a performance."

"Does Dale know you're here?"

"No, of course not, she'd throw a fit."

My mother had come prepared. She had a little pillow for her back and a thermos of hot tea with her. She poured a cup and offered it to me. I shook my head.

"Prepare yourself," she said. "It could be a while before she gets called on. It takes forever in the beginning, but then the group thins out pretty quickly after that. The real nervous nellies will turn green and bow out in the first ten minutes. Once they're gone, the talented kids really let fly."

"I can see you've attended these before."

She beamed. My mother's smile was infectious. I returned it. "Third one this year."

"So how does she do?"

"She's amazing. Really quite accomplished. I don't know where she gets it from."

"Grifting is just putting on a show," I said.

"She doesn't grift."

"It's in the blood."

My mother made an exasperated noise. "Stop it, you. I just wish she wouldn't always play the smaller secondary roles. I wish she'd go out for the bigger parts."

It had been years since I'd read or watched *Streetcar*. "Are there any smaller women's roles in this one?"

"No, which is why I'm so excited. I think she's finally going for the lead." She sipped and stared at me through wisps of steam rising from her tea. "So what brings you here?"

"I wanted to talk to her about Butch again."

We watched the first Stanley take the stage. He muffed his first line and asked if he could start again.

"So is he real trouble?" my mother asked. "Butch?"

"Semi-real trouble. You were right."

"So I should be worried."

"You should relax. She's smart. She'll kick him loose soon enough."

"And until then?"

"Until then I'll make sure nothing happens."

She had the presence of mind not to bother smiling. "You're a good boy."

"No, I'm not. That's why you asked me to check up on him. But if I wasn't here, the way I hadn't been for all these years, what would you have done?"

"Your father would have paid him a visit," my mother said. "If it was necessary."

"Sometimes you scare me, Ma."

We watched more kids foul their lines and nail their lines. A couple of them had real potential. Most of them didn't. A few of them knew it and were just there to have a little fun. The drama-coach-turned-director tried to move them along as quickly as possible. My mother had been right about that too. The group had thinned considerably already.

Finally it was Dale's turn. Unlike others, who'd read from their script pages, she'd memorized her lines. She was going out for Blanche. She and one of the Stanleys were doing the impending rape scene. One part of me was glad she wasn't doing the "I've always relied on the kindness of strangers" bit, which several other girls had already covered. She also wasn't playing Blanche with much of a southern accent. Another smart move, I thought.

My mother gripped my hand tightly, showing fierce pride. Instead of playing Blanche as a weak-willed naïve woman accidentally pushing the brutish Stanley over the edge, Dale characterized Blanche as a kind of seductress purposefully pushing the guy's buttons. Even when she defended herself and struggled against him, it seemed only another level of foreplay. When Stanley shouted, "We've had this date with each other from the beginning!" and leaped at her, I almost shot to my feet.

"She's so good," Ma said.

"Yes."

"What's the matter then? Your face is drawn."

"Isn't *Streetcar* a little . . . adult for fifteen-year-olds?"

"Maybe for my generation. But hers?" She packed up her items and stowed them away in her handbag. "I need to run."

"Why?"

"I don't want her to see me. You should go too. She'll get embarrassed and then overreact, trust me. Just go."

"I think I should talk to her."

"Okay, but be prepared." She kissed me on the cheek and went out through the side doors.

I followed a couple of minutes later. JFK was sitting beneath the flagpole. I'd only closed the window halfway and he'd shrugged himself through. I stood next to him and we waited. Dale and a couple of her friends came out about ten minutes later. I tossed the butt aside and stepped up to my sister.

She had the same reaction now that she'd had last night. Before she could snap at me, I said, "Relax. No lectures. I just thought I'd pick you up, maybe we could go out for a bite to eat or something. We could talk some more." Her friends shored up behind her, took her body language as a cue. "Bring your posse along with you if you like. My treat."

I watched the irritation drain from her face, replaced by that quaint smile she'd given everyone else. "I don't think I can today, Terry. We're all going over to Mary's to work on a science project together."

To their credit, no one broke into a grin, despite the obvious lie. A distant thrum of thunder broke across the sky and gurgled toward us.

"Hey, Dale, save that shit for Mom and Dad, right?"

She took a careful breath. "I'm busy, Terry. I'll see you at home."

"I want to talk to you."

She wagged her chin toward the auditorium door. "Did you see me in there?"

"Yes, you were good. Wonderful, really. Did you get the part?"

"We won't know until next week."

"We can talk about that too."

I met Dale's eyes. I tried to let her see that I wasn't being pushy for no reason. I wasn't trying to come down on her. I didn't mean to be a pain in the ass in front of her clique. JFK barked once. It broke the spell. Dale turned to her friends and told them that she'd meet up with them later on. They gave me disapproving glances and drifted off.

It started to sprinkle again. I went back and forth from loving the rain to hating it. I lit another cigarette, and before I could put the pack back in my pocket Dale reached in and grabbed one and waited for me to light her up. I did.

I searched my sister's face for the little girl I'd recognized last night at the lake. I didn't see her anymore. She appeared harder to me today, more adult. Maybe she always would, now that I'd seen her turn Blanche DuBois into a wild temptress.

She opened the car door, and JFK jumped into the passenger seat and refused to move. She shoved him into the back, where he stretched out on his side and yawned.

I started the engine but didn't pull out. We sat there smoking while the rain throbbed across the windshield.

"Was Mother watching too?" Dale asked.

"Yes."

"She always comes and sits in back. She doesn't realize how much we can see from the stage."

"She thinks she'll embarrass you."

"She does."

"Really?" I said. "You don't look embarrassed."

Dale finished her cigarette and crushed it out in the ashtray. She turned slightly in her seat so she could give me the full effect of her glare.

"What is this?" she asked.

"I'm showing concern."

"For what?"

"For you."

"I got that much. I mean, concern over what?"

I hadn't expected her to be so resistant. I should have. She was a teenager, and for the second time in two days I'd come from out of the shadows to pull her from her own crowd. It was stupid but I still wasn't sure how else I could've done it.

It was a rough hand and I didn't know how to play it. Should I soft-soap my worries over Butch or ask her flat out if she knew he was a punk working for Danny Thompson who might be a little too eager to step up?

I put the wipers on intermittent and watched the front doors of the school where I'd pretended to be a part of a society when I was actually an outlaw. I'd never believed I would need to get a joe job. I'd always expected to be able to boost and score and burgle my way through life. I'd fail a test and some teacher would threaten me with calling my parents, and I'd always think, Look at the scars on my chest, my old man made me this way. I'd feel a great love and a bewildering resentment for my father. I wondered if Dale felt the same way about him. And me.

She sat with her backpack on her lap. I had the sudden urge to yank it away from her and go through it. I had my nose in everybody's business. I didn't want to steal anything, I just wanted to pry and sate my curiosity.

She said, "I told you last night, Terry, I don't like you following me."

"Jesus Christ, I'm not following you, Dale. But I didn't think I'd need to make an appointment with your social secretary either."

"I have a life, you know."

"I know. I have no idea what it includes, but I know you have one."

"If you're interested, I'll tell you all about it."

I cracked my window and tapped cigarette ash outside. The smoke made JFK sneeze so hard he nearly rolled off the backseat. "I am interested. Of course I am."

"Stop playing coy, Terry. You're not here to take me out to the malt shop for a sundae. And you didn't come just to chat or to ask me how much homework I have."

She was laying it on the line. I had to do the same.

"Tell me more about Butch."

"You don't like him."

"I didn't say that."

An angry grin crimped her mouth. It was so abhorrent that I wanted to slap it off her face. "You didn't have to. You don't like him and Mom and Dad don't like him and the three of you are just buzzing around like wasps, aren't you?"

"No, I don't think that's what we're doing."

"He's my boyfriend. Isn't that enough for you?"

"No," I said. I tried to remember the days when I'd drive her to the ice cream parlor and everything made her eyes brighten. "Where'd you two meet?"

"At the lake."

I waited for more. There wasn't any.

"You know he's too old for you."

"Your opinion, Terry."

"And the law's. He could go up for seven on statutory-rape charges."

She tossed the backpack on the floor, put her feet on the dashboard, and crossed her ankles. "You worried about the law all of a sudden?"

"Not really. Are you being contrary for a reason?"

She turned her face away, took a deep breath, and let it out slowly. We Rands, we could work one another's nerves without even making an effort. "What did you do for those five years you were gone?"

"Worked on ranches, mostly."

"Why?" she asked.

"Why?"

"Yes, why? Did you like it? Is it something you always wanted to do?"

We were getting to places I didn't want to be. "I didn't mind it. And yeah, I thought about doing it before I wound up broke with a busted-down car on a road where the exits were thirty miles apart. But I didn't know what it would really be like."

She sounded genuinely interested. I wondered if she was just trying to find a way to hurt me. "So why didn't you get another job?"

"Because I was only killing time. I knew the call would come one day, I guess. I didn't know you'd be making it, but I knew it would come. And I knew I'd have to sit across from Collie and finally ask him the questions I wanted to know the answers to."

"Did you get them?"

"No. He's contrary too."

"I'm not being contrary. I just don't know what to tell you." She swung her legs down and planted her feet on the car mat again. "Start the car, let's go already."

I checked the rearview and spotted the security guy coming over to brace me and get me off school property. I threw the car in gear and headed back toward Old Autauk Road.

Dale was smart and mature and was running at least a small game on me, but I just couldn't manage to come out and ask her if she knew Butch was planning a heist. Or if she was involved in any way. I felt sick with myself for even thinking such a thing, but that didn't mean I was wrong.

"Why didn't you give Blanche a southern accent?"

"And be like everyone else? I was trying something new."

"It worked. You nailed it."

"Thank you. So you've complimented me, now comes the changeup when you ask me something you really want to know. So go on."

I wanted to know it all but I would never be able to convince her of that. Again that cruel smile played on her lips.

"Have you ever tried to visit Collie?" I asked.

"No."

"Why not?"

"Why would I want to? You didn't see him until I called you."

I didn't want to dig too deeply, but I thought the only way I'd ever learn anything about her, really understand her once again, was to discuss Collie. It tied us together and touched us in a way that it wouldn't touch anyone else. Collie was our older brother, and there was something exclusive in that.

"I don't feel the same way you do," she said.

"What do you mean?"

She used an index finger to draw a smiley face in the condensation of the passenger window. When she was done she wiped it away with her palm. "I didn't know him as well as you did. He wasn't . . . He didn't treat me like you did. He didn't read to me. He wasn't interested in me. He was out doing whatever he was doing. We had no real relationship."

"Dale, I know he was a prick, but still, he—"

"If you say that he loved me, I'm going to yank the wheel and crash us."

Maybe that was what I was going to say. Maybe Collie had loved her and simply hadn't known how to show it. Maybe he hadn't given a damn. He could've started slipping into the underneath years before he went mad dog. I seemed to remember him being around, taking her out for ice cream, buying her presents, hugging her and teasing her the way older brothers do. Maybe she just didn't remember, or maybe I was making too much of it.

"I wasn't going to say that," I said.

"Ask me what you really want to know."

"I'm not sure what I want to know."

"Yes, you are. You want to know if he replaced you at all. If in the last five years I visited him, wrote to him, phoned him. If I cared about him more than I cared about you." From second to second, emotions played havoc inside her, maybe the way they did inside all of us Rands. She moved from anger and insecurity to a need for proving herself self-reliant. "The answer is no, Terry. You were both gone. I felt the same way about you both. I didn't think about either of you much. I couldn't. You each deserted the family. I cared more about Gramp, right? At least he was there."

It hurt hearing the truth. This was why Rands didn't talk. Despite our stoniness, we were a sensitive, fickle bunch. I kept glancing at her. I kept wondering if there was any way to fix our relationship and if I even had the mettle to make the effort.

I said, "Dale, if you're ever in trouble, you don't have to face it alone."

She frowned at me, cocked her head like she hadn't heard right. "What?"

"You can talk to me. Really. I want you to."

It was the same offer that Mal had made to me.

"Terry, since you've been back we've hardly had what you might call a deep conversation."

"I'm trying to fix that right now. You can still talk to me. You're not alone. I'll help you. Whatever it is, I'll help you, if you're ever in trouble."

Her expression shifted a few more times, from perplexity to annoyance to something else I couldn't place. "Are you talking about . . . pregnancy?"

"Ah, no, not specifically, I mean—"

"Oh, God." She threw up her hands. Her nails snapped against the dome light, and JFK perked up like he'd heard a gunshot. "Is this your way of saying that you'll, what, help me get an abortion?"

"No, no, not exactly."

"Not exactly?"

I couldn't find the right words. I couldn't hold on to any particular thread of discussion. A pulse beat painfully in my belly. "I just mean . . . well, anything. Any problems. Anything you need help with. Ever. Whether it's with Butch or anyone else."

"You're fixated on Butch."

"I'm not fixated on Butch."

The rain came down harder now and splashed inside, but I liked the air and she must've too, because we left our windows open a crack.

"Do you want me to take you home or drop you off at your friend's? Or somewhere else?"

My sister gave me a long hard look. I let her do it. It went on for a while. I knew she didn't trust me. There was no way that she could after what I'd done. But she was trying to find common ground. She was at least willing to make an effort to forgive me.

She abruptly relaxed and asked, "Are you going back out west?"

I hadn't thought about it much. Now I did. "No."

"You're not leaving again?"

"No."

A scoffing sound eased up her throat. "Why?"

I thought of something we'd discussed at the lake. "This time I'm staying the course."

She laughed as if I'd just done something cute, reached out, and pressed her hand to my cheek. "My big brother, trying to make up for lost time. Okay. Okay, thanks. It's nice to know you'll be around in case I ever need you."

"I have a question," I said.

"Of course you do."

"Why was it you who phoned me at the ranch?"

"No one else wanted to do it. They were all afraid you'd be mad at them, or worse, that you wouldn't come home."

"Why didn't you tell me it was you?"

"I wanted to see if you'd know."

I tried to read her eyes. I sensed that she was a lot more worldly than she was letting on, but that didn't have to mean a damn thing.

She said, "You weren't just killing time. It wasn't just Collie. It had something to do with Kimmy too, didn't it? It had to. Why you left?"

"Yeah. She had a miscarriage."

Dale turned on me, waited a three count, then got up close. She jabbed me in the chest with a finger. It hurt.

"You . . . you . . . are a serious asshole! That just means she needed you even more!"

"I know."

"You abandoned her. You . . . you—"

"I know."

"But *why*?"

Her voice hit that same plaintive whine that mine had reached when I'd asked my brother the same question. I thought I might have an answer, but it wasn't a good one. And it might not even be the whole truth, but there didn't seem to be any great truth to it anyway. I missed a child that had never taken a breath. I saw her as clearly now as I had then, laid out and bleeding as if she'd been struck by a car because we hadn't been watching closely enough. I blamed myself, and I suppose I somehow blamed Kimmy as well. The tragedy had seemed greater in her presence. Her sobs had served to remind me that I couldn't protect my girls. My failures were forever on display. I was proven a liar. My love for her overwhelmed me until I thought I'd choke. I'd always believed I wanted to die in her arms, and holding her to me I was certain I would. But it wasn't possible to explain that to anyone.

Dale said, "And now you're telling me I can trust you?"

"You probably won't, not for a while. But yes, Dale, you can trust me."

She grunted like she didn't believe a word I might ever say. I wouldn't believe me either. I thought the ride might help to calm things down. I was wrong again. I took us out to Ocean Parkway. She didn't argue and say she was busy. She put her feet up on the dash the way that Kimmy used to do, and she let me open up the throttle and kick it up to triple digits in the rain. I knew she was a speed demon like Butch was. I could imagine her urging him on faster as he tore past the sand-strewn beach roads. It was a rite of passage. JFK hung his head out the window, and the rain spattered his thick old face and he panted into the wind. Occasionally he let out a bark. I wanted to do the same. We crossed the causeway and watched the bay thrash below us. It was primal and calming. It spoke to something inside both of us. I could see her readying herself to say something more. I wondered if she was going to admit to working with Butch or being closer with Danny Thompson's crew than I ever hoped she'd be. I spun through the traffic circle at the far end and drove back across the bridge much slower and more composed. Dale bummed another cigarette off me. She used a chamois cloth on the floor in back to wipe JFK's fur down. I waited for her to spill. I headed toward home and she turned her head twice in quick succession like she wanted to get a good look at me, maybe check my eyes, before saying the next thing she had to say.

"Okay, so tell me," I said.

She twisted a lock of her hair and drew it over her ear. "There is something, I think. I'm not sure."

I asked, "What?"

"I think someone's been following me, but I could be wrong. It's just a feeling."

"Cops?"

"They're easy to spot. No. Someone else. Maybe because of Collie."

"Reporters?"

"I don't know."

"When did this start?"

"I'm not certain. Nothing I can put a finger on. It feels like it's been there for a while but I can't pinpoint an exact time, you know? It's just been at the back of my mind and now it's sort of moved to the front."

"Someone angry at Collie who wants to take it out on his family? That kind of feeling?"

"I'm not sure."

"You ever see anyone?"

"No."

"When's it happen? At home?"

"Yes, when I'm coming home or leaving for school. And at other times. When I'm shopping at the mall with friends. I get a sense that someone is watching."

"Could it be someone from Danny Thompson's crew?"

She froze up for a moment, then seemed to slowly regain the power of movement as she nodded. "So you know about that. About Butch working for Danny."

"Yes," I said.

She nearly spit her words. "Of course you do. It's just small-time stuff."

"I heard. Has he had a falling-out with Danny?"

"No. Maybe. I'm not sure. He's . . . he's involved with something new. A job. I think Danny might be pressuring him for details. Or for money up front."

Dale spoke like she couldn't believe the truth of what she was saying, as if she was having déjà vu and hoping for some different outcome this time.

"And you're worried that he might be using you as leverage against Butch?" I asked.

"You tell me. You know that prick better than I do."

"I don't know him that well anymore."

She didn't say she thought it might be nothing. She didn't say it might just be all in her head and she might just be acting paranoid. She knew enough to trust herself, to be wary and on her toes. It was a part of being born into this bent life of ours.

"You ever spot a black Mercedes tagging around you?" I asked.

"I don't think so."

"Keep an eye out for it. Do you carry any kind of weapon, Dale?"

"What, like a gun or a knife?"

"Like pepper spray?"

"No."

We drove through neighborhood streets that had flooded. Trash spiraled in the gutters, the sewer grates boiling up like there were sharks under the water.

"I'll get you something," I said. "Maybe Mace."

"They don't sell Mace anymore."

"I might be able to get it. You carry it with you everywhere you go from now on."

"I want a knife," she said.

She laid it out flat and I wondered if she'd been lying to me. She might just want a knife because she was hooked up with Butch and his crew and she knew that if anything ever went down wrong she'd be able to play sweet and get up close and stick the blade in. At least she thought she could.

I felt my neck flush and straightened my collar to hide it. My Christ, what the hell was going on with this family?

"Maybe I'll get you a knife too," I said. "Something small. But you aim for the eyes and throat and it'll be effective. You feel like someone is following you again, you call me, wherever you are, day or night, you let me know. If anyone tries to grab you, you douse his eyes or you stab him in the face. Do you understand?"

"Yes."

We pulled up in front of the house. She didn't say, *I know you won't let me down.* She didn't say, *I believe in you.*

"Aren't you coming in?" she asked.

"I have to be somewhere. Take the dog, all right, Blanche?"

"Fucker."

She almost gave me that gentle empty touch on the arm that she'd trained herself to give the rubes. Instead, she leaned over and kissed my cheek.

Dale called the dog. JFK climbed out the passenger side and let my sister lead him up the walk. He turned back once and gave me a sad stare, like he had plenty of his own secrets to spill that would haunt us all forever.

Wes used to have a small apartment on the north side of Main Street, above a delicatessen that was one of Big Dan Thompson's fronts. Now he owned a nice house on the south side, right off the bay. A canal ran behind his patio deck. A twenty-eight-foot sailboat sat at a private dock. The sails hadn't been tied down properly and they'd become worn and frayed, flapping loose in the wind. The rails hadn't been polished in years and the deck had banged around so much in storms that I could see cracks worrying up from the keel.

The four-bedroom house was full of expensive, practical furniture. Chandeliers, marble tiling, a fireplace without an ounce of ash in it. A dining room that sat twelve. A living room with lush leather L-shaped couches, thick white carpeting, a huge plasma television and entertainment system. Coaster trays on every end table. The kind of room where you hosted large parties, serving martinis and canapés.

There were two fresh gallons of milk in the fridge but no beer. It told me that Wes either ate a lot of cereal or had ulcers.

No photos on the shelves, no pictures on the walls. No CDs or DVDs. Nothing that said he spent any time here relaxing. No sign of friends or family anywhere. No women's deodorant or Tampax in the bathroom. No drawer set aside for a girlfriend. No condoms in his nightstand. No spank mags in either of the bathrooms. No recreational drugs. I found the ulcer meds in his medicine cabinet.

Wes had moved up in the world but wasn't enjoying himself much.

He was out cold in the master bedroom. Like every syndicate guy who did business out of a bar or a titty joint, he didn't crap out until eight or nine in the morning and didn't get his day started until maybe five P.M.

He slept with a .32 snub under his pillow. I'd never known anyone paranoid or dopey enough to really keep a pistol under their pillow. He could sneeze or have a nightmare and put one in his own ear. Danny really had him knotted up inside. I unloaded the snub and left it on his dresser. In his closet I found a false back with an assortment of guns stashed behind it, including two .357 Magnums, a couple of Desert Eagle 9mms, and one semiauto rifle. They all appeared to be unfired.

There were banded blocks of hundred-dollar bills amounting to around fifty g's. If I was still a thief I'd be having a very good week. Between Chub's cache and Wes's hoard I could've set myself up in Miami and lived the righteous life for a year.

He also had five untraceable burner cell phones. I tried one and it worked. I pocketed it. In a small box were a couple of switchblades and a butterfly knife. I snatched the butterfly.

I watched him sleep for a few minutes. His hundred-and-fifty-dollar haircut still looked good after eight hours of tossing and turning. But his face remained scrunched into a harassed expression. I wondered why he put himself through all of this. He wasn't a born mob mook and he didn't have the disposition for the serious roughnecking. I couldn't see him ever killing anyone, but who the hell really knew.

I cleared my throat and said, "Evening, Wes."

He was a light sleeper. He snapped up out of bed and looked side to side. It took him a second to go for the gun under his pillow. He scrabbled at the mattress and then checked the sheets.

I said, "Relax."

His eyes cleared and he focused on me. Then he laid back down and rubbed his face. "Terry. Jesus God. You trying to juke me?"

"If I was I would've been long gone by now. Besides, Wes, you don't own a hell of a lot to fence."

His face fell and flushed so pink that it looked like a kid had dabbed him with a paintbrush. He wouldn't have minded me robbing him nearly as much as my finding out he was boring as hell. "I've been meaning to buy some new stuff."

"Right."

"Give me a minute. And get out of my bedroom."

He bounced away to hit the head and I went and sat on his nice couch in his nice empty living room. He joined me in ten minutes, freshly showered, wearing a clean suit, his eyes as red as if he hadn't slept at all.

"You've got a sweet touch," he said. "You must if I didn't wake up."

"Some skills you never lose."

He frowned at me. His knitted eyebrows made him look like he was about ten years old. "I don't appreciate you coming here like this. You could have just called or rung the goddamn doorbell."

"Don't get your feelings too bent out of shape or I might remind you that you've been parked at my curb, watching my house."

"I was only doing what the boss told me."

"I'm only doing what I have to, Wes. Next time I'll knock, right?"

He sat opposite me. "What do you want, Terry?"

I knew he wanted to get himself some milk. I wanted to tell him that it was okay, but I'd already embarrassed him enough. He wasn't my friend, but I didn't have to put him on the defensive like this. I'd been creeping around so much lately after so much time being out of the bent life that I wondered if I could go through a front door anymore.

"It hasn't been easy for you since Big Dan blew out his heart," I said.

"I get by."

"What is Danny into that's so off course from the way his father played the game?"

"You don't need to know that, Terry."

"You really ought to retire."

It made him laugh and glance around the room like I'd told a complicated joke to a large group of guests and he wanted to see if everyone else was laughing. "And do what? Garden? It's in my blood. Same as being a second-story man is in yours."

"I don't take ulcer medication or have two gallons of milk in my house."

He leaned in. "You don't have a house."

"Good point."

"So what did you do? Climb on the roof?"

"No," I said. "Popped out a basement window. It's easy to creep another criminal's house. They never have alarm systems hooked up to the police."

"I'll remember that." He held his arms up in a gesture of resignation. "So, you going to tell me what you want, Terry? We haven't been back to your dad's place."

"Let's table it. Tell me about Butch."

"Butch?"

"Started hanging around Danny's not too long ago. Thinks he's an outlaw. Twenty-one, skinny, busted nose, shaggy hair, pencil beard, smells like acne cream. Sounds like maybe he's taken down a few small scores."

"Oh, that kid. Yeah."

I could tell by the way he said it that he knew my sister was seeing Butch. That it was something they talked about around the Fifth Amendment. Maybe as a joke, maybe as something more. *Look at who the Rands are going to welcome into the fold—this dumbshit poser. What's that make him? How do we turn that to our advantage?*

"What's Danny got him doing?"

"Why are you asking?"

"You know why I'm asking, Wes."

He put his hand to his belly as if the acid were about to eat through his shirt. "If you've got questions for the kid, you should break in to his place. Not mine."

I waited. I wanted a cigarette but Wes didn't even have any ashtrays.

"He doesn't do much. He's an errand boy. Chauffeurs some of the guys around. Picks up food. We send him to the bakery. Gets the dry cleaning and like that."

"What crew does he run with?"

"No real crew so far as I know. But I don't know much about the kid. He comes in with losers, strings with a lot of third-raters."

"You know if they're moving up?"

He answered carefully. "If they are, Mr. Thompson will get a piece of it."

I nodded. It sounded about right. Danny wasn't pushing Butch and his crew into anything, but he wanted them to kick up in case they got away with a score.

"And my sister, Dale?" I asked.

"What about her?" Wes said.

I didn't want to form the words. "Has she been working for Danny?"

"Ask her."

"Hey, let's pretend I'm asking you, right?"

It got tense for a moment. We glared at each other. We were both good at holding a malevolent stare. The pause lengthened. It could go on all night. I let my eyes soften. It was a calculated move for an honest purpose.

"It's my sister, Wes," I said. "I need to know if she's in trouble."

"She's what, sixteen? Fifteen? Running around with a scumbag amateur punk who thinks he's up to raiding big scores. Is she in trouble? Is that really even a question, Terry?"

"I suppose not."

He smiled without any warmth. "Well, there it is then. But for the record, I don't know if she's involved with the crew."

"You don't know? You're Danny's right-hand man. You fucking run the crew."

He rubbed at his stomach again and grimaced. "Not so much lately. I handle his business and the main crew, but Mr. Thompson's . . . been dealing with out-of-towners."

"You mean he's having other syndicate guys whacked."

"There's some of that. But other things too. He's a little paranoid. It's not his fault. It's just the life. He has a lot of new help. Some of these guys, I barely know their names. He keeps them close. He includes me on most of it, but not all. I don't think he trusts me with some of the rougher stuff."

"Don't drink milk in front of him. You got any Mace?"

"What? Mace? No. Why would I have Mace? What the hell do you want Mace for?"

I got up and headed for the door. "Forget it."

Coming out of Wes's neighborhood, I took a corner too fast and Collie's folder came sliding out from under the passenger seat. The papers scattered across the floor mat. I tried to ignore them but they kept drifting, whispering, and drawing my attention.

I pulled over into a strip mall and watched folks going in and out of the stores. Kids still playing on those nickel rides that had been set in cement twenty-five or thirty years ago. A mini-helicopter that went up six or eight inches, then down, a couple of lights flashing. And the children excited as hell and clambering all over it while their mothers did their business in the stationery, the bakery, the laundromat.

I drew the butterfly knife and whipped the blade out, twirled it shut, then snapped the point out again. Dale would get the feel of it in five minutes. If she was going to hang around Butch and his crew and felt better with a little protection, then I wasn't going to deny her. I'd have to get her clear of them some other way. I didn't know how. She was on the edge, trying to decide which way she wanted to go. My stomach twisted at the idea of her getting in deeper with the crew, even if she wasn't running heists yet. Maybe the blade would wake her up to the fact that she wasn't playing a game. I thought how easy it would be for women to defend themselves if only men taught them a little about how it was done.

I put the paperwork back in order and paged through it. I wondered how much of it Collie's wife had access to. I remembered her in the prison, the way she used her hands to form compact, brusque gestures. The way her glossy black hair lashed the air. The way he had shrunk from her like a child being punished. She wasn't afraid of him. She had control over him. Maybe because he loved her. Maybe because he was locked up and needed someone on the outside to help.

How much help was she giving him? And what kind?

All I knew was that her first name was Lin. I dug through the file, hoping there'd be additional details. I didn't find any. I had to get to a library or hop on the Internet. I had to do a little research. Dale would have a laptop. I wondered if Collie's wife knew how to use a pistol or a blade. She seemed like the type who would.

Then I realized, Jesus Christ—Lin. Her last name would probably be Rand. Why not? Anyone who felt the need to go through a formal marriage even within the walls of a prison might be traditional enough to take her husband's last name.

I drew out my new cell phone and called information. They gave me her number and I punched it in.

There wasn't any ringing, just music. I waited for voice mail or an answering machine but nothing came up. Finally a woman answered with a crisp, "Yes?"

"Lin . . . Rand?"

Hearing her own name made her even more irritated. "Yes. Who is this? What do you want?"

I said, "This is Terry Rand."

"Oh." She brightened instantly. "Oh, Terry, yes, pardon me. My God. I wasn't sure if I'd ever hear from you. I'm so glad you called."

"I'd like to meet with you if I can."

"Yes, yes, of course. Are you free for dinner? We could—"

I didn't feel like spending an evening talking with a woman who had married a child-killer behind bars. "I'd like to meet now, if that's okay."

"Certainly. You could come by my apartment. I live in West Islip, off Sunrise Highway." She gave me directions. I knew the apartment complex. I'd boosted a few TVs out of there years ago. Who knows? Maybe I'd juked her place before.

"I'll see you in twenty minutes," I said, and hung up.

It took me fifteen. She had a ground-floor corner unit in the rear. Outside her door was a small but impressive garden and a couple of wrought-iron chairs that looked charming but impractical. I knocked and got an eight-count wait.

She opened the door, smiled at me, and said, "Terry, it's such a pleasure." First she held out her hand, and as I went to take it she drew me into an embrace. I didn't return the hug.

I'd noticed her killer heels in the prison, and now I saw how petite she was. She couldn't be taller than four-eleven and she wouldn't hit a hundred pounds if she had rocks in her pockets. I imagined Collie opening her letters, finding snapshots of her that would make him flinch after so much time in the can. She had a resolute poise but also seemed little more than an attractive wisp, her shining black hair gliding about her as if in slow motion, so that you felt if you looked away even for a moment you'd turn back and find that she'd evaporated.

Her place was clean and stylishly furnished. There were touches of formal Chinese setting. Mats, silks, bamboo, and a large framed painting of what appeared to be Hong Kong, taken from a junk in the harbor at sunset.

"What can I offer you?" she asked. She reached out and put three fingers lightly on my wrist. I could barely feel them. "A beer? A glass of wine?"

"You sounded terse on the phone," I said.

She nodded. Her glossy hair took a second to follow the motion of her head. "I've recently started getting a lot of crank calls."

"Because of Collie."

"Yes. Please sit." She directed me to a settee that was uncomfortably hard. She poured two glasses of wine and sat one in front of me. I didn't touch it. "He's in the news again all the time now. There's been a resurgence in interest. I did a few interviews with reporters, but they trim the coverage and edit out anything I have to say about the new details in Collie's plight. They make me appear to be an unbalanced . . . groupie."

I thought, Plight.

She went on. "People phone and tell me how next week they're going to be sitting in the dark, saving electricity to make sure there's plenty of voltage for his electric chair. They don't realize he's going to—"

"Get the needle."

"Yes."

She sipped from her glass, and her hair folded over her face like curtains at the end of Act I and she started to cry. I didn't know what to do. I didn't trust her. I didn't believe you could fall in love with a mass murderer through prison letters scanned by guards. I didn't believe you could have a legitimate relationship with a killer of nine-year-olds. But I'd abandoned the woman I'd loved and spent an entire afternoon watching her and her child from another man, jealous and sick and wishing I could steal her away, so what the fuck did I know?

"He told me to talk to you. He said you had information."

"Excuse me, Terry. I don't often get a chance to speak with someone who . . . understands. It's a relief." She wiped her eyes with her index fingers and took a slow deep breath. "And you look so much like him. It's a bit startling. Yes, information. About the other girls. Yes. Even so, it's nice to finally meet his family."

I smiled vapidly. Family. This was Lin Rand. She got up and walked out of the room. I wondered how she'd do feeding Gramp. I imagined her and my mother cooking together in the kitchen, boiling cabbage, providing plenty of leafy greens to my uncles. Her on the porch sharing beers with my old man. Giving JFK a flea bath. Paging through the photo albums, laughing at Collie when he was a kid. *Look at him here without his front teeth. Here with a foot up on the bumper of his first muscle car, wearing a T-shirt, a cigarette hanging out of his mouth.* Me in the background glaring, brooding, always angry with him. Her sitting with us on Christmas Day, opening presents, handing me a box. *Here, Terry, he wanted you to have this; he made it himself.* Me opening it and finding a license plate. TERRIER 1. I looked down and saw that the wine in my glass was full of tiny thrashing waves. I realized I was nearly panting, practically snorting.

Lin returned with an accordion folder like the one I'd grabbed at the precinct. She sat it in front of me and said, "This is some of what we've discovered." I flipped it open. Instead of official reports inside, there were dozens of pages of handwritten notes, newspaper clippings, obituaries. I took my time. I read through a lot of the data. I recognized the women that Gilmore had talked about. There were another three women listed, two who'd died before Collie's spree. I didn't know what to make of it. I had a hard time seeing one guy snuffing all these women without anyone catching on, but that didn't mean it couldn't happen. On the surface of it I saw a lot of disparate deaths, some clearly murders, others possible accidents. There were a lot of angry men in the world. So much of the focus of that rage would be women. I pictured insecure boyfriends diving onto these girls in a fury. I saw bitter, defeated men prowling, hunting, snickering, sneaking up. I saw my brother beating an old woman to death with his fists. I saw him strangling Rebecca Clarke and leaving her body in the grass.

"Terry," Lin said. "Your face."

"My face?"

"You're very flushed."

"Right." I shut the folder. "Why these women?"

"Pardon?"

"Why only these particular women? What's the connection between them?"

"They fit the profile. Young. Late teens to early twenties. Pretty. Brunettes."

I snorted. "Is that all?"

"We haven't discovered anything else to connect them."

I nodded and couldn't seem to stop. It was like the tendons in my neck had been cut. My chin hit my chest and it rattled my teeth. I couldn't catch enough air. "What about all the others?"

"What others?"

"The blondes. The ugly ones. The fat ones. The forty-year-olds. What about all of those women who've been choked or beaten in the last seven or eight years?"

"That's not—"

Gilmore had been right. It all looked like bullshit. The young women all bore a vague resemblance but other than that, there was nothing that tied them together. Maybe they were strangled, maybe not. I could almost hear Gilmore's finger coming down on the tabletop, *click click click*.

"This isn't evidence."

"It's part of the profile."

"You watch too much fucking television." I slid the folder aside. "You can force the facts to fit any profile, that doesn't mean it's real."

"But this—"

"What do you do?"

"Excuse me?"

"Your profession. What do you do?"

"Oh. I'm currently unemployed."

"You have a nice place. What were you before you were unemployed?"

There was the dull light of discomfort in her eyes, quickly replaced by defiance. "I worked for Child Protective Services as an investigator."

It struck me hard. I shuddered with the urge to laugh. I tried choking it back but a weird little giggle escaped my lips. I stood and thought, What the hell am I doing here? I took a step toward the door and the laughter came bubbling up, hot and wet, and I couldn't stop. She didn't know what to do. She crossed her arms in front of her chest. I leaned over and propped my hands on my knees, gasped until tears filled my eyes. I wiped them away and they kept coming. Then I wasn't sure if I was laughing anymore. Abruptly, I knew I wasn't. I faced her calmly and said, "You're goddamn kidding me."

"No, I—"

"They fired you when they found out you had married a mass murderer convicted of killing children."

"Yes," she admitted.

"Let me guess. You're suing them for losing your job. You consider it prejudice."

"No. I knew what I was doing. I realized I would be discharged."

I stepped away from her. "There's nothing here. My brother iced Becky Clarke. He's still running a game on me. And you too."

"I'm sorry you feel that way. I didn't expect you to be so . . . combative."

"It's the nature of my family. We're all contrary."

"Collie isn't."

That nearly got me laughing again, but I managed to curb it. She pulled the accordion folder closer, then sipped her wine. She didn't appear to be upset, merely disappointed.

I got to the door but couldn't make myself leave yet. I turned and asked, "Why did you write him in the first place?"

She looked me in the eye and said, "I don't think you would believe me."

"Tell me anyway."

She considered it. I drifted back toward the settee but didn't sit. I was drawn to the picture of Hong Kong. I'm not sure what there was about it. Maybe simply the openness of it. Talk about a city of thieves and murderers, corruption and money and beauty. Lin looked at me like she was looking at Collie. There was the light of love in her eyes, or maybe it was only self-deception.

"I wrote him," she said, "to tell him that I would be sitting in the dark, saving electricity to make sure there was plenty of voltage for his electric chair. I was one of those people. He killed a child. A little girl. A harmless old woman. All those poor people. I found him irredeemable."

"And now?"

She lifted her chin as if exposing her throat for the kill. "He's still irredeemable. But I love him."

I thought about it. "That's not why you wrote him. There had to be a reason. Something that set you off."

She held her glass of wine but didn't sip it. She looked like a mannequin posed in a beautifully mannered way. "Oh, that's right, you're someone who needs reasons. So I'll tell you honestly. I think it was his face. In the paper. His expression. He was handsome but unrepentant. He wasn't smirking like some of them do. He wasn't embracing the spotlight. And yet he also wasn't ashamed. He wasn't weeping. He didn't look suicidal. He didn't look like someone who would enjoy prison. He didn't look like a killer, but he was one. He wasn't terrifying. He also wasn't pathetic."

"What was he?"

"Himself. That's all he was. He was merely himself."

How profound. How authentic. Heartfelt, penetrating. The laugh was there in my belly, wanting out. I thought, And if he was terrifying or pathetic or suicidal he wouldn't have been himself? No wonder they'd found each other. They were both seriously nuts.

"He responded to my letters. They were . . . genuine. He takes the world on its own terms. His letters are direct but conscientious. You can read them if you like."

"Christ, no."

"I began to visit him. Due only to curiosity, of course, at first. I thought I might submit an article for a magazine. I dabble with journalistic writing. I was full of hate. I wanted to vent it. I wanted to put it down on paper, but more than that I wanted to show him for what he was, whatever that might be. I decided I should face him. I craved a chance to dig into him and make him feel something. I didn't realize that he felt everything, just like the rest of us. I've never met a man more emotionally honest and accepting."

"You don't get out much, lady."

She looked at me evenly. "It took months before the hate dropped away. I eventually began to look forward to seeing him. I fell in love with him. We can't ever truly know when it happens or why. We don't choose who we love, Terry."

"You're too easy on yourself."

She lowered her eyes. "Trust me, I'm not."

Trust was too hard to come by. I went to the painting again. I thought, Maybe that's where I need to go. That's where a man could get lost. They had world-class pickpockets there. I'd promised everyone in my family that I'd never run again, but maybe it was the only answer.

"Excuse me?" she said.

"What?"

"You whispered something."

I cleared my throat and coughed up the question. It was the same question. It was the only question.

"Why did he do it?" I asked.

There was a lengthy pause. "He doesn't know why. He just did. That's all there is."

"You sound exactly like him. He bought his gun the day before, did you know that? You don't plan something spontaneous and irrational. He must've said something about what happened that night."

"No," Lin said, and she watched me like she was watching a little brother who'd skinned a knee, as if she wanted to put a bandage on a little scrape, give it a kiss. "He never has. He simply says he did what he did and that's all."

"That's not good enough. Not nearly."

"It doesn't have to be good enough for you, Terry. You can keep asking, keep looking for answers, but you're only going to be hurting yourself. Don't you see that?"

"He's lying."

"Collie doesn't lie."

I rushed forward, grabbed her by the shoulders, and pulled her out of her seat. The glass went flying and hit the floor but didn't break. The spilled wine almost looked like it could be blood in this light. "You don't know shit about my brother. You're just one of those nutso fans who dig on serial killers because you think they're romantic outlaws. Marriage behind bars to a convicted murderer—do you know how pathetic you are? I know your kind. Every asshole on death row has fifty of you writing him every day, espousing love."

An expression of pity crossed her face. "You don't understand, Terry."

She wasn't bothered at all by my outburst. "Well, no shit, lady! I don't know you and I don't want to know you."

She took my hand and rubbed my wrist softly, the way you might touch a traumatized child. In a strange way it helped.

I managed to force the words out. "He kissed them. His victims. That day. On the forehead. He put his lips to their foreheads."

Nodding, she said, "I know."

"You knew?"

"Yes."

"But Becky wasn't kissed. There's evidence of that. That works in his favor, I think. Why didn't you tell me that?"

"It's in the files. I thought you understood."

"I thought you talked to Gilmore."

"I did. I begged him to check the evidence. He said he had but that he still wasn't convinced. He's . . . personally invested. He feels very betrayed by Collie. And by you, for that matter. I think . . . he almost wishes he was a part of your family. That he was your brother as well."

"He acts like it. Collie always stabbed me in the back. Gilmore goes for my kidneys."

"I don't know what that means."

"You don't need to. So Collie told you? About him . . . putting his lips on his victims?"

"Kissing them. Yes."

"When did he do it? When did he kiss them? Before or after he murdered them?"

She took a deep breath. "After."

"That rotten prick. That insane scumbag prick."

She kept rubbing my wrist. "This isn't good for you, Terry. You're going to make yourself sick."

I snapped my arm away. "Oh, shut up! You're calling me sick? You?" I dodged toward the door like I was going to run, then I turned and got up in her face again. "You? Your bridal suite was an eight-by-ten cell. Your husband ices little girls."

Again, that look of sympathy swam in her eyes. "You try to hide your pain by being as abrasive as you can."

I lifted my hands as if to put them on her shoulders. Or around her neck. She didn't flinch. My hands got closer. The pulse in her throat was in sync with my own heartbeat. I hissed, "You could have done it yourself. You could have snuffed those girls."

Her jaw muscles tightened. Her eyes lost that profoundly sad sheen. "That's ridiculous!"

"You could've done it just to help him out. Just to make the cops think there was another murderer out there. Drug users, meth-heads, prostitutes. Those sound like the kind of people you'd run into while working Child Services. How many crack babies were you visiting on a daily basis? How many skells did you run into out in Riverhead?"

Nothing I said rattled her. Maybe she really was an icy-blooded psycho like Collie. She said, "These other murders aren't helping him. Nothing can help him. He's doomed. He's going to die for what he did. He's all right with that."

"And are you?"

"Yes."

"Then why do you care about Becky Clarke? And these others, assuming they are connected?"

"Because there's someone else out there killing women. It has to be stopped. You looked at the data I've collated—"

She grabbed for the folder again. She smacked it against my chest. She reached for my hand and forced me to take it.

"There's nothing here."

"They're going to murder him," she said.

I'd used the same word while I'd stood in line to get into the prison to see him the first time. "It's not murder. Murder is an unlawful killing. *He's* the murderer. This is an execution. He deserves to die."

"He's your brother."

"He's an asshole. And you worked Child Protective Services? You should be mortified. Hang your head, lady. Put your nose to the ground."

"He wants you there, Terry. At the execution. He wants you to be a witness. Maybe he'll give you the reason you need then. Maybe they'll be his last words."

"Fuck the both of you."

I threw down the paperwork and beelined out the door. I swept past her garden, got in my car, and tore ass out of the lot with the tires smoking and squealing. I went over the curb and the shocks took such a hit that my head bounced hard off the roof. I saw white stars that turned red and ran into the gutters.

I went home and Gilmore was sitting out on the porch with my father. I was surprised to hear my old man laughing, but there it was. It sounded real.

I knew that Gilmore's romanticized concept of family, twisted by his youth, had somehow led him to us. I wondered what would have happened if he'd been lucky enough to live in middle America with a boring-as-fuck-all family perched on a plastic-covered couch, watching *Lawrence Welk* repeats. Would he have been better off or worse? Would we?

"Hello, Terrier."

"Gilmore."

My father took a deep pull on his beer, then said, "We were just talking about that time Gramp got caught on the bay with a stolen kayak and some silverware. His car died over on Oak Beach. Thought he could land the kayak at Fire Island and instead got caught in the ferry channel—"

Gilmore showed a lot of teeth in his smile. It wasn't nearly as bad as his grin. "—and almost wound up pulled into the props of a boatload of gay activists planning a parade at Cherry Grove."

"He spent the day with them, said they had good barbecue and knew how to laugh."

"I arrested him after he stole a clam boat and tried to make a getaway." Gilmore swung himself aside in his seat to face me. He leaned in and motioned for me to do the same. "He didn't realize it had no motor and he had to pole himself back to the mainland. He got tired halfway across and sent out an SOS. He didn't know the water was only three feet deep and he could've walked back. Not one of your better-planned jukes."

"Old Shep was never much for ocean activities," my old man said.

I didn't remember the story. It sounded made up. It sounded like my father was being ingratiating, using Gramp as a punch line just to keep Gilmore smiling. I wondered why he would bother.

I wondered if Gilmore was here to square off with me again, in some way using my father as leverage against me. I sat, took a proffered beer, and waited for the questions. I was surprised when the men continued passing anecdotes. Stories of stupid burglars and cops on the take who got nailed with their hands in the evidence locker. They didn't try to engage me in any way. I even found myself joining in a bit. Finally I wished them good night.

I stepped inside and went up to my room and then padded downstairs and took up a perch by the front window, where I could listen to my old man and Gilmore talking. The night-light over the kitchen sink didn't reach my dark corner. I sat on the floor and dropped my head back against the cold wall.

"He looks well," Gilmore said. "He say anything about his time away?"

"Not much. Just that he was enjoying himself."

"That's good. Anything about where he settled?"

"A farm," my father said. "Milking cows, feeding chickens, all that. Raised corn." My father cracked open another bottle, took a sip. "Can't picture him doing it, but he's healthy, and that's what matters."

"You don't think he's back simply to get into trouble, do you?"

"No, I don't, Gilmore."

"Good, that's good to know. But there's something about home that brings it out in him again, huh?"

"I don't think so."

"All right, then. But I wish you hadn't called him." Gilmore sounded wistful. "I wish you would've let him go."

"I did," my father said, "but his brother needed him."

"Collie's going to get him involved in something bad."

"Collie's gotten us all involved in something bad already. Terry's just doing right by his family."

I got the sense that they both knew I was listening. I kept waiting for

Gilmore to mention my taking the files and the incident at the Elbow Room.

My mother came out onto the porch to ask them if they wanted anything to eat. She didn't notice me there in the dark corner of the kitchen. I felt like a kid again, playing a child's game, hiding from the grown-ups and having difficulty understanding their intentions. Mal came in and got himself some leftover fried chicken, nodded to me, then went off to eat in front of the television.

Gilmore and my father continued talking about small somethings and next-to-nothings. Finally I heard Gilmore stand and move to the porch steps.

"You have a good evening, Pinsch."

"You too."

"Thanks again for the photos."

My father kept up the geniality, but his voice sharpened the smallest degree. "Don't mention it. Drive safe now."

I got up and glanced out the window. Gilmore got into his car and waved. I was surprised to see my father lift his hand in response. After Gilmore drove off down the street, my old man stepped into the house. He immediately turned his head to where I sat. I asked, "What photos?"

"You shouldn't have been listening, Terry."

"You knew I was here. You wanted me to listen, Dad." We stood in the shadows and faced each other. "What photos did you steal for him?"

"I didn't steal any." My old man sounded a little strained, maybe a little embarrassed. That worried me worse than almost anything that had happened so far. "I took some of his kids."

"You staked out his ex-wife's house?"

"It's his house."

He opened the fridge, drew out another beer but didn't open it. The refrigerator light showed me a hint of his hidden pain. "Why would you do that? What's he got on us?"

"Nothing. I did it because I know what it's like for a man to lose his family. You think I wouldn't have asked someone to take pictures of you on your ranch if I could've? Or Collie, even now?"

Mal walked in and deposited the chicken bones in the garbage. My father followed him into the living room. I moved to the kitchen table and continued to sit in the dark, wondering something I had never wondered before. I wondered if my father was lying to me.

The house stank of boiled cabbage and chicken grease. I headed for my room and made it halfway up the stairs before I heard the phone ring. My mother answered and my belly tightened. She moved to the bottom of the steps and saw me there, held the phone out toward me with a slightly apprehensive expression, the same kind she wore when I was in junior high and some girl called the house. "For you."

I was tired. I felt feverish. The stink was killing me. "Who?"

"Take it."

It was my uncle Grey. He asked, "So, you busy?"

I hadn't spoken to him in half a decade but he sounded like we'd shared an espresso twenty minutes ago.

I didn't know how to answer. "Not really."

"You hungry? Meet me at Cirque d'Outre. Nine o'clock."

"Cirque d'Outre? The hell is that?"

"Torchy's."

Torchy's was our in-joke for a restaurant down on the water in Glen Cove. Since the fifties it had been owned by various arms of the syndicate, changing hands every few years. The wiseguys insured it up the wazoo, opened it as a high-class establishment, brought in the yacht and sailboat crowd, and slowly skimmed off the top until they were so far in the red that they had to torch the place. It had been built up and burned down again under four names that I was aware of.

"How soon until the next fire?" I asked.

"A few months at least. You don't have to worry about getting your toes roasted, you know those boys have never picked up a murder rap off a firebug scheme."

I wanted to talk to Grey. I missed his action, his energy. He was already lightening the load I felt. "I'm not dressed for it."

"So put on some nice clothes."

"I don't have any nice clothes that fit anymore."

"You can raid my closet."

"I don't think I'm in the mood for a big night."

"What big night? A chance to sit and relax. Break bread. Have a nice meal. Talk with a beautiful woman."

"What woman?"

"You've been home for days and I haven't seen you yet. Enough with the dodging out the back door. Nine o'clock sharp, right?"

"Sure." I hung up.

My mother wafted in close, sponging down an already clean table. She kept her back to me. That meant she had something to say that she didn't want to say but would eventually get around to if I stood where I was long enough. I hung back and waited.

She said, "Watch out for him."

She spoke with almost no inflection. I couldn't tell if she meant I should watch out *for* him or watch out for *him*. She didn't look at me. I slid aside and she raised her chin. I tried to read her face and saw almost nothing there now. "What do you mean?"

"He's been going out nights. More and more. And not just with the ladies. I think he's working on some kind of scam."

"This is news?"

"It worries me."

My mother had become a nervous woman, with good cause. Collie's arrest, my abandonment, having to care for Gramp, Dale blossoming into a young woman and all the problems that presented. Now the chance that Mal and Grey were both getting ill. She was the strongest of us.

"What kind of scam?" I asked.

"I don't know. But he gets that look in his eye like whenever one of you Rands is working a racket."

"You're a Rand too."

"You *male* Rands," she said. "You *born* Rands."

"I'll see if I can find anything out. It seems like he's set up a double date for us tonight."

She went to the sink. It was empty. There were some dishes on the drainboard drying. She looked like she wanted to keep busy. Her hand went to a clean glass and she put it in the cupboard. Then she moved it to the left. Then to the right. Then she closed the door and looked at another glass in the drainboard.

"Ma, it'll be okay," I said.

"He'll be with that pretty reporter."

"He's probably just diverting her attention."

"No, he's trying to hold on to his youth with that one. He likes how interested she is in him."

"That's a bad thing?"

"Yes, because she's more interested in the story. That's why he's bringing you there, really. You're part of it. She'll have questions."

"I know how to handle myself."

"I know you do."

She turned and looked at me, and a charge passed through the air between us. She was trying to shield and guard me through her own force of will. Her hands wandered to my collar, then my throat, and then she placed both palms firmly on my cheeks and kind of smooshed me. My lips pursed like a fish and she gave me a quick kiss. Then she ruffled my hair like I was six years old and left me alone with my own trepidation.

I took a shower and then checked Grey's room. He was a clothes horse. He had at least twenty tailored suits in his closet. I found a classic white shirt and black suit combo that fit almost perfectly. When I shot my cuffs I looked like any other Rat Pack wannabe circa 1962.

He had a separate cabinet for ties. There were hundreds. I didn't see the point. After you got through about twenty, they all started to look alike. He had a real fetish. Or maybe his various women all gave him the same Christmas gift each year. I found a thin black silk one and grabbed a pair of shoes that pinched my heels only a little.

I checked myself. Flo had been right. I did look a little like Grey.

He'd stand in the mirror when I was a kid and I'd watch the slow and significant ritual of his grooming. The way he'd use two wooden brushes, one in each hand, to style his hair. Slapped aftershave to his cheeks and massaged his skin, always giving himself a few chucks under the chin right before he finished. Then he'd dab himself with cologne at the hollow of his throat. He'd have a suit already laid out on the bed but would often try on five or six shirts, sometimes all the same color, before he made his choice. He'd hold up ties against his chest and check his reflection from different angles, in different lighting. When he was done I'd be fascinated with the intricacies of tying a double Windsor knot. It was like a stage performance. He'd catch my eye in the mirror and say, "The clothes don't make the man, the man makes the clothes. But they have to be the *right* clothes and the *right* man."

Headlights washed against the window. I pulled back the curtain and spotted Dale and Butch sitting in his Chevy, parked at the curb. They were arguing, their faces animated in the harsh dashboard light. I went to my room, pulled out the butterfly knife, and left it on her nightstand.

I walked downstairs and stood at the front door. I looked down at myself dressed in my uncle's clothes, on my way to a date I didn't want to go on, and abruptly felt like a moron. I should be helping Dale. I should be preparing myself to tell Collie to go fuck himself. The list went on. I should be making sure that Danny Thompson wasn't still plotting to pull forty grand out of Mal's ass. I should either be figuring out what to say to Kimmy and Chub or I should let it go. I had to watch out for Fingers and Higgins. Sweat broke out on my upper lip. Maybe Gilmore was right. Maybe my coming home had only stirred up all this trouble. And instead of fixing it, here I was playing dress-up.

My father came up behind me, gestured with his chin at the muscle car, and said, "Your mother right about him?"

"Yes. He's a bank-heister wannabe."

Two, three beats went by, then he let out a disgusted grunt. "So that's why he gravitated toward her."

I didn't have to say it. He said it for me.

"Or her to him."

"Yeah."

"Won't be able to stop her from seeing the little shithead."

"No, probably not."

The rest of the equation passed between us silently. Someone might have to convince him to stop seeing her.

I started to undo my tie. My old man put a hand on my arm and said, "Hey, no. Go have a night out."

"Dad, I should be—"

"You should be out having a good time with Grey. He invited you. You said yes, right? So go. The reporter is cute. You can field her questions. And she'll have a cute friend. What's so wrong with that?"

Maybe nothing. I took the parkway up to 25A and drove down to the sound. The party boats coasted in on moonlit water as calm as a sheet of glass. They docked behind Torchy's, and wealthy couples strolled across the massive deck, arm in arm, all pearls and five-thousand-dollar Italian fashion. A ten-piece band led by a young Dino look-alike played fifties crooner tunes. I was twenty minutes early. Grey would already be inside with his date and her friend. They'd be at the bar and he'd be regaling them with stories and letting them drink in his beauty. I let him do his thing and parked on the street for a while, listening to "Till There Was You" and "More" and "A Blossom Fell." Then I drove in and let the valet take my car.

Inside, the place wasn't quite as different as I'd been expecting. But a lot of ritzy restaurants right on the water had the same feel. Large windows so you could watch the party boats coming, an emphasis on seafaring decor that you really couldn't get away from. Ocean-blue walls, portraits and ancient photos of whalers, framed centuries-old maps of Long Island, seascape oil paintings. This one had a three-tiered setup with a lot of mirrored and well-lit staircases, like they expected Fred Astaire and Ginger Rogers to put on a show.

The host wore a black suit that was only a touch more retro than mine. He asked for the name of my party and I told him.

We got two steps toward the table when Grey appeared at the foot of the bottom staircase, slick and handsome with all the cool and style in the world, owning everyone and everything around him, including me.

"There's the boy," my uncle said.

He was sixty-two and looked ten years younger. He wore dashing and debonair the way other men wore desperation. I could smell his moisturizer, exfoliants, veggie conditioners, and skin toners. His eyebrows had been trimmed. He was holding a glass of Glenlivet, his favorite liquor. With his free arm he pulled me into a tight clinch and kissed my forehead.

"It's good to see you, Terrier. You know I should break your ass for dodging us the past few days."

I hadn't seen him in five years and couldn't think of a thing I wanted to say to him. I clenched him back and my head felt emptier than it had been since the ranch. I felt protected and fortified. Hugging him was like hugging my father, who never hugged anyone. Grey clapped me on the back and I did the same to him. He shot me a smile and I returned it.

"Whatever's been on your mind, let it go for the night," he said. "All the same shit will be waiting for you when you come back to it. But for now let's get soused in style."

I stalled and held back a step as he turned for the dazzling staircase. Maybe I did have questions after all. They started buzzing me all at once. I wanted to know what kind of game Grey was running on the pretty newscaster and why he hadn't kept her out of the family's hair. I needed some perspective on what my parents had endured. I wanted to ask if he'd been to the doctor like Mal and how far the disease had progressed. He shouldn't be drinking, that much was obvious. But I knew he wouldn't stop, it was too much a part of who he was. Grey might not answer. He might freeze me out for ruining his night. But of all the Rands he was the one who'd learned to chatter the best. Usually just to play the ladies, but I thought if anyone might shoot the heavy breeze with me, it was Grey.

As we walked up the steps he said, "You like older women, right?"

"What?"

His chuckle broke deep in his chest. "Sure you do."

"Look, I just wanted to—"

"They're worldly. They're self-affirming. They know their own needs, their likes and dislikes, and they aren't afraid to share them with you. Don't be put off."

"Is this about infiltration?" I asked.

"If you're lucky." He sipped his drink. "The twentysomethings, even the thirtysomethings, are usually still trying to figure themselves out, and they think daytime television and therapy and *Redbook* quizzes are the way to do it. The forty-year-olds, they're not called cougars for nothing."

"Grey, the hell are you talking about?"

He looked me up and down. "You chose a nice suit. Wrong tie for it, but you did pretty good."

We walked to the top tier and he led me to a table at the far corner. I supposed they were the best seats in the place, looking down on everyone else, with the best view of the sound. You could see clear to Westchester, the lights of the party boats bright and inviting.

The pretty blond newscaster was sitting there with another woman, those azure eyes full of eager delight. A soft scent of citrus danced along with her, tangling with Grey's cucumber-and-aloe deep pore cleanser.

I glanced at Grey but he was giving her the sloe eye. I wondered if she had her tape recorder running in her purse.

Like I'd done yesterday morning when she and her news crew accosted me, I held my chin up.

Grey either didn't notice my discomfort or didn't care. "Terry, this is Victoria Jensen. Vicky. I believe you've already met."

She held her hand out and smiled brilliantly at me. "If it's not the Freddy's Fix-It guy."

I did my best to smile back but I knew I wasn't making it. She let out a warm laugh that had probably driven a dozen men over the edge. "That's me."

"Terrier, I'm glad we can finally say hello."

I took her hand. She was looking right through me. "My brother is scheduled for execution in ten days. Do you still want to know what I think of that? And if I have a message for the families of his victims?"

"I was doing my job."

Grey cleared his throat. "Let's keep it light for the night, shall we?"

Maybe it was he who'd been played. I thought perhaps she'd maneuvered him into asking me along tonight, but then I realized—she was looking through me, all right, but it was only because she was eyeing him with that perfectly loving gaze. I decided no, not her, the other one.

The friend. I gave her my full attention.

Grey said, "And this lovely lady is Eve Drayton."

I nodded. "Another reporter."

"We prefer the term *journalist,*" Eve said.

She didn't stand. She offered me her hand and I took it. She was on the north side of forty and still quite captivating. Twenty-five years ago she'd been a beautiful teen but had settled into a well-aged attractiveness. Deeply black hair framed her face, with a few strands of silver here and there. There was a bold assurance and natural radiance in her eyes. She was dressed in a classy black dress that hugged her curves but didn't stifle.

She openly studied my face and body. Her lips tilted into the barest self-satisfied grin. I sensed a sharp intellect at work, biding its time, already covering the angles. Despite myself I stood a little straighter.

"How do you do, Terrier," she said.

"Hello, Miss Drayton," I said.

"Please, no formalities on such a lovely night. Call me Eve."

There was something about her I liked, and that spooked me. Maybe it was the attention. Or just standing here in clothes that weren't my own. I looked over at my uncle. He was canoodling with Vicky. Perhaps Grey did have real feelings for her. You could never figure out someone like him. He always switched up the game.

The waiter came around to take our drink orders. He was a small, limber guy with a lot of pep in his stride. I thought he had to be in shape in order to run up and down all those stairs so many times in a night. Grey ordered me a Glenlivet. I hated the taste of it, but for some reason we were clearly trying to make an impression. He jumped the gun and ordered fresh lobster all around.

The waiter asked, "Would you like to come downstairs and choose your own from our tank?"

Grey said, "Only if you install an elevator."

Vicky kept a hand on Grey at all times. He didn't seem to mind. Before my arrival she'd been in the middle of a story, and now she continued. It was about a celebrity actor she'd interviewed out in the Hamptons only minutes before the guy's wife backed over the mayor's dog. It wasn't much of a story. The mayor had screamed, the dog had been crippled, and the actor and his wife had taken off and caused a six-car pileup in Bridgehampton.

Grey gave her a loving stare. He gave every woman a loving stare. He packed his gaze with a sweet longing and a casual indulgence. It was natural to him. The world came easily to Grey. He knew how to have fun.

I wanted to know what information was being passed on in the sugary words he whispered into swooning women's ears. Was he giving away family secrets? Was he doing it and forgetting that it had been done?

The drinks arrived. I sipped while Vicky laughed. It was a lush and bratty giggle that made my teeth ache.

"She left out the most significant part," Eve said, like a mother trying to correct a child's mistold joke. "The mayor's dog, faithful Banjo, wound up being featured in a children's movie the next summer. Banjo has a little wagon now for his hind legs. The movie grossed three times what the actor's next film made, and he's still doing community service for his role in the traffic accident. He puts in ten hours a week at a no-kill shelter."

Maybe it was a true story. We all laughed like it was. I hadn't laughed in a long time and it felt good. Eve smiled pleasantly at me. Vicky and Grey went into a huddle. She pointed across his lap at the water and Grey said, "It's Westchester, sweetie, not Jersey."

They were being capricious, acting giddy, the kind of playfulness that would've drawn attention if we hadn't been at the top of the restaurant. They whispered together.

I finished my drink. I wondered if it would be easier to phone the host and tell him to send up another.

"Grey's told us that you've been away from home for a while," Eve said to me.

She'd checked into the family. She knew I'd been gone. But she tried to personalize the fact. I wondered if it was a reporter move or if she was just being polite. "I have."

"We've kept up with the Rands in a professional capacity. But I must confess I don't know much about you."

"But I bet you've checked my police jacket," I said.

"Yes, I admit I have," she said, grinning, which brought the dimples out. "You're not so bad."

"So far as you know."

"Can I get a few words from you on record about your brother?"

"No," I said. "Sorry."

It was a knee-jerk rebuke. I knew she'd work on me for the story. It was her job. I tried not to hold it against her. I still felt tight and guarded, but I liked her lips and I kept staring. I felt strong but foolish.

"I understand," she said.

I wondered if she really did. I wondered if anyone could understand the conflict I felt over Collie, and how much a part of me wanted to rant about it, and how the rest of me would be mute forever. "Do you?"

She sipped her drink. "I think so. Most people enjoy talking about themselves and telling us their stories. Whether they're just cultural filler or something deeper, more relevant on a personal or even social level, they want to share their tales." She leaned back in her seat, but she held me with her acute focus. "It's only the tragic cases where people prefer to say nothing. They're too overwhelmed."

"And always will be."

She gave the slightest, most feminine of shrugs. "Perhaps."

She had watchful, intense eyes. I liked the way she looked at me. "You've visited your brother in prison," she said.

At least we weren't going to have the usual so-tell-me-about-yourself kind of conversation. In one way I was glad for that. In another I thought, When he's dead, will they stop wanting to know about him?

"Yes," I told her.

"Twice. I'm curious as to what he had to say to you."

"The same thing he's been saying for five years. Mostly. He now states he didn't murder Becky Clarke."

I didn't know why I told her. I turned and looked out the window. I thought that maybe I should run again. I'd promised not to, but since when did I keep promises? North this time, somewhere it was cold and white. Maybe I'd just picked the wrong direction the first time.

She touched my wrist and I turned back. She smiled, dropped her gaze. That bothered me. She said, "He never admitted to it."

"But now he flat out denies it."

When she glanced back up at me, she tried to give off an air that she knew all my secrets. "And you don't believe him."

"I don't believe much of what I hear."

She interviewed me without making it seem like I was being questioned. She made flat statements that filled in for interrogatives. She had a well-practiced rhythm to her cross-examination. It was subtle and she tried to up the ante by being even more indirectly flirtatious. It wasn't an act. It was just the way she came at life, unable to separate herself from the job. Few people could. She put three fingers on my wrist, the same way Collie's wife, Lin, had. Where Lin was almost a will-o'-the-wisp, Eve put weight and energy into the touch.

"Have you met his wife?" she asked.

"Yes."

Grey perked up and snapped out of his lovers' huddle. His cheeks were pink from all his kissy business with Vicky. "What's this now?"

"He married a pen pal in prison a year ago," I said.

"Your father never said anything."

"My parents didn't know. I met her this afternoon."

"And what's she like?" Grey asked. He appeared genuinely interested. "Or do I really need to ask?"

"Not what I expected," I told him. She hadn't been, but I only realized it now. All of the anger I'd felt had faded, and I replayed my conversation with Lin.

"What did you make of her?" Eve asked.

"I'm still not certain."

Three waiters brought the dinners up, along with another round of drinks. They set a lobster in front of me still in its shell and provided a nutcracker and bib. Vicky put hers on and tore in. Eve crossed her legs and bumped my leg with her heel. It gave me more of a thrill than I would've thought.

Grey sipped and sat back, clinking ice cubes. "All the worst killers have their fan clubs. The ones who want to know what it's like. Who get excited from the prospect of writing to or meeting with or, Christ, actually marrying someone who's crossed that line."

"I don't believe she's like that," I said. My voice sounded strange to me because just a couple of hours ago I had been convinced that she was.

"Either that or they want the gratification of bringing another one into Jesus's fold. They want to prove that nobody is beyond redemption. They weep and praise God and think they're saints for putting time in on lost causes."

"She's not like that either. She said Collie was irredeemable."

"I really hope she doesn't start showing up for the holidays."

"I met her once," Eve said. "She came down to the television station, trying to prove he was innocent of the Rebecca Clarke murder."

Vicky touched the back of Grey's hand, as if she had to soothe him due to the nature of the conversation. Her fingers were dappled with a sheen of butter sauce. "That's right. We let her talk on camera for a while but she made some wild accusations. She believes another killer is loose and the police aren't investigating properly."

Grey caught my eye and said, "Sounds like a ruse to throw off the scent at this stage of the game." His face clouded. He slowly dug into the lobster, chewed it as if he refused to let anything ruin his night. He had a staunch capacity for pleasure.

"He admits the others, just not that one," I said.

"It's a new game he's running. You don't wait years to tell someone you're innocent of murder."

"He doesn't claim to be innocent of murder. Just that one."

His voice was beginning to thicken with alcohol. "It doesn't matter. They'd have to retry his entire case. Who knows, maybe it's what he was after all this time. I didn't think he had it in him, the patience to do it this way, but it's a nice maneuver, if that's what he's after. A hell of a gambit. I give him a lot of credit for holding off until the last week. Eat, Terry. You're too thin."

"He looks good," Vicky said.

"Yes, he does," Eve agreed, and the dimples flashed again.

I ate without enjoyment and without putting the stupid bib on. Grey kept things lively and the women responded. The conversation shifted to other news topics that I hadn't been following. Eve asked about my tan and I told her about working on a ranch. I didn't know why. Maybe she was right and everyone wanted to tell their own story, so long as it wasn't laced with tragedy. My life out west had been boring but not tragic. I mentioned the one time I tried to break a bronc and wound up with a concussion. They all laughed and eventually so did I. Once the table was cleared, Grey and Vicky decided to go for a stroll on the deck and listen to the band. I could hear them playing "Carolina Moon."

"Back in a few minutes," Grey said. He didn't wink but it felt like he had. He thought he was doing me a favor. I turned to Eve. The window behind me vibrated. The breeze was picking up. It was about to rain again.

Her purse was carefully propped against her hip, slightly open. I suspected a digital recorder. Reporters wanted a statement one way or another, but it didn't faze me. I was glad that she put her job first and foremost. It clarified things. I wasn't ready for a real double date. I couldn't imagine trying to begin a relationship and making the small talk that led to enduring times.

"I've been flirting with you all night," Eve said. "You don't seem to enjoy talking much. Or is it that you just don't enjoy talking to me?"

"To any reporter or recording device."

She lifted her purse, opened it, and withdrew a miniature recorder. "It's not on. I'm eager for a story, but not to the point of deception."

"Some journalists play a low game."

"Yes, they do. But put it in perspective. Are they lower than the games a family of professional thieves plays?"

I went to finish off my drink and it was already empty. "Are you asking my opinion?"

Her grin eased into an expressive smile. I wondered how many stories she'd gotten out of men who never wanted to say a damn thing. "I bet if this wasn't already turned off, you would've cased my house and stolen it while I was in the shower."

"I would've waited until you were asleep."

"I see. Well, if that's the case, let me save us both some embarrassment and I'll tell you now that I sleep in the raw."

It made me laugh. She wasn't flirting so much as she was trying to break through my hard shell, and I knew it. "I certainly appreciate your concern for my emotional well-being."

There was a real affection in her expression, the frown lines smoothing, her face opening. But her fertile eyes were still trying to pin me down. "You were going to be the centerpiece of my report."

"We'll both survive the letdown. So will your viewers. You were bound to bore the hell out of them anyway."

The tension between us thrashed and built and lessened like the sound waters. "People can't understand your brother. What he's done is too hideous. But you, they'll sympathize with you. They'll identify with you."

"Why would they want to? Because I'm not so bad? Or because I'm not as bad as him? He's going to be dead in a little more than a week.

He'll be forgotten two days after he's in the ground. There are better stories for you to chase."

"That's a wonderfully honest response."

"They've all been honest," I said. "They just haven't been what you wanted, sadly."

She ran a hand through her hair, and the silver strands caught the light a little more brightly. She turned her face away for a moment and something in her strong profile seemed to call to me. The set of her lips or the distinct arc of her jaw.

Grey and Vicky returned. They were both flushed, their faces streaked with sweat. Grey was an amazing dancer. He'd tried to teach me over the years, but I had no rhythm. He used to say, "No woman will ever take you seriously if you can't lead or keep up with her on the dance floor."

The waiter appeared and presented Grey with the dessert menu. He ordered seven or eight items, more than we could eat, and said that we would share. We moved over to white wine. The chatter became even more casual. It wafted past me and I responded adequately and had no idea what I was saying. Eve spoke of her daughter, who was training to be a vet technician. She took out her phone and showed us photos that her daughter had sent her of a litter of newborn Rottweilers. Grey and I chuckled and talked about how my father had boosted JFK from a puppy mill he'd accidentally broken into. It was, to my knowledge, the one and only time my old man had ever called the cops.

The chocolate layer cakes and cheesecakes and pie à la mode arrived. We ate from one another's dishes. Eve fed me forkfuls of icing. She leaned in a little farther. She continued her sweet yet powerful assault on my will.

I waited for Grey to use the men's room. When he excused himself I gave it a ten count and then pushed away from the table.

"Excuse me, ladies, I need to use the house phone."

"You can borrow my cell," Vicky said.

I stood. "Okay, I lied. I want to talk to my uncle about you two."

"Stay here and ask us instead," Eve said.

"Sure," Vicky concurred. "We'll tell you anything you like."

I grinned and turned away and headed for the men's room.

Grey was in a stall. There was a towel guy who looked like he'd been put together from pieces of driftwood washed up in the Bay Shore marina. He could've been anywhere from forty to eighty, his rough-hewn skin colorless, his face pudgy and soggy from years of alcohol abuse. He glanced up at me as I entered, and his whole life story was in his glazed eyes. Condemned for his sins to sit in the corner of a shitter and hand out towels to rich men.

He nodded to me. "Sir."

"Can you do us a favor and give us a little privacy?" I asked.

"I'm not supposed to leave, sir."

"How about when you need fresh hand towels or more soap or something?"

He cocked a thumb at the stacks of towels, toilet paper, hand creams, soap, and cleaning products behind him. "We have plenty, sir."

He made *sir* sound like *fuck you, shitheel.*

I pulled out my wallet and dished him a fifty. "You just ran out, right? Take ten minutes."

"Certainly. Thank you, sir."

He tipped off his stool and clawed for the door handle, his vision burned out by hours of blinding porcelain-tile reflection.

I stood outside Grey's stall and said, "So what's this all about?"

"I'm busy at the moment, right?"

"I knew you had a thing going with Vicky, but why did you invite me along? Why expose us this way?"

"You like Eve, don't you?" he asked.

"She's sharp. She's insistent. Forceful."

"So why's that bending you out of shape?"

"It's not," I admitted. "But we don't need another pair of eyes on us."

"Ah, she does have beautiful, enchanting eyes." He sounded like he was half in love with her himself. "And since when do you speak for the whole family? You've been back a few days and you're taking over the entire house? You running the show?"

"I didn't mean it like that."

"Eve is a lovely woman. I thought you'd like her."

"I do."

"See how easy that was?"

"But—she wants a story."

"So feed her one."

"That's not what I do."

He sighed. "I'm sorry, Terrier, I'm not sure what it is you do anymore. I thought you might like to come out and enjoy yourself for a night."

Thunder broke over the sound, and the echo picked up such strength on its way to shore that it was like a colossal hammer coming down on the restaurant. The acoustics in the bathroom made it even worse.

"Jesus Christ, what are you doing in there?" I asked. "Giving birth?"

"It would go faster if you'd quit diverting my attention."

"Sorry," I said.

He finished up and unlocked the stall door and spent a long time washing his hands and staring at himself in the mirror. He combed his hair, smoothed down one eyebrow. "You're going to have a good time with her. She's very witty. She's also very creative in bed."

I shook my head. "Oh, Christ, did you really have to tell me that?"

"Go frolic. Have some thrills. Infiltrate. It'll be an agreeable experience. Trust me."

"Stop saying shit like that, Grey."

He laughed and finished duding himself, checked the knot on his tie, and walked out. I followed.

Grey didn't sit again. The bill was on the table. He said, "Are we ready?" He didn't look at the check, just counted off six C-notes and laid them down. I wondered what he thought he was getting for his payout. He didn't need to impress the women. Was he trying to impress me?

He held his hand out to Vicky and helped her put her wrap on. Eve began to put her own jacket on, and I realized there was no reason to be rude and I held it for her while she shrugged her arms in. Then she lightly touched my elbow, squeezed it twice, and then released me. I wondered what my play should be. I wanted to talk with Grey longer. I was worried about his health. I wanted to know if he'd seen a doctor as well. He hadn't had any leafy greens with his dinner. He should be taking fish-oil capsules. Lobster wasn't fish, it was crustacean. I thought maybe it wouldn't count.

"I think Vicky and I are going to walk down to the beach and sit in the moonlight for a while," he told me. "Eve came with me. Do you think that—"

Eve interrupted and said, "It's all right, I can have the host get me a cab."

"Nonsense," Grey said.

"I'd be happy to drive you home," I told her.

"Thank you, Terry, that's very sweet of you."

The valet brought my car up. We got in and I pulled off and drove a little stiffly. I was surprised and a bit uncomfortable that I felt some attraction for her. She didn't put her hand on my thigh. I thought she might. I sort of expected it.

She said, "I live in Head of the Harbor. Just take 25A east."

It was a ritzy area on the North Shore. "I know where it is. Northern State is quicker."

"And more dull. Besides, it'll give us time to talk."

"Sure."

I drove east on 25A. We were going to hit a lot of lights. The traffic was fairly heavy and it grew worse around Huntington when the rain started to come down again. I remembered driving Kimmy down the shore on dark storm-filled nights like this. Eve asked about my youth and I answered honestly, what I could remember. So much of it was always right there on the tip of my tongue, in the front of my mind, and yet so much of it seemed gone forever. I talked about my dad, about climbing drainpipes and jugging safes. There was no inflection in my voice no matter how much I tried to sound lively. Maybe once we got

Collie out of the way it would be different. Or we'd be done. I turned on the radio and Eve shut it off. I glanced at her and she smiled. I thought she would smile no matter what I might say or do.

"You want to discuss him," she said.

I turned and looked at her face in silhouette. "Christ, no."

"I think you do. It seems to be what matters most to you right now. That much is obvious, Terry." Her voice rose a bit with a tinge of anger. I wasn't sure if it was for me or Collie. "You're thinking about it right now. Anybody can see the pressure you're under."

"He's not what matters most."

"Then what does? I'd like to hear."

I thought I might talk about Kimmy and Scooter. I thought about telling her to interview Cara Clarke again, because there was a girl who had a lot of pain to purge.

Eve said, "Why did you feel the need to visit him a second time?"

It had to come back to my brother. "He asked me to."

"And that was all you needed to prompt you."

"Yes, I suppose so."

"Will you see Collie again?"

I turned and snapped, "Who the hell are you to use his name?"

She relaxed and fell back in her seat, opened her purse, drew out a cigarette, and lit up off my car lighter, the way Kimmy used to do. I almost wanted to put my arm around her. "You're protective of him."

"I just don't like to hear his name."

She was in shadows, the smoke catching the light and drifting across my face. "Did he tell you why he killed those eight people?"

I thought, Seven. He says it was only seven. But I don't know. How the hell am I supposed to know?

Already there were several accidents on the road. Late dark night, wet country roads, you had vehicles wiping out into one another like they were playing bumper cars. Cops in their rain gear directed traffic. The flares left flaming streaks across my vision as we passed by.

"That's not how this is going to work," I said.

"What do you mean?"

"You're not going to get anything out of me because I have nothing to give, Eve."

By the burning red glare I watched as she nibbled at her bottom lip with her front teeth, held on for an instant, then slowly let out a small sound that wasn't quite a sigh. "I want your perspective."

"I can't give that either," I said. "I'm too close. What do you really expect me to say? I have no more insight into Collie than anybody else does. I'm at even more of a loss, right? Because I never expected this to have ever happened. So I'm worthless to you. But you're not to me."

She kicked off her shoes, shifted in her seat, got more relaxed. I turned the heater up and opened the vent onto the floor so she wouldn't get cold.

"Okay," she said. "I'll listen. What can I help you with?"

"Did you interview the families?" I asked.

"The victims' families? Yes, of course."

"All of them?"

"Yes."

"Anything to connect them?"

"The police say no."

"I know what the police say, Eve. What do you say?"

"I say no."

The same images scuttled through my head. The little girl, twisting away from the barrel of his gun. The old woman, meeting my brother on the sidewalk, passing him without a word, fearful of such a large man, and Collie spinning the full force of his strength on her with his fists. Her breathless grunts beneath the awful sounds of her bones snapping, screams choked in the center of her flailed chest. I held on to the steering wheel at ten and two, a conscientious driver. I was worried that the images were already losing some of their power over me. Another accident was coming up. I rolled down my window partway and the rain sluiced in and wet the side of my face.

"Give me something I can use," I said.

"To what end?"

"To the only end, the very end. I need to know if he did them all or not."

She drew her knees up and angled closer to me. Her breath warmed my neck. "I think you should just accept that he's guilty of killing them all. It would be easier for you."

"Maybe, but I'm not sure."

"Your father is still robbing houses," she said.

It took me so off guard that I nearly missed a bend in the road. Shining reflectors appeared across the dark expanse of a guardrail. I eased my foot off the gas and maneuvered into a tight turn. "How do you know?"

"He was detained three months ago for breaking in to a home."

"Whose home?" I asked, and my voice was sharper than I intended.

She looked aside at the wet empty woods flashing past as if she had to think hard to come up with the name. She was deciding whether to tell me or squeeze me for another angle at the story. Our attraction for each other was secondary to a night of murder and the continuing fallout. She glanced at the side of my face. I turned and she read something in my eyes, despite having nothing more than the dashboard light to read them by.

"The Wright family. Do you know them?"

I didn't let my expression change. My scalp prickled with sweat, and a sliver of ice worked itself into the small of my back. My father had crept Chub and Kimmy's house. I imagined him parking in the same spot where I had parked in front of their place. Watching them as I had watched. Seeing Scooter race by on the front lawn. My old man that close to her. I watched him popping out a screen window and sliding through, wandering the house in the darkness while Kimmy and Chub slept. Or made love. My old man listening. The fuck was going on?

"You said detained. He wasn't arrested?"

"No, Terry. But it's on record."

Had Gilmore shown up to talk Kimmy or Chub out of pressing charges? Had she or Chub simply shown mercy? I wondered at the fear in her face, awakening in the night to see her ex-boyfriend's father at the foot of her bed. My hands tightened on the steering wheel, and a muscle spasm made me tug right, then left, the tires chirping on the wet road.

"Who was the cop on scene?" I asked.

Eve reached for my knee in a show of concern. The rain sprayed my temple. I was driving sharp but fast. I wanted to go faster. I wanted to take the next right and head back home and confront my father. I thought, This means something, this will paint your old man in a way you have never seen before. My stomach twisted. I'd never been angry at my father, not even when he'd torn my rib through my flesh. But now I was chewing my tongue and tasting blood.

"I don't remember," Eve said. "Is it important? Who are the Wrights?"

"What did he take?"

"Nothing."

"Then he wasn't robbing the house."

"So what else could he have been doing there?"

The stink of burning flares continued to fill my nostrils. I glanced at Eve. She was watching me intensely. She said, "Terry . . . please, slow down." This whole scene might turn up on page three. The way I folded under questioning, how I sweated and barked. My mother would want to break Grey's ass for putting me in this position. My sister would think I was a dunce. Lin would pass word back to Collie that I had been wooed. I didn't know what my father would think. It seemed a little pathetic that I wouldn't know what my father would think.

We got to Head of the Harbor and she directed me along a series of back roads to her isolated neighborhood. She looked at me like she knew I had boosted a lot of TV sets out of houses like these, but it wasn't true. There were too many private security forces and it wasn't worth the risk.

She lived in a beautiful home that wasn't more than five years old but had been built in the Victorian style. Three floors with arched windows set in squared-off bays. The front door was centered in an elaborate porch, and the roof featured gabled ends edged in a decorative carved timber.

"Come inside for a drink," she said.

"I'm not going to tell you anything you can use, Eve. I'm sorry I wasted your evening."

She kissed the edge of my mouth. "You haven't. Not at all." It was prim by any standard of kissing, but there was a controlled heat to it. I turned to her and she thumbed her lipstick off my cheek. She placed a hand on my forehead like she was checking for fever and then leaned in and kissed me again, much more passionately. I didn't entirely return it but I could feel something loosening within me. Our tongues rested against each other for a time. I liked not having to talk. She drew away.

Not everything had to lead back to Collie and death. I could have something of mine. I wanted her. I could have her. There was nothing wrong with it, and I tried to believe it.

"Is there a Mr. Drayton?" I asked.

"Mr. Drayton is shacked up with a twenty-year-old theater-arts major in Miami. He won't be bothering us. Come inside for a nightcap."

I shut off the engine. The pulse in my throat snapped. Kimmy had been on my mind so much that the very idea of sleeping with another woman somehow felt like a betrayal. Eve noted my resistance. She also saw my desire. She brought my lips to hers again. I fell into it and started reaching for her hungrily.

My conflict heated her even more. She liked a little obstinacy. She lifted a knee and swung closer to the driver's seat and ground herself against me. I started to groan. The pictures in my head continued shuffling. I hugged Eve tightly and licked beneath her ear. It made her laugh. I liked the sound of it. Her laughter got louder and poured itself down my throat.

In the dark, when we were about three quarters of the way through the funky stuff, I heard the front door open. I thought maybe Mr. Drayton had returned from Miami a sadder and wiser man. My thief's instincts took over. I extracted myself from Eve and hopped off the bed. I looked at the door. I looked at the window. We were on the first floor and I wondered if I should climb out. I looked for my pants. She caught her breath and turned on the nightstand light.

I thought of Mr. Drayton wearing a bright-yellow shirt and holding a 10-gauge. I pictured Collie slipping through the tight rooms. Someone moved up the hall toward us. I scanned for my pants but couldn't find them.

"Relax, Terry," Eve said. "It's my daughter, Roxie. She works late for an emergency animal clinic."

"Oh yeah." I remembered the photos of the newborn Rottweilers.

"I think I mentioned that she's training as a vet technician."

"That's very . . . professional," I said.

"Yes, she is. Come back to bed."

Roxie's footsteps continued to the door. She knocked quietly and asked, "Mom, you still up?"

"Not now, Rox," Eve said. "We'll talk in the morning, all right?"

"Sure thing. Good night."

"Good night, honey."

Roxie headed up the stairs, and a door on the second floor opened and shut. A stereo turned on in a distant corner of the house, and quiet music made the ceiling thrum.

"Come back to bed," Eve said.

I slid in under the covers and she rolled into my arms. She inspected the black and yellow bruises over my kidneys. "My God, I didn't notice these before. Who've you been tussling with?"

"The cops," I said.

I shouldn't have, but I was still a little miffed at Gilmore and the truth slipped out. She was right. I guess I did want to talk.

"I can do an exposé," she told me, her voice tight and serious. "I started my career investigating a sergeant in Bedford-Stuyvesant who had raided his own evidence locker. Give me the officer's name. I'll visit him with a news crew every day. I can have him walking a beat in Cudahy, Wisconsin, this winter."

"No," I said. "He's a good cop. He's not hurting anyone else."

"How do you know?"

"He and I just had some personal issues. And I might still need him."

"What for?" she asked. "A burglar needing a cop is an odd state of affairs."

"I need him to keep looking into the Rebecca Clarke murder."

"Then you do believe your brother is innocent."

Her body was taut and well muscled, but soft in the appropriate places. She put in a lot of time at the gym. I spotted some oddly pigmented areas at her neck, breasts, and hips that might have been very faint surgery scars. Her breasts were large and didn't sag much. Her belly was trim and tight and slightly freckled. She wore a thin golden chain across her midriff that chimed so faintly while we'd been making love that I thought there might be a cat walking around the place with his tags tinkling. Legs lean, calves well defined as she arched her toes out and her whole body tightened with a yawn.

"Whatever I believe, I don't want to talk about it now," I said.

She ran her hands over my stomach, my chest. "How could you stand it?"

"It was only two sucker-punches."

"No, not that." She kissed my chest. "This."

I thought she meant my scars, but then I realized she was talking about my tattoo. "Yeah, it hurt like a bitch."

"It's so intricate."

There had been a lot to cover. I nodded. She ran a hand through my chest hair like she was petting the head of the hound. She pressed her lips to the dog's eyes, his nose, then licked across the teeth of its open, barking mouth. She laid me back against the set of thick pillows and ran her tongue down from my navel. I started to pant. I took hold of her head and gently guided her lower. She went with it for a moment, then resisted.

"Why are you all named after breeds of dogs?" she asked.

"Why in the hell are you asking that now?"

"I'm curious."

Upstairs, Roxie closed a bathroom door. A fan went on, water ran, and the pipes groaned in the walls. Her phone rang and she answered and immediately began arguing with someone. The rain kept spraying against the windows, like it was being cast off by a woman whirling her wet hair against the glass.

"No one seems to know," I said. "It's just been the way of our family for at least the last four generations."

I brushed her hair back with my fingers. She kissed my inner thigh. She flicked her tongue against my flesh and murmured and giggled. She nipped at me. She turned her face upward at me. I thought, Jesus, she's going to keep me vibrating like a cello string all night long.

"Isn't it degrading?" she asked.

"I thought you liked it," I said.

"Not this. Being named after a dog."

"No. It's my name."

She tried to be ingratiating, whispering cutely the way real lovers do. Upstairs, her daughter was on the verge of yelling and then must've hung up. The pipes kept groaning. Eve made me groan too. "Still, if you're named after an animal, doesn't it make you feel like you should act like an animal?"

I didn't know what she was asking, if it was a risque way of saying I should be more aggressive or if she was going deeper than that, asking if I ever felt the temptation to go mad dog. Let the beast loose.

"Playing timid isn't your strong suit," I said.

"You might be surprised, Terry."

She began to stroke my thighs again. She used her skilled hands to make me sip air. She continued trying to distract me in an effort to make me more pliable. Her eyes were amused and bright.

This time we kept the light on. Afterward, she walked naked to the kitchen, got me a beer, poured it for me in a tall glass, and snuggled beside me while she sipped two fingers of Glenlivet. I noticed now that she was shaved, oiled, well powdered despite the sweat streaks, and I wondered if it was really for me. Grey had admitted to sleeping with her. I wondered how often and how recently.

I finished the beer. We fell back into bed and went another round, this time much smoother and suppler and maybe even a touch sweeter. I hated drinking scotch, but for some reason I liked the taste of it on her lips.

After, she said, "You're a good man, Terry."

"How would you know?"

"Because I've met a lot of bad ones. I've interviewed them and covered their court cases and done follow-ups through the years. I once visited Manson for an hour-long prime-time special. Five minutes in his presence and I knew we'd never air it. I knew you could see the fear in my face. You're a good man at your heart."

I let out a chuckle. "Because I'm not as nuts as Manson?"

"You don't have to worry about being like your brother."

"Eve—"

"One doesn't have to be very astute to know what's so heavy on your mind. It would happen to any of us. It does happen. It's why people like Dahmer's father write books. They feel a need to understand where that kind of evil comes from."

Evil. It was a word I hadn't used in connection with Collie yet. He was a mass-murdering prick, but I hadn't thought beyond the act itself to imagine him as truly evil.

"This is some kind of fucked-up pillow talk," I said.

"I was just trying to put you at ease."

"I think falling asleep in each other's arms would be more helpful."

Eve held me tightly and said, "Say no more."

She dropped off to sleep first. I thought about Chub unwinding himself from Kimmy and sneaking back to his garage to pore over his getaway maps. Checking up on the roadwork conditions, which lanes would be shut down tomorrow, where the detours were. I had to talk to him. I felt myself drifting, Eve's breath glancing off my chin. I started to dream before I was fully asleep.

My sister had been right. I had a head as full of snakes as when I'd left. Now I clung to memories that weren't mine. I couldn't be sure if I was awake or out cold. My stomach burned. The smell of whiskey seemed overwhelming and made me gag. Eve's soft snores pounded at me. I saw hands pulling a sash around a young woman's throat. In her dead eyes I saw my face.

I snapped fully awake with the sense of someone watching me.

I knew the feeling well, probably because my mother liked to watch me sleep. I opened my eyes into slits. It was still dark. I checked Eve and she was sleeping soundly. The door remained shut.

I waited.

Moonlight splayed against the walls, the silver hue blurred by the intermittent rain. I considered that Torchy's was undoubtedly mobbed up. Danny might've gotten word that Grey and I had been out on the town. It could've miffed him. He might want to brace Mal again. He might want to push me for showing up with attitude at the Fifth. I couldn't imagine Danny sending Wes around in the middle of the night, but Wes had admitted there were nastier goings-on that he wasn't a part of. Danny had a lot of worse boys around still trying to make their bones. I hung my hand over the edge of the mattress and felt for my pants. A shadow broke against the moonlight.

Someone was standing at the window, peering in.

I slipped out of bed on a roll and slid my trousers on in a fluid move. The forward momentum carried me across the bedroom. I rushed to the window. There was a patch of glass that the water diverted around, like someone had wiped it down to see inside better and the oil from his fingertips had caused the rain to deflect.

I turned the latch and hefted the window up. The screen stopped me. If I was outside trying to get in, I could pop it loose in half a second. But right now I was so keyed up that I couldn't get it to unlock from the track.

Eve woke and said, "What is it? What are you doing?"

The sound of someone running across the wet lawn made my heart hammer, and I finally just put my shoulder to the jamb and bulled my way through the screen. The metal track squealed and the molding cracked like a gun going off. I took a header into the bushes and lurched across a lawn gnome that practically impaled me. I tasted dirt. I came up in a crouch and wasn't sure which way to go. I didn't have my bearings yet.

Eve hadn't put on the outside light, and the streetlamp didn't provide much illumination. I spit out blades of grass.

An engine started up the block. Trying not to slip in the mud, I loped in that direction, but it was already too late. A car pulled away from the curb a couple of houses away. No headlights, no shouting, and no mad screeching as he turned the corner. I couldn't tell the make or model. Whoever it was accelerated smoothly and popped on the lights just as he faded from my sight.

I ran to my car but it was a lost cause. Eve's porch light came on.

She stepped out onto the veranda, dressed in a robe, and hugged herself as I walked back to her. She gave me a perplexed grin. "I've had guys try to skip out before breakfast, but you even left your shoes—" Then she caught my expression. "What is it? What was it?"

"Someone was staring through the bedroom window at us."

"Who?"

"I didn't get a good look."

She was nervous but tried to play it off. "Well, we were certainly worth watching, especially during the second go-around, but—"

I put my arms around her. "It's okay, Eve."

"No, it's not. I'm actually spooked. Come inside."

We walked back into the bedroom. I reached over the windowsill and pulled the busted screen back up. I'd wrecked it good. "I'm sorry."

"Oh, who cares about that. Are you all right?"

"Yeah."

She stared over my shoulder at the dark front yard. "What did you see?"

"Just a shadow."

At the door was a knock. "Mom?"

"It's all right, Rox."

"What's all the noise?"

"Nothing, dear."

Roxie huffed in agitation. "You're sure?"

"Go talk to her," I told Eve.

She left the bedroom and spoke with Roxie for a few minutes, then returned. I asked, "You have any jealous boyfriends that might be hanging about?"

"None."

"Your daughter have any dirty-minded beaux? I heard her arguing on the phone."

"She's twenty and it's her first serious boyfriend. They're discovering all the joys and pains. Perhaps it was one of your fellow unsavory types?"

Leg-breaking I could understand. But not window-peeking.

Someone had simply been watching Eve and me sleeping.

"I don't know," I said, my pulse driving harder through my throat, my scars burning as I thought about my father creeping houses again, standing at the bottom of Kimmy's bed, watching her, moving silently to Scooter's room, looking down at the baby sleeping in her crib.

I got dressed. Eve offered me an early breakfast but I declined. I held her for a while and we kissed deeply, but I think we both knew this was a one-night venture. We didn't promise any further rendezvous.

"Take care of yourself," she told me.

"I'm not the one cracking beers with Manson," I said. She laughed and I pressed my lips to her forehead and cut out.

I caught a few hours' sleep at home. I woke up late, almost nine A.M. I showered and came downstairs feeling refreshed but a little out of sorts. A lot had happened yesterday and I hadn't had any time to sort through it.

My mother was cleaning dishes. All she seemed to do was cook and clean dishes and stuff Old Shep with cereal. She was making a big breakfast for the family but no one was around. She said, "Sit. In ten minutes I'll have pancakes and scrambled eggs. But no bacon, we're out of bacon."

"Don't bother with it, Ma."

"It's no bother."

"Have you eaten yet?" I asked.

"Of course I have. All I do is eat."

My mother, beautiful as she was, looked tired and too thin to me. The morning light caught in her auburn hair, the red highlights blazing. She gave a soft smile. She was worried about me. She had always worried about me, but now I was back under her roof, within reach. She would share my burden willingly.

"Ma, coffee is good. Leave the—"

"You talk like I need to get to the office, Terrier. As if I have to check my daily organizer first to see if I can fit in making a meal for my son. Sit, drink some milk, eat." She enjoyed waiting on her children. I knew that every time she turned around and looked at the kitchen table, she'd see Collie in his usual place opposite me.

She poured me a glass of milk and stirred pancake batter. I thought, There's plenty of money. They could put Gramp in a home. They could hire a nurse. "Did you have a good time with Grey?"

"Yes," I said, but I'd hesitated a half second too long.

"What happened? Trouble?"

"No. Is he here?"

"No. He stayed out last night."

"He set me up on a double date. That reporter and a journalist friend of hers."

"That Vicky." She nodded and stirred eggs around in one pan with a spatula, then flipped a huge pancake in another. "You'd think he suddenly wanted to be in the limelight, for them to write about us again, after all this time. Maybe he does. It's attention, and he loves attention. Did they give you a hard time, asking questions?"

"Nothing I couldn't handle."

"He should know better."

"He does know better, but I think he genuinely likes her."

"Grey doesn't genuinely like anybody. But she is young, and that's a powerful bouquet to a man like him."

"Who's 'a man like him'?" I asked.

"An older man who can't let go of his own youth, who's preoccupied by the past. He acts like he's twenty. Too much silk and not enough sand."

"Do women like sand?"

"Women *love* sand."

"Well, he's got style anyway."

"He looks foolish running around with dim girls like that Vicky."

I'd never heard her say anything like that before. I drank my milk. My mother finished cooking and set the food down in front of me. She pressed syrup in my direction. She didn't sit but started cleaning up immediately. I wondered about the grandparents I never knew. I tried to imagine what would have happened if my mother had listened to them and stopped seeing my father. She'd be married to a stockbroker and be vacationing every year in Saint-Tropez.

When she'd drained the sink and folded her gloves neatly across the drainboard, I asked, "Why don't you and Dad ever travel?"

"Travel?" The word appeared to be poisonous in her mouth. "What do you mean? Where would we go?"

"I don't know. Anywhere."

"Why would I want to go anywhere?" she asked. It was a genuine question.

"People do. They go on vacation. They visit Europe."

"But what would we do in Europe?"

"I don't know what you would do in Europe, Ma. You'd be a tourist. You'd eat European foods. You'd see the sights of the world. The Coliseum. The Eiffel Tower. Go look at the Rhine."

She pulled a face like I'd just suggested the silliest thing she'd ever heard. Maybe I had. Either way the topic was dead.

She said, "I need you to run to the store for me."

She handed me a list of items she needed. A lot of green leafy vegetables, bottles of vitamins, ginkgo biloba, and fish oil. Plenty of chicken. Turkey burgers. Salmon. A frozen turkey. I knew I should get used to eating this stuff.

She also had listed a lot of munchies. Potato chips, cocktail peanuts, candy, and mint chocolate chip ice cream, which was my favorite. "I don't eat this crap anymore, Ma."

"You're too thin. Here." She tried to shove money into my hand but I refused to take it.

"I've got it, Ma."

"Don't steal the groceries."

"I'm not going to steal groceries."

She squinted at me. "I still have to shop there."

"I'm not going to steal the goddamn groceries."

I drove over to the market. Out in front were those same nickel rides that had been in the strip mall by Wes's place. These I'd ridden myself twenty years ago. A rocket ship that went up and down, beeping with lights blinking. Kids were tugged past by their parents. I flashed on Scooter giggling excitedly, with me cheering her on. I thought of Kimmy and Chub bringing her to the Mother Cabrini Feast. It was a tradition when we were kids, fronted by St. John's Church. A second-rate carnival that still seemed like something special. Chub and I used to warn the rubes away from the worst of the rigged games.

It took me twenty minutes to get everything on my mother's list. I hated boiled cabbage, but I would start eating it. I would have to. I picked up bottles of vitamin A and C and E. Flaxseed. They all helped with memory and cognitive function. I'd have to learn to start taking them.

I paid and carried out the bags. I got to the car and was halfway through loading the groceries in the trunk when I saw Higgins coming for me.

Fingers had been too tight to hire another goon. He really should've sprung for somebody better, like I'd told him.

Higgins had no cool. He'd taken our fracas too personally and his anger made him stupid. He hadn't given his foot time to heal. His face was swollen with bruises, and his lip was badly split. He came gimping along on an intercept course with a Glock held down tight against his leg. His new sunglasses burned like twin camera flashes in the sunlight. There were kids around, families walking to their cars.

He started to raise his gun. He wasn't going to make any kind of a speech or take the time to get off a wiseass tough-guy phrase. He just wanted me iced. I was a little surprised by his single-mindedness.

I did the only thing I could do. I hurled the frozen turkey at him.

It was a huge twenty-five-pounder. It struck him high on the shoulder and I heard his collarbone snap. The pain was so intense he couldn't quite scream. A choked groan stuck in his throat, his mouth open as he tried to suck air through the agony. His arm went dead and he dropped the pistol. I was shocked it didn't go off.

I made it to him in three steps and hooked him twice under the heart, then put a forearm into his face. His glasses broke and flew off. I hadn't noticed before that his eyes were beady and black and too close together.

No wonder he kept them covered. I grabbed the gun and dragged him into the space between my car and the one parked next to me. I reached into his back pocket and came up with his blackjack and put him out.

He'd be unconscious for hours. I stuck him in the passenger seat and grabbed up the dropped groceries. At first I was surprised as hell that no one had seen anything, but then I realized the fight had lasted no more than twenty seconds. I pulled out and drove over to the mall, parked close to the main doors, and started roaming various stores and shops. Within twenty minutes I'd clipped three wallets from daddy fat cats who didn't look the type to ever be intimidated and were bound to make a serious stink.

Higgins was still out cold. I transferred the credit cards, driver's licenses, and cash to his wallet. I wiped my prints off the gun and stuffed it back in his pocket. Then I drove him over to Gilmore's precinct, dumped him at the curb, and split.

The cops wouldn't know what to make of him at first, but they'd hold on to him tight. His record would speak for itself, as would his association with Fingers Brown and the skirted gunrunning allegations. Loaded with fresh charges, they'd sniff around the bowling alley again and Fingers would spook and cut him loose. The only question was whether Fingers was angry enough to take a run at me on his own. I didn't think he had the heart.

I drove home and carried the groceries in. As my mother started unpacking them she said, "This turkey's starting to thaw." She looked up at me in surprise. "Something happened, I can tell by your face. Where've you been? What happened?"

"Nothing happened."

"Your cheeks are flushed."

"I'm fine."

Her face hardened. "I hate when I'm lied to."

I helped her put the groceries away. Everything went in the same place as when I was a kid. That would never change, not in five years, not in fifty. There was something comforting in the familiarity. Another minor symbol of saccharine sentimental value.

"Where is everyone?" I asked.

"Mal and Grey, who knows. Your father's in the garage with his collection."

It stopped me. "What collection?"

She turned and grinned. "Oh, you haven't been introduced to his hobby yet?"

"Dad's got a hobby?"

"He has for some time. Go look at it."

"It?"

"Them. Go ahead. In the garage."

"Am I going to want to see this?" I asked. I didn't know what I thought might be out there, but I had trepidations. My father with a hobby? What might that entail? Stamps? Coins? Empty beer cans from around the world?

The other day I'd worried about him being bored after his retirement. Now I knew he was still doing a little second-story prowling, and not just to keep himself busy. But was there more going on?

"You look scared," my mother said.

"I'm not scared, I just never thought of him as having a hobby."

"It's not porn."

"I didn't think it was porn. And I don't think porn can actually be a hobby either. And it wouldn't scare me."

"I'm just telling you, that's not it," she said.

"Okay."

"Retirement gives people too much time to think. They have to do something to stay busy and focus their attention."

"How about you?" I asked. "What focuses your attention?"

"I take care of the family," she said simply. "I've got an old man inside who needs as much care as a newborn. I've got a teenage daughter dating a creep. Worrying about her is a full-time job on its own. And I have to clean a house three times bigger than we need, because half the space is for loot. I even clean the loot sometimes. It's all junk. We should get rid of it, but it would take as long to dig it out of the house as it took to put in. You know some of the shit that's hidden away? But who knows, there could be a de Kooning or a Pollock stuck in these walls. Those three, they don't want to get rid of any of it, because they think the police are watching. The cops who were chasing all that crap have been dead thirty years. We should have a garage sale and really put some money in the bank."

"I agree," I said.

"Well, when you get out there, try to talk your father into it."

I went out and around to the garage. The side door was ajar. I stepped into the huge work area where my grandfather and his brothers had done most of the woodwork for the house's secret rooms. JFK heard me and clambered to his feet and moseyed over.

I was expecting rebuilt classic cars. My old man hadn't been much of a car thief, but he had taught me how to boost the muscle speedsters of his teenage years. I thought he might be looking to the past and trying to get back in touch with his youth.

It wasn't a car.

My father was spraying glass cleaner and wiping down an enormous display case with six lengthy glass shelves and mini-track interior lighting.

He glanced over his shoulder and said, "Hello, Terry. So what do you think?"

"Well . . . it's not porn."

Inside were figurines. I estimated there to be at least a hundred pieces. Most of them were of Asian men and women and children, pulling rickshaws, feeding barnyard animals, playing with dogs. I didn't find them beautiful. I didn't think them ugly. I forced myself not to frown. I made myself keep my hands at my sides instead of reaching up to scratch my head. My father opened the case and started spraying the inside of the glass door with no-streak cleaner.

I said, "Can I touch them?"

"Sure."

I picked one up. It was hollow and very light. It felt cheap to me. There wasn't a speck of dust on it. I turned it over. I was surprised to see the words "Made in Occupied Japan."

"Why these?" I asked.

"I don't know," my father said. "Gramp had a couple of them around when I was a kid. They caught my attention somehow. I'd snatch one every now and again from some house, kept them in a cache hole in one of the crawl spaces. For the last couple of years I've been hunting through antiques shops. Gives me something to do with myself."

"Why keep them out here? Why not bring them into the house?"

He shrugged. "They're not really for show. They're just for me. I like looking at them. They're something delicate made during a terrible time."

He sounded a little embarrassed, like he expected me to think less of him.

"Tell me about them," I said.

"Nothing too interesting to tell. They were produced by U.S. forces from '45 to around early '52, at the end of the occupation. It was a short production period so these pieces are fairly scarce. The bisque figures are less common than the porcelain, and usually they're of higher quality. You saw the import stamp on the bottom. They were all required to have the 'Made in Occupied Japan' or just 'Occupied Japan' mark."

"How valuable are they?" I asked.

"Depends on the individual piece," he said. "Piano babies can range from twenty-five to a hundred dollars. Toby mugs from, say, ten to maybe eighty-five dollars. There's a couple of shops out in Southampton that really try to gouge you. Salt-and-pepper shakers list for up to maybe forty dollars a pair."

I didn't know what a piano baby or a Toby mug might be, but my father was actually excited to be talking about the figurines, so I let him go on. I'd imagined they must be expensive antiques worth in the thousands. To hear him price them at ten or twenty bucks really stunned me.

He went on about the salt-and-pepper shakers, poodles, boy with begging dog, boy with fish on line, girl holding flower, and how thousands of pieces had been copied in European styles. I wasn't really listening. I was watching him. He looked happy and animated. There wasn't much in the world for him to be buoyant about, so I was glad he had this.

My father was too short to wipe down the top few inches of the case, so I did it for him. When I was finished I stared at my reflection and watched the man behind me. It was the only way I could meet his eyes.

"Dad," I said.

There was something in my voice that warned him. I turned and watched as his shoulders hitched. He cocked his head slightly. I knew his body language like I knew my own. He was setting his resolve, waiting for the pain. I waited too, for the confidence to ask the question. It took time to find it.

"Why did you boost Kimmy's place?"

"I didn't boost it," he said.

"You went there."

"Yes."

"And you were caught."

He almost smiled. "Yeah."

My old man rarely did anything that got under my skin, but that smile did it. I threw down the dust rag. I took a step toward him. My blood surged and I got up close, in his face, thinking, Am I about to hit my father? Is it possible I can do that? If I can do that, then he could watch me making love to a woman through her window.

"You had to have wanted to be caught. You're too good otherwise."

His lips slid into a self-effacing grin. It only masked the truth. "I'm getting old."

"That's not an answer."

"Do you really want one, Terry?" he asked.

"For Christ's sake, yes."

The grin dropped. His eyes filled with emotion. It was something I wasn't quite prepared to see. A quiver of fear went through me and I was suddenly sorry I'd decided to face him at all.

His shoulders slumped again, and he walked to the worktable and sat heavily on the stool there. "I heard Kimmy had a baby. I wanted to see her."

"Why?"

His face tightened. "I've got to explain everything to you?" There was a hint of anger in his voice. When I was a kid, that used to terrify me. Now it was even worse. "You leaving us . . . and Collie about to die . . . it's got me . . . I've been . . . been—"

He couldn't put it into words. He hit the wall. It had been so long since he'd opened up about anything that I could see the confusion and fear in his expression as he tried to talk. His eyes shifted back to his figurines as if they helped to ground him.

I wanted to put a hand on his shoulder, perhaps even hug him. But that would be too much. It would overpower him. It would suffocate him. I waited in silence with him, and when the silence got to be too much I said, "Go on, Dad."

"I always thought I'd have grandkids. I've been thinking about that some lately. Kimmy . . . I thought when she got pregnant that . . ." He drifted to a close, his thumbs brushing across his fingertips like he was getting ready to jug a safe.

"You knew about that?" I asked.

"How stupid do you think we are? Of course we knew. She was family. The baby—" He regained some composure. "Anyway, I'd been thinking about her and the kid she and Chub had. I just wanted to see her."

"You could've knocked on the door."

"No, I couldn't have. Anyway, the little girl kicked off her blanket. I pulled it back over her. Stood there a few seconds too long, Chub caught me in the room. He was understandably . . . uh, irritated and called the cops. Kimmy tried to talk him out of it but it was too late. So I got hauled in. Chub dropped the charges an hour later. I played like I was getting senile and walked in to the wrong house. It was an easy sell, what with Gramp. So there it is."

He hadn't told me because I'd asked, I knew. It had been something inside him that needed out. Now that it was, he didn't look angry or indignant. He hadn't been looking for any kind of forgiveness or absolution from me. He'd only explained himself because he'd wanted to.

I did put my hand on his shoulder then, for an instant, and then walked back into the house.

I helped my mother feed my grandfather his lunch. I'd just managed to get the last forkful of chicken salad down his throat when a news flash broke in on his cartoons. Instead of his chin dropping, he lifted his head a little higher, his eyes dark and alert. Vicky was on the scene at the park. She looked gorgeous and smiled endearingly.

Cara Clarke's body had been discovered hanging from a tree in the same location where her sister Rebecca's strangled corpse had been found five years earlier.

They put up a photo of Collie. We looked like twins.

The crime scene was a quiet bedlam. Hundreds of people had turned out to stand behind the police lines and watch the cops working the scene for evidence and taking photos of Cara Clarke's body. Some were on their knees weeping. A lot of them were praying. Flowers were already on display. They'd stack them up on the spot for years to come.

Vicky and her film crew were still covering the story. I made sure she didn't spot me, or she would have beelined for me. Gilmore walked past twice, looking angry and in command. I tried to get his attention. We had to talk.

The heat was going to come down on me now. After five years away, I return home, visit my brother twice in prison, and now the sister of one of the women he'd been convicted of murdering was dead in almost the same way.

I tried to imagine what could have happened. The reports said she'd been hanged. They were playing up the fact that she was on antidepressants, and they hadn't even found her extra stash or the stolen scrips yet. A lot of trauma victims tended to revisit the scene where they'd lost a loved one to commit suicide. Psychiatrists were on camera, discussing the rise in teen suicide.

I stepped up to one of the uniforms standing guard around the scene. I said, "Tell Gilmore that Terry Rand is here."

"Detective Gilmore is extremely busy right now, sir."

"I have information he'll want to hear."

The guy actually sighed. I didn't blame him. They were going to be getting hundreds of tips an hour from all over the place. "Of course, sir. We'll be happy to take your statement. Simply line up to the left, please. Someone will be with you shortly."

"It's important and it's real."

"Yes, sir."

"Seriously, don't brush me off. He needs to hear this, and he needs to hear it now."

"Line up to the left. Or you're welcome to come down to the station, sir."

I slipped under the crime-scene tape. It was a bold move. Five cops descended on me in an instant. They wrestled me back, saying, "Sir, sir, please, you are not allowed on this side of the tape!"

"Let me talk to Gilmore. My name is Terry Rand. He'll want to hear this."

The disturbance caught Gilmore's attention. He came over. The other police officers dispersed. He shook his head at me. "Terrier, today you're just being a pain in the ass. If this is about that nonsense with your brother, I'm going to give profound consideration to running you in."

"Is this your case?"

"For the moment it's everybody's case."

"Let me spill what I know. Then you decide."

"Okay, but make it fast."

I told him the truth. All of it. Starting with me watching the Clarke house, creeping the place, getting caught by Cara, staring down the .45. If I caught another beating for it, that was fine by me. I was used to pissing blood. I was less accustomed to murder.

He listened intently. His little grin dropped from his face, but his lips were still busy, curling and uncurling. He looked at me and his expression shifted into earnest worry. I knew what he was thinking. That maybe I had snuffed Cara in order to help my brother. That this was my confession. I held his gaze. I thought he might arrest me on the spot. I was ready to lie on my belly again and put my hands behind my head.

"Let's go talk in my car," he said. "I want to hear you repeat everything you just told me. Everything."

"In your car?"

"In my car. Come on, Terry."

He should've dragged me to the precinct and gotten me on video. He was cutting me some slack, but he should've known better. We marched over to where his car was parked on the lawn. I didn't want to see Cara's corpse, but I couldn't help staring. Forensics was still working on her, so they couldn't cover her up yet. Her face had gone an ashen gray, and her protruding tongue looked exceptionally pink against her darkened chin. Her eyes were only half open but had bulged forward from the sockets. I stifled a groan. I was probably acting very suspicious. I was probably sealing my own doom.

He said, "In back." We both got in the back, and I kept looking at the police crawling all over the area. Forensics was working on the tree limb, taking photos, checking the scuffs on the bark. Cara Clarke had been tall, nearly six foot, the branch was fairly low. It wouldn't have been difficult for a strong man to heft her up and make it look like she had hanged herself. I couldn't spot anything that Cara might have leaped from, but she could have conceivably climbed onto the branch herself.

"How was she done?" I asked.

"Hanged."

"They said that on the news. But how?"

"Terry, I can't talk about that with you."

"I might be able to help."

A squall filled Gilmore's face. "How in the hell are you going to do that?"

I saw several thoughts whip through his eyes. He thought about grilling me. He thought about giving me friendly advice to get out of town. He thought about raiding the Rand house and seeing if there might be something around to implicate me in the girl's murder. He was an almost-bent cop. That meant he picked and chose when he'd cross the line and when he wouldn't. You never knew when he might go by the book and when he might not.

Surprisingly, he settled on simply answering my original question. "A nylon cord, the kind used to tie dock cushions and bumpers to the sides of boats."

"Does her father own a boat?" I asked.

"Yes. A twenty-four-foot Wellcraft cuddy. Keeps it docked at a marina but apparently hasn't taken it out in years."

"Cord in the garage?"

"We're not discussing this further."

I thought of Sharon, the youngest sister, who would now be coddled obsessively by her parents. They were going to hold her close but not close enough, because the ghosts of her sisters were always going to get more attention.

"Did you find the .45?" I asked. "Or any gun? She was tough. She knew how to fire a gun. Check her hands for gunpowder residue."

"I don't need a career thief to teach me how to do the job of a police officer. She didn't pull the trigger on you. You managed to talk your way out of it."

"I wouldn't have been able to talk her into showing up here. Was she done on the spot or strangled elsewhere and left here?"

Gilmore snapped his fingers under my nose. His expression had hardened. His eyes weren't full of sadness anymore, they were like shale. "Focus now, Terrier. You don't ask the questions. You answer them. You assure me of your sincerity and maybe I won't throw you in jail tonight. Or maybe I will. Did you have anything at all to do with this?"

"No. How long's she been dead?"

"Get out and go home."

"Tell me, all right?"

He turned away for a moment, and when he turned back he stared deeply into my face, trying to read whether I was someone he could trust. I wasn't, of course, but he was still giving me leeway. I knew why. On some level he was acting like I was his younger brother, the punk always getting his nose dirty but who was forgiven for it. He looked away again, and when he faced me I could see that he'd come to a decision.

"Early this morning," he said. "And just so I know, Terrier, where were you this morning?"

I didn't want to drag Eve Drayton into this but there was no choice. I told him about Eve and even my father's figurine collecting, but I left out the bit about Higgins. Gilmore nodded.

"Your old man, he likes his Toby mugs."

"How the hell do you know that?"

"He's showed them to me before. Now, give me the names of all the antidepressants again and exactly where I can find them in her room."

I told him about the false outlet and the five-inch-deep cubbyhole.

Gilmore nodded. "She only had legal prescriptions for the Zoloft and Valium. All of those others, in combination—self-medicating on stolen pills, maybe expired—who the hell knows how someone will react with all of that in their system."

"So you think she really offed herself?" I asked.

"That's what it looks like so far," he said.

"I don't think she would do it."

He frowned at me, his face mottled with emotion. "How do you know?"

"I just feel it."

"You met her for what? All of fifteen minutes?"

"It was enough," I said.

He scoffed. He seemed to take a dim kind of pleasure in schooling me on the realities of the world. "No, it's not. Twenty years isn't enough for you to really know someone, or do I need to remind you of that?"

I held my hands up in a gesture that might have been anger or helplessness. "No, you don't."

"She was a screwed-up kid taking powerful meds in dangerous amounts. With all the renewed coverage on the case of her sister's murder, she was probably hurting worse than ever. And you showing up in the middle of her bedroom couldn't have helped any."

"Listen to me, she was sharp, she was on the ball, she—"

"You don't know a thing, Terrier. Now go home. Don't mention any of this to your journalist girlfriend or I'll—"

"She's not my girlfriend."

"—pull you in on obstruction. Do you understand me?"

"Yes."

"Do you?"

"Yes."

"Then go."

I got out. I walked toward the crime-scene tape. I glanced back at Cara. Figures in blue uniforms and white gloves worked over her excitedly. Who had iced her? Why now? I thought, My Christ, has he been watching me? Is he following me? Is he that close even now? Her dead eyes were aimed in my direction.

I headed back to my car. I sat heavily behind the wheel. I scanned the faces in the crowd. The only one I recognized in the area was Gilmore's.

Is he that close even now?

The dead girl continued to watch me. My body was a little ahead of my mind. I glanced in the rearview and saw that my face was pale.

I imagined Gilmore sitting with my father, playing cards with my uncles, being friendly with my brother. I saw the two of them out at the Elbow Room together, sharing stories, frustrations, fears. I thought of him opening up to Collie about his marital troubles. Gilmore had told me, *Anytime you get too curious about what was going on in his head, remember where that kind of thinking leads.* Maybe he'd gotten close enough that the underneath had swallowed him too.

My father had said, *He's got too much time on his hands. I don't know what he does with it all.*

I gripped the steering wheel, my thoughts burning. I tried to turn myself away from what I was thinking, but I couldn't.

He'd tracked me to the Elbow Room. He hadn't worked the cases, he'd told me, but he'd looked into them. But what if he was already familiar with them? The whores, the drug addicts, the women presumably murdered by their boyfriends. Gilmore would know exactly what to do to make those cases look like accidents or suicides. He'd know how to plant evidence to point at a husband or a pimp.

I shook my head to shake the questions off or to line the pieces up in place. Was that why his wife had left him? After he'd killed Rebecca Clarke in the park, did she know her husband had gone off the big ledge?

I thought about Gilmore wanting to become a part of my family and what that might actually mean. What if he'd been following Collie?

He was always around, always in our business. He'd spent so much time projecting that big-brother vibe that I was starting to pick up on it.

Except my big brother was insane.

Gilmore could've been shadowing Collie around that night. He could've sensed what was going to happen. He was going to lose his wife and kids. He was already heading out onto the edge.

I said the name once out loud. "Gilmore."

Christ, it was crazy. I shook my head again. Collie had me so twisted up I didn't know what to think anymore. Gilmore. Was it possible? Why was I wasting time even considering it?

My cell phone rang. I'd never heard it ring before and it took me a second to figure out which button to push to answer.

"Hello?"

"You heard about Cara Clarke?" Lin asked.

"Yes."

"Do you really believe that I'm killing those girls in an effort to somehow help your brother?"

"No," I said.

She let out a deep breath. "Then you accept there's a murderer out there?"

"No," I said. "I'm still not sure about that."

"What? Why not?"

I wondered if I should mention Gilmore. But I wasn't sure of a damn thing. "It looks like Cara Clarke committed suicide."

"That's just the killer covering his tracks and obscuring the facts!"

"Maybe," I said. And again, "Maybe. But you don't know for sure."

I could hear the tremor in her voice. "But it's—it's so—"

"Don't say 'obvious,' Lin. Nothing about this is conclusive."

"Will you go to the police anyway?" she asked.

"I already have," I said.

"Do you want my files? Something here might help them."

"They've already gone through your files, right? They've already written you off as a nut. I might stop by to go through them again. I'll call you if I learn anything more."

The anger and disappointment seemed to have tightened her mouth. She could barely get the words out. "Thank you, Terry."

I snapped my phone shut, sat in my car, and watched the mob thin as the cop cars came and went. I kept thinking I should have done something differently. Cara had been a kid in pain and I could've reached out to her more. I could have advised her better. The same was true about my own sister. I needed to watch over her more carefully. I couldn't make the same mistake again.

Gilmore.

I'd memorized his address from the rent receipt in his desk at the precinct. I thought of Gilmore working my kidneys, full of fury but trying to control it. Hating me, maybe the same way that Collie did. A man on the edge who'd been dipping his toe into bloody puddles.

I drove over to the complex. It was nicer than I remembered, with a large open court full of flowers and trimmed hedges. He had a one-bedroom corner apartment. There were three locks on the door, looked like two of them were fairly fresh. Did that prove he had something to hide? Gilmore should know that putting in your own locks often made it easier for someone to break in. Locksmiths got sloppy, didn't cut out the perfectly sized holes for the latches and bolts. The work sometimes loosened the door in its frame, giving a little extra play in the setting. There was no one around. I felt strangely calm considering my suspicions. It took me fifty seconds to get through all three locks.

I crept the place. I searched for anything that might tie Gilmore to the Clarkes or the other women. I checked all the obvious and inconspicuous places. I searched for kill trophies. I checked his cereal boxes again. No cash, nothing. He'd wised up. He wouldn't keep money around the place anymore. So where was the extra cash that he made off Danny Thompson? Was he flying straighter now or did he have a secure lock-box someplace?

He didn't take his work home with him. There were no files, no paperwork. I went through his computer and discovered nothing encrypted. All I found were photo albums of his kids, hundreds of pictures of better times with them and his wife at the beach, trick-or-treating, opening Christmas presents. I found the photos that my old man had taken of Gilmore's daughters, the two of them standing near their mother's car, as if waiting to be driven to school. What did that say about Gilmore? Was he obsessing over his kids? Over girls or women in general? And what the hell did it say about my father? Was it as creepy as it seemed? Or was it just further proof that lonely men with too much time on their hands will do strange things to alleviate their average sorrows?

It wasn't hard to push a good man off the big ledge. It happened every day. Heartbreak could make you a murderer. So could losing your job, drugs, or having one beer too many. Or maybe nothing at all, like Collie kept saying.

An hour after I'd entered, I relocked his door and got back to my car. I phoned information and got the number for the television station where Eve and Vicky worked. It took me ten minutes to wade through the menu and finally get Eve. She answered on the first ring.

"You've heard about Cara Clarke?" I asked.

She wasn't someone who needed the quiet hellos and the after-sex small talk. I wondered if I did, if I normally would want it if I hadn't just seen the body of a murdered teenage girl.

"Vicky's been on scene," Eve said. "We're busy here now, Terry. Your brother's story was big before, but now—"

"Off the charts."

"Yes."

I had difficulty saying it. "I need your help."

"Anything," she said.

"In exchange for an in-depth on-camera interview, right?"

"No, Terry. I know you'd probably agree to sit for one, but it would be a lie. I'm a professional but not a shrew. Hopefully we're at least a few steps along the road to being friends. So what can I do to help?"

"The cop I mentioned. His name is Detective Gilmore."

I could hear her perk up in her seat. In the background there was a din of voices, the sound of a lot of activity. I wondered what other kind of fallout Cara's death would bring.

"You said you still needed him. That you didn't want me to do an exposé."

"I just want you to dig. Find out what you can about him."

"Why?"

Because, I nearly said, *my brother is manipulating me into being suspicious of everyone, and it's making me as crazy as he is.*

"A screwy hunch. It's probably nothing, but I've got a gut feeling I can't shake loose."

"And what am I looking for?"

"I'm not certain. See if his jacket has gotten sketchy in any way over the last five years. If there've been any off-duty collars in places where he shouldn't be. If there's been any kind of internal investigation into him. If he's had a psych evaluation."

I could tell that she held the phone a little tighter to her lips, got herself away from the noise of the newsroom. Now there was something like concern in her voice. "You suspect him of something. What is it?"

"First let me know if anything pans out, then I'll fill you in if I can."

"You ask a lot," she said.

"Everyone does."

"Give me a couple of hours."

I disconnected. I had to keep moving. I was close to the address that had been on Butch's suspended driver's license. I had to keep an eye on the punk and his crew and see if Dale needed something more than a butterfly knife to protect herself. I had to see who his connections were.

It was a nice house, obviously his parents' place. His Chevy wasn't around. I rang the bell, and when his mother answered I told her that I was a high school buddy of Joe's and wanted to catch up on old times. I figured she wouldn't call him "Butch."

Despite the gray streak and a few extra years, I was young enough to look like we'd run together. I turned on my most winning smile. She looked at me like she knew I was lying but that everyone who hung around her son lied to her. Her face went hard and drained of all interest and concern. She told me he hadn't been living at home for some time and shut the door in my face.

Next stop was the Fifth Amendment. Butch wasn't around. Nobody knew where he might be. Danny was holding court with his crew in their usual spot. A lot of fat cats with lit cigars were rolling their sleeves up. It looked like a big poker game was on the agenda for later tonight. Maybe someone had Butch out picking up some fresh baked goods. I split.

From the road I phoned the house, hoping to talk to my sister. My father answered and put Dale on.

"Where's Butch?" I asked.

"Why?"

"I wanted to ask him something."

"What?"

"What to get you for your birthday."

"You're full of shit."

"Where is he?"

"I'm not pregnant. You don't have to beat him up. And he didn't defile me either. I wasn't a virgin when I met him, you know."

Some things men weren't meant to imagine, and a sister's first time was one of them. "Shut up! Christ! Tell me where he is."

"No," she said. "And thank you for the knife." Then I heard her turn on her blow dryer and she hung up.

I staked out my own house and parked down the street, mostly hidden by a curtain of brush. Dale fixing her hair meant she'd be heading out soon.

Butch picked her up around seven o'clock and I tagged along. There wasn't much need. I figured they'd be heading over to the lake. Butch parked pretty much in the same spot as before. They reenacted everything that they'd done the other night, except that Butch seemed to be drinking a lot more. Maybe the pressure of the heist was getting to him.

I didn't spot anyone. I kept the lights off and the music low and I tried not to let myself drift too much, but I couldn't help it. I kept thinking that I could've saved Cara Clarke somehow. I didn't know how, but I had botched the job. Maybe I never should have visited her. Maybe I had led the killer to her door. Maybe I had brought the underneath along with me and she'd gotten swept up in it too.

I stared at the headlights of the kids' cars and watched them dancing and drinking in the firelight until it felt like my eyes were full of splinters. Maybe this was the beginning of Alzheimer's.

It was a school night and my sister left early enough to make my mother only moderately unhappy. Butch wove around on the road a little and kept crossing the center line. They parked in front of our house and argued for a few minutes, maybe about his drinking, and then made out for a while. Then Butch split.

He was knocking back beers as he drove home. I followed. I wanted to drop a dime on him for drunk driving with my sister in the car, the prick. He pulled into a low-class apartment complex in Wyandanch known for its drug market. I watched him weave up the sidewalk. I sat out in front and waited for ten minutes, then I went to have a look.

I couldn't even say I crept his place. The lock was broken and his front door was halfway open. The stink of rotting food made me gag.

Butch was passed out on the couch. He had a three-inch doobie still burning in an ashtray. His pad was a catastrophe. Empty beer cans and old bags of Chinese takeout, ribs, burgers, were everywhere. I could hear the roaches skittering. I hoped to Christ my little sister didn't spend much time here.

There wasn't much to the douche. He had a .22 with a warped front sight tucked down between the couch cushions where he slept. He had a new wallet. It had someone else's ID and about a hundred bucks in it. The idiot had juked somebody but hadn't tossed the driver's license. Maybe he thought he could pass himself off as Carlos Ortiz Arroyo.

Right out in the open, scrawled on a grease-soaked pizza box, were the name and number of Stan Herbert. He was a fairly small-time fence who took the dirty items nobody else wanted. If you boosted a church, then you brought the silver chalice to Stan. Butch and his string were relying on the wrong guy to move their jewelry. Either Butch was running the heist into the ground or they were all a bunch of amateurs or morons. Danny would want a fat hunk off the top and there wasn't going to be much cheese left for the rest of them. Even if they got away with it, they weren't going to want to give out such a big cut. That would put them on the wrong end with the Thompson crew. They were as good as caught or dead. The cops would sniff out Dale. Whether she was involved or not, it would go bad for her just because of the Rand name.

Butch was a dim bulb. I wasn't going to be able to scare him into laying off the heist. I wasn't going to be able to talk any sense into him.

Five men in all. I wondered if he'd picked up his fifth yet or if he was still looking. A family-owned jewelry store. Small shop, a lot of employees. Four minutes inside. I tried narrowing down which shop it might be, but there was no way. I looked over at Butch on the couch and tried to see what my sister saw in him. She could do much better. If she went for bad boys she could still go for smarter. Maybe she just dug the Chevy.

As I was heading home, my phone rang again. The noise of it startled me. I didn't think I'd ever get used to carrying a cell and I couldn't wait to get rid of it as soon as I could. When that might be I had no idea. Maybe as soon as Collie was dead. Since I was still doing a lot of creeping, I thought maybe I should set the fucker on vibrate.

"Hello?"

"We've got a little trouble, Terry," Wes said. "And don't bother asking me how I got this number, it's my goddamn phone. I knew you wouldn't be able to resist juking me."

"Taking a burner isn't juking you, Wes. What's the trouble? Something with my sister?"

"No," he said. "Your uncles are here at the Fifth."

"Ah, shit. The poker game."

"Right. They just walked in a few minutes ago. You're the one who put it in Mr. Thompson's head that when Mal and Grey are together they're cheating. He said you mentioned cross chatter and keeping the marks distracted."

"What a fucking idiot I am."

"If you get here fast, maybe we can calm the situation before anything starts."

"Danny throwing his weight around?"

"No. It's all nice and mellow so far. But you know Mr. Thompson holds a grudge."

"How much have they won so far?"

"Nothing. Nobody's much ahead yet."

That's how it would start. My uncles were just loosening up a little. They'd run the hands evenly for a while. Take a pot or two and then feed a couple back to the other players. The next step was to start losing slightly, then more heavily. After they'd gotten five or six grand deep, the others would get in a good mood and grow even sloppier, and then my uncles would come in with the serious rips and finish the fat cats off fast.

"I'll be there in five minutes. But tell me something else first."

"What is it?"

"How deep is Gilmore into Danny's pocket?"

I could almost hear Wes's stomach rumbling, the acid splashing around. "You don't need to know things like that, Terry."

"I really do, Wes. Has he ever pulled a trigger for you?"

"What?" Wes's voice tightened, and he put some frost into it. "Terry, I don't understand what's been going on with you, but this isn't the kind of thing we should be talking about."

"Is that a yes, then?"

"Doesn't the guy eat at your house and drink beer with your father? I thought you knew him."

"I thought I did too, but I'm not so sure anymore."

"There's a lot of that going around. Hurry the fuck up and get here, would you?"

It took me ten minutes. A sign on the front door said PRIVATE PARTY TONIGHT. That had always been Big Dan's euphemism for a major game. It just proved that Danny was still walking in his father's shadow, afraid to strike off on his own.

I walked in anyway. I started over to Danny's table, and one of his soldiers stepped up and blocked me. Danny watched it happen but kept me waiting. Wes saw it too and knew he had to let the boss throw his weight around a little. A few minutes went by. I tried hard to be patient.

Danny had a new suit on, one that looked a couple of sizes larger and fit him more comfortably. His paunch was well hidden. He'd used some kind of thickening gel to give his hair more texture. He still couldn't keep from thumbing back his widow's peak.

Mal had one of his stogies lit. He smoked it without ever pulling it from his mouth. Just sucked air through his teeth and then blew smoke out one side of his mouth. In front of him was either a Bloody Mary or a glass of tomato juice, garnished with a stick of celery.

Grey had stopped off at home at some point and now wore a charcoal suit and a power tie. If possible, he looked even sharper than he had last night. He wore his best jewelry. Rolex watch, diamond pinkie ring, a gold bracelet. He said it all served as distraction and decoy. The more flash you wore, the more chance that someone was looking at the shine and not at your four-card pull. It went counter to everything my father had taught me. You wore nothing on your hands so that no one looked at your hands. Both methods seemed to work pretty well.

The fat cats appeared to be having fun. I recognized two of them as mob guys who used to hang around with Big Dan. Both from Chicago, in town for a few days doing business. I suspected Mal was right again. The Chi syndicate was here pulling the Thompson crew apart and stealing their business.

Danny's boys hung close but not too close. The mook in front of me had on an enthusiastic expression like he was daring me to try to run around him. I thought about picking up a chair and cracking him across the face, but I thought that probably wasn't the best way to proceed. I was there to keep things from getting out of hand, not to start a riot on my own. I waited.

Finally Danny glanced up from his cards and waved me over with two fingers. The soldier moved aside and a path was cleared to the table.

"What, no dog this time?" Danny asked. "Figured you had him trained to read cards and bark out the suits. *Arf arf!* Queen of diamonds! *Woof woof woof!* Nine of clubs!"

His boys laughed because they had to. The Chi guys went along with it and smiled even though they had no clue.

My uncles knew exactly why I was there. Mal seemed a little disturbed but Grey was curious, his eyes a bit hot, wondering how this would all play out. He grinned at me and gave me a nearly invisible head wag. He wasn't telling me not to join in. He was saying, *You've got balls, kid, getting laid last night must've really fired you up to jump back into the game.*

There was an empty chair on Danny's right. I swung it around and squeezed in on his left.

"So deal me in," I said.

"You need ten g's to join us."

Like his father, Danny didn't bother speaking in code the way some of the other outfit guys did. They would've said *ten bags of cement* or *ten slices of bacon* or something equally stupid. Big Dan didn't believe in speaking stupid in his own place, even if the feds were tapping him. Danny was following suit.

"My uncles will spot me," I said.

"Sure," Grey said. He gave me the wag again. His eyes were even brighter. He was enjoying himself. He paid ten grand, collected the chips, and set them in front of me. They didn't amount to nearly as much as I would've thought.

Danny's dealer did have a three-card bottom drag, just like Mal had said. The guy kept folding the aces back into the deck to feed Danny. It didn't mean anything to Mal or Grey. I saw Mal cut the deck once and knew he'd snapped a face card out and palmed it. I had to fight to stay in the game, though. I sat next to Danny so that I could pull his discards and load myself up. I had wide pockets and kept them stuffed with at least one card each. Danny had a penchant for going for flushes. It was dumb, but it made it easy for me to cheat on his behalf. Once I knew what he was after, I could aim a suit in his direction.

Grey and Mal both had the minutest of tells. No one else would be able to pick up on them, but I could see exactly when my uncles were about to squeeze a pot or feed each other cards. Their cross chatter distracted the others, but I tuned it out. I managed to upset their juke and steal some cards they needed along the way. I fed the pot when they wanted to go light and I threw in my cards when I shouldn't have.

I was down a couple of grand, which wasn't so bad considering how little I cared about my own hands. I wasn't nearly the card manipulator my uncles were. Not even as good a player as a couple of the fat cats. But I was lucky during the game. I managed to swing some tight inside straights and pulled a full house twice on the last card.

Danny had been worried that with three Rands in the game he and his friends would be cut to ribbons. Instead, he was up, with the Chi guys down. I think it made him feel secure, like he was getting back at them a little, showing them that, like his father before him, he could be in charge and take their money whenever he wanted.

Every now and then the conversation would get risque and someone would tell a dirty joke and Grey and Mal would feed into it like it was the funniest thing ever. Mal's heavy laughter resounded across the Fifth and made heads turn. The girls kept coming around with drinks and taking food orders. I knew they were shills who would be glancing at our cards and giving Danny the information with coy body language. Wes kept mostly clear of the scene, popping over only every once in a while to make sure nobody was getting too badly bent out of shape. He was a good man to have around. I wondered how many times he'd kept Danny from going to war.

My nerves were tight. I tried not to make eye contact with my uncles. Grey still seemed to be having a good time, talking women, talking about the best places in Chi to eat, to score, to shack up. Mal didn't talk much when he wasn't chattering with Grey. He looked too intimidating. No one ever wanted to start a conversation with him.

It was never foremost about the money for them, just the skill of working the cards. They had as good a time fighting me for control of each hand as they would have had scooping in the pot.

About three hours in, the effort started to put a real strain on me. It was exceedingly difficult trying to keep everything as even as possible, to shield Danny from my uncles' maneuvers. I wasn't going to be able to hack it for much longer. Grey knew it. He nodded to me, a sign of respect.

I'd done my part. Danny still kept giving Mal the stink eye from time to time. Maybe he was showing off. It made sense. If he wanted to look hard in front of the Chi syndicate, he would've picked the biggest, meanest-looking guy in the room. Every so often he'd try to embarrass us the same way the guard at the prison had, by saying our entire names. "Malamute, you want another celery stick or are you going to step up to carrots now? Greyhound, I like your aftershave, reminds me of a good time I spent in a Parisian whorehouse when I was seventeen." The Chi boys were used to fucked-up names and didn't cut a grin. Their current boss was Nicky D'Amico, who'd been nicknamed "No Nose" because he suffered from asthma.

I'd been in the game long enough. If anyone's luck changed too radically at this point, it would look extremely suspicious. Mal and Grey weren't going to be able to juke Danny or the mob tonight. I wasn't sure what I'd accomplished really. I'd screwed my uncles' score. They weren't going to like it. They were going to come right back here during the next big game and steal another forty grand, minimum. Maybe more to make up for their loss tonight. I'd bought a little time and pissed them off in the process.

It was after midnight. I cashed out. I'd won an extra two hundred bucks and left it as a tip for the waitresses.

Danny said, "Calling it quits?"

"I know better than to push my luck."

"I'm not sure about that, Terrier. There's a lot of things I might say about you. But that you know when to fold probably isn't one of them."

"I do tonight."

I stood. I gave a nod around to the other players. Mal and Grey eyed me and I knew how it would go down. They'd play another hour, maybe win a grand or two each, and then fold up. I was going to get an earful.

"Maybe that's good then," Danny said. He thumbed his widow's peak, took a swig of his drink, and wiped his face down with a cocktail napkin. I got the feeling he was working his way up to saying something that wasn't going to be nice. I thought I should scram fast.

"Right. Have a good night, Danny."

"So tell me, Terry. Did you snuff her?"

I froze. I knew he was talking about Cara Clarke. His timing was bad but he was asserting himself again. Mal and Grey both stared at him like they wanted to give him a smack. Everyone had heard the news. It was on everybody's mind.

Who's the guy who'd come home after five years and talked to his mass-murderer brother right before one of the victims' sisters had been snuffed in the same place and pretty much in the same way, hmm?

I wondered if I should answer. I wondered if I might wind up with a little more cachet with these guys if I kept them guessing.

But I suppose I needed to clear the air. "No."

"Sure about that?"

"Is that the question, Danny? If I'm sure I didn't ice the girl?"

"Just thought I'd ask."

"Looking out for the community now, is that it? You're a real *padrone,* huh? Worried about your neighbors' daughters?"

"You laughing at me?"

Wes had a lot of guts. He tried to edge between Danny and me. He wasn't afraid to get in the middle of things and he was smart enough to know when he had time to ease some of the pressure.

He said, "He isn't laughing, Mr. Thompson. He isn't even smiling."

"That's where you're wrong, Wes. He is. You don't know him like I do. He's laughing. He's smiling."

I said, "This the way you want to play it, huh, Danny?"

"When I make a play you'll know it. You got anything to say to that?"

"Sure. Fuck you."

He banged his fist down on the table. Cards jumped and chips rattled onto the floor and drinks spattered. "I told you already, Terry! Don't talk that way to me!"

Mal and Grey cashed out. They stood and pressed their chairs back and moved to me. Grey on my left, Mal on my right. Mal balled his hands into fists and let them rest against his legs. Grey put his hands in his jacket pockets and made it seem like he might pull a nickel-plated .38, something that matched his nice suit.

The tension grew. Danny's boys moved in. A couple had opened their jackets to make it easier to draw from their shoulder holsters. They kept looking to him for orders. Danny did nothing. He sipped his drink some more, let the ice click off his teeth. The Chi guys looked worried. They didn't want to get caught in the middle of a shoot-out.

I started to say something, I'm not even sure what, and Grey put a hand on one of my shoulders and Mal put a ham hock on my other and they easily turned and shoved me along and followed me out the door.

Once we were in the parking lot, Grey let out a humorless laugh. He lit a cigarette and took a deep drag and said, "Been a while since we've been backed up to an alley wall like that. I used to think I missed it. I don't."

Mal braced me at my car. "You feel like telling me if you were just honing your craft or if there was another reason for that?"

"I was worried that if you juked Danny another forty large that—"

"Thirty-seven."

"—he might not be so forgiving this time."

"You see what we have here?" Grey asked. "You see how our nephew looks out for us? This is love. Our boy gets laid last night and suddenly he's all balls."

He winked at me and I felt my face flush. "Like I said, I was worried."

"And that makes it all right?" Mal demanded.

"Say what you want, I did it for you. For us."

"We've been doing this a lot longer than you, kid."

"Yeah, but Danny doesn't hold to the same code as his old man."

Mal frowned, his craggy face falling in on itself like cliffs toppling during an earthquake. "Big Dan once gutted a man because his baked ziti didn't have enough cheese on it. You're giving him more credit than he's due. He had no code. There is no such thing as a code with these people, Terry."

"All the more reason not to score them."

"It's what we do."

When you got down to it, that was the answer to everything. "I wish you people would all get off that. You've all got enough cash to live large for the rest of your lives. Why don't you relax a little? Go on vacation. Visit Europe."

He glared at me. "What would we do in Europe?"

"I don't know what the fuck you would do in Europe!" I shouted. "Why do you have to do anything in Europe?"

"Why are we talking about Europe?" Grey asked. "You planning some kind of score going on over there?"

"No, Christ, there's no goddamn score. Forget it. Forget I said anything."

"Sure." Grey checked his left cuff, brushed a bit of lint off. "Right after you apologize."

"Apologize? For what?"

"Did you see all the mooks getting ready to yank their guns or did you miss that?"

"I saw it."

Grey regarded me like he had something important to say but this wasn't the proper time to say it. It's how he used to look at me when I had a big date in junior high. He was still grinning. His eyes were still hot. I knew what was going to happen about a second before it did.

His hands were fast and powerful. He slapped me so hard that my eyes filled with a white glare as if lightning had struck in front of me. My ears rang and my head shook so badly that my nose started to bleed.

Mal handed me his handkerchief. They were probably the only two guys in the world who still carried handkerchiefs.

Still, he gave Grey a disapproving glance.

Grey said, "No matter what your reason was, you never ruin another man's juke. Especially when we're talking about family. It's rude, Terry. It's disrespectful."

"I know. I'm sorry."

"See?" Mal said. "He apologized. I knew we taught him better than that."

"Of course. He's our boy."

Mal squared his shoulders. He drew a fresh cigar from his inside jacket pocket, chewed off the end, and spit it out. He focused on me. "You know anything about who might have offed the sister?"

"Now *you're* asking me if I did it?"

"Is that what I said?"

My nose kept bleeding. I couldn't look either of them in the face, because I was so angry I thought I might actually take a swing at them. I shut my eyes and breathed deeply. "No. I don't know anything. I talked to Gilmore, though."

"And what's he say?" Mal asked.

"Nothing. He told me nothing."

"He never tells anyone anything, that prick."

"Collie's girl," Grey said. He tightened his tie knot. Even after three hours of high-stakes poker and working the cards, he still looked fresh, not a hair out of place. "The wife. The groupie. He could've talked her into it."

"I don't think so," I said.

"It's what they do. It's a fact. Half of them are copycats in the making."

I wagged my chin. "I'm pretty sure not her."

Mal looked puzzled. "What girl? Collie's got a girl? A wife?"

"He got married in prison," I said.

"Did you tell me that?" He got agitated, moved in close on me. His massive hands came up in a shaky gesture of distress. "Did I know that?"

"I don't think you did, Uncle Mal."

"If you mentioned it, then tell me you did. I need to know when I'm being forgetful."

"I didn't mention it," I told him. "You didn't know about it."

I almost brought up the fact that I'd crept the Clarke house, my suspicions about Gilmore, my worries about my old man. But I kept thinking, What can they do to help? What's the point of explaining? These two popping their vitamins. What was added stress going to do to them?

I thought, This is who I am. I am going to become one of these old men. I'll have nothing. No wife, no children, no family. I'd lost Kimmy. Worse, I'd given her up. And Chub was going to lose her as well, the fucking fool.

Mal sighed. He placed an enormous hand on the back of my neck and pulled me to him in a half hug. "It's late, let's go home."

"I can't," I told him. "I have something I need to do."

Nothing had been shifted around in either of Chub's safes. I sat at his office desk and picked up the phone. "Home" was #1 on his speed dial. I punched the button and wondered if Kimmy would answer. I wasn't sure what the hell I would say if she did. I realized as the line connected that I hadn't put much thought into this plan.

Chub gave a very tentative "Hello."

He saw that he was being called by his own garage, after hours. I thought perhaps I should say my name at least, tell him to meet me. But I didn't. I felt safer in my anonymity. I was afraid of my own best friend. I was a cowardly fuck. I hung up.

It took him fifteen minutes to tear ass over from his house. He was driving a '64 Shelby Cobra 289 Roadster, another classic muscle car he must've restored himself. Some he sold, some he kept.

He was a disciplined planner when it came to getaways, but he didn't know what to do when entering his own garage that had mysteriously called him and hung up in his face. I watched him standing out there in the dark, wondering which way he should play it. Whether he should come in the back or through one of the bays or just unlock the front door. He finally decided to try the front. He didn't even bother calling out a hello. He checked his desk, picked up the phone, listened to the dial tone, kept looking around.

"Chub."

He spun, his left hand going for his back pocket. There was no bulge of a pistol, so he must've been packing a blade.

It was stupid of him to carry anything except an automatic with a hair trigger. The only bastards who were likely to come after him were the crews he was working with. Some paranoid mook who wanted to take care of all witnesses, anybody in the know. As soon as Chub laid out the plans, the mook would lever up something small, probably a pop-gun .22, and go for the head shot. Even if Chub saw it coming, what the hell was he going to do to stop it with just a blade in his hand?

I snapped the lights on.

When he saw it was me he cocked his head, drew a deep breath, and took his hand out of his pocket. A sad grin played across his lips but never fully settled there. He wore an expression that said he should've known it was me. He'd been waiting for this. I suppose I was predictable. I was the guy who didn't have whatever it took to face up to people the normal way. I couldn't knock on a door. I couldn't stand by my girl. I couldn't save my brother. He eyed me but didn't approach.

"Terry."

All of the jealousy and anger I felt moved through me second by second like a storm on the open water. It bobbed to the surface and then fell away. A thousand good memories all scrambled through my head. I thought we would have to shake hands. We would have to do that much. I put out my hand and he took it. I moved in a little closer and could feel his heart hammer against my own. He took a step away. As I waited for my anger to return, I realized it was already there.

"How long have you been home?" he asked.

"A few days."

"Heard on the news about the girl. The sister of the one that—"

"I didn't do it," I said.

He gave a puzzled expression. "I never thought you did."

He was too skilled to let his eyes shift toward the safe. He walked to the front of the desk and leaned against it, facing me, blocking me from the safe. I heard his folded knife thunk against the thick wood. He crossed his arms.

I remembered how he'd walked with a light step, almost skipping out of the car and rushing after Scooter, who squealed and playfully tried to run from him. How he'd swept her into his arms and set her on his shoulder and twirled and whirled across the lawn while her fingers brushed the buds of tree branches. The way he had kissed Kimmy and pressed his forehead to hers.

"Why are you here?" he asked.

"Collie asked me to come back and I did."

"Was that all it took? Someone asking?"

"It was more than that," I admitted.

He nodded, but the tension between us grew. He looked into my face until I turned away. "You ready to talk about it?"

I said nothing.

"You don't think you owe me that much, Terry?"

There was too much clawing around inside me, like a wild animal wanting out. He shifted and the blade clunked again.

I said, "You once told me that Kimmy . . . she'd send me up or set me straight. Which is she going to do for you?"

"What do you mean?" he asked.

His face was blank. He swallowed thickly. His throat was dry. He knew.

"Give it up, Chub. She deserves better than to watch you get taken down by the cops. Your daughter needs her father."

He stood and took two steps forward and got nose-to-nose. "This is the first thing you say to me in five years? Out of everything, that's what you choose to say?"

"It's the most important thing I can think of."

His mouth folded into a sneer. "That's sad, then."

"Maybe it is."

"You don't know shit, Terry."

"I know they're doing roadwork out on Vets Highway, and if you send a crew down there they'll get snagged in traffic and get scooped up."

He gave a disgusted laugh. "You went through my stuff. I should've known. If anyone could find a second safe, it would be you. That's why you're in the garage. That's why you decided to play it this way. You thieves, you think you've got a God-given right to stick your nose up everyone's ass."

"You're a thief too, Chub."

"No, I'm not."

Maybe he was right. You could look at it that he was just a guy who aided others in pulling their scores, without really getting his hands too dirty. The cops would still give him at least a nickel upstate.

"You've got no reason to keep playing the game, Chub."

"Who the hell do you think you are? What I do is my business."

"You don't need the extra cash."

"You don't know anything, Terrier. I have my reasons."

"Unless you're going to tell me that your little girl has a rare blood disease, then you don't."

Chub was on me in a second. He shoved me hard against the wall. He pinned me there with one hand locked on my throat and the other on my right wrist. I didn't struggle. Sweat dappled his bald head.

He said, "You know where I work. You must know where I live. You've seen my daughter. You've been watching us, haven't you?" I didn't confirm or deny. He paused, his face mottled with rage. "Did you know your old man cased my house a few months ago? I woke up and found him talking with Kimmy. Said he was checking up on her. At three in the morning. After breaking in to my house. I should've pressed charges and sent him to the joint, but I felt sorry for him. He looked lost." Chub tightened his grip on me. I started to gag but I still didn't fight him. "So what happens? You do the same thing to me. Just where the fuck do you people get off?"

I choked out, "It's time to change."

It sounded stupid and overwrought even to me. It got another ugly laugh out of him. "You're telling me that? You? First thing you do when you get back home is fall to type. Just like your brother and uncles and father. You couldn't wait to break in here, could you? I bet this isn't even the first time. You've been here before, haven't you?"

"Chub, I—"

He didn't let it go, his voice tight and hard. "Haven't you?"

"Listen to me."

"Haven't you, Terrier?"

"Yes."

He backed away from me and wrapped his arms around his chest as if to hold in his frustration and hate. *"Jesus fucking Christ!"*

"Listen to me," I said. "Forget about that."

"Forget about that?"

"You have a kid. I don't. Think about Scooter."

"Scooter?" He was practically screaming. *"Who the hell is Scooter?"*

"Your girls. Think about your girls. Chub, don't wreck your life. Don't you know how easy it is to lose everything? Take it from me."

His eyes were full of rage and disappointment. He was so hurt and appalled that he couldn't even look at me anymore.

"Take what from you, Terry?" he asked. "Why don't you explain? What life lessons have you learned since you abandoned Kimmy? Since you left her to go through the most difficult time of her life all alone? Since you vanished without a word. Guide me with your newfound wisdom. What else do you have to tell me?"

There was nothing else to tell him, nothing further that I could elaborate on or account for. There was no way for me to articulate the all-consuming panic of being trapped in the underneath. The pure crystalline clarity of the terror that had made me run.

I said, "Don't make my mistakes." I knew exactly what my brother had meant about making ghosts. It hadn't been that difficult to figure out. I had understood without wanting to face it.

The night of his spree he was compounding all the failures of his life, sustaining the sins, building the deeper, awful memories that he would carry to the grave with him. The underneath had welcomed him and he'd gone to it. That was the result of all that blood. He had taken his own life without putting a bullet in his head. I said, "Don't get caught, Chub," and left.

Just as I was about to pull into the parking lot of the Elbow Room, my phone rang. It was Eve. I answered and was surprised at how much I looked forward to hearing her voice.

"It's late," I said. "I didn't think I'd hear from you tonight."

"I work late," she said. "And talking to contacts on the night shift is the best time to get honest answers from them. They're bored. They're just hoping to find an ear they can bend. So I did some digging into your friend Gilmore. He's under IAD investigation."

That didn't surprise me. "For anything in particular?"

"They think he's tipped off some mob boys about police raids."

"He has. Anything about his wife? They recently separated. Anything like a restraining order? Abuse?"

Eve paused. I knew she was still wondering how this tied in with my brother, with me. "No, nothing like that, Terry. It appears to be amicable. Neither of them has filed for divorce. Maybe they're working it out."

"Anything else? Anything worse?"

"What do you mean by worse?"

"You tell me."

I could hear her lick her lips. The sound heated me up a little. "You're worrying me now."

"Don't be. I'm probably wasting my time. And yours."

"Well, there was nothing I could find, and I dug around pretty well. I could pull in some favors, if you like, but that might get me onto Gilmore's radar. Do you care about that?"

"Yeah, I do. You've done enough, Eve. Don't put any more into this."

"What were you hoping to find?"

"I wouldn't say I was hoping to find anything. Thanks, Eve."

Her voice hardened, but not much. No one liked to pull favors for a one-night stand. "Of course. You can pay me back with dinner sometime."

I said, "I promise," and I meant it.

I walked into the Elbow Room and found Flo perched at the bar in the same place as the last time I'd been there. She had lipstick on her teeth and still smelled of Four Roses. She was chatting up a john who stared at her like she was every woman in the world he'd ever hated, from his mother to his first girlfriend to his wife. She didn't seem to notice his brooding, intense glare. I wondered, Is this the place every guy comes to right before he goes out of his skull and butchers a helpless stranger?

I stepped over to her and snapped a fifty in front of her face. I nodded to an empty corner in back. She whispered a few cooing words to the john, but he didn't seem to notice. She followed me and put her hand on my ass.

"Hey, honey," she said, "you got a car in the lot? You look so melancholy, just pining for the one who got away, huh? You won't even remember her name after me. Let's go to your car and—"

I turned and she breathed whiskey into my face. "You remember me?"

She didn't yet. She smiled and placed her hands on my chest and tried to take the money from my grip while humming empty promises. I gripped her by the shoulders and gave her a solid shake. Her expression tightened and her eyes focused.

"Know me yet?" I asked.

"Yeah. The white streak. Like your brother. You have a bad temper too. Buy me a drink."

I held on to her. Her sweaty skin felt like wet clay. "No, you're already stewed. You can earn half a C-note by not fucking with me and just answering a couple questions. Then you can get back to your other business, right?"

She looked back at the bar. The john was glaring at her empty seat, like he still saw her, or some other despised woman, sitting there.

She said, "All right, all right, let me go."

I released her. "You know a cop named Gilmore?"

"Sure."

"When was the last time you saw him?"

She grinned and showed me her red waxy teeth. "The night he beat the piss out of you."

"Right. Is he a regular around here?"

"No, nothing like that." She licked her lips in what she thought was a seductive manner. It made my stomach crash. "Him and a few other cops come around every once in a while. The bar's pretty close to the precinct. When they do I usually head out the back door. But like I said, it's not often. Not regular."

"He ever roust any women?" I asked. "You ever hear complaints about him? Following women? Anything like that?"

"No. What are you going on about? What are you getting at?" She moved for the money again, and this time I let her take the bill and crush it down into her cleavage. She put her hands back on my chest and tried to push me off. "I don't like talking about cops. I don't want nothing to do with them."

"You said you were here the night my brother killed those people and was arrested."

"Yeah."

"Was Gilmore here that night? Think hard. And don't try to bullshit me. There's no more money to be made, so don't string me along."

A disgusted giggle floated up from her chest. "You don't want bullshit then I'll tell you I don't remember. I remember your brother only because of what happened. I don't know who else was here. I don't know if Gilmore was around. I know he wasn't one of the cops who arrested your Collie. I would've remembered that. But whether Gilmore was here having a beer, I have no idea. Did you really expect I would? That anyone would?"

It had been a stupid long shot, but it was all I had to play. "Okay, thanks."

I walked her back to her seat. The john continued to drunkenly glower, lost in his bitter stupor. I took two steps toward the door. The fucking bartenders in this place never seemed to cut anybody off. Flo sat beside the guy and let out a laugh that made the flesh between my shoulder blades crawl. I got the hell out of there.

The drive home went by so fast it almost felt like it didn't happen. My brain was on autopilot. I drove without thinking, without seeing the road. I couldn't shake the vision of Gilmore strangling Rebecca Clarke, slowly squeezing the life out of her as she choked and gasped, and then five years later coming back to do the same thing to her sister.

I sat in the driveway without realizing I'd pulled in and parked. Maybe it was the slap Grey had given me, maybe it had rattled my brain loose. I put my head down on the steering wheel and started to drift again. I figured I'd better get inside to bed before I woke up on the Cross Bronx Expressway doing ninety-five onto the George Washington Bridge.

I barely got my clothes off before I hit the bed.

I dreamed of Kimmy. I would always dream of Kimmy.

She didn't want to rush it. We weren't speeding along. I had called the Montauk Lighthouse and asked a few questions about wedding ceremonies. I had the judge's name. I knew what paperwork we needed to bring.

We were in the mall, moving past the huge plate-glass window of Fireside Jewelers, when she unlaced her fingers from mine and stopped in her tracks.

She glanced at me and gave a grin. I returned to her side and we stood shoulder-to-shoulder and stared through the window together.

She had her eye on a half-carat diamond bordered by twin sapphires. Not too expensive so far as these things went, but more cash than I'd ever dropped on anything in my life. My fingertips itched.

"I can get it cheaper," I said.

"You can't steal an engagement ring."

"Why not?"

"Is that the question you're asking me? Why you can't steal my engagement ring?"

"Nope."

We stood there for what seemed like a long time. I held her to me. Moments like these, I thought I could go straight. I wanted to offer our children a life, a future, something besides a house full of decades-old loot that nobody wanted. I imagined the ring on her finger. It looked like it would hurt if she brushed it against my back while we were making love.

We stepped inside. She tried the ring on and held it up and I kissed her finger and I kissed the piece of ice. I thought I had just enough cash in my wallet to at least make a down payment. I was wrong. They wanted twice as much. Kimmy reluctantly took the ring off but she remained giddy. I put my hand to her belly. My girl inside wasn't moving yet.

I reached for her.

Sweat slid onto my lips and I heard voices in the backyard. The taste of salt reminded me of kissing down the length of Kimmy's back that night while she giggled and eyed me over her shoulder and said, "That's it, that's it, worship me like a dirty goddess. Kiss me like I'll die tonight." I coughed and thought I should go to the window, I should see who's out there, but I wanted to return to my girl. I rolled over. I pressed my face into the pillow. The voices stopped and the breeze carried only the scent of storm.

Part III

THE
LAST
KIND
WORDS

I leaped out of bed to the sound of screams. I hit the stairs and jumped down three at a time. JFK rounded the corner, barking insanely. I'd never heard him like that before. He knew something I didn't. My mother hung wilted against the back-door jamb, hunched over but with her knees angled outward like she was about to push out a baby. Beyond her, my old man was hauling something heavy across the yard, gasping, struggling, the way he had when we'd pulled up tree stumps together. JFK circled and chewed at his hindquarters. I watched my father dragging Mal's massive and rigid body through the dirt, guts trailing behind. His brother's dead weight was too much for my dad, and his eyes flitted in a wild panic as he searched anywhere for help. His wet gaze finally landed on me but he was too out of breath to say anything. He mewled what could've been my name. My father had finally lost control. I took a step off the back porch and my knees nearly went out from under me. My mother moved to me, turned away, and tightened her arms around herself, her eyes shut tight. Grey hurtled from the back door like a ballet dancer, covering an unbelievable distance in four or five bounds. He was in a white T-shirt and boxers, which were immediately soaked through with red. Grey's voice cracked to pieces as he shouted, "Call an ambulance!" It was too late for that. It was too late for anything. My mother wailed in response. Dale appeared at my side. She wasn't sobbing, but the tears ran into her mouth. "Don't move him. You're disturbing the . . . the . . . forensic evidence. The police—" My father and Grey dragged Mal on his back, flattening the grass and digging gouges in the rain-softened earth. Mal's head bounced across the ground, which made his tongue jut and withdraw like he was testing soup that was still too hot. His eyes were half open and perfectly focused. He seemed puzzled, a little uneasy, but not too concerned about any particular thing. His face tilted and I caught his gaze. He still had something to tell me. I rushed forward and tried to help and they batted me away. I reached for my cell phone to call Gilmore and realized I was naked.

It rained like a son of a bitch the day we buried Mal. Some of his old grifter and heister cronies showed up and stood there in the downpour, sipping from flasks and sobbing.

The young priest knew our family's reputation and went full out with a morality lesson as he stood over the open grave. He had thick glasses spattered with raindrops. He had trouble reciting certain passages and stumbled over the words, misspoke them, chased after them, his voice rising dramatically. He reached for hellfire but stammered too badly to get the proper rhythm down.

Dale hung back with Old Shep. He was in a wheelchair and dressed to the nines, and she kept her hands on his shoulders. He wore a white fedora that my mother had placed on his head to keep him warm, and the rain ran off the ends of it. Within the etched sorrow of Dale's face I thought I could see a hint of anger. Butch was a no-show.

Beneath her umbrella, my mother let out occasional gasps of disbelief. I thought I could almost hear my father's heartbeat above the wind. I kept a watchful eye. I was afraid that my old man might strangle the priest with his own rosary.

Gilmore stood behind my mother like he was one of the family. I knew it was insane to think he was a killer, but he reminded me so much of Collie that I couldn't let go of the fear and suspicion. There were at least five officers scattered through the cemetery, all carrying the same umbrellas and pretending not to survey us. The cops had given us hell for moving Mal, but they seemed to accept that my father and Grey had simply been too upset to think rationally. We spent four hours answering questions. They collected all the knives they could find in the house, which was maybe half. If my family had been trying to cover up the crime, there were a thousand square miles of marsh from Sheepshead Bay to Fresh Kills where we could've tossed the corpse.

I stood in Grey's suit and ill-fitting shoes. I wore one of his raincoats as well. I hadn't knotted it properly and the tails flapped in the wind. Lin showed up and mostly hid herself under her umbrella. She didn't introduce herself to the family and I didn't do it for her. I probably should have, but the timing couldn't be worse.

Victoria and Eve each held on to one of Grey's hands, the three of them stooped beneath Grey's umbrella. Eve met my eyes once and gave a sad smile. I nodded back.

Somehow we got through the service. They lowered Mal in and everyone passed by and tossed roses into the flooded grave. His grifter friends threw in other bits as well. Coins, photos, goodbye notes they'd written, pocket Bibles. They were more emotional than I would have guessed. A few were openly crying. One fumbled his way toward Grey and nearly knocked him over. Another drew my father into a wild bear hug. My mother appeared to know them both and whispered and consoled them until they clumsily moved off.

The rain hissed like water in a pan simmering on a stove. I was tired of the noise.

Grey's hand trembled so badly that when he walked past the grave and threw in his rose it fell short. His knees started to buckle and he nearly went headfirst into the hole. My father and I both rushed to him and kept him on his feet. Victoria wrapped an arm around his waist and he clopped back and laid his head against her shoulder.

Large puddles had formed at the edge of the grave. Grey's rose swirled around twice before a stream carried it to the lip, where it hung and quivered before finally dropping away.

The image had an impact on me. The deep-red flower disappearing into the black pit. I knew I would have sporadic dreams about it for the rest of my life. Because it looked to me as if, at the last instant, the rose had been snatched into the grave.

The line of mourners continued to snake away. I waited until everyone else had walked off toward their cars, then I reached into my pocket and pulled out a fresh deck of cards and tossed it in. It was a stupid gesture, but I was a man full of stupid gestures. I was about to make another one.

When the priest turned to go, I reached out and grabbed him by the wrist.

"The last kind words ever spoken to Jesus were spoken by a thief."

"Excuse me?" He tried to pull away but I held on. "You're—you're—"

"We were the first let into heaven. Thieves are pardoned."

I tugged him toward me and enjoyed the pained expression on his face. Then I released him and left him there with his certain knowledge of God and hell. I walked away in my own bitter confusion.

Most of the mourners came to the house and ate. Gilmore begged off and said he had to get back to work. He shook my hand and I held on an instant too long. He frowned at me in puzzlement and misread my intention. He gave me a quick, awkward hug and left.

My mother and Dale kept presenting hors d'oeuvres and platters of cold cuts. A few folks spoke to me. Some I recognized. Most I didn't. I think I responded, but I had no idea what I might've said. I searched for Lin. She hadn't shown. I realized it was important to introduce her to the rest of the family. She was my brother's wife. I wasn't thinking clearly and knew it.

My father began to get hold of himself. He started to take charge, passing out drinks, his voice growing louder. He and the heisters told anecdotes. There were even a few chuckles as they ate and drank together. I kept thinking about Mal and me crashing backyard birthday parties, him taking over the grill and cooking hamburgers, the two of us singing happy birthday to Timmy or Holly or Bob when nobody knew who the hell we were. It almost got me smiling.

I stuck close to my grandfather's corner. I sat beside Old Shep, and his glassy eyes remained fixed on the television for a minute. He still had the hat on. I liked seeing it on him. It was a throwback to the good old days when he was nearly as stylish as Grey.

He slowly inched his head toward me. I didn't know what it meant. He was almost looking into my eyes. He was freshly shaven and the suit looked good on him. I knew he was in there somewhere. Maybe he wanted to talk. I said, "Gramp, if you—" and he slowly turned back to the TV. I put my hand on his knee. I hoped he would snatch my wallet again. I stood and turned my hip toward him, praying he would reach for me. He didn't.

Grey was still devastated but reeling himself in. He looked like he was half dead himself, drained of color and energy. It was the only time I'd ever seen his hair mussed. He hugged Vicky to him, but I thought I could see in her eyes that she knew this was it, the end of the line for her.

Eve stepped to me and said, "There's only one question a person can ask after a funeral. It's a foolish one but it's the only one. How are you holding up?"

I hadn't spoken all day long except for what I'd told the priest. It was difficult forming words.

"I suppose there's only one answer to give," I said. "I'm doing the best that I can."

She put a hand to my chest. "Terry, whatever you're thinking about doing, don't."

"I'm not thinking of doing anything."

"Yes, you are. I can tell. You've got blood in your eye."

Her fingers massaged me through my shirt. I shut my eyes and lost myself for a moment in the human contact. Then I took a breath and turned aside. "Eve, you showed me a very nice night, and I should thank you for it. It's been a long time since I had a chance to hold a beautiful woman close and fall asleep in her arms. But how about if you don't pretend as if you really know me."

"All right. But I meant what I said the other night. I do believe you're a good man, at heart."

"But you keep qualifying it as 'at heart.' "

"Only because I realize you're under an incredible strain."

She was being thoughtful and kind but I felt the way I'd felt during the times I'd been arrested and kept in the county cage. I wanted to shrug my shoulders and hurl the world from off my back. "I won't do anything rash and I'm not going to get hurt."

Eve saw something in my eyes that must have felt like an invitation. "You can talk to me if you like, Terry. About anything, at any time. This has nothing to do with my job. Please know that. Please believe that."

"I do."

I knew I would never see her again unless it was on the day of Collie's execution.

Grey tried to tell a story about Mal but it fell apart about halfway through. My old man picked up the slack and finished the tale, and the old grifters all laughed appropriately. Grey eventually went to his room. Vicky must have thought he was coming back, but after a half hour she thanked my mother and Dale for the food and said goodbye.

There was still a lot of meaningless chatter, but somehow the emptiness and quiet of the house deepened. All the many secret rooms carried with them a brooding silence across the decades and generations of Rands.

My parents broke from the others and found me with Gramp. My father said, "I'm worried about Grey. He has no one now."

"He has us," my mother said. "He has his girlfriends. They help keep him happy."

"No, we have each other, but he's alone. Despite all the women, he's alone. His health, it'll get worse now."

"We'll make sure he goes to the doctor more often."

"He won't go."

My dad looked out the screen door. There was no sun, but he turned away with a hand shielding his eyes as if he'd seen something he couldn't take. Maybe Mal out there demanding action.

"Who?" he said, his voice firm. "Who the hell could have done this? And why?" My father looked at the floor, and then his gaze settled on me. "Do you have any idea?"

"No."

He nodded, because that's all any of us could really do. Nod as if we were in complete agreement with some larger force that would do whatever it wanted with us whether we consented or not. Then he and my mother walked back to the dining area and became proper hosts again for their guests.

Dale gravitated toward us. She said, "Gramp needs to be changed. Ma usually handles it, but I thought I'd give her a rest and do it myself."

"That's very considerate."

"Can you help me get him to his room? On the bed?"

I wheeled him there, eased him out of his chair, and got him onto the bed. Dale got out a set of pajamas and an adult diaper. We turned him over on his belly and she cleaned him like a newborn. It was loving and illuminating. It was possibly the worst thing I'd ever witnessed, because all the time I was watching Old Shep I was seeing myself down the road.

My sister finished up and got Gramp back into his chair. I made sure we put his hat back on him. He deserved a little cool. Back in front of the TV, he perked up a little.

Dale glanced at me and said, "You're going to do something, aren't you, Terry?"

"Yes," I admitted. "Tomorrow."

"Good," she said, and slipped off.

I went up to my room, changed out of Grey's suit, and put on my own clothes. I didn't remember crying but my face was covered with salt tracks. I washed up. JFK stood in the door and growled. I looked in the mirror and made the same sound.

Wes had tried to reinforce his basement window so that I couldn't pop it again, but I easily finagled past his lackluster efforts. I hit the stairs and tried his closet again. He'd moved his stash. It took me five minutes to find it in the central-air conduit in his living room. He'd chipped some paint around one of the vent screws. It was as clear to me as a beacon in the dark.

I snatched up both of the Desert Eagles and extra clips. I counted out forty thousand from his cache and stuffed it in my jacket. I drove over to the Fifth Amendment, walked in, and approached Danny's table with my hands in my pockets. He and Wes and a couple of his soldiers were eating dinner and drinking wine. I could smell the veal Marsala, spicy garlic tomato sauce, and the fried calamari.

One of his boys—the same mook who'd stopped me during the poker game—lazily moved up in front of me and said, "Hold on, you can't just—"

I drew the Desert Eagle and shot him in the thickest part of his thigh. He shrieked and fell down, clutching the wound. There was less blood than I'd imagined. I'd never fired a gun before. It was easier than I'd expected.

The rest of his crew started going for their hardware and I rushed up and jammed the pistol under Danny's left ear.

"Let's converse," I said.

Fear twisted in his eyes but he held himself together. "Don't you think this is a bit much, Terry? You Rands don't use guns."

"I've had a change of heart."

He tried to turn but couldn't do it with the barrel wedged into that ganglia of nerves. "Sorry to hear about your uncle."

260 | Tom Piccirilli

"I came to pay off," I said. I drew the stacks of money out of my pocket with my left hand and tossed them, one after the other, onto the table. They bounced and fell into his veal, then into his lap. "Here's the thirty-seven g's my uncle owed you."

"But Mal—"

"Plus a little interest. Count it, Danny. And count it slow. Make it last as long as you can."

Wes very quietly said, "Terry, listen to me now. Don't do anything crazy. Just think this through."

"I have."

"No, no you haven't, Terry. No, you haven't at all."

"You really think this is the best time to argue with me, Wes?"

Danny tried to scoot out of the way of the splashing Marsala sauce but he had nowhere to go. "Wait, just wait," he said. I finished emptying the cash onto his plate. "You're smarter than this. You're much sharper than this."

"Who was the hitter?" I eyed everyone sitting with him. They all looked like your average mook. None of them stood out from another. None of them had any style or hipness or grace. Any one of them could have been the knife man. I looked for shoulder-holster bulges. It didn't prove anything. Plenty of hitters carried guns and then made examples of their victims with blades. "You think your father would approve? Hiring a knife fighter to ice an old man? Two in the head is too clean for you now? My mother and father found him dying in his own shit. You brought my mother into this."

My vision started to light up with red. I moved the barrel of the gun and pressed it hard into Danny's left eye.

"That hurts! For Christ's sake! Stop acting so nuts!"

"Who's acting?" I said.

"I didn't do it, Terry! I didn't order it done! Listen to me. I didn't do this. Grief has made you stupid. I know something about that."

"I want the name. If he's sitting here, tell me now."

"I have no name to give you. Nobody here does that kind of work. You need to start listening to me."

"Why's that?"

"Because we're friends."

"We haven't been friends since the eighth grade, Danny. You're not counting your money. I wouldn't want you to think I cheated you. Mal said it was only thirty-seven, but there's forty. You keep the change, right?"

The guy I'd shot was still rolling around on the floor in agony. The crew started getting antsy. Someone was going to make a move soon. I grinned at them. I pulled the other Desert Eagle out of my waistband and held it on them. I knew at least a couple of these pricks wouldn't mind seeing Danny go down just so they could skip to another syndicate outfit, head off to Chi or L.A.

One mook really knew how to give a death glare. He was drilling it hard into my forehead.

I let out a chuckle and whispered, "Come on, you."

Danny knew the scene was a second away from detonating. He held his hands up in front of him and tapped the air, trying to get us all to simmer. Half of his crew looked at him like they hated his guts. I wondered if he noticed.

"If you take me out, you're doing it for nothing. I didn't cap your uncle. I didn't give the word. Whoever did it will still be out there."

"Your father would be ashamed of you," I said. "You've got no cool, Danny. Your dad wouldn't have given much more than an asskicking for snatching thirty-seven g's during a dirty game. Not to someone who deserved as much respect as Mal did."

"I thought it might come to this. I thought you might think it was me, but you're usually more levelheaded. I didn't expect you to take it so far."

"You've got to work on your presentation," I told him. "You're not very convincing."

"I don't know what else you want me to say."

Big Dan had done some rotten things in his time but he never crewed up with a psycho hitter who used a blade like that. Mal had thrashed around in his own guts for five minutes before he finally gave in.

And I had heard him talking to someone. I had turned over and gone back to Kimmy instead of looking out the window. All I'd had to do was go to the window and maybe he'd still be alive.

I backed up a step. I checked Danny's eyes one last time. So far as I could see, he was telling the truth. It didn't mean anything. He was nearly as adept a liar as I was. I said, "We're done now, Danny, for good."

I backed up farther. I kept the guns trained on everyone. The mooks looked a little disappointed that I hadn't pulled the trigger.

"Take your money, Terry," Danny said. "I don't want it."

"It's not mine. It belongs to Wes."

Wes sucked down the rest of his wine and poured himself another glass. "I knew you were going to juke me," he said. "Did you go in through the same window? I don't care if it *does* look bad, I'm getting a fucking security system put in."

I backed out all the way to the front door. Nobody got to their feet. Most of them went back to their food. No one was going to come after me right now. Danny might decide later on that he couldn't let so brazen a move go without some kind of answer. He had to save face in front of his men and the other outfits. But I thought that maybe this was the breaking point. His men were already jumping ship, and this might make the rest of them go. He wasn't cut out to be a boss. He couldn't handle this kind of stress.

I cleaned the guns down and threw them both into the backseat of Wes's car. I hadn't accomplished a thing. Just as I was leaving, I saw Butch pull in. I thought, Fuck him, let him drop, I don't give a shit. He hadn't even shown at the funeral to help support Dale, the prick.

But I wasn't going to let my little sister go down with him. She was an actress. I imagined her with a plastic mask over her face, her hair styled short, more boyishly, a padded shirt filling her out with a male physique. I saw her carrying a gun Butch gave her that still had the serial numbers intact. I saw her lying in the backyard with her hands clutched to her belly.

I had to make sure she was safe from coming anywhere near the underneath. I couldn't let what happened to me and Collie and Mal happen to her.

I drove around town for a while. I turned on the radio. I listened to the news. Cara Clarke's death had officially been listed as a suicide.

In the morning I drove over to Stan Herbert's pawnshop. He'd bought out the stores on either side of him and had upped his game. He had a lot of old flea-market type crap but he'd expanded into the real deal. Old TVs, DVD players, DVDs, CDs, iPods, laptops, cell phones, BlackBerrys, digital cameras, and other computer equipment. He still wasn't going to be able to give Butch's crew what they were expecting for the ice. Maybe he'd lied to them and planned on making excuses when it was time to pay up.

There were a handful of people in the place, some customers wandering around and a couple of young employees who were rearranging stock. Stan was in back, in his office, sitting in front of his computer and going through ledger sheets.

"Hello, Stan," I said.

He looked up and the screen continued to glow in the reflection in his glasses. He'd lost the rest of his hair, but he'd picked up a few pounds and looked healthier and happier than I remembered. He wheeled his seat back and looked me up and down.

"Well, you're a Rand, I know that much," he said. "Not sure of the breed, though."

"Terrier."

He nodded. "Okay, I think we've met before."

"A couple times when I was a kid, helping my father unload laptops and stereo systems."

"Not so loud. The boys up front don't know I was ever a part of the bent life." He got up and closed the door, sat again and steepled his fingers. "Heard about Malamute. Saw it on the TV. Hell of a waste, him going out like that. Hell of a card player. Hell of a finger man."

"Right. Can we talk?"

"I don't move your kind of product anymore," he said.

"What kind would that be?"

"The illegal kind."

"Oh, you've gone straight. Good, glad to hear it." I raised my voice and projected toward the door. "Then you're not going to try moving any ice you might get from a five-man crew that's taking down a family jewelry store and expecting to get paid mid-six figures—"

"Christ, not so loud," he hissed.

It was probably true that he'd gone mostly legit. But like every other fence in the world, he'd never turn down a good heist when he was going to pull in a major percentage and do almost no work for it.

"What's their score?" I asked.

He shrugged and shook his head. "I don't know."

"Stan, you do know. I know you know. Just tell me and I'm out of here. What is it?"

"I don't rat. I don't do that."

"It's ratting if you go to the cops. I'm not a cop. Besides, you're already going to rob them blind. You lied about the payout and they're only going in because they think they're about to be rich. Even if they pull it off, they have to kick up to the Thompson crew. They're going to walk away with peanuts and they won't be happy. They might even try to take it out of your ass."

"Jesus." He opened the bottom drawer of his desk and my stomach tightened. I got in much closer and watched him carefully. He pulled out a bottle of J&B and poured himself two fingers in a dirty glass. "Why do you care?"

"That's my business, Stan. Your business of the moment is to tell me who's running the string."

"You Rands, you used to be a good family to work with." He threw back half the glass and made a face. "But now you're all sick in the head, you know that?"

I leaned on his desk. "Yeah, I know it. Now, who bosses the string?"

"Some kid."

"Which kid? Use names, Stan. Butch?"

"No, not that one. He's a moron. He only goes by Butch because his last name is Cassidy, can you believe it? Fucking idiot. No, the boss is another guy. Young, like Butch, but smarter, you know? His name is Harsh. That's all I can tell you."

"Is it his score? Did he put it together?"

Stan finished his drink, put the bottle back in the drawer, pushed the glass away from him. "I think so."

"Is it a tight string?"

"Who knows? I can't be sure with this new kind of punk."

"Contact info."

He tried to stand, but I blocked him and he dropped back heavily into his seat. "You can't foul the juke, Terrier. If you do and it traces back to me—"

"I'm not going to foul it. I'm going to make sure it goes off without a hitch. Give me an address."

"I don't have one, but I can give you a number."

He pulled it up off his computer. "Password protected and encrypted. Better than a floor safe in the corner."

He read the number off. I memorized it and said, "They're packing."

"So far as I know, yeah."

"So what happens when they find out you're not going to give them anything more than a dime on the dollar, Stan?"

His eyes danced with amusement. "It'll work out."

"A guy named Harsh might be eager to use his piece. You shouldn't have lied to them on what you were going to be able to move." I got up and opened the door. "Hey, you have any piano babies or Toby mugs?"

"What? Porcelain?"

"Yeah, I think so."

"I don't deal with that kind of crap."

"Who does?"

He thought about it for a second. "Try Rocko Milligan."

I left, got in my car, and headed north on Route 231. I called Harsh's number. When he answered I said, "This is Butch. Meet me at the Rail Cross Diner on Commack Road."

"This doesn't sound like Butch."

"I've got a cold. Twenty minutes."

"Who is this?" Harsh asked.

"Come find out."

"How will I know you?"

"I'll be the one calling out, 'Harsh, you asshole, your jewelry-store score is on the fucking skids.' Twenty minutes, right?"

Harsh showed up on time. I was having a cup of coffee and relaxing in a back booth. It wasn't hard for him to guess I was the one who'd called him. It was a small joint and I was the only one sitting alone.

He was a little older than Butch, maybe twenty-three or -four. Buzz-cut blondie wearing a tight white T-shirt under a loose jean jacket. He had wraparound shades on. Everybody and their shades. It must be a retro thing, guys falling back on what was hip in the seventies. They were all watching too many DVDs, trying to pick up on classic style. He scanned the place, spotted me, and took his time stepping over.

It looked like he was carrying a .38 in his jacket pocket. Right off, that meant he wasn't a pro. I could've been a cop. He could get a couple of years just for having a piece on him. You never packed unless you knew what you were packing for.

He stood before me and I said, "I'm Terrier Rand."

"I've heard of you. Your people have been in the news. I don't like that."

"You don't like that?"

"I don't like being seen with guys who might have reporters following them."

That was actually pretty smart of him. I reassessed Harsh a bit. He sat and the waitress zipped over and he waved her away. He took off his shades. His eyes were youthful but he was trying to keep them mean. I guessed that he'd been in the game since he was young, had pulled a couple of jobs that had gone well, and then he'd impatiently struck off on his own. That's the only reason I could imagine that he'd taken on a punk like Butch.

"You know my sister?" I asked.

"Yeah, I know her."

"How well?"

"Not too well. I never touched her if that's what you mean."

It wasn't, but I decided to take it at face value. I pulled an envelope out of my pocket and put it in front of him.

He didn't make any move toward it. That was another good sign that he wasn't a complete moron.

"What's this?" he asked.

"Three grand. You're going to pay off Butch and cut him out of this jewelry-store score. Take a thousand for yourself and give him the rest. Tell him it's his cut for helping out as much as he did and that you'll hire him on for the next job."

He studied me coldly. "Why would I do any of that?" he said, neither affirming nor denying anything.

"Because he's going to be unable to assist you. Find another man."

Harsh let out a slow grin. There was more than a hint of cultivated savagery to it. "You, I suppose?"

"No. I don't want in. I don't want to know anything about it. I already know too much. Because Butch talked out of turn. He approached me thinking I'd jump on board. It was a mistake. Not an unforgivable one, but bad enough. He also wrote Stan Herbert's name on a pizza box and left it out in the open for anybody to see."

"And you know Stan."

I nodded. "And I know Stan. Whatever he promised you, you won't get more than ten percent of the ice's worth in cash."

"He said twenty-five."

"It'll never happen."

Harsh started running other schemes in his head. His eyes flashed with possibilities, trying to find a way to squeeze more money out of the deal. I could see he already had other scores in the works as he started mentally shuffling through them, wondering about other fences, other people he could talk with.

"Why were you working Butch's place?" he asked.

"Finding out what I could. Is it your heist? You put it together?"

"Yeah."

"How'd you wind up with Butch on your string?"

Harsh wasn't sure how much he should tell me. I drank my coffee. I looked out the window onto Commack Road. He would either trust me a little further or not. There was nothing I could do to force his hand.

Finally he decided he didn't have much to lose by discussing things with me. "I asked Mr. Thompson for a man who might be willing to help out on a job here and there."

"And he actually suggested Butch?"

"Yeah."

Danny should've either stepped up and offered one of his own men or kept out of the score altogether. But he wanted to have a thumb in every pie without putting in any time or effort, even if it only ruined the pie. "You should have known better right off."

"I did, but I didn't know how plugged in Butch might be with the Thompson crew."

"He picks them up from the airport."

"I know that now. I wasn't comfortable kicking him off the job. He's good enough to do what I need him to do."

"You hope. What's Danny's cut of the action?"

Harsh looked away, a little bothered having to talk numbers. "Mr. Thompson gets fifteen percent of our net."

"His father used to take ten."

"His father is dead. And there's no time to find another man."

"You've still got a couple days," I said. "I can even provide you with some names if you like. Either way, you've got no choice."

"I don't like being braced."

"Nobody does."

He put his shades back on and ran a hand over his buzz cut. "You're not going to ice Butch?"

"No," I admitted.

"Just hurt him a little."

"Less than a little, but it'll be enough."

"Right. How do I know you're telling the truth?"

"What would I gain by lying? Like you said, you know who I am."

He squared his shoulders. I didn't need to see his eyes to know he was thinking about it. "Okay, you're paying me a wad of cash. You've got to have a reason."

"I do."

"Your sister."

"That's right. I want her unconnected."

"She's as connected as they come. She's from a family of thieves. One's on death row and due for the needle, and another just bought the farm." He pushed away from the table and stood. "You people are bad news. You think you're doing her a favor? You're doing me one."

Butch's door was open again. He was inside, smoking a joint, listening to his iPod with his earplugs in. His eyes were closed and he was singing loudly and badly along with music I couldn't hear.

I still had Higgins's blackjack. I stepped up behind Butch and caught him on the sweet spot. He slumped over without a sound. I took off his right shoe and tapped his ankle once. He made a little noise in his sleep like a colicky newborn. His foot began to swell.

There was nothing in his freezer except a half tray of ice. There were no dish towels in the kitchen. I walked the apartment. There were no towels on the rack in the bathroom. Butch certainly led the life. I found a dirty T-shirt on the floor of the bedroom and wrapped the ice cubes in it, then pressed it to his ankle. He'd be off his feet with a minor fracture for two weeks. The score would go down without him. If it went bad and Harsh and his crew wound up in the bin, Butch would be in the clear, and so would Dale.

I searched the place again. I looked for signs of my sister. I found nothing. Before I left, I dumped the melting ice cubes in his sink and threw the dirty shirt back on the floor.

When I got home, my parents were sitting at the kitchen table, dressed in black again. They'd just gotten back from the cemetery. I put my chin to my chest. The funeral had been yesterday and already they were visiting the wet grave again. My mother looked at me like she knew it was too much but she had to do it for my father's sake.

He grinned at me without any humor and said, "You okay?"

"Sure."

"That's good."

I wondered if he was going to ask me again if I knew who had killed

Mal. He got up and walked out the door, headed to the garage, still in his suit.

I followed him. I thought I should stick close.

He said, "Four months until the stone is ready, can you believe it?"

"Guess there's a backlog."

"We got a nice one, did your ma tell you?"

"No."

"Not sure how to describe it. Big. Square but rounded at the top. Has a kind of silhouette of his face on it. The profile. Not really his face, just sort of his face. Who the hell would want that face on marble? Not him. Nobody. And no angels, nothing like that. But . . . well, anyway, it's nice."

"Right."

My father stood before his treasured figurines. He seemed to be showcasing a couple of new ones. A Japanese boy pulling a wagon. And a rooster just standing there. I looked at the rooster and tried to figure out why any artist skilled in making porcelain figures would make a rooster just standing there and why anyone would want it.

I wanted to tell him I'd heard voices that night, but I didn't know how it might help. I sat in the garage, watching him at his hobby, cleaning the pieces and rearranging them, and I could feel the waves of fury coming off him. I thought, One of these days he's going to pick up a hammer and smash the shit out of each one of those pieces. In a week, in a month. He'll destroy the display case and it still won't be enough. He'll cut himself. He'll be slashed and bleeding and won't even notice. There will be a thousand pounds of glass on the ground and he'll stamp on it. He'll take the hammer to the walls, to the windows, and he'll keep at it until he's too tired to hold it anymore. It'll fall from his sweaty, bloody, trembling hand and he'll drop to his knees but he won't weep.

My mother will find him like that and go to him and hold him, and they'll both continue to carry their burdens separately and together. They'll bandage his wounds and clean up the shards and continue on with their day. She won't cry either, not in front of him, but when she's in the laundry room, a week or a month later, she'll drop and sob into a dirty towel for maybe twenty or thirty seconds tops, and she'll finish throwing in the fabric softener and then go make lunch.

"Should I show up?" my dad asked. He was moving the rooster around. He tried it on one shelf, then another.

"Show up?" I said. "To what?"

He dipped his chin, shuffled more pieces about. "You know. The execution."

"Jesus Christ," I said. "No. Don't do that."

"Collie shouldn't be alone."

"I'm going." I hadn't realized that I'd been planning to attend, but there it was, and it was the truth.

"You don't have to," my father said.

"I think he wants me there."

"That doesn't mean anything."

"It means something, Dad."

He finally settled on where the rooster should go. He closed the case. He appeared to be extremely calm. I looked over my shoulder at the workbench and thought I should hide the hammer. "To you or to him?"

"Maybe to both of us."

My old man placed a hand on the back of my neck and pulled me into a half hug, the same way Mal had done outside the Fifth Amendment.

We walked back into the house together. My father went to change. My mother was cooking. Dale stood waiting for me. While our parents were busy she took my hand, drew me in to the living room, and said, "Something happened to Butch."

"What do you mean?"

Her grip tightened. "He fell while he was stoned. Banged his head up and broke his ankle. He doesn't want to call an ambulance, and I don't want him driving himself to the emergency room with a bad foot. Plus he's got no money or insurance and . . . well, his license is suspended and doesn't have his current address on it. Will you drive me over there and help me get him squared away at the hospital?"

"Sure. Where's he live?"

"I'll show you."

I went to one of my caches in the house and pulled out two grand. It should cover the emergency-room costs. Dale got into the car. So did JFK.

She said, "God, does this dog have to always drive around with us? What if someone sees me?"

"They'll think better of you being with John F. Kennedy than with Butch."

She pulled a face. "You don't know my crowd."

"No, I don't." I decided to ask her the question that was still going around in my head. "Do you love him?"

Dale grimaced, her lovely features falling in on themselves. "Are you nuts? Hell no. But he's sexy. In a dumbass kind of way."

"I thought he was your beau?"

"I'm getting a little tired of his shit, to be honest."

I liked hearing it. I hoped it was true. I tried to imagine her studying hard and nailing the SATs and worrying about university acceptances, but I just couldn't do it. There was still time for her to break away from the rest of us.

"Did you get the role?" I asked. "Blanche?"

She twisted a lock of her hair and drew it over her ear. "No, but I'll be helping out as stage crew."

I squinted and almost chuckled. She was lying to me again. Toying with her hair was her tell, I could see it now that I knew what I was looking for. She'd gotten the role and turned it down. It was an act all right, for our mother's benefit. Dale knew Mom came to watch the audition. Now my sister could mislead our parents and say she was at rehearsal while she was really out with Butch. It wasn't a big lie. It was a rather average lie, the kind any teenage girl told her family.

I nodded. I took a breath.

"Let's talk about Mal."

"I don't want to."

"I think we probably need to."

Dale pressed herself as close to the passenger door as she could. She burst into tears.

"I don't want to talk about Mal," she said.

"I need to know if you saw anything."

"I would have told you!"

"You told me that you thought someone has been following you. You said it was just a feeling." She still had her face turned from me, the back of her hand to her mouth with tears dripping across her wrist. "Were you telling the truth?"

She screwed up her face and regained some control. She sniffed hard and gasped for air. Then she glared at me.

"No," she said. "I just wanted a knife."

"Why?"

"Protection, Terry. Even before Mal was murdered in our backyard, I could feel things slipping."

"What does that mean?"

She weighed her words carefully. "Dad sneaks out at night sometimes. Grey is hardly ever around. Mal stole some money from Danny Thompson. We lived in this house with Collie Rand, Terry. What if he was home in bed when he decided to go on his rampage?"

I'd had similar thoughts myself. "Right, but that was five years ago, Dale. He's—"

And then I understood.

My brother's legacy was to make us all suspicious of one another. To worry that at any minute any one of us could be overwhelmed by the underneath.

"You wanted to protect yourself from me," I said. "The knife was for me."

Her tears were completely gone and she sat straight up. In typical Rand fashion, her expression was nearly blank and her eyes empty of emotion.

"I'm sorry, Terry."

"Don't be. It was a smart move."

She nodded.

I had to be careful not to make turns until she gave me the proper directions. We pulled up in front of Butch's place. Before we climbed out I handed her the cash and said, "Here." She took the money without counting it and pocketed it. She said, "Thank you," and kissed my cheek.

I stepped into his apartment and tried to act like I'd never been there before. Butch was on the couch with two squares of toilet paper stuck to the back of his head. His foot was up on the table atop a pillow leaking stuffing. He was angry with himself and kept saying, "I'm so stupid. I've fouled up everything."

"No worse off than you were before," Dale said. "Except you'll have a limp for a while."

"No, babe, no. I don't even know what I did. I can't figure it out. What'd I trip over? Where'd I bang my head?"

"Maybe now you'll listen to me when I say you smoke and drink a little too much."

Butch checked the toilet paper, looked at the small spot of dried blood, crumpled it, and tossed it on the floor. "Don't start."

He put an arm around each of us and hopped while we carried him down to my car.

"Jesus, you brought the dog?" Butch said. "Why'd you bring the dog? I need to lie down back there."

"The dog isn't going to bother you," Dale said.

"He's already bothering me. He won't move. Can you get him to move?"

I snapped my fingers and JFK jumped into the passenger seat. Dale and Butch sat in back, sort of cuddling while he groaned and she whispered. There was a strange kind of music to it. It was a song I knew. Halfway to the hospital I looked at my sister in the rearview. She had Butch's head in her lap. He had shifted to moaning but not too loudly.

"You'll need a ride back," I said. "I'll wait for you."

"Don't bother," Dale told me. "We'll get a cab."

"If I survive," Butch said.

"You're going to survive, honey." Dale shushed him and made gentle noises like she was singing him a lullaby.

"I'll wait," I said.

She glanced out the window. We passed some jocks jogging past and she watched them. I had worried about what being a Rand was going to do to her. She was a popular, beautiful girl. She was a teenager. She was fickle. She was scared. She was smart not to trust strangers, even if they were her own blood. She was mature and harder than she should be. She was going to be all right, but she'd made a misstep with Butch. She wasn't in on the heist, but just hanging around a crew stupid enough to have Butch along might bring the brick wall down. With Butch out of the way, she was going to be safe for the time being. Maybe she'd turn her sights on the team quarterback. Maybe she'd go after some other badass. I'd keep watch.

She turned her head and her brunette hair brushed the glass. She caught my eye in the mirror and said, "What?"

The dead don't drift. They're rooted, irresolute, and inflexible as your own past. Sometimes your ghosts chased after you every minute of the night, and sometimes they just couldn't keep up. I saw Butch back to his apartment and my little sister back home.

Another day passed. Collie was that much closer to his death. I got up early and followed Gilmore to the station, then sat in the parking lot for an hour, watching the cops come and go. I no longer had even a gut feeling about him. He simply reminded me too much of my brother and I couldn't let a crazy idea go. I wondered if this was Collie's plan from the beginning, to run me so ragged that I'd explode the way he did. Was it possible that he hated me that much? To wind me up and let me spin out of control over the edge? And then I thought, Yes, it was. It had to be, because I had no other answer.

I started the car and drove without direction. I had no idea where I was going, but my autopilot seemed to have all the usual destinations mapped out. My stomach was still twisted up. I still didn't know if Collie was telling the truth. I went by the high school, the lake, the Commack Motor Inn. I wove in a wider and wider radius but always returned to the same pattern. I drove past Kimmy and Chub's house. I never broke 40 mph. I eased along and the hours passed. I put three hundred miles on the car. I thought no one, not even my brother, was wasting his life as badly as me.

I parked across the street from Eve's house. She wasn't home yet and I was glad for it. I didn't want to talk to her. I didn't want to talk to anyone. I noticed she'd had the window fixed. The lethal lawn gnome had been moved back out in front of the bush.

I played the radio low and listened to some oldies station and my mind went along with it, rolling on the tide of another time. Whenever some image hit me, I pressed it away. There seemed to be no good memories. Everything brought pain. A man should be composed of more than his heartaches, his failures, his missed opportunities and regrets. Even Collie knew love. I turned the radio up. I nodded for a bit.

When I opened my eyes, I saw a little red Mazda come zipping into the driveway. I watched a young woman get out, dressed in blue scrubs covered with pictures of different breeds of dogs and cats. She dropped her purse and stooped to pick it up. It was Eve's daughter, Roxie. She had curves in all the right places, her long brown hair swaying lightly in the breeze as she grabbed her sunglasses, cell phone, iPod, and stuffed them back into her purse. She looked the way I imagined her mother had looked twenty-five years earlier. But, more than that, she looked pissed.

She took another step toward the front door and her cell phone rang. She answered, angled her face down, and listened for a moment. She said, "Well then, why don't you just go fuck yourself?" Her voice carried to me as clearly as if she were in the backseat.

Roxie fumbled for the disconnect and stared at the cell phone like it was the face of a lost lover. She tried to stuff it back into her purse and dropped it again. The phone hit the walk and she gave it a nice kick that catapulted it into the garage door, where it broke to pieces.

It was the kind of thing only your first and greatest love could make you do. This would be the pain and passion by which all other pain and passion would be measured through the rest of her life. I thought of what kind of scars and marks Butch would leave upon Dale's understanding of men. I thought of my eternal draw to Kimmy, Gilmore shattering over Phyllis, and Grey's never-ending heartbreak at being left at the altar.

I snapped off the radio.

My attention dispersed, then refocused.

My exhaustion over the past several days was making it hard to keep my thoughts straight. My instincts were off. I didn't know whether Collie had played me across some elaborate game or not. Was Gilmore really a killer, or a bent cop who was closer to my father than I was? I saw

Mal crawling across the grass almost directly beneath my bedroom window. The same dream called to me. Go with Kimmy. Drive away.

I looked out the window at Roxie Drayton.

She looked like her mother, the same dark intensity, the same lovely features—

She looked like—

She looked a little like Becky Clarke.

She looked a little like Cara Clarke.

She looked a little like—

She looked a little like Dale.

I shut my eyes and twisted my face aside.

She looked like Eve.

My sister had said, *Dad sneaks out at night sometimes. Grey is hardly ever around.*

I heard Flo's voice, as loud in my ear as if she were in the backseat. *He still comes in here sometimes. Handsome. A touch of class. He knows how to treat a woman.*

I knew then who else was trapped in the currents of the underneath. I knew because it was my blood tide. I knew because we looked just alike.

I threw the car into drive and pulled away from the curb. The transmission moaned so loudly that Roxie dropped her purse again. I sped off. I called home and my mother answered. I asked, "Is Dale home yet?"

"Out with that Butch, I think," she said with disappointment. "I hope the next boyfriend's a doctor. Is that asking for so much?"

"The next boyfriend's going to show up next week. Just keep your hopes in check that he's a B student. Who else is home?"

"Who do you expect to be here? Your father's in the garage. You want to talk to him?"

"No," I said. My voice was too blunt. I tried to soften it up. "That's okay. What about Grey?"

"He's been out all night."

"With Vicky?"

She let out a small noise of exasperation. "How would I know? Since when do any of you tell me anything about where you're going?" The irritation and frustration were taking hold. She'd been through so much, and it wasn't over yet. She'd given everything she had to holding us together, and we kept falling further and further apart. I heard her place the phone against her chest, the heavy beating of her heart somehow calming me. "We need to sit down as a family again."

"Pencil me in, Ma. I'll call again later."

"We'll be here."

I disconnected. I let my mind wander in ways it hadn't before.

I heard my father's voice.

I think your uncles have a touch of Alzheimer's too. I've found them out in the yard in the middle of the night a couple of times, looking dazed.

Who could get up that close to Mal to do what had been done to him? Who would Mal trust?

I shook my head as if I had an earache. I slammed my fist down on the steering wheel. I was wrong, I had to be wrong. I phoned Vicky and Eve's television station. Like the last time, it took me ten minutes to work through the menu. Finally I got her.

"Hello," Vicky said. "Victoria Jensen."

"This is Terrier Rand. I'm looking for Grey. Is he with you?"

"No, he's not, Terry, I haven't seen him."

I shook my head again. My throat was beginning to constrict. I coughed and licked my lips. "You haven't seen him?"

"Not since the funeral." I waited, and the pregnant pause took on all kinds of meaning. I had a feeling I knew what she was going to say next. *He's no longer interested in me.* But no beautiful woman wants to admit that out loud. "I've been very busy with work. I just haven't found the time to return his calls. And you know, Terry, I don't want to speak out of turn here, but you and Eve make a wonderful couple. I think that—"

I cut her off. "Vicky, this is something of a rude question, and I'm sorry for it, but did my uncle stay with you that night we had the double date?"

"No, Terry, he didn't. He said he didn't feel well."

"Thanks."

"Tell him I'll talk to him soon."

I hung up.

Grey had slept with Eve. He had met Roxie. I thought about the peeper at Eve's window watching the two of us in bed. Becky Clarke strangled during Collie's spree. The missing knife.

Grey with his ladies'-man looks, owning a thousand women but not the one he'd truly wanted, the one who'd rejected him forty-five years ago. Like any of us, he was capable of violence.

"No," I said. "No."

Where had Grey been spending his nights?

I drove home. I'd been thinking of someone close to the family, someone who might have followed Collie that night, someone who knew our ways. I'd been thinking of Gilmore. I stepped harder on the gas pedal and jockeyed through the traffic. I kept pushing. Someone said, "No." Someone had been saying that for a while. I checked the rearview. My lips were moving, but I didn't know the voice.

I slowed when I got to the corner of our block. I eased up to our house and saw Grey's car in the driveway. I pulled in, got out, and stepped up the porch. I wondered if I'd gone over the big ledge. I wondered if I was finding madmen around every corner because I'd already become one myself.

My mother and father were in Gramp's room, cleaning and changing his pajamas. My grandfather's eyes were focused on the ceiling but it still felt like he was looking at me.

My parents glanced at me. I didn't know what to say. I wasn't sure about what I'd found out or if I'd found out anything at all. The pulse in my belly was throbbing heavily. My father said, "Don't stare, Terry. Old Shep's got some pride left."

"Oh, sorry."

I turned away and started back down the hall. I moved to the bottom of the second-floor stairs. I looked up and could see shadows playing against the corridor wall. I heard the creak and thrum of water rushing through the pipes. I took a step, thinking, Maybe I should wait.

"Jesus God, what the fuck am I doing?" I whispered.

"Who's that?" Grey called.

I climbed the rest of the stairs and stood in his doorway. Grey was stripped down, with a towel around his waist, about to step into the running shower. He was laying a suit out across his bed. Steam coiled through the air.

I said, "Can we talk for a minute?"

"Let it wait until I come out, right? This goddamn floor is like ice."

"Sure."

He padded to his bathroom and shut the door. I had maybe ten minutes to search the room. I hit all the key spots where anything of importance might be hidden. I found forty g's in cash split among three caches but nothing else of note. If Collie's knife was here, I couldn't find it. No trophies, no newspaper clippings. I needed proof. I needed to know for sure. His wallet was on the corner of his bureau. I went through it and discovered nothing that mattered.

I checked the suit he was about to put on.

I reached into the inside jacket pocket and found a photo.

It was old. It showed a pretty teenage brunette smiling happily, head half turned over her shoulder, her hair a wild flurry in the wind, dark and blurred branches of shaking trees in the background. I didn't have to guess who she was. The only girl he'd ever truly loved. She looked a little like Rebecca Clarke. Roxie Drayton. Dale. All this time later, all the times I'd heard the same story, and I still didn't know her name. She'd left him at the altar and broken his heart, and in his sickness she continued to haunt him, crawling through the seams of his mind. Every young pretty brunette became a part of the same obsession. My mother had said it herself. *An older man who can't let go of his own youth, who's preoccupied by the past . . . Too much silk and not enough sand.* She just hadn't realized how far he'd gone.

Inside jacket pocket. Right over his heart.

I could see him putting the suit on, working the tie until it was perfect, then slowly dragging his thumb across the left side of his coat like he was touching the cheek of the woman.

Maybe I should do a more thorough search, check the rest of the house, his car. Maybe I should wait and watch him longer now that I suspected.

But I wasn't a patient man. I couldn't imagine leaving him alone in this house another night with my sister near him. I didn't know how far into the underneath he was. I didn't know if I was right or wrong about him. Maybe Collie was going to his bunk each night laughing himself to sleep that I was out here running in circles. Maybe Gilmore hid his trophies elsewhere. Maybe there was a killer in the woods watching the house right now. Maybe my father had gone to see Kimmy for some other reason.

I had to get Grey alone.

I went to my room and shut the door. I thought of all the years I'd spent here feeling safe, surrounded by my family, my father and uncles on watch. I could feel the underneath tugging at me, that insane sense of panic trying to make me jump the wrong way. Vertigo made my legs wobble and I reached out to touch the wall. Behind it was our legacy, three generations of junk.

I sat on the bed and put my head between my knees. When the dizziness passed I called information and got the number for Rocko Milligan's pawnshop. He answered on the fifth ring with a flamboyant, "Yallooo?"

"Rocko, this is Terry Rand."

He sucked air. "Holy shit, a ghost from the past. Let me guess, you're on the narrow and you met a girl you want to marry, and now you need a good deal on the ring. You know I'm the man to talk to about that."

"Not entirely on the narrow yet, Rocko, but if I ever gear up for marriage, I'll get the ring from you. Now listen to me. Do you ever sell my father figurines?"

Rocko coughed out a chuckle. "Terry, not for nothing, but your father is loopy for the fucking things. I don't get it. They're not worth shit."

"When was the last time he came by?"

"He hits me up every month or two. Been a while. I think he goes out east, checks the antiques shops in the Hamptons for this crap. The old ladies out there like their porcelain too. Or they did years ago. Now their grandkids are inheriting it all and dumping it at garage sales."

"I want you to call him for me," I said. "Tell him you've got a few nice pieces in."

"I never call him, Terry, he just comes in on his own."

I listened to Grey moving around in his room, getting dressed across the hall. I almost hung up because it all suddenly seemed so stupid to me. I'd been wrong about everything so far, why should this be different? But I continued to clench the phone to my ear. "I'll square up with you and make it worth your time."

"My time's worth two C-notes," Rocko said.

"Fair enough. Call him now."

I walked downstairs. My parents were on the couch, watching a news channel, with Gramp in his chair beside them, a blanket over his lap. His hair had been trimmed. His face was clean and pink. He smelled of baby powder.

My father turned his head in my direction as if to say something, but he didn't get the chance. The phone rang and he stood to answer. I took his seat and pretended to be interested in the news. My mother was tsking and saying how terrible, how sad. My father asked Rocko what was so special about the pieces, and Rocko must've known what to say, because my dad actually said, "Oohh," with a great delight. It was a sound that at once amused and alarmed me. It was further proof I didn't know my old man as well as I thought I did.

He hung up and reached for his jacket off the back of the kitchen chair. "Rocko Milligan's got some bisque figurines from '46. Another buyer is interested so I'm going to run over there."

"You should go too, Ma," I said. "I'll watch Gramp."

She frowned at me. "What? To a pawnshop?"

"The two of you can go out to dinner."

"He didn't ask me to dinner."

My father looked a little embarrassed, but his expression quickly shifted to one of enthusiasm. The bisque figurines had put him in a tenuous good mood. It was an overreaction in the face of Mal's death, but I was glad for it. "You want me to take you out to eat tonight?"

"I didn't say that. I've still got half a roast in the fridge. Why would we go out to dinner?"

"Leave the roast. We haven't gone out together in a while. We can eat at the Nasgonset Inn. We always liked their Italian."

"They have a good house wine. All right. Let me get dressed and put my face on."

"You look fine," I said.

"He's right," my father agreed, "you're beautiful. And I don't want to wait two hours or we'll never get out of the house. Come on."

My mother reluctantly agreed with a timid smile. Once again I grew aware of just how burdened they both were by how ugly things had become over the past few years and my part in that. This might be her last smile, the last I'd ever see. My name would be spoken with shame from now on, just like Collie's. I almost took a step toward her, but my dad gripped her hand and led her out the door. She looked over her shoulder once and met my eyes. I watched his back muscles moving beneath his shirt as he walked onto the porch. Outside, JFK lumbered to his feet and licked my father's hand. My mother gave the smallest of waves. Then my old man tugged her across the porch and to the car. I watched my parents pull out of the driveway.

I looked at the ceiling and listened to Grey's footsteps. My breath hitched. I shut my eyes and tried to center myself, but too much flashed across the screen of my mind. I kneeled beside my grandfather's chair. I had no idea what he'd seen, what he knew. Maybe he did have some shame left, maybe not. His chin was resting against his chest. I reached for the remote and turned the cartoons on for him with the sound down low. His head lifted.

I smelled Grey before I saw him. His vegetable moisturizers, after-shave, citrus conditioners, the minty mouthwash. He was ready to go out. I didn't know where. Which woman would he chase tonight? A few thin shafts of sunlight crossed behind him as he moved into the living room. He was in a charcoal suit, white shirt, and power tie. A shiver passed through me. There was something chilling about seeing him so well dressed now.

He didn't notice me kneeling on the floor. He didn't seem to notice anything. He went to the kitchen and poured himself a glass of Glenlivet. He took a deep pull and then let out a sigh.

"Pinsch?" he called. "Ellie? Anyone still here?"

There was a hint of desperation in his voice. He sounded lonely, even forlorn.

He cocked an ear, waiting for a response. When there wasn't one, he stepped to the screen door and stared out at the rest of the world. He was cool and handsome, hepcat aristocratic. He was dashing like they didn't make them anymore, sophisticated swank and suave as he sipped his drink in the sunlight.

After a minute he seemed to soften and slacken a little. He pawed at his face. He said something I didn't catch. It might've been my father's name again. It might have been mine. His grip on the glass eased and it began to slide out of his hand. I thought it would hit the floor but he managed to hold on. His breathing deepened.

I looked into my grandfather's eyes. He wasn't watching the cartoons anymore. He was staring at my face.

I stood and spoke Grey's name.

He didn't respond. He seemed to almost be sleeping on his feet. I spoke again, louder. He turned his head toward me.

"What the hell are you doing there?" he asked. "Does he need a change?"

It was like I'd woken him in the middle of the night. He took a deep breath, cleared his throat, took a sip of his drink, and straightened his tie.

The neckties. Maybe I should have known just from the necktie fetish. I thought of him knotting them around his fists, snapping the material in his hands. Following Collie around town on the night of the underneath, guessing what was going to happen.

Worse, I wondered if Grey had somehow actually *pushed* Collie into the underneath.

"You want a drink, kid?"

He must've been excited after our night out together at Torchy's. He had sensed the underneath tugging at me too. He thought it might lead me to going mad dog. He'd wanted to see what I was capable of, if I was ready to be drawn down the same way Collie was. It's why he pushed so hard for the double date. It had been Grey out there in Eve's yard. He'd stood at the window and peeked in on me having sex with Eve. Did he want me to attack her? Had he expected me to kill her?

I remembered Grey's hot eyes during the poker game. I remembered how he had slapped my face and looked at me like he had something to say but was unable to say it. He'd watched me at work during the game, the tension high, ready to fight, ready to snap. He saw me baring my teeth at Danny Thompson, going for his throat.

It had somehow aroused Grey's sickness. His dementia needed a catalyst to activate it. Since I'd come home he'd been waiting for the underneath to take me down too, so that he could follow along in my blood-drenched wake the way he had in Collie's.

Mal must've seen the agitation in Grey, the growing chaos. After the card game that night, he must've recognized how detached Grey was becoming. I imagined him finding Grey outside in the yard, holding a necktie twisted between his fists. I could see Mal reaching for his brother out of love and terror. He'd discovered him out back before, wandering the yard. I could picture Mal being as afraid for his brother's sanity as for his own.

Maybe he knew what was happening. They had spoken quietly. I could see Grey admitting what had happened, mentioning Rebecca Clarke's name. Then reaching into his pocket and drawing out the knife.

Collie's knife, the one he'd yanked out of Douglas Schuller's chest in the gas station men's room. Staring at it in the moonlight, I could see the vastness of the truth being too huge for Mal to handle. I imagined him going to grab his brother, maybe to shake him, to hurt him, or only to clench him tightly. So physically strong that the first couple of stabs might've only felt like wasp stings. Once he realized he was being murdered, he might have embraced the pain, accepted it, unable to fight against the person he loved most in the world. Thinking, How is this possible? How is it possible that I'm being killed by my own brother? And Grey still stabbing Mal like he was trying to kill whatever was wrong in himself. So divorced from himself that he not only didn't know himself but didn't know who he was killing.

As much as I hated Collie for what he'd done, as much as I'd said that I wanted him to die, in my heart I would never be able to kill my brother.

I backed away.

Grey said, "That drink, yes or no?" He furrowed his brow at me. Not a hair out of place.

I thought of Lin's files. Could Grey really be responsible for all those murders? Or had he only killed Becky Clarke on a dark, insane night that consumed him and my brother? I thought of Collie pleading with me, setting me in motion. Had he wanted this? Had he spotted Grey behind him at some point during his spree? Had he known about Grey all along?

"Terrier, you're shaking. You're pale. Sit down."

"No, I'm all right."

"You're sweating. Let me get you that scotch."

He started to move across the kitchen and I held my hand up, gestured for him to stay still.

"No," I said.

"You all right? You sick?"

"Me? Yeah, maybe." I checked his eyes. He was back, but did his conscience know what he'd done? Was he aware of it, or was the truth hiding deep in his head? "I need to know the truth, Uncle Grey."

"The truth? The truth about what?"

"About what you've done."

"What I've done? What the hell have I done?"

A rush of despair moved through me. I crossed my arms tightly over my chest and held back the flood. "You killed Mal. You snuffed Becky Clarke."

He grinned crookedly like it was a bad joke and he couldn't figure out the punch line. He scoffed and let out a chuckle. Then his face hardened. He finished his drink and slapped the glass down hard enough that it rang like a bell. "What the hell are you saying?"

"You did it, Grey."

"You've got to calm down, kid."

"I am calm."

"Your imagination is working overtime. You're bent all out of shape. Is this what's been on your shoulders? This is what talking to your brother has done? No wonder you're acting flighty."

He moved toward me and I backed up. He kept coming and I kept backing up into the living room. He unbuttoned the top button of his collar. His hands moved incredibly fast. He continued smiling. I stood a little straighter. I stopped trembling. "Don't do it, Grey."

"Don't do what?"

"Look at your hands, Grey."

He looked down. He found that he was holding his tie twisted between his fists. His chin came up again and he met my eyes.

"Terrier, you need to listen to me. Just calm down, kid. You need to calm down."

"I am calm."

"Talk to me."

"Do you even know what you're doing?" I asked. I could feel the tears in my throat. "Do you know who I am?"

"Talk to me, Terrier. We can talk this out. We need to talk this out. I'm here for you. I'm here to listen to you."

"Do you even know who you are anymore?"

He came at me so casually, his face passive. He let the tie go slack between his hands, winked at me the way he used to when I was a kid sitting beside him at a ball game and the team he'd bet on had won the game. He never lost that kind of bet, it was always a sure thing. He'd sit back in the stands with a beer halfway to his lips and he'd give me a wink and hit me with that grin, the one that said nothing could stop us, nothing could ever beat us. I took another step backward. He brought his hands a little higher. I whispered his name. I was strong and fast. He was sixty-two. He had powerful hands. I could outrun him if I could just get my legs to work. I backed up and passed in front of the television screen. As I blocked out the cartoons, Gramp's head fell forward, then came back up. I wanted him to look at me again. I wanted him to tell me I was right. I hit the far wall. Maybe I'm wrong, I could be wrong. Grey came closer until our chests were nearly touching, like he wanted a hug.

"Don't make me do this," I begged.

"Do what?" Grey asked. "What are you going to do? Tell me."

He got the tie up to my throat and began to press. He couldn't get much purchase. He tried to turn me, hoped to get behind me. I coughed and said his name again, tried to push him away. We wrestled across the room, knocking pictures off the wall: Collie graduating from high school, smirking, thinking he had the world by the balls with his stupid blue mortarboard and tassel; Dale and my mother grinning into the camera, my sister about six, missing one front tooth, really giving it her gleeful all; Gramp at twenty-one, hip and not quite handsome, but with amused eyes like he'd already snatched the photographer's wallet. Glass shattered on the floor.

We bashed up against a curio cabinet that almost went over. I got a flash of Gramp's eyes and thought I saw a hint of sorrow in there. I wondered how much of his family's destruction he would hold himself accountable for. I thought of Scooter fifteen years from now, when she'd be a beautiful young brown-haired woman jogging in the park. I thought of Grey still on the prowl. He said, "Stop it, Terry!"

I croaked, "Let go," and drove the heel of my hand under his chin. It wasn't enough. I hit him again. Two rivulets of blood poured out the sides of his mouth, but he wouldn't stop. JFK started barking like mad outside, leaping at the screen. I hooked Grey twice to the belly and he pulled away. His eyes were fiery but without personality. Without any of the Grey I knew in them. He'd vanished that quickly into the underneath.

I hauled off and hit him in the face again. He dropped his tie on the floor and fell back, reaching out to steady himself against the card table. He touched his jacket pocket and drew his hand away as if he'd been burned. The symbols of our life intensified over time and controlled us right to the end.

He went for his trouser pocket, moving so fast that I barely saw him draw out Collie's knife.

It was a switchblade. A weak choice—the thin blade tended to break easily—and I wondered why Collie had bought one off Fingers Brown in addition to the pistol. Did he need the feeling of sawing through flesh?

Grey snapped it open and rushed me. I dodged but not quickly enough. He stabbed me in the side. I screamed, or tried to, but the sound stuck in my throat. He tried again, and I lashed out with an uppercut that raised him onto his tiptoes and forced him away. I dropped to all fours and clenched my right hand over the wound and tried not to writhe. As I scurried back, my left hand touched Grey's tie. I snatched it up and got to my feet. My uncle was coming for me again.

The latch on the screen door snapped and JFK burst through. He barked frantically without any idea of what to do or who to do it to. He circled us as we faced off again.

"Grey—"

"Just calm down," he said, his jaw broken, the words flailing from his mouth.

He stabbed at me again and I tried to wrap the tie like a cord around his wrists, bind them together, but he fought free. He slashed me across the belly and I barely felt it. My rage and panic were loose. I'd either hauled him down into the darkness or he'd done it to me. We were both going to die and I was fine with that.

I hissed, "Not Scooter, you prick."

He got me in a choke hold with his left hand and pushed me back against the front window. Glass cracked behind my head and I started to bleed into my ears.

I heard footsteps. I glanced over and saw Dale rushing us, her expression frightened and then not concerned but furious, bitter, as if she too were showing her true self. I could smell beer on her breath and the sweet scent of marijuana on her clothes. She'd been out with friends or

Butch again, and the guy had dropped her off at the curb. By the time she made it to the porch she'd heard the action inside. Instead of running off or calling the cops, she'd jumped into the fight.

JFK continued to bark, so frantic now he was practically out of his head.

The switchblade danced in front of my belly. Grey shifted his weight, ready to thrust through my guts.

My sister's eyes met mine. I saw her pull the butterfly knife from her pocket, the one she'd wanted for protection. I wondered if she was going to help Grey kill me. I saw a flash of her teeth. I started to count off the major grudges she held against me, but there could be a thousand more I wasn't aware of. Collie would never know all my resentments. No one would.

I closed my eyes and waited for her to slide her blade into my belly a moment after Grey eased in his. Maybe they'd leave me in the backyard crawling around on the lawn in my own filth. I couldn't bear the idea of my mother seeing that and I let out a gurgling moan.

Dale shoved the knife into Grey's back.

He cried out and glared at her over his shoulder. She said, "Oh God—"

She had trouble withdrawing the blade. It stuck between his shoulders for a moment before she finally managed to wrench it loose.

"What are you doing?" she said, her eyes full of confusion. She looked at Grey's blood on the knife and covering her hands. Then she looked up at me. "Why did you make me do that?"

Grey glowered at her as if seeing her for the first time. A vicious, humorless leer widened across his face like a deep scar. Without turning, he prodded me again with his left hand and I went a little farther through the window. He let out a laugh as the switchblade in his right fist flailed in front of Dale. I'd never heard a laugh like that before. I reached for his wrist, but his hands were so goddamn strong and fast. It took everything I had to move him off a foot, then two, then three, just trying to get him away from my sister.

He wasn't seeing Dale. No more than he'd seen Becky Clarke when he'd strangled her in the park. Or Eve's daughter, Roxie, when he was drinking Glenlivet and slipping through her house. I was certain now. I could see the murder in his eyes. He was seeing the woman who'd broken his heart. I could tell that it was a sweet pain he was feeling. All of his hate flooded through him. The memories, fantasies, and impulses were a riot in his head. I pushed him harder, gagging, and we bumped into Gramp's chair. Old Shep blinked twice and angled his chin at me. Dale came at us again, trying to break Grey's grip on me. She held her own blade the wrong way, too tightly instead of loose across her fingers. She slashed at his back twice.

Grey grunted softly and whispered, "There's no need for that. Everything's going to be fine now." His blade quit wavering and I knew he was about to kill my sister.

And then the knife wasn't there anymore.

Grey didn't notice. He stabbed forward with nothing in his fist. Dale squealed as if she'd been skewered, then looked down in surprise and started to back away in a run. I looked down at Gramp and saw the switchblade in his hand. He was snapping it shut. His eyes were still on the television.

I screamed something. I didn't know what. I sounded crazy, much more insane than Grey. My belly was hot with pumping blood. I swung around behind my uncle and got the sweet silk tie around his throat, put a knee in the middle of his back, and pulled.

Dale screamed, "Terry, don't!"

JFK spun in circles and howled as if in agony.

Grey twisted and fell aside and I dropped on top of him. The knife wounds in his back were spurting blood. Dale had done real damage. I held on. He contorted all across the floor and I held on. He whispered a word. It might have been "Why?" I'd never be sure. Dale kept shouting, her face wet, her hands red. Eventually I felt the cartilage in his throat beginning to crack. His struggles weakened. There might still be time to save him. Doctors, psychiatrists, maybe it was possible—and then? Prison? Then he started to convulse and I let go and watched him choke down his last breath.

His body relaxed and I sat up and drew him into my lap. I thought about Kimmy and wondered how I would ever look my father in the eye again.

I dropped over onto my back and JFK licked at my face and my belly. I sucked air in and tried to breathe even while I sobbed. Gramp snicked the switchblade open and then shut it again, and then opened it again.

Dale entered my field of vision. Her eyes were red-rimmed but she wasn't crying anymore. She leaned down and gripped my shoulders. She said, "What happened? Tell me what the fuck just happened!"

"He killed Mal," I said.

"No . . ."

"And Rebecca Clarke. He was sick . . . the Alzheimer's . . . it . . . he—"

"No, it can't be. Not Mal! Grey would never do that!"

"He couldn't help himself."

"Oh no, no . . . bullshit! Maybe it's you who's crazy!" She stared at the drying streaks of blood smeared up her forearms. "Maybe we both are."

There was no reason for her to believe me. I was practically a stranger, whereas she'd seen Grey every day of her life. I'd done hardly anything to make her think of me as her older brother. I'd done nothing to make her believe in me. I looked and acted more and more like Collie. She already had one lunatic brother. She had to be wondering if she had two.

JFK wouldn't come near us. He sat on the rug and stared at me with a harsher judgment than I'd ever felt before.

Dale's eyes flashed with theories and blazing possibilities, trying to put it all together. I propped myself up against the wall, hands clutching my belly. I was leaking fast. I explained everything as quickly and quietly as I could. What I knew and what I suspected. If she didn't buy it, she'd call the cops and that would be that.

"He was gushing blood," she said. "I killed him."

"You saved my life, Dale."

She dropped her head back, the tears tracking down her face. I knew what she was thinking. I was thinking it too.

"Oh Jesus, oh God, poor Dad . . . poor Daddy. What's Dad going to think? What's he going to do?"

I struggled to get up and couldn't do it on my own. She eyed me closely. She would always look at me like this from now on. She would never be completely sure of me again. The tears shimmered and slowed.

"Terry, you're bleeding."

"Not so bad."

"Yes, it is."

"Go get bandages."

"Bandages aren't going to stop this. You need to go to a hospital. We have to call the police."

"No. Help me up."

She did. I rested my weight on her and she groaned beneath me. She helped me to the bathroom. I tore a couple of towels into strips and made a bandage to knot around my stomach. The wounds hurt, but the black burden of what we'd done blunted everything else. The guilt was just beginning for us. I was drenched in cold sweat. Dale lathered up in the sink and washed Grey's blood off, then helped me to clean up as well as I could. I found some outdated pain meds in the cabinet and popped a handful.

There was a lot to take care of. We'd already had too much tragedy in my family. My old man wouldn't be able to handle losing another brother. He was about to lose his oldest son in three days.

Grey was going on the long grift. I wasn't much of a forger, but I wasn't going to have to be. Grey's letter would be short and to the point. I had been gone for five years. Grey could vanish for a few himself. It was a better ending than the truth.

I opened a closet door and found an old black denim jacket. It was tight and hurt like hell to put on, but once I had it buttoned up, constricted against the shredded towels, I felt a little better. I picked the butterfly blade up off the floor and stuck it in my back pocket.

I checked the window. There was blood on the cracked glass. We had to do something about that. I examined the screen door. The latch was broken and would need to be replaced. The jamb looked fine. My old man would be glad to get out his tools. He wouldn't even be curious. I could tell him I stumbled. I could tell him I got angry and kicked the door in. One stupid story was as believable as another.

"What are you doing?" Dale asked. "What are you going to do?"

"I need you to clean the house. Ma and Dad are out at dinner." I checked my watch. "We've still got a couple hours."

"They don't go to dinner."

"They went tonight, Dale. You're going to clean the place. Put everything back the way it was. Wipe the blood up." I pointed to the living-room window. "There too. Change your clothes. Throw everything bloody into a plastic bag and put it in my trunk."

She looked over at Gramp. "Poor Old Shep, he saw it all. He filched the blade. He saved my life."

"Both our lives." He wouldn't have snatched Grey's knife if he had any doubts. "He's still in there someplace." I put my hand to his stubbled cheek. "Thanks, Gramp."

Dale glanced at the corpse on the floor. "What are you going to do with Grey? We need to call . . . I mean . . . we can't just—"

"I'll take care of him."

"Terry, no." She reached up and took me gently by the collar, forced me to look into her face. "You can't. You're not going to—"

"I'll take care of it."

"Not this too."

"Yeah, this too."

I blitzed out the back door and got a shovel out of the shed. I looked off at the woods. A shiver went through me so violently that I had to slap the shovel down into the dirt and prop myself up with the handle. I walked back in and Dale was smoking a cigarette.

"This isn't the way to do it, Terry."

I couldn't imagine dumping him in the ocean or burying him on some construction site under a thousand gallons of cement. "Leave him in Sheepshead Bay? I can't do that."

"It's the safest way. We can't keep him on our property."

"I can't let him go. He needs to stay at home."

"You're going to get caught."

"That's better than the alternative," I said.

She shook her head. "I'll be an accessory, damn you."

"No, you won't. I'll keep you clear of it."

"You're not thinking straight. You can't even lift him."

"Yes, I can."

But she was right. I got him into a seated position, hooked my arms under his, and dragged him to the back door. I managed to push his body to the top step of the porch, hunch down under it, swing his arms over my shoulders, heft him up behind the knees, and get him into a dead man's lift. It was possibly the hardest thing I've ever done in my life. I carried him through the woods, his lips pressed against the back of my neck. Gases gurgled and escaped his mouth like muted curses.

JFK followed, sniffing at Grey's ankles. I dug a grave behind the log where Mal and I'd had our lengthy conversation. The ground was soft from all the rain. It was easier than putting in fence-post railings. It wasn't going to be deep but it would be deep enough for the time being. It took me only a half hour. I rolled Grey's corpse in. At the last second, just before I threw the first shovelful of dirt on top of him, I grabbed the photo from his jacket pocket. I didn't know why I wanted it, but I felt strongly that I had to keep it. I covered him over quickly but well and shifted the log over the grave.

When I was finished, I started back to the house. JFK stared at the muddy spot until I called him to me. Halfway through the woods, I had to stop to vomit. I was feeling light-headed and feeble. Dale met me on the back porch. She'd changed into a summer dress. She looked beautiful and very young and innocent.

"Gilmore's here," she hissed.

I used the backyard hose to wash the dirt off my hands and spray the sweat from my face. I opened the jacket and looked down at the red-stained towels wrapped around my belly. The blood was starting to soak through but you couldn't really tell with the black denim.

"Did you finish cleaning inside?" I asked.

"Yes, but—I hurried. I might have missed something."

I doubted it. She was too sharp for that.

"He's got a pizza," she said. "He does that sometimes. Brings food for when they play cards."

"It's okay, just go tell him that Dad isn't here."

"He knows you're home. He saw your car. It's got the bloody towels and sponges and some of my clothes in a bag in the trunk. That window in the living room is broken. I cleaned the blood off and closed the curtains over it. And the front screen is busted to shit."

"Tell him Butch did it. You broke up with him and he came here and kicked the door in. I beat the crap out of Butch and sent him home."

She nodded. One side of her mouth lifted in a pained half smile. "Good thinking. In case there's any blood left around. Or on you."

"I'll be inside in a minute. You split."

"No, I'm not leaving you alone," she said.

"You've done enough, Dale. I'm sorry you've been dragged into this."

I couldn't say any more. This was family. These were the things of which we do not speak.

She went inside. I put on my game face. I knew I didn't have much of one, but I made the effort. The pain meds were wearing off and my belly burned. Every time I moved a little, I could feel my skin splitting further. I waited another minute, then followed her in.

Dale had cleaned the place up fine. You couldn't tell there had been a fight in the living room. You couldn't tell a man had died here. Gilmore was sitting at the card table, holding a slice of pizza, the box open and turned to the seat opposite. He looked up at me and said, "Thought we could share a pie. You hungry?"

"Starved."

I got a couple of beers out of the fridge. I checked the clock. I hoped my parents would be gone at least another half hour. The thought of facing them weakened my resolve. I sat down, passed Gilmore a bottle, and he gave me that fucked grin.

I wondered if I should play up to him, smiling and kicking back, wasting time until he got his fill of the Rands for the night and took off. But looking at his teeth I was overwhelmed with rage. I wanted to scream at him. I wanted to scream. I picked up the beer and pressed it against my lips and drank deeply and tried to fight off the urge.

"Your old man went out?"

"To dinner with my mother."

Gilmore nodded like a proud father whose son has just gone off on his first date. "Good for them. I keep telling them they should do that kind of thing more often. Spend time together out of the house."

He really did think of himself as some lost begotten son. I wiped my mouth and said, "What's the word on Mal's murderer? Anything yet?"

"It's an ongoing investigation."

"You bastard. You actually said 'ongoing investigation' to me?"

He quit grinning. "I'm not on the case. And even if I was I couldn't tell you anything pertinent. You know that."

I nodded. This had nothing to do with cards, with friendship, with checking up on my father. Gilmore was reaching out. He couldn't do it with his wife and kids, so he came here. Pizza is what you had on family nights.

"How's your father holding up?" he asked.

"As well as can be expected."

"He seems like the rock, rugged, solid, but your mother is really the strong one who can handle the serious hurt. She holds it all together. Your old man, he's a little softer than you might think."

"Because he takes photos of your family for you? Because he crept my old girlfriend's house?"

"He told you about that?"

"No."

"But you found out anyway."

I wasn't in control and I knew I was going to make a bad mistake. Maybe I already had. Gilmore's expression could mean anything. I reached over and slid a slice of pizza out of the box and chewed a hunk off. My stomach surged with bile, but I kept eating.

He wasn't a fool. He saw me sweating. He could sense the bad news coming. The question was whether he'd follow up or let it drop. He scanned the room. He checked out Old Shep. He eyed me carefully and I kept on chewing.

"You're bleeding," he said.

"Your asskicking scraped me up pretty good."

"Dale said you got into it with her boyfriend."

"Nothing major."

"It looks like he did some damage."

"It's tough to make a stoner see reason."

"A lot of people refuse to see reason."

He took a last bite of his crust, then sat back and stared at me. His shoulders shifted a little. I fed the rest of my slice to JFK and cleaned the grease off my fingers. I saw that I'd left the slightest dab of dirt under a pinky nail. Then I took another slice. I forced myself to down it bite by bite. I thought of Grey out there in the mud. My brother would be dead in three days. My sister and I would share this sin for the rest of our lives. I heard the faint sound of metal snapping against metal. It was Gramp playing with the switchblade.

Gilmore pursed his lips. "You're in trouble. You can talk to me, Terrier. I can help you, if you want. You've been looking in all the wrong places for a killer. I can imagine what you've found. Or what you think you've found. I heard about you pulling a piece at Danny Thompson's place. That was really fucking stupid. A Rand with a gun—I never would have believed it. What if he comes after you?"

"What if he does?" I said.

"You don't need that kind of grief."

It almost got me laughing. "Anybody question him about Mal's murder?"

"Of course. And they'll stay on him."

"Even if it turns up dirt on you?"

Gilmore leered at me with surprise. "You think if he killed Mal I'd hush it up to hide my dirt?"

I looked into his eyes. They were like tidal pools heavy with flotsam. A couple of days ago I'd thought he might be a serial killer. Now I almost felt sorry for him. And I feared him. In his own way he had loved Mal the way he loved my father, the way he loved me. Like a child standing outside in the snow, staring through a window at a family he wished he was part of on Christmas Day. I thought, This guy is crazy, but he's not our kind of crazy.

"You're making bad moves," he said. "Like with Cara Clarke. She hanged herself, but who knows what pushed her buttons. Who pushed her over the edge. You think you might've had something to do with that, Terry?"

I kept eating. We were just two pals enjoying some pizza together.

"You never should have come home," he said.

He wasn't going to get an argument from me there. He shifted his weight. I thought, If he takes another poke at me, even if he is a cop, I'll break his jaw. He must've realized it, because we each held our ground.

I still had the butterfly knife. I wondered if this was the moment when I became my brother, when I became my uncle. What would I do to stay out of prison? What would I really do to protect my sister? Gramp's snicking blade beat into my temples until I could barely hear myself breathing. Gilmore was here because he wanted a family, and we Rands were losing ours, one by one.

Dale sashayed into the room then. She'd been listening. She'd done another quick change and had on the clothes I'd seen her wearing the other night at the lake. The tight leather jacket, the sexy pants. She looked twenty-five and gorgeous as she paraded in front of Gilmore. "Ugh, anchovies and onions?"

Gilmore kept glowering at me. It was his default expression. Dale bent over the table, grabbed my bottle, and took a long sip. Beer leaked over her chin. I wanted to tell her not to overplay it. He's too crafty. He shifted his gaze to her. He looked at her hips, her chest, her pulsing throat. He wasn't thinking about reading tween vampire romance novels to her now.

"Where are you heading out to this evening?" he asked. "The lake?"

"No, I'm going out on a first date."

"No wonder Butch crashed your door. He seems like the jealous type."

She worked the bottle around her bottom lip. "He's history now that Terry shooed him off."

"Good, you're too young to settle for someone like that punk. This new one a football star?"

Dale smiled sexily, her face full of amusement. "No, he just got out after a nickel in Sing Sing for armed robbery. But he's completely reformed. Wants to go to night class and become an IRS auditor."

Gilmore blinked and shrugged. "Well, that's . . . good."

She said nothing. I said nothing. But we'd closed ranks. You could feel the change in the air as we waited for the next thing to happen. Gramp kept playing with the blade beneath his blanket. It sounded impossibly loud to me but no one else seemed to hear it. Finally Gilmore stood.

He wasn't a fool. He was a solid, sharp cop despite his vices. He knew us. In a very real way, he was us. His gaze whipsawed around the room one more time. Even with the cleaning, we'd left a million clues for him to spot. I tried to hold my leaking guts in. His knowing grin faded. He carefully wiped his hands off with a napkin, crumpled it up, and tossed it on the table. He frowned at Dale. She was a good actress but not good enough, not after having helped kill a man. A man she had loved. Gilmore's gaze hardened. He shook his head like he was very disappointed in her. He went stone-cold-killer cop. He even looked at JFK, who let out a moan in the corner. The dog knew we'd botched it. Gilmore glanced at Dale again, made sure she had her hands in view. He turned his hip to me so he could draw his gun easily. He zeroed in on the dirt beneath my pinky nail. He read the guilt in me. He was a bad boy. He was bent. He might've even been in on a few body dumps himself, who knew. I wondered if we would have to get rid of him too.

He said, "So who did you two kill?"

I told Gilmore everything. It was nearly word for word what I'd said to Dale only an hour earlier. All that I knew and all I suspected. It fit together and made perfect sense, if you were willing to go along with it. Gilmore wasn't. He didn't believe me. He hadn't seen Grey's face as he'd tried to strangle me. Whatever I said sounded like a coward's lie. His disgust was written in his face. I was no better than my brother. He kept looking at Dale, and I could practically hear the sound of his heart breaking. It was no different from my own.

We brought him to Grey's grave. Gilmore huffed air and said, "Jesus fucking Christ. You buried him in your own backyard. You both want to wind up in the chair too? That what this is about?"

"No," I said.

"Your mother. She came to your brother's trial. Think she'll show to yours? Or will she finally wash her hands of you once and for all?"

I remembered him saying that my mother had wept the whole time but had still tried to put in the righteous word for Collie. I wondered what she would say about me.

"I did it," Dale whispered. "It was me. I stabbed him. I had to. Grey was strangling Terry. He was out of his head. He didn't even recognize me. He would've killed both of us. It's the truth. I had to do it."

I wasn't certain when Gilmore had drawn his gun but he held it loosely in his hand. So we were heading down that road already. He was going to call in backup.

I pleaded with him. "At least leave her out of this."

"How can I?" he asked.

He stared at Dale for a very long time. In her he saw a younger sister. In her he saw his own daughters. His expression was heavy with tragedy.

She couldn't bear up under the burden of her guilt and the force of his reproach. She wavered where she stood. I watched her folding, inch by inch, but I was too slow to catch her. Gilmore spread his arms and she dropped into them, sobbing, but he kept a grip on his gun, pointed at my chest.

It was true, he knew I'd never punch a cop, not even in self-defense. Not unless I had to, in order to save my sister. He watched me warily. I could tell he wanted to pat Dale's back, do something to soothe and placate her. I wasn't going to be fast enough, but I'd have to try, no matter the cost.

I shifted my stance.

He shook his head slowly and said, "Don't, Terrier."

His eyes remained dark and lonely. All he had in the world were the Rands. We both realized it. I could see that he was trying to imagine his own empty future now.

"I ought to take you apart," he said. "I ought to take you apart and bury you next to him."

"It was Grey," Dale said, wiping her face with the back of her hand. "Terry didn't—"

"Shut up," Gilmore snarled. "Both of you shut the hell up for a minute."

I thought about what he had said when we'd first met up again outside the Elbow Room. *There are lines you cross and those you don't.*

I told him, "This wasn't a line, Gilmore. It was something that had to be done. It wasn't his fault. He was ill. You were right, there was no serial killer. There was just Grey, drawn along in Collie's wake. If Collie hadn't gone mad dog, neither would Grey. He wouldn't have crossed paths with Rebecca Clarke and she wouldn't be dead. This is what's best. Just turn around and walk away."

"I can't do that. I'm a cop."

"You're on the Thompson payroll."

"That's minor shit."

"I know."

"That's nothing like this. I've never done anything like this."

"I know."

"Let's go."

"Leave her out of it. You can do that much."

"It was me," Dale said. "I did it. I stabbed him. But I had to."

Grey probably would've survived the knife wound in the back if I hadn't strangled him. I knew Dale was protecting me just like I was protecting her. Or maybe we were both intent on blaming ourselves.

Gilmore backed away toward the house. He gestured with his free hand for Dale to follow him and motioned with the gun for me to do the same. I did. I was limping now. The pain was quickly becoming agony. I could barely maneuver the back porch stairs. I got to the door and Dale hung my arm across her shoulder and led me inside. JFK stayed close by. He sensed the danger to our family. I thought he might go for Gilmore's throat. One of us might have to.

We all stepped into the living room. Gilmore still hadn't gone for his phone. He turned and stepped backward. I could rush him. JFK would probably do the rest. But Gilmore eyed me again and I had trouble seeing the outcome. I didn't think I had it in me to murder him, not even to save Dale. I'd failed my family again. What in the hell was the point in coming back, I thought. I've done nothing but kick our home off its foundation.

Gilmore wagged the gun at me to get me moving again. At the edge of my vision I saw a flash of metal in Gramp's hand. Some instinct was pushing him along as well, taking on the responsibilities I couldn't handle. Beside him, JFK crouched like he was ready to leap.

I shoved Gilmore out of the way. He spun around and stuck the gun under my chin just as I plucked the switchblade out of Old Shep's hand. I said, "Thanks anyway, Gramp, but we're not going to do that."

He blinked at his cartoons.

Gilmore pulled that tight, nasty grin again. He held a hand open and I put the knife in it. He snapped the blade shut and stuck it in his pocket. The false chuckle rang hollow in his chest. He said, "You know what this is going to do to your father?"

"Yes."

"And you don't even care, do you, you little bastard?"

Enough was enough. I made my move. I lunged forward, swung wild, and connected with his chin. It was a beautiful shot, one I'd been waiting to give him since he'd sucker-punched me in the parking lot of the Elbow Room. It was the last bit of reserve I had. I went down on my face on the rug, groaning and panting.

I started to puke but Dale got a wastebasket and helped me to my knees. When I could breathe again, I reached into my pocket and took out the photo of the woman who had jilted Grey forty-five years ago and put the splinter in his mind that had gone deeper and deeper until it cut him in two. I hoped she was alive. I hoped she hadn't been Grey's first victim.

I handed the photo to Gilmore and said, "I don't know her name or anything about her, but check on it. See if she was murdered. Grey . . . he might have . . ." I looked down and streams of blood were pulsing down the front of my jeans. Dale pushed her way in and said, "Oh God, Terry, you're—" She grabbed more towels from the kitchen and pressed them to my stomach. My mother was going to wonder where the hell all these towels went.

Dale started tying off my wounds. Gilmore said, "They won't hold."

"Do something," she begged. "Help my brother."

He winced as he rubbed his jaw and finally came to a decision. Covering over Grey's murder was the lesser of two evils. It was between that and the promise of a completely empty life. We Rands were all he had.

"All right," he said.

"We have to get rid of some other things," Dale told him.

"I know a place."

We were going to be seeing a lot more of Gilmore from now on. He owned us, and we owned him.

He and Dale helped me to my feet. Maybe I would die anyway. Maybe I wanted to die. Maybe that was the perfect choice to make.

I visited Collie one last time. I requested that we meet in the area where I'd first spoken with him, where we could talk on the phone and there would be reinforced glass between us.

The screws brought him in and took their time unlocking his chains. He must've come straight from the gym. He was still sweaty and the veins remained knotted all across his arms, twisting red and black in his throat. He smiled at me through the glass but he knew something was wrong. I was a little heartened to realize he could still worry about something even now.

The screws left and Collie spun his chair around, sat backward as usual, and snatched up the phone. I took a breath and reached up to mine. I moved stiffly. It had taken twenty staples to close the jagged tears in my side. The emergency-room docs had done an excellent job patching me up. They told me the scars wouldn't be bad. The dog tattoo would need some touching up, though.

"I wasn't sure if I'd see you again," my brother said.

"I didn't plan on coming back," I told him.

"So why are you here?"

I could feel that old singular pain rising once again. My foolish mantra returned to me. It beat along with my pulse. I can do this. I can do this.

"You were right," I said. "Someone else snuffed Becky Clarke."

He let go with a chuckle that grew wilder until it became a whoop. It got the screws looking in at us. "I knew it. Lin was right. My girl is sharp as hell. Idiot cops couldn't figure it out, but she did." He raised his chin and eyed me. "Did you find him?"

"Yes," I said.

He waited for me to continue. I didn't. I decided there was no need to tell him that I thought Lin had been wrong too. I didn't believe Grey was a serial killer. Instead, there was a world of mad dogs like him, husbands and boyfriends who couldn't contain their rage, whose hands had learned how to batter and strangle. The world was littered with dead young brunettes.

His face emptied of its usual high-strung emotion. He looked at me with some real attentiveness. "Did you take care of it yourself? There's been no word here. Nothing on the circuit. Lin hasn't said anything."

"I handled it. Nobody else knows."

"Right. But I can see you're holding back. You've got more to say."

I nodded. "Why didn't you tell me about how you kissed them?"

Collie looked away in embarrassment. His face flushed until it glowed pink. I had never seen my brother embarrassed about anything. It was a revelation. I had learned something new about him on the eve of his death, and that disturbed me. I didn't want to believe that there was more I might learn about my brother, if we had more time.

"I didn't know they knew about that," he said.

"Forensics did their job. Did you really think they'd miss that?"

"I don't know."

"It was in the files. Your attorneys should have used it."

"I didn't care. I didn't want to fight. I didn't want them to fight for me either."

"You should have told me anyway. Maybe it would have helped convince me that you hadn't iced Rebecca Clarke."

"Nothing was going to convince you one way or the other. You were either going to help or you weren't."

He was right. I couldn't argue the point. Right from the beginning I knew I was going to help. Even before he asked me. Despite my own protests. He called me and I had come running home.

"Why'd you put your lips on them, Collie?"

"I just did, Terry."

We were bound by our rituals. The underneath forced him to kill with viciousness, but perhaps it couldn't steal all of his love from him.

Maybe it was his way of begging forgiveness from them. Or him forgiving them for allowing themselves to become his victims and the impetus for his own destruction.

"So tell me," he said. "What happened? Who was it?"

I leaned so far toward the glass that he actually drew away on the other side. "I want the truth from you, Collie, do you understand? Don't run any kind of a game on me. Don't hold back. Don't lie. Talk straight. If you've got any kind of a heart, use it now. You owe me that much."

"What the hell do you mean, Terry?"

I enunciated every word very clearly into the phone. *"Did . . . you . . . know?"*

"Did I know what?"

"Did you have any idea at all who it was?"

He shook his head. "No, of course I don't know who it was. If I'd known I wouldn't have needed you to check into it. What happened? What did you do?"

I said, "Does it really matter?"

He glanced away again. "No, I suppose not."

I looked at my brother for so long that his expression shifted several times. He smiled, then frowned, then a hint of real concern began to ply his features.

"What is it, Terry? What do you need to say?"

My throat was raw. I swallowed several times. I looked at my reflection and then realized it wasn't my reflection. I was staring at my brother. We were the same. Maybe it was the onset of Alzheimer's, maybe it wasn't. Maybe there really was no reason. Maybe Grey had none either. It might not have been the girl who broke his heart. It might have been anything at all. And me. And me. Was I going to wind up collecting Toby mugs or would I murder young women who reminded me of Kimmy? I was already a murderer. I should be sitting on the other side of the glass. I had a premonition that I would be someday.

"What is it?" he repeated.

I sucked air like I was suffocating. "Collie, I have to tell you something."

"Okay. That's okay, Terry. You can tell me anything you need to. Go on. What is it? Tell me."

I said, "I love you."

He couldn't have been more shocked if I'd opened all the doors and ushered him to a limousine and driven him out of there. His face grew a healthy, youthful pink again. It took ten years off him. He looked like a kid again. "What?"

"You're my brother and I love you. But I can't forgive you. Do you understand? I'll never forgive you. When they put you on the table, when they put poison in your blood. When they murder you, Collie . . . I'm sorry, but I'm going to be glad. What you see when you look at me that last time? You're going to see someone who's wishing that you burn in hell. But I'm not lying. I love you."

I put my hand to the glass and fanned my fingers. His eyes were wide and his mouth had dropped open. He looked frozen in the glare of open emotion. He didn't respond to my gesture. I hung up the phone. The screws came and put chains on my brother and led him out. I watched him shuffle through the door. He started to turn his silver head and look back at me but didn't complete the motion. I sat there until one of the screws told me to leave.

The next day Collie gave it one last romp for posterity's sake. He was going to go out having some fun. He fought them with a huge smile on his face. I knew he wasn't really trying to hurt anyone. He was just putting on one last show for his own entertainment. The screws wrestled him down to the floor and fell over themselves. The priest stepped away and kept reading from the Bible in a shaky voice.

I concentrated on Collie. I put my will into it. I focused all my attention and directed it with all my mental wattage and tried to find him in the distance between us. I thought maybe it would be enough for him to make a last-ditch effort to connect with me.

Collie glanced up once and grinned at me through the window even while they swung their billy clubs at his back.

They strapped him down to the table and stuck the needle in. He had no last words. Not even for his wife. Lin sat expressionless beside me. I wanted to jump out of my skin but she seemed relaxed, almost serene. She'd married him knowing this would be the final outcome.

I didn't know any of the other witnesses. I had wondered if the Clarkes would show up. I wondered if anyone else here was a relative of one of Collie's other victims. I tried to read their expressions. I couldn't. We all looked about the same kind of haunted.

His eyes were stone, but I imagined what it must be like staring at a group of pitiless people who all wanted you dead. Even your own brother. It felt like they wanted me dead too.

The machine took no time at all.

Collie shut his eyes and then it was over.

As we were leaving Lin folded up and almost fell. I reached out and took her in my arms and turned her to my chest. I let her sob for both of us. It went on for a long time. When she was done she pushed off me and walked away.

There was cheering outside. People hooting and flashing their headlights. Protesters were holding candles and singing hymns. It was an emotionally charged moment. I didn't know which camp I fit into more. Vicky and her news crew were interviewing folks. I thought Eve would be on hand but she wasn't. Maybe she'd already moved off to a new story.

Gilmore stood out beyond the gate. I walked over to him. He was smoking a cigarette. He was a touch pale. It only peripherally had to do with my brother. I knew he was thinking about family again, the family an orphan like him had never had, and the family that he couldn't hold on to himself.

He said, "I don't know what to say, Terrier."

"You don't have to say anything. In fact, I wish you wouldn't."

"Your mother, she—"

"What happened between you and Phyllis?" I asked.

He looked down and let a stream of smoke out. When he looked back up it was like he'd forgotten I was there. It took him another moment to respond. "She left me."

"Any chance you can win her back?"

"I doubt it."

"Is it what you want? To have her back?"

He paused. He wasn't thinking about the answer, just whether he should tell me. "More than anything."

"Then do whatever she needs you to do, right? Quit the force if it's that. Be a straight arrow if it's that. Be a better father if it's that. Spend more time with the family, whatever it is she needs. Do it."

"It's easy advice but hard to change." He shook his head. "She won't take me back."

I thought about him bringing my father into his ordeal. My old man breaking in to houses again, but not to juke the places, just to snap photos or to stand among the dreams of what might have been, the wreckage of our reality. "Then move on. Stop hanging around executions and people like the Rands."

His lips crimped into that fucked grin again. I wanted to slap it off like it was an insect that had landed on him. "Why are you saying this? You know how ridiculous you are, Terry?"

"As a matter of fact I do. That's proof that I know what I'm talking about, Gilmore. I'm Exhibit A."

I walked away. He had as good a chance as anyone at pulling it together and getting himself back on track. So long as he stayed out of our backyard.

I got into my car. I sat there in the lot, watching the crowd. From a distance I couldn't tell the divergent groups apart anymore. The moon climbed into the night sky. The candles went out one by one. I turned the key and threw the car into drive, then put it in park again and turned off the engine. My brother was still inside somewhere. I thought I would wait with him a little longer.

My mother phoned. She spoke my name and then said nothing more for a time. I couldn't speak. I didn't know what to tell her, how much detail to give. A heavy numbness had settled on me. It was lulling and I shut my eyes.

She finally managed to ask, "Did he say anything?"

"No."

"Are you all right?"

"I will be."

"Come home."

I went home. A couple of news crews were out in front. They jumped in my face. JFK barked his ass off. I said nothing. It was three in the morning.

I walked in. They were sitting in the kitchen. My mother had prepared food. It seemed right. We all took our usual places. The three empty seats seemed not to be empty at all.

No one said anything. No one asked me anything. Dale almost got up the nerve at one point but backed out. I was glad. My mother fixed me a sandwich and I ate without tasting. I helped with the dishes. She'd bought a crumb cake. It was Collie's favorite. Dale cut us each a piece and put them on plates and we sat and stared. Eventually my mother cleaned the table again.

I was her only son now. I thought I should make some kind of grand familial demonstration. I didn't know what it should be, so I did nothing.

My father took his beer cooler out onto the porch. The news vans were gone. I sat with him. We drank in silence. JFK circled the yard restlessly, cutting in and out of the brush and prowling the property line. My father got drunk enough that he nearly passed out. I helped him to bed. My mother feigned sleep as I laid my old man beside her.

I passed Dale's door and heard her crying. I knocked softly and she quieted. I walked in and sat on the edge of her mattress the way I used to do when reading those vampire romances to her. I pulled a blanket over her shoulder. I rubbed her back until her breathing softened and I knew she was asleep.

I laid down beside her but couldn't keep my eyes closed. I stared at the ceiling and thought of everything and thought of nothing. I got up at dawn and went for an easy run around the college campus with JFK. My staples pulled and bled a little but there was no major damage. When we got back I showered, got dressed, and went shopping.

When I returned home, my parents were sitting in front of their cold, untouched breakfasts.

I handed them an envelope.

"What's this?" my old man asked.

My mother pulled out the tickets. "A cruise?"

"Yes," I said.

"What are we going to do on a cruise?"

"I don't know what anybody does on a cruise. Drink piña coladas and visit tourist dives. It goes all over the Caribbean. Two weeks."

"I think I'd be afraid to be out there on all that water. This is very thoughtful, Terry, but really—"

"You live on an island, Ma. You're always surrounded by ocean. You're going on a cruise."

"This isn't a good time," my father said.

"Why isn't it a good time?"

"It just isn't."

"It's a good time. It's the only time, Dad."

"What about Gramp?" my mother said. "What about Dale? I need to cook for Grey."

"Dale can handle herself. Gramp is getting a nurse. You don't need to cook for Grey."

"There's no insurance for a nurse."

"There's money," I said. "There are caches and cubbyholes stuffed with money. We're cleaning them out. Old Shep is getting a nurse and you two are going to the fucking Caribbean if I have to row you there in a goddamn kayak."

"What are you getting so angry about?"

"I'm not angry!"

"You seem angry."

"I'm not angry."

"A cruise," my mother said.

"What the hell," my father said.

I parked in front of Kimmy and Chub's house. JFK was curled up in the passenger seat, relaxed but watchful. He'd hopped in and I needed a friend. There was no reason for me to be here. I wasn't family. I wasn't even a friend anymore. Three of the men closest to me in my life were gone, all within the last week, one by my own hand. My blood had thinned considerably. I climbed out and JFK stepped along with me. The weight of what I'd done hit me all at once and I bent over, holding my arms across my guts and fighting down the urge to scream. I clamped my teeth shut and made noises that no sane man should ever make. When the moment passed, I was covered in sweat and my driver's-side window was flecked with my tears. JFK had his nose pressed against my knee. I stood at the bottom of the driveway. I didn't go any farther. JFK waited and finally laid down. I almost turned around. The front door opened. Kimmy said something about the drive-in and Chub said it might rain.

Scooter ran a few cantering steps down the walk. She didn't watch where she was going and was headed right toward me. I thought, This is not my daughter, she's not my girl. Kimmy's smile dropped and her eyes widened. I couldn't read what was in them. Chub stood beside her, a little out in front in a protective manner. They really were a good match. Strong and partnered, tight together. I wondered if I was going to weep or rage or run away again. I wondered if I would even remember this scene a few years from now when it was my turn to disappear into a dark corner.

There were names set against my tongue. I would say them on my deathbed even if I didn't know what they meant anymore. Mal. Grey. Cara. Becky. Collie. Scooter. Kimmy. She tilted her head at me as if I'd spoken aloud. I thought she would ask, *What do you want?* And I would say, *Kiss me like I'll die tonight.* Perhaps those would be the last kind words. I was a man of vivid dreams and wondered if this was one of them. I bent as Scooter ran to me. I wasn't insane yet. I could keep control. She rushed into my arms, laughing. I hugged her for an instant and her face fell at the sight of a stranger. She backed up and looked as if she might cry. I suspected I looked the same. She turned around and ran back to her parents and hid behind Chub's legs. One of these days the cops would crush him and he would howl for his girls. Scooter spotted JFK and let loose with a giggle and some chatter I didn't understand and peeked out from around her father's knee. The dog yawned and sniffed. I didn't smell the storm anymore. Kimmy said, "Terry." It was still my name, and to hear it on her lips loosened my chest and let me breathe deeply in a way I hadn't for weeks. Maybe not in years. I stood and waited for the dream to end or for the world to move me once again to where I needed to be.

ACKNOWLEDGMENTS

I'm indebted to Bill Pronzini, James Grady, Max Allan Collins, Brian Keene, Alethea Kontis, Linda Addison, Gerard Houarner, and Dean Koontz for giving much-needed encouragement during a particularly difficult time.

My editor, Caitlin Alexander, for her wise editorial reading, sage advice, and astute guidance (but no salty bagels this year, wtf?).

My agent, David Hale Smith, who talked me off the ledge a few times (and actually talked me onto it at least once or twice).

Finally, thanks to Ed Brubaker, Ken Bruen, Norman Partridge, Eddie Muller, and Ed Gorman, my brothers in noir.